By Linda Howard

A LADY OF THE WEST

ANGEL CREEK

THE TOUCH OF FIRE

HEART OF FIRE

DREAM MAN

AFTER THE NIGHT

SHADES OF TWILIGHT

SON OF THE MORNING

KILL AND TELL

NOW YOU SEE HER

ALL THE QUEEN'S MEN

MR. PERFECT

OPEN SEASON

DYING TO PLEASE

CRY NO MORE

KISS ME WHILE I SLEEP

TO DIE FOR

KILLING TIME

COVER OF NIGHT

DROP DEAD GORGEOUS

UP CLOSE AND DANGEROUS

DEATH ANGEL

ICE

By Linda Howard and Linda Winstead Jones

WARRIOR RISING

Veil of Night

LINDA
HOWARD

VEIL OF NIGHT

A NOVEL

**Doubleday Large Print
Home Library Edition**

 BALLANTINE BOOKS · NEW YORK

BALLANTINE and colophon are registered
trademarks of Random House, Inc.

ISBN 978-1-61664-534-2

Printed in the United States of America on
acid-free paper

**This Large Print Book carries the
Seal of Approval of N.A.V.H.**

Veil of Night

Chapter One

Six weddings in five days. *Holy shit.*

All Jaclyn Wilde could think was that her mother, Madelyn, who was her partner in Premier, *the* events planning firm to hire in the greater Atlanta area if you wanted your guests to be impressed, must have been sipping a couple or twelve champagne martinis when she'd accepted so many bookings so close together. It wouldn't have been nearly as bad if the bookings had been anything other than weddings: a party was simple in comparison to a wedding, because they were relatively free of emotional turmoil. A wedding, on the other hand, was fraught with every emotion known to man. It wasn't just the brides; it was the bride's mother, the groom's mother, the maid of honor, the bridesmaids, the parents of the flower girl and the ring bearer, the cousins who weren't invited to be in the wedding party, what colors to choose, the date, the location, the damn *font* on the friggin' invitations . . .

"Jaclyn Wilde," the clerk called, interrupting Jaclyn's increasingly stressed and frantic thoughts.

The clerk's voice was too cheerful. Didn't she realize it was inappropriate to sound cheerful when you were collecting payments for traffic violations? Maybe it was asking too much that she sound glum, but she could at least sound bored and noncommittal, instead of all but dancing with glee at taking someone's money.

Jaclyn stifled her irritation; it stemmed more from the almost impossible workload facing her during the coming week than it did from paying her speeding ticket. Adding to her stress was the fact that *because* they'd been working so hard, she'd forgotten to mail in the money for the speeding ticket, and today was the day it was due, so she'd either had to take time off from work—thereby increasing the stress by getting behind—or have a warrant issued for her arrest. Yeah, that would be a real stress-reducer.

Being late was her fault. If the city of Hopewell, where she lived and where she'd received the ticket, had been set up to receive online payments, she could have handled it that way, but it wasn't. She got up, silently forked over the cash, and a minute later was striding down the hall, the speeding ticket already forgotten because that particular item had just been checked off her to-do list.

She glanced down at her watch. She had just enough time to get to her next appointment—Carrie Edwards, a bitch for all seasons, and one of the reasons why six weddings in five days was looming as Mission Impossible. Carrie's wedding wasn't even one of the six; her wedding wasn't for another month, but Carrie was taking up way too much of their time with her histrionics and constant flip-flopping on decisions. One bridesmaid had already told her—Carrie, not Jaclyn—to go fuck herself, which was a first in Jaclyn's experience. Usually, no matter what the bride did, the members of the wedding party would grit their teeth and see it through. Even when they did drop out, they'd make polite excuses. Not this girl; she'd let Carrie have it with both barrels, and hadn't minced words.

When the blow-up happened, Jaclyn had stepped out of sight, allowed herself a wide smile and a fist pump, then schooled her expression and returned to try to forestall a hair-pulling, eye-gouging catfight. She'd have loved to see Carrie with a black eye, but business was business.

If she hadn't been so wrapped up in her thoughts she might have been faster on her feet, but when a door suddenly swung outward she was caught by surprise and slammed into the tall, dark-haired, dark-suited man who stepped into the corridor. She gave a short, sharp "Oomph!" The impact knocked her briefcase from her hand and sent it spinning across the gray-tiled floor. She felt one foot, elegantly shod in three-inch heels, begin to slip, and in panic instinctively grabbed the man's arm to steady herself. Her free arm slipped inside his open jacket and she grabbed a handful of shirt fabric, holding on for dear life. The side of her arm brushed against something very hard, and there was a very brief glimpse of leather before she made the startled identification of *holster,* followed by *gun,* then *cop.* Considering she was in city hall, the conclusion was both logical and inescapable.

The arm she grabbed turned to iron as the man immediately tensed it to hold her weight; he half-turned, his other arm sliding around her waist to catch her. For a brief moment, no more than the second needed for her to catch her balance, she was held firmly against a very warm, very solid, indisputably male body.

He released her the moment she was sure-footed, but he didn't back away. Not immediately, anyway. She blew out a shaky breath. "Wow. Whew." Her heartbeat, thrown into high gear thanks to the collision and almost falling, was pounding against her rib cage so hard she could feel the thuds. A spill on the floor of city hall would've been par for the course on this perfectly crappy day, but the last thing she needed right now was to break an ankle or something. Even a sprained ankle, at this point, would throw Premier into a time crunch they simply wouldn't be able to handle.

"Are you all right, ma'am?"

He bent his head down as he spoke, and his breath, scented with spearmint chewing gum, brushed her temple. His voice was a warm baritone, with a slight rasp that roughened it just enough to take the tone from mellow to something . . . more. She didn't know just what that *more* was, just that it was there— Wait a minute. Had he just called her *ma'am*?

Did she look *that* haggard?

Jaclyn squashed her initial annoyed re-action. The badge he wore explained the "ma'am." Actually, being almost any-where in the South explained it. He wasn't commenting on her appearance; he was a cop, a civil servant on his best behavior. She blew out another breath, and realized she hadn't yet released her grip on either his arm or his shirt. He *couldn't* step back, not as long as she clung to him. She forced her fingers to unclench from both shirt and arm, and she took the necessary step back to put some distance between them.

"I'm fine," she said as she looked up at him. "Thanks for catching me. I wasn't paying attention to where I was going." A small part of her brain, the part reserved for hormones and irrational decisions, gave a wolf whistle. Abruptly she felt both overheated and overexcited. Damn, he was fine-looking, in a way that wasn't at all boyish and depended more on strength and an air of competency than it did on regular features. There were boys, and there were men. This was a *man.* This was a man who had *it,* that indefinable quality of sex appeal, maturity, and strength all mingled together into a potent whole.

He gave a slight smile, a nice and natural, easy curve of his lips. "Not the best layout here, as far as traffic goes."

"Don't mention *traffic* to me," Jaclyn said, almost under her breath.

He shot a quick glance of comprehension in the direction from which she'd come, and his smile widened a little. She liked that smile more than she should.

In her line of business, Jaclyn met a lot of men; unfortunately, they were usually about to get married. Not always, of course, but it took something special to get her

attention this way: a certain look, an unexpected chemistry . . . and to be honest,
it had been a very long time since she'd
had the time to admire any man.

She didn't have time now, either. She
had to really hurry, or she'd be late.

"Thanks again. Sorry I almost smashed
you flat." She gave the polite cop a quick
nod of her head, a friendly—but not *too*
friendly—good-bye, then looked around
for her dropped briefcase.

The case had spun all the way across
the wide hall, coming to a stop against the
far wall. Before she could reach for it, a
man in stained jeans and a dingy T-shirt
stretched tight over an enormous beer
belly laboriously bent down and picked up
the case. "Here ya go, ma'am," he said,
holding the slender case out to her in one
meaty paw and smiling a ridiculously
sweet smile for such a rough face.

"Thank you," Jaclyn said as she gripped
the handle, giving the burly guy a warmer
smile than she'd given the cop, because
she wasn't attracted to him at all, so being
nice to him didn't seem as dangerous as
being nice to the cop. As she strode away
down the hall she mused on how cockeyed

that reasoning was, on a logical basis, but how rock solid it was on some gut-level feminine instinct. She didn't have time for the cop, didn't have time to be attracted to him, so she wasn't about to do anything that might attract him.

As she walked away, she was almost certain that he was watching her, but she didn't dare turn around to look. She didn't *need* to turn around; she could practically feel the bull's-eye his gaze was painting on her back.

She hurried out to the parking lot, using her remote to unlock her steel-gray Jaguar just before she reached it. In almost one motion she opened the door, tossed her briefcase onto the passenger seat, and slid behind the wheel. Her first action then was to hit the door lock, a safety precaution she'd taken so often it was second nature to her now. As she turned the key with one hand, she was pulling the seat belt into place with the other.

She didn't need another ticket, so she kept an eye on the speedometer. She especially wasn't going to speed on the way to a meeting with Carrie Edwards; it was all she could do to keep the car heading in the right direction, and even then she flirted with the idea of calling her mother and saying, "I'm throwing up, have hives, and probably the measles; can you handle my meeting with Carrie?" So what if Madelyn was occupied with getting the final details in place for a wedding tomorrow, and had the rehearsal to get through? Madelyn was the one who had taken Carrie's booking in the first place, so it was only right she should share some of the joy of dealing with her.

Jaclyn sighed. No, she couldn't do that to her mother. Well, maybe she couldn't. She certainly wasn't in a hurry to meet with Carrie, who was the worst of the worst in a business that often seemed to bring out *the* worst in some women. Sometimes a client would be a delight from start to finish, but just as often one of the principals would make her think there really was something to be said for getting married at a courthouse or an all-night chapel in Vegas—not that she'd be foolish enough to say so aloud. After all, weddings were her bread and butter.

Today's meeting with Carrie was at Premier's office, located in Buckhead, but tomorrow there were several consultations—with the caterer, the cake-maker, and the florist—that would take place at the reception hall in Hopewell. Carrie's initial orders had been made months ago, but there were several last-minute decisions to be made and Bride-zilla was dragging her feet. The bride should be going to the vendors for these consultations, but Carrie had insisted on holding court and making them all come to her. In her mind, she was Important, which meant people came to her instead of the other way around.

Because this was a big and very expen-sive wedding—the groom was the son of a state senator—they'd all agreed. And natu-rally, the bride had insisted that Jaclyn be there as well. Carrie Edwards did a lot of insisting. Tomorrow was shaping up to be another crappy day, just on the basis of dealing with Carrie, plus she had the first of those six-weddings-in-five-days to get through. Even though Madelyn was han-dling the wedding, inevitably there were last-minute emergencies that required ex-tra help, even if it was nothing more than spending time on the phone locating an emergency replacement for a limousine that was the wrong color, or wouldn't start, or the flower girl threw up on the groom and a new tuxedo was needed. On the day of a wedding, they had to be ready for literally anything to happen.

Jaclyn arrived at the office barely five minutes before the scheduled meeting. Naturally, Carrie was already there, waiting in her private office. Diedra, Jaclyn's assistant, sat at the outer desk, which was piled with books and fabric swatches and photographs. She gave Jaclyn an exaggerated expression of sympathy, and frustration, as she nodded toward the office door.

Jaclyn squared her shoulders and turned the door handle. She didn't have a chance to step into the room before Carrie turned, an expression of dissatisfaction on her beautiful face. She was truly stunning: a curvy, perfectly proportioned figure, golden blond hair, smooth skin, clear green eyes. Her personality, though, ran the gamut from nasty to mean. "What kind of coffee is this? Surely you can afford a better brand. This is too bitter. And I have to say, your secretary—"

"Diedra isn't my secretary, she's my

assistant," Jaclyn interrupted as she stepped inside and closed the door behind her. She ignored the comment about the coffee, which she personally liked very much. No one was holding Carrie down and pouring the coffee down her throat, so she was free not to drink it if she didn't like it. After all, she could have chosen from a variety of flavored teas, or even soft drinks.

"Well, she was rude." Carrie didn't like being interrupted. She also didn't like not getting her way in all things. She was still carrying a grudge because Jaclyn hadn't been able to book Michael Buble for the reception. *Get real.* Jaclyn hadn't embarrassed herself by even trying.

"In what way, dear?" She made her tone soothing, and tacked on the "dear" even though her tongue almost shriveled with distaste when she forced herself to say it. Sometimes a comforting "dear" or "honey" could soothe the most fractious of clients—then again, some clients would have required a tranquilizer dart. Carrie would probably need the same dosage one would use on a mad rhino.

"She tried to make me wait outside, instead of in here."

"That's because I don't like people in my office unless I'm also here," Jaclyn said calmly. "I'm sure you understand."

"Don't be silly. Why should you care?"

"Because I keep confidential information in here. I suppose I'll simply start locking the door. I should have been doing that anyway." The confidential information wasn't anything relating to security or credit card numbers, but rather the details of weddings—and, yes, some clients would pay dearly to find out what so-and-so was planning, or how much someone else paid. Weddings were a cutthroat business.

Carrie gave her a hard, cold look, but evidently realized she wasn't going to get any traction on this issue, so she moved on to her next complaint. "I've changed my mind about the bridesmaids' dresses," Carrie said. "The shade of the fabric is too plain, all of them in gray like a line at West Point or something. I think it would look better if the one closest to me was in black, then the next dress would be a shade lighter, the next one a shade lighter than that, and so on. That would be really dramatic, don't you think? And instead of having the sashes in pink, I think I'd like teal. Pink is too *Paris Hilton.* I want something more sophisticated, like teal. But not a greenish teal, I want something more on the blue side. You can take care of the problem, can't you?"

Jaclyn bit her tongue. The poor bridesmaids had already paid for the hideous dresses, and Carrie, of course, hadn't chosen an inexpensive fabric. The color wasn't hideous, but the design certainly was. She'd tried to steer Carrie away from flounces and bows, but if Carrie ran into anything even remotely resembling good advice, so far she'd invariably run in the opposite direction. When the unfortunate bridesmaids found out about this change—when they found out they were going to have to pay for another dress, and this time a hefty charge for a rush order would be included—they'd probably all storm out. The girl who'd let Carrie have it and quit the wedding party was apparently the smart one.

"Carrie," Jaclyn said in a purposely soothing voice, "it's really too late to make this change. I think you'll be very happy with the look of the bridesmaids' dresses, when you see them with the flowers you've chosen."

"I'm thinking of changing the flowers, too," Carrie said, a gleam in her eye telling Jaclyn she was actually enjoying being difficult. "They're just not right. I was studying the sample pictures last night, and they look like someone vomited Pepto Bismol. I saw the most wonderful arrangement in a magazine. If I change the flowers, then I also need to completely redo the bridesmaids' look."

"This will be quite an expense for your friends."

Carrie's lips pursed, her eyes narrowed. "They won't mind. This is my special day, and they'll do whatever I want them to do." In her tone was an unspoken *or else.*

"If you insist, you can call the dressmaker and—"

"I want you to do it," Carrie said carelessly. "I don't have time." She opened her expensive, oversized handbag, withdrew a fabric sample, and slapped it onto the desk. Jaclyn could tell at a glance it was a fine, heavy silk—another expensive choice, something that would set each bridesmaid back several hundred dollars, perhaps even more than a thousand. "Besides, when I called her this morning to discuss the matter, she was hateful and unreasonable."

Dealing with the dressmaker technically wasn't in Jaclyn's job description; she handled the details of the event itself. But she knew Gretchen pretty well; they ran in the same circles, they very often worked the same weddings. Gretchen was never hateful or unreasonable, but then again, Carrie Edwards had the ability to bring out the worst in everyone.

"I'll see what I can do, but I won't make any promises. We're running out of time, to the point there literally may not be anything you can do other than buying the bridesmaids' dresses off the rack—"

"No. Never."

"Then you may have to go with your original choice. Now, as far as the flowers are concerned, the floral designer has already put in a lot of time making sure every aspect of the wedding and reception are well coordinated and original, as you requested," she reminded Carrie. "If you change your mind about the bridesmaids' bouquets it will affect the bridal arrangement and the boutonnieres, as well as the arrangements for the reception." Bishop Delaney was a genius. He also had a very low bullshit threshold, and if he walked it would be difficult to find someone reputable at this late date. "If you insist on making changes, be prepared to pay quite a bit more than you were originally quoted."

"Why?" Carrie demanded. "If I don't use the other flowers, why should I pay for them?"

"Because the designer has already spent a considerable amount of time making arrangements, and he shouldn't have to take a loss because you changed your mind. His initial order has already been placed, I'm sure, but I'm not sure that he'll be able to cancel." Tomorrow was supposed to be about Bishop showing photos and drawings of his grand plans, not a point to start from scratch. Jaclyn did not want to be between Bishop and Carrie if they butted heads.

Sometimes she felt as if she was instructing a wayward, willful child in manners, but the gleam that was still in Carrie's eyes was too calculating. She was so demanding because, all too often, she'd gotten away with it. Probably a lot of people finally gave up and took the loss rather than keep dealing with Carrie, which meant she'd learned to double-down whenever anyone called her on her behavior. Acting badly usually got her what she wanted.

Now she wrinkled her nose and sniffed, before waving away Jaclyn's point, petulantly. "We'll discuss it with the florist tomorrow. I'm sure *he'll* be reasonable. At the moment, my main concern is fixing the problem with the bridesmaids' dresses."

Jaclyn took a deep breath. In. Out. She was not going to let this spoiled, nasty little twit get the best of her. "Why don't we meet with the dressmaker tomorrow and discuss our options?" Maybe together, she and Gretchen could convince Carrie that it was much too late to make this change, that there simply wasn't time to order the fabric and get the dresses made—not that reason and the bridezilla were well-acquainted. Jaclyn wasn't sure they'd ever even met. In order to save Gretchen from another phone call, she said, "I'll call this afternoon and make the arrangements."

Carrie rolled her eyes. "Well, duh. That's your *job*."

Jaclyn had dealt with difficult brides in the past, but Carrie was a one-in-a-million pain in the ass. One of the advantages of being her own boss, however, was that she could decide when enough was enough. She very slowly stood, planted her hands on her desk, and said, "It's also a job I can walk away from. I won't take any abuse, and my assistant won't take any abuse. Are we clear on that?"

Carrie gave her an affronted glare. "*Abuse?* I haven't abused anyone. I simply want my wedding to be spectacular, and I don't see why—"

"Instead of spectacular, it's going to be a disaster if you don't stop changing your mind," Jaclyn said bluntly. "I'm saying this because it's my *job* to make things run smoothly, which means pointing out when you're about to go off a cliff. I'm not saying the floral designer absolutely won't be able to change the flowers at this late date, I'm saying that doing so might cost you quite a bit more, and you should really find out from Gretchen if it's physically possible to have new bridesmaids' dresses made before you do anything about the flowers. You might also check with your bridesmaids, because no matter what color you've decided you prefer, one or more might drop out rather than pay for another dress they'll never wear again. Now, if *you* want to pick up the expense for new dresses, I'm sure none of them would mind—"

"Don't be ridiculous," Carrie snapped. "The bride doesn't pay for the bridesmaids' dresses."

"Under certain circumstances, she most certainly does. Changing her mind at the last minute is one of those certain circumstances." Maybe, Jaclyn thought optimistically, if she started playing hardball with Carrie, the young woman would either stop being such a pain in the ass or fire Premier. Jaclyn could heave a sigh of relief, and Carrie would set her sights on some other poor event planner who would let the promise of a big paycheck blind her to the true situation.

"I know my friends," Carrie said. "None of them would be that petty." She tossed her long blond hair, then reached into her handbag and pulled out the sample menu she'd already decided on for the reception—if she could only make up her mind about the kabobs. Beef or lamb. How freakin' hard could it be? "And another thing . . ."

Jaclyn kept her expression calm, but as Carrie went on and on about what was acceptable and what wasn't, she mentally checked out and made one very firm decision: before this day was over, she was going to need a good, stiff drink.

Chapter Two

Detective Eric Wilder sat at the bar in his favorite watering hole, Sadie's, which was his favorite because it was the closest to city hall and the police department, therefore the most convenient. For most of the other cops in the long, dim, narrow room, that was the main attraction for them, too.

Over time, business and clientele had adjusted to each other, so now Sadie's made allowances for the cops, and the cops made allowances for "Sadie," who happened to be the scrawny redneck bartender. "Sadie" obviously wasn't his name—that was Will Aster—and whatever ambience he'd been trying to project by choosing a woman's name for his bar had long since been swamped under a tide of uniforms, weaponry, and testosterone. Sure, some of the female cops came in, and sometimes one of the guys would bring in a wife or girlfriend, or civilians would wander in, but Sadie's was now solidly a cop bar.

If Will had ever intended his bar to be more sophisticated, he'd long since given up on the effort. The drinks served were mainly beer and bourbon, and the food offerings didn't have much variety but tended toward the hefty side. You could get a basket of fried chicken fingers and fries in Sadie's, but you couldn't get a salad; peanuts were available, but not popcorn. Occasionally, if Will was in the mood, there would be "Wing Night," and nothing was served except hot wings. The limited menu was fine with Eric, because he didn't come to Sadie's to eat.

He liked the place, liked the way he could relax here. The atmosphere was almost cavelike, with dim lighting, dark red-brick walls, rough tile flooring, and a row of small black tables along the wall. An

aisle about six feet wide separated the
long bar from the tables, giving the two
waitresses room to maneuver. A jukebox
stood in one corner, and that was Sadie's
nod to the idea of entertainment. There
wasn't a dance floor, but if enough people
were in the mood they'd shove the tables
to the back of the bar and make themselves a space for gyrating. The bar was
usually noisy with loud laughter and sick
jokes, which was how cops unwound after
a rough day. Whenever Eric stepped
through that door, he could almost feel the
tension begin to ease from his neck and
shoulders. By the time he'd made it to the
bar, Will would have pulled him a Bud and
was ready to slide the foamy glass to him.
You couldn't beat service like that.

After a day spent testifying in court, he
needed a beer before he headed home.
There were few things that frustrated him
as much as lawyers and the entire court
system, even when the outcome was a
good one. A bad outcome was when some
slick legal eagle got a drug case dismissed
because some unimportant *i* hadn't been
dotted, which pissed him off big-time, and
he wasn't above hoping that the druggie

would then burgle the lawyer's house looking for quick-sell items to support his habit.
Today, though the cases had been relatively minor and justice had prevailed, he'd
still had to spend too many hours hanging
around just to give five minutes of testimony, when he could have been out working cases. It was all part of the job, but it
was the part he liked least.

He'd been there about fifteen minutes,
long enough for the pleasure of not doing
anything to begin seeping into his muscles,
when the outside door opened, letting in
street noise and warm humid air. All the
cops in the bar automatically glanced over
to check out the new arrival. It was reflex,
an unconscious threat assessment: Was
the new arrival friend or foe, cop or civilian?
Eric did the same, and immediately recognized the newcomer. A warm jolt hit his
midsection. No doubt about it: she was
the woman he'd bumped into that morning
in city hall, just outside one of the munici-
pal courtrooms. She was still wearing the
same stylish black suit, which meant her
day had been as long as his.

He liked what he saw now just as much
as he had in the hallway at city hall. Every-

thing about her said "classy," from the suit she wore to the way she pulled her thick black hair into a smooth, heavy knot at the back of her head. She had legs, capital *L,* holy-shit, wrap-them-around-me Legs: long, shapely, nicely muscled and toned. He could almost feel the interest level in the bar rising several notches as the guys looked her over. The women cops who came in almost always dressed down, suppressing their femininity not only so they'd fit in better with the guys but so they'd be taken more seriously by the disorderly element of citizenry they dealt with the most. This woman didn't downplay anything. Neither was there anything gaudy or obvious about her, which made her even more attractive, because "class" and "Sadie's" didn't usually collide.

She paused briefly in the doorway, scanning the row of tables as if looking for someone, then she strode toward the back where there were two unoccupied tables close to the restrooms. The three-inch heels she wore meant she wouldn't be able to run, but she sure as hell had a way of walking in them that made it almost impossible for him to look away from the sway of her hips. This morning in city hall when she'd walked away he'd had the same problem looking away from her ass, but then again, a sight like that was worth savoring.

She chose an empty table and sank into one of the chairs, positioned so that he had a view of her profile and her back was to most of the bar, which told him she either didn't have the survivor instinct to watch the door or she didn't want to make eye contact with anyone. When she was seated she visibly exhaled, rolling her shoulders and tilting her head from side to side to ease tense muscles, as if her purpose in being there jibed a hundred percent with that of most of the patrons.

From where he sat at the end of the bar, Eric could easily keep her in his field of vision without turning his head. She wasn't paying attention to any of the other patrons, had chosen her seat so she actually couldn't without turning around in her chair. She was probably waiting for someone else to arrive. He found himself surprisingly interested in who she might be meeting in a cop bar. Was she dating a cop? Or had she and a boyfriend simply arranged to meet here for convenience, then they'd move on to their dinner date, or whatever?

He glanced at his watch, because appointments were normally made for the hour or half-hour. It was eight-eleven. If she was waiting for someone, the odds were that she was roughly twenty minutes early. He felt that little *ping* of increased alertness he always felt when he noticed something that was even a little out of the ordinary. Most women would rather wait in their cars until their dates or appointments arrived, rather than sit alone in a bar. Maybe it was a sense of self-consciousness, a safety issue, or they simply didn't want to deal with any unwanted attention. For this woman to come in alone, twenty minutes before a logical meeting time, didn't fall within his mental parameters of most common behavior.

He automatically assessed her physically: five-seven, between a hundred twenty-five and a hundred forty, black and blue. Her hair was true black, and even though he couldn't see their color now, he remembered the clear blue of her eyes, the paleness of her skin: Black Irish coloring at its finest. She was tall and slim, dressed like a million bucks, and, he kept coming back to the word, classy.

No wedding ring, either. She wore a slim gold watch, and small gold hoops in her ears. No rings at all. If he got closer, whether or not he'd see a pale circle or an indentation on her ring finger was up in the air, but from where he was sitting he couldn't make out any telltale sign.

One of the waitresses approached her table, slapped down a cocktail napkin, and waited with a poised pen for the order. Eric couldn't hear what she ordered, but a few seconds later the waitress slid the order across the bar to Will and said, "Margarita on the rocks."

There weren't many froufrou drinks served at Sadie's, but Eric supposed a margarita on the rocks was kind of middle ground: not so swishy that a man wouldn't drink it, but not in the same class with a bourbon and Coke, either. When the drink was carried across to her, he watched as she took a sip, savored the taste, and sort of relaxed deeper into her chair.

She took her time with the margarita, sipping slowly, probably deliberately nursing the drink while she waited, and he watched the clock hands move toward eight-thirty. But eight-thirty came and went, and no one arrived. Neither did she check the time on her watch, so she wasn't feeling anxious about the passing time. She never looked around whenever the door opened. Huh. Evidently he was wrong that she'd been waiting for someone. Maybe she'd come in for no other reason than she wanted to unwind over a drink, just like almost everyone else in the bar.

He thought about approaching her table, speaking to her, but even though his interest was piqued he was way more cautious with women now than he used to be. At his age, thirty-five, he wasn't led around by his dick any longer, and he'd been through a divorce, all of which should make a man see the wisdom of not rushing in.

The fact was, she looked expensive, and he wasn't in the mood for an expensive complication. Women were always complications, bless their perverse little hearts. He enjoyed women for a lot of reasons, but he also enjoyed the simplicity of his bachelorhood. A man didn't even have to marry a woman to lose his bachelorhood; all he had to do was be in a somewhat steady relationship with her, and he'd find himself structuring his free time to accommodate her. And God forbid you actually move in with a steady girlfriend; you might as well get married. He knew, because he'd tried all the variations: married, not married but living together, steady dating, semi-steady dating . . . it all boiled down to the same thing, meshing their lives together. For right now, he wanted his life unmeshed. Some day, yeah, he'd probably get married again, but he wasn't in any hurry, and when he did take that step he'd make damn sure they were more compatible than he'd been with his first wife. There should be a law against people getting married before they were at least twenty-five.

There was one other possibility for Ms. Classy, too, one that made him doubly cautious. Maybe she was a cop groupie. Some women got off on having sex with a cop. It had something to do with the uniform and the weapon, whether it was the one in the holster or the one behind the zipper, or maybe both. Some cops, especially newbies, let the increased sexual attention go to their heads, which could wreck both careers and marriages. Eric had always steered clear of that, even when he'd been in uniform. Now that he was a detective, he was looking ahead to other promotions, and he wasn't about to let a piece of ass, even a prime piece, mess with his good judgment and common sense.

The temptation got to someone else, though. A chair scraped back; he watched Blake Gillespie, a street cop still in uniform, approach Ms. Classy's table. Eric controlled a scowl. It wasn't any of his business if Gillespie tried his luck, and if she was a cop groupie, better Gillespie than any of the other guys. At least Gillespie was single. That didn't mean Eric had to like watching another man make a move on a woman he'd spotted first, even when he didn't intend to make his own move. Okay, so men were territorial sons of bitches. Inform the newspapers, call the TV stations, and see if anyone gave a shit.

He watched as Gillespie made his move, with the easy smile and an invitation to join him. Ms. Classy glanced up without a change of expression, then calmly shook her head and said, "No, thank you," before looking away as if the matter had been settled. Eric couldn't hear what she'd said, but easily read her lips because she'd formed the words so firmly and plainly.

Okay, so she wasn't a cop groupie. Gillespie was a young guy, worked out all the time to pack his uniform with muscles, and he wasn't butt-ugly, either. If she'd been looking to bag a cop in the sack, Gillespie would be sitting beside her now instead of shrugging and heading back to his own table. At least he hadn't got pissy about her rejection, which upped Eric's opinion of the young patrolman.

She wasn't waiting for anyone, and she wasn't looking to get picked up. Hell, maybe she was simply a woman who'd wanted a drink. He could relate to that. Not the part about being a woman, but wanting a drink was definitely relatable.

Eric turned his attention to his beer, studying the amber liquid for several long minutes. He should probably finish it and head home. The last thing he should do was waste any more time trying to figure out what a woman was thinking, even a woman with world-class legs and a drool-worthy ass. But— "What the fuck," he muttered under his breath as temptation grabbed him by the dick and hung on. He slid from the barstool, grabbed his beer, and headed toward the classy, expensive complication.

Out of her peripheral vision, Jaclyn saw another man approaching. She could hope that he wasn't really headed her way, that he was on his way to the men's room which *was* just past her table, but it certainly seemed that he was walking directly toward her. He had a drink in his hand, so she was almost certain he wasn't going to the restroom. Why couldn't a woman stop after work for one drink without men— some men, anyway—assuming she was willing to be picked up? At least the first guy had been decent, taking himself off without an argument when she'd said no, so she could only hope this guy would do the same. She purposely didn't look his way, hoping he'd take the hint and keep moving.

"Small world."

The two words jarred her, because they weren't what she'd expected. She looked up, her cool expression still in place, but when she recognized the man standing in front of her her mind kind of went blank for a minute. She never sputtered, but she came damn close to it as she mentally scrambled for something to say, and what finally came out was a far cry from the stone-wall dismissal she'd planned. "Don't call me ma'am again," she said, her eyes narrowing in warning.

The cop smiled, that same slight but humorous curve of his lips she'd noticed before, and something in Jaclyn unwound. There was something *real* about him, a straightforwardness that didn't scream *pickup* or any other kind of game playing—and, damn, he was fine. That description seemed to be the best she could come up with. He wasn't handsome, but all her hormones and little chemistry receptacles or whatever were sitting up and paying attention. They were saying *Man!* in all the best ways. She wasn't the type to moon over a man, and God knows she'd never been a giggler or much of a flirt—much—but that didn't mean she couldn't appreciate a man's body and face, if he had a body and face worthy of appreciation.

This cop had both.

She found herself giving him a small,

rueful smile in return, and explained, "It's just . . . on a bad day, being called ma'am by someone near my own age makes me feel old. You have good manners, and I shouldn't hold that against you."

"I hope your day improved after you left city hall," he said.

"Not really." She had to crane her head back to look up at him. The dim lighting in the bar, and the shadows his position created, kept her from getting as clear a look as she'd like at his features, but her memory was good. She'd known he was tall, because with her heels she was about five-ten, and he'd still been three or four inches taller than she was. She liked the breadth of his shoulders, the mature and muscled depth of his chest. Her memory provided a too-sharp sensory image of how hard and warm his body had felt against hers in that brief moment when they'd collided, and she mentally shied away from the intimacy implied.

Her hormones didn't know their collision had been an accident; they just knew they had liked her contact with this man's body. She might have felt this sharp a physical attraction before, but at the moment she couldn't remember when. The fact that what she felt was so strong both compelled and repelled. Part of her was excited, wanted to respond, wanted to see where this would take her; another part urged her to run like hell. When she thought of what she wanted from a relationship, what came to mind was comfort and compatibility, a sense of ease, of fitting together—along with physical attraction, of course. If the physical attraction was so strong that it clouded her mind, that couldn't be good.

"That's too bad."

His comment so neatly dovetailed with what she'd been thinking that it took her a moment to reconnect to the conversation. "But at least I didn't smash into anyone else this afternoon."

"That's a plus. Another one, and I'd have to cite you for a moving violation." The dryness of his tone made her smile again, even while she was having the usual arguments with herself. She didn't know him. Aside from the fact that physically he really did it for her—like she was going to tell him that—they had nothing to talk about. Before you knew it, they'd be discussing the weather, or he'd ask for her astrological sign. She really didn't want to do that two-step, but there was something about him . . . and she wasn't ready to let him go. Not yet.

"Please, have a seat," she said, motioning to the empty chair at her table.

He sat, placed his drink on the table with a solid thunk that almost seemed as if he was staking a claim to the spot, and looked her in the eye. His face was no longer shadowed, as it had been when he'd been standing. Nice jaw, a mostly straight nose, dark level brows, and a penetrating intentness to his gaze. Dark hair, and she thought his eyes were probably hazel, though in the dim bar she couldn't really tell. But most important of all, this man was confident. He was accustomed to getting his way, which could be off-putting, but somehow he projected those qualities without coming off as arrogant. She suddenly had the thought that his good manners were kind of a camouflage, hiding a dangerousness hinted at by the piercing intensity of his eyes.

"Are you waiting for someone?" he asked, double-checking even though he was already seated.

"No."

"Good." Settling more comfortably into his chair, he extended his hand. "I'm Eric Wilder."

Amused, she started grinning even before she placed her hand in his. His big, warm fingers wrapped around hers and she willed herself not to get totally, completely, sucked in by the feel, even though it was a sensation that would be very easy to get lost in. "Wilder?"

"It's just a name, not a comment on my personality or lifestyle."

"Pleased to meet you, Eric Wilder," she said. "I'm Jaclyn Wilde. It's just a name, not a comment on my personality or lifestyle." He'd turned his hand just a little, the subtle movement changing their grip from that of a handshake to something more . . . intimate. Her heartbeat jacked up, and she fought the sudden urge to lick her lips.

He laughed, his eyes crinkling and his head tipping back a little, revealing a strong, tanned throat. "For real?"

"For real."

"It really is a small world, isn't it?" He let go of her hand, and as much as she hated to release that warmth and strength, she couldn't very well grab his hand and hold on. Then he deliberately caught her left hand and lifted it, checking out her ring finger. She lifted her brows, then coolly gave him back as good as she got, pointedly checking out his left hand, too. Not that the absence of a wedding ring was a sure sign that a person was single, but it made for a safer bet.

He leaned back, lifting his beer for a sip. "So, Jaclyn Wilde, why did you have a bad afternoon?"

She sighed and reached for her margarita, mirroring his actions. He was probably sipping for pleasure, though, while the mere thought of Carrie Edwards made her need more liquid fortification. "I'm a wedding planner, and I had a long, miserable meeting with probably the worst client I've ever had in my career. She has the ability to turn the gentlest of people into raving lunatics."

"You don't look like a raving lunatic."

"No, but it was close. I did feel the overwhelming need to stop for a drink on my way home, thanks to bridezilla. That's not something I usually do." She didn't want him to think she was a lush . . . not that it really mattered what he thought. She'd share a drink with him, then she'd head home and that would be that.

Men didn't make Jaclyn nervous. She knew who she was, and that was all that mattered . . . usually. Eric Wilder, though, made her nervous. Not jumpy nervous, not uncomfortable, just on edge and sharply *aware,* as if her skin had become too tight and too sensitive. Looking at him was suddenly too much, so instead she glanced around the bar with a nonchalance she was far from feeling.

"Wedding planner," he said. "Sounds like an interesting job."

"I'm technically an events planner, but most of our business is weddings. And I have to admit, some days are more interesting than others." She forgot about nonchalant and looked directly at him, which delivered another jolt to her nervous system because he didn't look away. Instead, those intense eyes—yes, they *were* hazel—remained locked on hers.

"In my experience, a wedding is a really crappy way to start a marriage," Eric said.

"This opinion is based on what?" she asked, both amused and a little testy because there was a possibility that he could be right.

"My own wedding," he said bluntly. "The entire weekend was a nightmare. I think I'm the only one who didn't cry, and we're not talking tears of joy, here."

The bottom dropped out of her stomach. Jaclyn could feel her spine straighten, her unexpected enjoyment of the conversation shutting down. "You're married?"

"Not anymore. Divorced. Six years, now." He lifted his beer. "You?"

"Divorced, too."

Thank God, that little detail was out of the way. They were both divorced and, apparently, available. Not that availability was required for a simple conversation, but it was nice to know.

"Were you a wedding planner when you got married?"

"I was. Mom and I had just started the business."

"So, does a woman who plans everyone else's wedding go whole hog with her own? Or were you already tired of the whole deal?"

"To answer in reverse order, I wasn't, and I did," she admitted, and added wryly,

"The marriage lasted only slightly longer than the ceremony. But, no, I don't get tired of what I do. When everything turns out just right and everyone has fun, it's something to remember. . . .

"And in case you're wondering, I didn't cry at my own wedding," she added, teasing.

"I don't imagine you did."

She took another sip of her margarita, and Eric signaled for the waitress. "Let me get you another drink."

Jaclyn shook her head at the girl who was headed her way, covered the top of her glass to signal that she didn't want a refill, and turned to Eric. "Only one drink for me. I'm driving."

"You didn't come here to get lost in a lime and tequila haze?"

"I never get lost in any kind of haze," she said.

"What do you get lost in?" he asked, and she could almost feel that intense gaze boring beneath her skin.

"Work," she answered with honesty, though a part of her, a part that had been dormant for a long while, realized that she could very easily get lost in Eric Wilder. "You?"

"Work."

"Better a workaholic than an alcoholic," Jaclyn said, thinking of her father's struggle with booze. It wasn't an accident that there was no liquor in her house, that she always limited herself to one single drink. She'd never had a drinking problem, but she was always aware of Jacky Wilde's weaknesses and the possibility that she might've inherited a penchant for obsession. Or, heaven help her, addiction. But she didn't want to think about her dad—she loved him, but a little of him went a long way—and she'd talked enough about herself. She wanted to know more about him. "How long have you been a cop?"

"Thirteen years. I joined the army straight out of high school, got my degree while I was in, and took my civil service exam as soon as I left Uncle Sam's employ."

"Your job is probably way more interesting than mine. At least the people I deal with usually stop short of committing a crime."

"Usually?" His dark brows rose.

"You don't want to know."

He did, though, so she found herself

telling him about the time the entire wedding party had been smoking pot before the ceremony, the time the groom had waffled and the bride's mother had pulled a freaking *knife* from her purse and threatened to skewer his anatomical pride and joy if he backed out after all the money she'd spent, and other tales from the dark side. He laughed in the right places, a deep sound of genuine amusement that invited more confidences. He told her some of his own war stories, and she was aware that he kept things light, that he didn't get into the darker, more disturbing details.

Talking to him was easy. Despite the heat of physical chemistry that could completely burn her up if she let it, she was somehow able to push that aside and simply enjoy being with him. There weren't any of the usual awkward silences between new acquaintances. For the moment there was nothing except the pleasure of talking to him and feeling the heated tingle of attraction. She'd felt it from the instant she'd collided with him that morning, and closer acquaintance hadn't dulled any of the sharp edges. She'd walked into Sadie's for no other reason than she'd been driving by and seen it, a parking place had been available, and the idea of some downtime with a nice, soothing drink had been too tempting to resist. She was glad she hadn't resisted, glad she hadn't moved on to one of the more fashionable bars.

If she'd been thinking she would have realized that, this close to the police department, the odds were a bunch of cops would be here. She didn't *think* her subconscious had led her here, hoping she'd see him. Her day had been so hectic he honestly hadn't crossed her mind again . . . but if her subconscious *had* been at work, then all she could say was, good job. She was glad she'd stopped here, and glad she'd run into him again.

She finished the margarita, but she wasn't quite ready to leave. When the cocktail waitress came by to scoop up her empty glass, Jaclyn ordered a cup of decaf. Eric was still nursing his beer, and she was glad to see that he didn't knock it back and order another one. Like her, he was very much in control.

It wasn't like her to get comfortable with a man so quickly, but the sense of ease went both ways. From war stories, she moved on to telling him about her business, her mother-slash-business partner, and the absolutely insane schedule she had for the next few days.

He rolled his almost-empty glass between his palms, then glanced up at her. "So I should wait until next week before I call?"

Those hazel eyes were so intent her heart gave another of those disconcerting little thumps, and her mouth went dry. Her first thought was that maybe it was time her personal sexual drought ended. Her second thought was that she bet he'd be an excellent drought-ender. Her third thought was that, damn it, she didn't have *time.* But when she opened her mouth, what came out was "Not necessarily." Then her common sense kicked in again, and she sighed. "But, yes, next week would be better. Six weddings in five days doesn't leave me with any free time, even though Mom and I share the work."

"You have to eat," he said, his voice low and easy and slightly gruff. It was the kind of voice that would be capable of talking her into, well, anything. Oh, damn, he was either good or dangerous, or both.

"Yes, I suppose I do." Maybe the smartest thing for her to do was get away from the testosterone he was throwing out like a force field, so she could think more clearly. Besides, like it or not, it was getting late and she needed to go home and get to bed. She hesitated, then opened her purse and extracted her gold card case. "My card," she said needlessly, placing the cream-colored business card—with *Premier,* along with her name and numbers, in gold foil—on the table and sliding it toward him. "My office and cell numbers are both here."

He glanced at the card, holding it up to catch the light so he could see it clearly. "Not Wilde Weddings?"

Jaclyn smiled. "That's not the image we're trying to project."

He studied the card. "Classy." His gaze flicked back to her. "Like you."

Before she could respond, he reached into his inside jacket pocket and whipped out his own business card. It was black and white, a plain font, all business. It said as much about him as her card said about her. He turned it over, took a pen from his pocket, and scribbled on the back. "My cell number. Call me any time."

She dropped the card into her purse, stood, and said good night. "You'll be hearing from me," he said, and she didn't doubt it. As she walked toward the exit, she could feel him watching her, just as she had that morning. This time she looked back and smiled . . . and sure enough, his gaze was locked on her. The way he looked at her was enough to make her bones go to butter.

Damn.

Chapter Three

The streets were all but empty at this time of the evening on a weeknight, so driving didn't require nearly enough of Jaclyn's attention as she headed for home. Maybe if there'd been a line of traffic to maneuver through, or maybe some careless pedestrians, she could have kept her mind on mundane matters, but no one was obligingly suicidal enough to step in front of her. Not that she wanted to actually hit anyone, but the evasive maneuvers would at least have transferred her interest away from a certain cop.

No matter what she did to push him

aside, Eric Wilder remained lodged front and center in her thoughts. It was everything about him: his voice, his eyes, and, she might as well be honest with herself, his body. She liked his height, the breadth of his shoulders, and, well, everything. He was the kind of man who'd stand out in a crowd no matter where he went; he would draw her eye in any courthouse, in any bar . . . anywhere at all. The problem was, the very last thing she needed to complicate her life right now was a relationship of any kind, whether it was sexual, romantic, friendly, unfriendly, whatever—even if the man in question occupied her thoughts as she drove home. She didn't need to be thinking about men, not about him in particular or about men in general. She needed to mentally run through the next day's work plan, because she and Madelyn were about to enter the insane portion of the week's schedule, not the least of which was the meeting with Carrie Edwards and the poor, abused vendors she'd selected. After Carrie's wedding was over, Jaclyn figured she owed each and every vendor an abject, and heartfelt, apology.

Current insane schedule aside, Jaclyn

wasn't against the idea of having a man in her life. In fact, she wanted one. She didn't want to live her life alone; getting married and having kids someday were definitely in her long-range plans. Someday she'd find a man she loved, and who loved her, and they'd make it work, have one or two kids, and grow old together. Her first marriage had failed, but that didn't mean she'd given up on men; she was just more cautious. Okay, maybe *too* cautious. Someday, though . . .

But this wasn't "someday," this was *now,* and she had her hands full. A man like Eric Wilder was a time-suck; she instinctively knew it, even though she'd spent little more than an hour, if that much, in his company. He might not insist on having a woman's undivided attention, but she had the feeling that the sheer force of his personality would make him as hard to ignore as an elephant in the living room. Just because he'd been playing nice tonight didn't mean she couldn't see the force beneath that civilized veneer. As a general rule, the meek and mild didn't become cops. And as another general rule, cops were almost perpetually on call even on their days off, worked long, irregular hours, and, like marrying a doctor, a woman should go into a relationship with a cop accepting that the job wasn't a regular nine-to-fiver in either schedule or importance. Having Eric around would do nothing but muck up her orderly life.

Not that she'd mind being mucked by him.

Crap!

Exasperated by the way her thoughts kept going back to him, Jaclyn rummaged in her bag, snagged her cell phone, and hit the speed dial for her mom.

Her mother answered with her usual, confident "Madelyn Wilde," her husky voice touched with a Southern accent deeper and richer than Jaclyn's. Madelyn had the type of accent that could turn a two-syllable word into four, slow and redolent with a lazy charm that was in no way reflected in her personality. Madelyn was charming, beyond a doubt, but she was also tough and ballsy. She'd been a rock for Jaclyn during the tough days when her marriage was disintegrating beneath her, though maybe that was more along the lines of returning the favor, because Jaclyn had comforted her mother more times than one could count during Madelyn's own breakup with Jaclyn's dad.

"How did the rehearsal go?" Jaclyn asked. Sometimes she and her mother shared the duties of an event, if bookings were slow, but when things were busy they would split up. This week, things were way beyond merely "busy."

"As smoothly as can be expected," Madelyn drawled, her tone calm and amused. "The groom was late, the bride went into hysterics because she thought he was leaving her at the altar, never mind that they weren't even at the altar yet, and one of the bridesmaids showed up with a black eye. A door, she said, but no one believed *that* story. I heard she got drunk at one of the showers, knocked over the punch bowl, and the ladle hit her in the eye."

Jaclyn took a moment to imagine that scenario, and couldn't keep the smile out of her voice. "Since you didn't call earlier with bad news, I'm assuming the groom arrived and the wedding is on."

"Yes, and Peach called a friend of hers who's a whiz with makeup. She made an appointment for the girl. Tomorrow evening, no one will realize that one of the brides-maids is sporting a shiner."

Peach was Madelyn's friend and assistant, and together the two women could work wonders. It was a large part of the reason Premier not only survived, but thrived. Between the two of them, they knew almost everyone who was anyone in the Buckhead area—and in Buckhead, everyone was someone. What made Premier different was their ability to handle any situation with aplomb, and Jaclyn was definitely her mother's daughter.

Middle-of-the week weddings were unusual but not unheard-of. The happy couple had been able to snag the reception site they wanted for a bargain price, and they hadn't been forced to wait months for the church to be available for the ceremony. The affair wasn't one of the big, extravagant presentations, but Premier handled weddings in all price ranges, and how many duties Jaclyn and Madelyn handled depended on how much the bride wanted to spend.

Madelyn sighed, and asked the inevitable question. "How did your meeting with the bride from hell go?"

"I didn't kill her, if that's what you're asking," Jaclyn said drily. Even though she was the one handling Carrie Edwards's wedding, no detail was unshared. Madelyn and Peach knew everything about the problems with Carrie.

"Diedra talked to Peach this afternoon, and brought her up-to-date. It's a bad sign when no one has anything nice to say about the bride. Makes you wonder if the groom has lost his mind. Even if she can suck the chrome off a bumper, there's no blow job good enough to be worth living with her." While Jaclyn was still snorting with laughter at the incongruity of the bawdy insult drawled in Madelyn's lazy-Southern-lady accent, her mother added, "It's a big wedding, the money is nice, but I swear, if we'd known how much trouble this wedding would be, we would've tossed it back like a stinky fish."

They were all counting the days until Carrie's wedding was over and behind them. In their years of business they'd dealt with some doozies: angry brides, demanding brides, brides who cried at the drop of a hat, brides who probably heard voices telling them to kill. Then there were the mothers of the brides, who could be even worse, and the toxic bridesmaids, the grooms, the grooms' parents, the squalling flower girl and/or ring bearer . . . the list went on and on. But never before had they all been so anxious to be rid of a client. Carrie Edwards would be legend; she would be the bridezilla against which they'd measure all future bridezillas for pure meanness.

Jaclyn sighed. Most brides were perfectly wonderful, happy women; some were even a joy to work with. It was a shame that a few bad apples had to stain the reputation of so many.

"You're on your cell. Are you in the car?" Madelyn asked.

"On my way home."

"I thought you'd be home by now; were you working late?"

"I stopped at a bar for a much-deserved drink."

"I should've done the same after the rehearsal, but I was anxious to get home and take my shoes off. I rubbed a blister on my foot today. If you ever see me wearing those navy blue shoes again, slap me."

Madelyn had been invited to the rehearsal dinner, but as usual she'd declined. After a long day, blistered foot or no blistered foot, a frozen dinner in front of the television was always preferable to being "on" for a couple more hours. Besides, without official duties to keep them busy, attending the rehearsal dinner meant hours of casual conversation with people they didn't know and would likely never see again once the ceremony was over, so neither of them usually attended unless the bride specifically requested that they do.

Jaclyn considered telling her mother about Eric, but really, what was there to tell? *I met a nice guy who's maybe more wolf than lamb.* Jaclyn shivered, just a little. More accurately it would be, *I met a guy who makes my toes curl,* which wasn't a conversation she wanted to have with her mother. They shared all the details of work, but definitely not the details of their love lives. She didn't want to think about her mother *having* a love life, though she knew Madelyn dated—much more often than she herself did, as a matter of fact—and she imagined Madelyn felt the same about her.

They made plans to meet at the office in the morning before they both got busy with their workday, said good-bye, and Jaclyn ended the call as she pulled into the one-car garage that each condo possessed. To her, having the garage space was worth the cost of the condo. Though they weren't rolling in money, she and Madelyn each made a nice living from Premier. She lived in a nice place: spacious but not huge, sort of upper middle of the road, if such a thing existed. Overall she was very happy with her life and home, and the business they'd built.

There was something innately satisfying about what she did. She made sure marriages got off to the most spectacular, beautiful, and trouble-free start possible. She planned and executed wedding ceremonies and receptions that were events to remember with fondness if everything went right, and it was her job to make sure everything did. Relationships were her business, in a way, and yet she didn't have time for one of her own.

She was pretty sure that made a statement about her life, but she didn't know exactly what the statement was.

Eric had remained sprawled at the table after Jaclyn had left, staring at his empty beer glass and wondering if he should order another. No, he had to drive home; one was his limit. And if he wasn't going to order another beer, he should be nice to the waitress and get his ass out of the chair so the table would be available to customers who actually intended to order something.

Someone slid into the empty chair across from him, and he glanced up to see Gillespie leaning toward him, his expression one of good-natured mischief. "Okay, old man, what did you say to her that would make a woman like that talk to someone like you, when she gave *me* the brush-off?"

Eric snorted. Old man, his ass; he was only seven or eight years older than Gillespie. He could tell by the small pool of silence around them that eager ears were listening, hoping to hear something they could use to rag Gillespie in the locker room tomorrow. Not that the patrolman wasn't well-liked—he was—but an opportunity was an opportunity, no matter who the target was.

"Listen closely, Grasshopper," he intoned, holding up one finger as if to focus the attention of a thick-headed student.

"I'm listening, Master," Gillespie said in a falsetto.

"One must be subtle with women," he continued, raising his voice just a little so their audience could catch every word.

"Subtle." Gillespie refrained from snickering. Eric wasn't exactly known for his subtlety; he was more of a kick-ass type of guy who'd had to learn restraint.

"Anything overtly sexual is a turnoff, not a come-on."

"Roll up your pants legs, the bullshit's getting deep in here," came a loud whisper from their audience.

"You're going too fast. Let me take some notes," said Gillespie, pulling out his notebook and pen and flipping to a blank page. He wrote down one word. "Okay: subtle. I got that. What else?"

"There's one thing about me that gave me a big advantage," said Eric, and their surrounding buddies erupted.

"Come on, Wilder, it ain't *that* big; we've all seen you in the shower, remember?"

"Yeah," added a black detective, grinning. "You're not even the right color, man."

Eric kept his tone solemn. "Confucius say, sleeping tiger look small; attacking tiger look big as fucking rhino." While everyone was still hooting with laughter, he slid his chair back and stood. When the bar was quiet enough, he looked at Gillespie and said, "But I wasn't talking about the size of my dick. There was something else."

"Yeah? What was it?"

"We'd met before," Eric said, grinning, and walked out of the bar with their laughter and groans following him.

He stood on the sidewalk in the thick, humid heat of a summer night, taking a moment to look around at the city lights, his immediate surroundings, the passing traffic. It had been a long day, and he'd killed more time in the bar than he'd intended, thanks to Jaclyn Wilde. He should be hitting the sack pretty soon, but he still felt antsy, coiled with tension.

He didn't want to go home, not yet. Normally he looked forward to the peace and quiet, when he could kick back in his recliner, turn on the television, and watch some baseball or a fishing show, maybe a thriller, or read the newspaper he hadn't had time to look at that morning. But not tonight; tonight, he wanted . . . something else.

Hell, he knew what he wanted. Her. Ms. Classy. Jaclyn Wilde. Expensive complication or not, he wanted her naked. She was easy on the eyes, easy to talk to, and unless he missed his guess she was as attracted to him as he was to her. She'd also made it plain she put her business first and wouldn't make time for him until her schedule wasn't as hectic.

He walked to his car, restlessly jingling his keys in his hand. Like all cops, he paid attention to everything around him, all the noises, the cars driving by, anyone he saw on the street, but it was as if he did so on autopilot. A big part of his brain kept seeing Jaclyn's legs, and thinking of sliding that black skirt up them.

To hell with it.

He pulled out his phone and her card, and thumbed in her cell number. After two rings she answered with a crisp, "Hello."

"I don't want to wait a week," he said bluntly, not even identifying himself. "Invite me over."

There was a pause during which he could feel his heart beating and his balls and dick getting heavier with every second, waiting for the yes he knew she wanted to say, a pause that went on so long he began to think she might say no instead.

"Yes," she said, her voice low. "Yes. Come over now."

What the hell have I done?

Jaclyn stared at the phone in her hand. Oh my God. She hadn't asked him if he'd lost his mind, she hadn't simply given a polite "no," instead she'd actually told him to come over. It was as if her mouth had been acting independently of her brain . . . and her brain was nowhere near being on the same page as her body.

For a moment she seriously considered calling him back and telling him that she'd changed her mind, or that she'd been suffering delusions and had just regained her senses. Either way, the end result would be to send him elsewhere, anywhere but here. Every functioning brain cell, and admittedly she didn't seem to have a lot of them right now, told her she was crazy to get involved with him, or any man, in any way. It wasn't logical for her to trust a man she'd just met. Cop or not, polite or not, he was a stranger.

But her instincts were whispering—hell,

singing—a different tune. She wanted him pressed against her, into her. She wasn't ready for the night to end; she wasn't ready to let him go. She didn't often ignore her common sense in favor of gut instinct, but tonight she was going with her gut.

Her brain whispered, *That's* not *your gut you're listening to.*

She didn't care. Tonight she simply didn't care. For years, the most impulsive thing she'd done was when she and Madelyn decided to open their own business, even knowing the horrible percentage of new businesses that failed within the first five years. Premier was almost seven years old, was stronger than ever, but she and her mother had worked their butts off for those seven years and tonight she didn't want to be sensible, she didn't want to take things slow, she wanted . . . hell, she wanted *him.*

There was a small sense of disorientation as she placed her cell on the end table and walked into the bathroom, not hurrying, but not dawdling, either. After getting home she'd stripped off her business suit, removed her makeup and washed her face, then taken a quick shower and put on her comfortable thin white pajamas—a simple tank and loose-fitting pants. She'd taken her hair down and thoroughly brushed it, the strokes of the brush easing the last bit of tension from her scalp. Her scintillating plan for the evening had been to relax in front of the television for an hour or so, watch something easy like *House Hunters* or maybe the Food Network, then lights out. Tomorrow was going to be a very busy day.

Now . . . this. Eric was coming over. For a moment she stared at her reflection in the bathroom mirror, wondering if she should slap on some makeup again, maybe spritz on a little perfume, put on some clothes. It didn't take her long to decide. No, this was her, fresh-faced and un-adorned, her shoulder-length black hair hanging loose. She glanced down at her bare feet, glad she'd recently had a pedi-cure. Her toenails were a bright red, the only splash of color on her body tonight.

As for putting on clothes . . . who was she kidding?

She *did* brush her teeth, before return-ing to the living room to wait for him. Should she put on a pot of decaf? No. That would be just as ridiculous as rushing around to put her clothes and makeup back on. Eric Wilder wasn't coming here for coffee and more conversation. He was coming for sex, because he wanted her and she wanted him. They were adults, they both knew what this was about, and there was no reason for her to play games.

Her toes curled in anticipation.

When the doorbell rang she didn't jump, not exactly. Her heart jumped; something deep and low within her jumped. She took a deep breath, walked to the door, and, just as a precaution, she glanced through the peephole to make sure it was him before opening the door wide.

They stood there facing each other almost like adversaries, gunslingers standing in the street, each waiting for the other to make a move. Eric had loosened his tie, but nothing else had changed in the short time since she'd seen him last. Because she was barefoot now, he was a lot taller. Well, to be accurate she was shorter, but the end result was the same. He towered over her a good seven or eight inches.

He looked her over, blatantly, without an

ounce of discretion or subtlety or pretense, just the way he'd looked at her ring finger. His gaze traveled up and down, then slowly back up again, taking his time, lingering on the places of most interest to him. Jaclyn took a deep breath, then backed away from the door, stepping out of his way, inviting him inside. He strode forward two steps, into the room and closer to her, and then he closed and locked the door behind him.

His eyes were slightly hooded, his gaze pinned on her—her face, at the moment, which was good form on his part because she knew damn well her erect nipples were evident against the thin fabric of the white tank. Then again, he'd already seen all he could see while her clothes were on. "I couldn't stop thinking about you," he said.

Ditto. "Good . . . I think." She didn't know anything for certain, except she felt as if her skin might blister at any moment from the heat building inside her. Everything else was moving both too slow and too fast, events jumbling and bumping against each other even while time crawled.

He looked her up and down again; his

gaze lingered on her toes for a moment. "Good God, I could eat you up."

Butterflies fluttered in Jaclyn's stomach. It had been years since she'd been nervous or anxious enough to suffer from butterflies, years since she'd simply let go and *felt.* "So what's stopping you?"

"Nothing, thank God," he said roughly, catching her wrists and sliding his palms up her forearms, then cupped her elbows and pulled her forward until her progress was stopped only by his muscled body, the thin fabric of her pajamas doing nothing to cushion the impact or protect her from his heat. As naturally as if they had been together forever, his hands moved from her elbows to her back, down to her bottom, gripping and urging her hips forward until she was nestled against the hard length of his erection.

She drew a deep, shaking breath, savoring the feel of him, then tipped her face back and went up on her toes, meeting him as he lowered his head. As first kisses went, this one was like lightning, bright and hot and explosive. Maybe it was because they both knew where this was heading, knew there was no holding back. The kiss was deep and hungry, tongues tangling, one big hand in her hair, her fingers clasping the back of his strong neck. He bent his knees, wrapped one arm around her butt and the other around her back, and lifted her so her feet came off the ground and her head was more level with his. Automatically her legs parted, coiled around him, and he made a rough sound deep in his throat as his penis pushed hard against the softness between her legs.

"Where's your bedroom?" he asked, the words so low and rough-edged they were almost a growl. His hand slid down her spine, thrust inside the loose waistband of her cotton pajama pants, stroked over her butt.

"Back there," she said, freeing one hand to indicate where "back there" was. He turned and began striding in that direction even as his rough fingers delved lower, probing, and she gasped the last word. Oh, God. What was he— *Oh, God!* Her legs tightened around him and she instinctively lifted herself a little, though whether she was trying to escape or giving him easier access, she couldn't have said. Her breasts rubbed against his shirt, turning her nipples into aching points. What he was doing set off explosions all along her nerve pathways, making her squirm and arch and whimper, and they weren't even on the bed yet.

He maneuvered her through the doorway into the bedroom and put one knee on the bed, then took her down to the mattress with her still locked around him, his heavy weight crushing her. She'd left on a lamp, preparatory to going to bed; the mellow light washed over them as she pulled at his shirt; he peeled her tank off over her head, then went for her pants. While he stripped them down her legs his mouth closed hungrily over one nipple, sucking strongly, his tongue rasping around and around the puckered point until she almost couldn't bear it. She made a raw, wordless sound and her back arched, her hands leaving his garments to clasp each side of his head. The hot smell of his skin surrounded her as surely as his touch did, dragging her down beneath the rising tide of sheer need.

He fought his way out of his clothes and they were both, finally, naked. She felt as if she'd been waiting forever, as if the feel of his hot bare skin against her was something she'd been craving to the edge of madness. Panting, she clung to him, her hips lifting, searching for the inward thrust that would bring them together.

"Fuck!"

With that one explosive word, Eric moved away from her, *damn* him, and just as she was about to grab his ass and pull him back, she realized that he was reaching for his pants, delving in his pocket and pulling out a few condoms. He tossed a couple of them on the bedside table and tore open the one in his hand. *Thank God,* she thought weakly, horrified that the basic safety measure hadn't even occurred to her. At least one of them had a few working brain cells left; she wished she'd been the one, but she was grateful nevertheless. Even though she was on the Pill, a condom was a requirement.

He pulled her into position under him, spread her legs, braced himself on one arm, and with his other hand guided his penis to her. *At last, at last.* She was wet, ready, so close to the edge she thought she might come without him even making it inside her, if he didn't hurry. With one quick short push he had the head in, and she gasped as she discovered maybe she wasn't quite as ready as she'd thought.

It had been a while for her, so long that she couldn't immediately think of the last time; maybe that was why the discomfort was so sharp, why for a moment she wavered on the very edge of pushing him away. But need outweighed any other consideration, a need that had her clinging to him even though a whimper of distress almost escaped. She bit it back, and dug her nails into his shoulder muscles as he pushed deeper, his movements slow now, easing him deeper inside. His penis was hot and thick, so thick her flesh quivered around him. She blew out a breath, tried to relax. When he was seated to the hilt he let his weight down on her and framed her head with both hands, his fingers threaded through her hair. "Okay?" His voice was low, the word a breath across her lips.

"Give me a minute," she murmured, turning her head to find his lips again. How could something feel so wonderful and so . . . *upsetting* at the same time? She felt as if her flesh was under so much stress she might fly apart, but she didn't want him to stop.

He gave her the minute she'd asked for, and more. He kissed her, seducing her even though he was already inside her, courting her with his mouth and stroking hands, enticing her until her inner muscles eased and began to clasp his rigid length, until her breath came in rhythmic gasps and her hips began to move. "Now," she said in a choked tone, clinging to him and closing her mind to everything else except him.

For tonight, for now, there was nothing else, just the man and the night, and that was all she needed.

Chapter Four

Jaclyn slipped out of bed at five o'clock the next morning and, bemused, stood there listening to the slight snoring sound Eric was making: not really a snore, but more than just breathing. It sounded almost like a soft growl rumbling, barely audible, in his throat: a subconscious warning to any nearby predators maybe?

She silently picked up her pajamas, guided by the faint glow of the night-light in the bathroom, and tiptoed out of the room—not just to let him sleep, but because she didn't want to startle him awake. Last night when she'd let him in she'd been so focused on the feel and smell and taste of him, on satisfying that incredibly strong sexual urge, that she hadn't noticed anything else. After their second bout of lovemaking, though, she'd gotten up to go to the bathroom and spied the big black pistol lying on the bedside table. How could she have missed *that* when they were fighting to get each other out of their clothes? She felt as if she'd stepped over a rattlesnake without seeing it, or something like that.

She was uneasy with guns; she didn't know anything about them, and didn't want to learn. Never mind that she was a born-and-bred Southerner; she didn't go hunting, she went to the theater and shopping, which perhaps was a different kind of hunting but so far hadn't required any weapon other than a credit card.

Her father wasn't an outdoorsman, and neither was her ex-husband. In fact, the closest her ex came to the outdoors was when he went to a football game and actually sat in a stadium, drinking beer and feeling manly even though he didn't particularly care for football, and did it only because it enhanced his image as a lawyerly good old boy. His saving grace, Jaclyn remembered, was that he'd had a sense of humor about it. Steve wasn't a bad guy, he just wasn't the guy for her.

The fact was, she'd never been around guns, had never slept with a man who came to bed armed. What would happen if she shook him awake? Would he grab for the gun? She didn't want to find out, so she was extra careful not to make any noise as she eased the bedroom door closed.

Now what?

That was a question with as many layers as an onion. The first and most obvious answer was to go to the second bathroom. After relieving herself—and noting that sex was evidently like exercise, that unless you did it regularly an energetic bout made you sore—she put on her pajamas, got a drink of water, and combed her fingers through her hair because her brush was in her bedroom.

Next up: coffee.

She put on the coffee, and while it was brewing she stood in the kitchen with a hundred things running through her mind. Thinking about Eric made her uneasy, so she focused on work. She had a lot to do today, which meant she had to get an early start. Getting an early start meant she had to dislodge the cop from her bed and send him on his way so she could get ready. Dislodging him meant she had to wake him up. Waking him up meant she might be taking her life in her hands, depending on how jumpy he was, though probably he didn't go for his gun first thing. After all, if cops regularly shot the women they slept with, it would be all over the news.

Well, that was a comforting thought. Not.

Too late, she realized that she should have awakened Eric before she ever got out of bed, but she hadn't been thinking clearly. She hadn't wanted him to see her with bed head, or maybe try to kiss her while she had morning breath, or, God forbid, hear her peeing. None of that ever seemed to bother men, but it sure as hell bothered her. She didn't know him well enough to let him hear her peeing. Never mind that they'd had sex three times: first the hot, frantic sex, then relaxed sex, and the last time had been sleepy, cuddly sex at two in the morning— she still didn't know him. She knew a lot of things about him, mainly on the physical level, but she didn't know *him.*

What she did know was that she needed to shower and get ready. She needed to be in the office by seven; she had to move, and move fast. She needed to get the cop out of her bed and out of the house so she could do this, and she didn't have time for chitchat.

The coffeemaker finished its burping and spewing, beeping to let her know the coffee was ready. Gratefully she grabbed two cups, then paused and gave them a thoughtful look. Yeah, that would work. She knew just how to get him moving out the door, with a minimum of fuss.

Eric woke up when Jaclyn eased out of the bedroom. Through slitted eyes he admired the lean, graceful curves of her body just before she slipped out of sight and carefully closed the bedroom door. There wasn't a lot of her, but what she had was shaped just right, from her small, high breasts with those tight little nipples to the round curve of her ass. And her legs . . . holy fuck, her legs were a wet dream by themselves, slim and firmly muscled, and satiny smooth. He might never recover from the high of having those legs wrap around him and hug him tight.

But he should have gone home last night and not stayed in bed with her. Now what? He hated the awkwardness of the morning after. Did she want a morning quickie? He'd be glad to oblige her, except he needed to get home, shower, shave, and change clothes, and get to work, and women tended to get pissed if a man turned them down, no matter how good an excuse he had. Maybe she'd just want to cuddle or—God, he'd rather have a kick to the balls—talk about last night. Why did women always want to talk about the night before, at least if there had been sex involved? Just let it be. They'd had the hots for each other from the minute they'd collided at city hall, he'd asked, and she'd said yes. It wasn't any more complicated than that.

He wanted to see her again, yeah, but he didn't want to dissect everything he'd said and done last night . . . not that he'd said much. Neither of them had. Between bouts of sex, they'd both slept. When they'd met up in the bar she'd talked easily and with confidence, but after they were in bed talking had been kept to a minimum. It was nice, being with a woman who didn't think a good time to have an in-depth discussion about anything was while she was having sex. He liked that, liked her . . . so far.

But because he wanted to see her again, he figured he couldn't just get up, get dressed, and leave. He'd have to pave the way, make sure he didn't do anything to piss her off—such as getting up, getting dressed, and leaving. Which was why he should have done just that last night, with a hug and a kiss and a promise to call her later. For some stupid reason, women didn't seem to mind a guy leaving at night, but if you stayed until morning all sorts of weird rules kicked in, and damn if he knew what they were.

He rolled over and looked at the clock, and his eyebrows rose. Just after five. She'd said she was busy this week, and if she had to get up at five o'clock she hadn't been exaggerating. He had no idea what a wedding planner had to do that took up so much time—how hard could it be?—but she was conscientious about the job, and he liked that. Too many people these days blew off their responsibilities as if only stupid people actually did their jobs to the best of their abilities. Of course, being a cop meant he pretty much dealt with the dregs anyway, but he ran into that privileged, smart-ass, *I'm entitled* attitude every day in people who hadn't earned a tenth of the regard they thought they should have.

He couldn't hear her moving around anywhere in the house, but he caught the faint aroma of fresh coffee, which was enough to get him out of the bed. A quick visit to the bathroom, then he began pulling on his clothes. He had on his underwear and pants, and was sitting on the bed putting on his socks and shoes, when the door opened and Jaclyn came in, carrying a big mug of coffee in one hand and a . . . to-go cup in the other.

"I don't know how you drink your coffee, so I brought two packs of sugar and two creamers, and a stirrer," she said, extending the to-go cup to him. Startled, he automatically took it. The sugar, creamer, and stirrer were in a plastic sandwich bag, along with a neatly folded paper napkin. "I'm really rushed, I need to jump in the shower," she continued. "Could you make sure the door locks behind you as you leave? Thanks, you're a sweetheart. Call me in a week or so." She bent down, brushed a quick kiss across his forehead, then disappeared into the bathroom. He heard the snick of the lock as she turned it, and a moment later came the sound of running water.

Huh.

He sat there on the bed, staring at the to-go cup in his hand. *Get up, get your clothes on, and leave.* The only way she could have been any plainer was if she'd pushed him out the door.

He guessed it was safe to say she wasn't interested in talking about the night before. For a moment he wavered between relieved and . . . well, *fuck!* He was a little pissed. Women were supposed to want to talk about it; that showed they were interested, that they were feeling the vibes and the heat. What was he supposed to think now? That Jaclyn had wanted sex but nothing else, and now that she'd been laid she wanted him gone?

He set the coffee on the bedside table and finished dressing. As he slipped his service weapon into the holster on his belt he wondered if the pistol had spooked her. She wasn't a cop groupie, so maybe she hadn't liked it that he'd automatically placed the weapon within reach. He'd developed the habit when he'd been on the Atlanta P.D., and now it was so ingrained he hadn't even thought about what he was doing.

She didn't seem like the skittish type, but he didn't know her well enough to decide. For whatever reason, she didn't want him hanging around for breakfast. Okay, he could oblige her. It wasn't as if they didn't want the same thing.

He looked at the closed bathroom door and muttered, "I feel so used." Then he grinned, shrugged, grabbed the cup of coffee, and headed downstairs.

Eric let himself out of the town house, making certain the door was locked behind him. A light rain was falling, and the streetlights gleamed on wet pavement. The predawn air was cool, with a damp breeze blowing from the west; maybe the clouds would hang in there and the day wouldn't be so miserably hot. He hadn't heard any weather predictions so the rain kind of surprised him, but it was a pleasant surprise. The officers working traffic might not agree—he'd always hated a rainy day when he was on traffic detail—but as far as he was concerned, any break from the heat was good.

He stood for a moment on her small, covered front porch, looking around to make certain everything seemed normal—no suspicious cars, no suspicious people—before going down the steps and down the short sidewalk to his car. This was a good area, so a clunker car would be a jarring note. No one was out and about yet, though some of the other town houses had lights on inside, indicating more early risers.

Once he was in his car, he removed the lid from the cup of coffee, dumped in both packs of sugar and one of the packs of creamer, then used the little plastic stick to stir it all together. He lifted the cup to take his first swallow. Then the coffee hit his taste buds and he spewed the coffee back into the cup, shuddering. Holy hell, what was that shit?

Something flavored, and not a good flavor, either. What was it with women, messing with coffee? What was wrong with coffee that tasted like coffee? Who needed maple-strawberry-peanut-whatever? Even worse: not only was the flavor weird, but it also tasted weak. The woman had great legs, but she didn't know how to make decent coffee.

In a strange way, that made him like her more. If she'd made great coffee, she would have been too perfect. This was better. God knows he wasn't perfect, so the fact that her coffee sucked put them more on the same level.

But he seriously needed a cup of coffee, and no way was he swallowing so much as a sip of that poison. There was an open-all-night service station/convenience store just down the road, though, that would have coffee—maybe not the freshest in the world, but he was used to old, bitter coffee; that was why he used both sugar and creamer, to make it drinkable. Too bad sugar and creamer couldn't do anything to disguise the awful flavor of Jaclyn's brew; if they actually started seeing each other on a regular basis, he'd have to take over the coffeemaking, because he couldn't drink that swill even to be polite.

When he got to the convenience store, a guy dressed like a construction worker was putting gas in a dusty Ford pickup. A ten-year-old black subcompact was parked off to the side; probably the clerk's ride. As Eric pulled into a parking slot, the construction worker finished fueling and stood for a moment waiting for his credit card payment slip from the pump. He tore it off, carefully folded it, and put it in his wallet, then got in the truck and drove away.

Going inside, Eric nodded to the clerk, a skinny guy with a receding chin who had been watching through the window as the construction worker gassed up, and went straight to the coffee counter at the back of the store, where the motor oil, gas additives, and windshield washing liquid were shelved. The clerk looked faintly alarmed, and edged back behind the checkout counter.

Eric caught a glimpse of himself in the shiny surface of the coffee machines, and grimaced. No wonder the clerk looked a little worried. Not only did he need a shave, but he hadn't even dragged his fingers through his hair before leaving Jaclyn's. He hadn't tucked his shirttail in—after all, he was going home to shower and change clothes, so he hadn't seen the need—but he'd pulled on his jacket to cover his weapon. All in all, he looked as if he'd just had a mug shot taken.

He pulled a tall cup from the stack and dumped in two sugars and one creamer, then filled the cup to the brim. As he was fitting a black lid on the cup he heard a vehicle with a loud muffler pull up to the store. The engine didn't cut off.

Shit. What were the odds? What were the fucking odds?

Instinctively he ducked down, hiding himself from whoever came through the door. Maybe it was nothing. Maybe the driver was having trouble getting the car started, maybe the battery was low, so he didn't want to take the chance of cutting off the engine and not being able to get it started again.

He heard the chime over the door as it opened, and momentarily the sound of the running motor was even louder. It was nothing, he thought. Even an idiot would notice the car parked practically in front of the door, and realize someone else was in here with the clerk. And only a cop would hear a car left running outside and immediately think *Quick getaway.* His Spidey sense had short-circuited after a hot night of sex, that was all. Traffic outside was picking up as dawn came closer, not a good time for a robbery, any fool knew that.

It was noth—

Crash!

Something was knocked over, the harsh sound exploding in the small building along with yells and swearing, then a hoarse voice yelling, "Gimme the money, mother-fucker, or I'll blow your fuckin' head off!"

Fuck. It was something.

Damn it, he *knew* it, he'd known it as soon as the car pulled up outside. His weapon was in his hand, and he didn't remember drawing it. It was just there, because instinctively he'd known that car meant trouble. Just as instinctively, he'd noticed the clerk's position, and could tell the robber was between him and the clerk. He could fire, but if he missed he was likely to kill the clerk.

And if he discharged his weapon, there'd be forms to fill out for the next month, even if he didn't hit the fucking robber, and if he *did* hit him he'd be relegated to desk duty while an internal investigation took place.

Just as quickly as he'd drawn his weapon, he shoved it back into his holster, grabbed a can of motor oil from the shelf in front of him, raised it, and whipped it toward the robber's head with every ounce of strength in his throwing arm. The guy wore a black hooded sweatshirt, with the hood pulled up over his head—had to be hot as hell—but even with the hood to cushion the impact, the can hit his head with a sound like a cantaloupe being dropped on the floor. The robber went down as if he'd been pole-axed—or, in this case, motor-oiled.

Eric drew his weapon again and bolted for the door, hitting it with his shoulder and skidding to a stop beside the getaway car, his weapon leveled through the open window at the driver, who turned out to be a girl wearing a tiny green halter and a pair of Daisy Dukes. "Police!" he barked, identifying himself. "Turn off the engine and put your hands behind your head."

She stared at the impressive barrel of his service weapon, aimed right at her. Her lower lip began quivering, her face screwed up, and she began bawling. "He made me!" she squalled.

"Yeah, right," Eric muttered. His damn coffee was getting cold, he needed a shower, it was obvious he hadn't been home, which was going to give everyone something to talk about, and here he was, stuck with Bonnie and Clyde. He took a quick glance over his shoulder; he could see the clerk had come out from behind the counter and was talking on the phone. The robber was still down for the count.

"I said turn off the engine!"

Still sniveling, she did.

"Okay, now get out of the car. We're going inside with your boyfriend."

"He's not my boyfriend!" She got out of the car, and all the time he was cuffing her she kept babbling about how she didn't even know the guy, he'd gotten in her car at a red light, he'd held a gun on her and made her drive here, she hadn't known what he was doing—

"And that's why you didn't just drive off when he came inside?" Eric asked drily as he ushered her inside where he could keep an eye on her. The clerk jerked around, evidently not as reassured as he should have been by the girl being cuffed, his eyes widening at the sight of the weapon in Eric's hand. "Police," Eric said, briefly flashing his badge. Hell, why couldn't the moron put three and three together, and come up with "cop"?

The guy on the ground was moaning, beginning to stir. He'd have a headache from hell, probably a concussion, but Eric used his extra set of cuffs to secure him anyway. He could already hear sirens; good response time, he thought. But then, Hopewell wasn't Atlanta, and the night shift didn't have a whole lot to occupy its time.

Less than thirty seconds later two squad cars slid into the parking lot, lights flashing and sirens blaring. Eric stared down at his two prisoners and the freaked-out clerk, and heaved a sigh. All he'd wanted was a damn cup of coffee.

Chapter Five

Jaclyn determinedly did *not* think about Eric Wilder as she finished getting ready—not much, anyway. Completely dismissing him was impossible, partly because she had pink beard burns on her breasts and a similar tender spot on her jaw. She soothed the irritated places with aloe gel, carefully covered the place on her jaw with concealer, and wondered why physical intimacy with a man was such a contact sport that a woman almost needed a helmet and protective padding. And he hadn't even been rough. In fact, he'd been remarkably tender, considering the hungry way they'd gone at each other. Still, she should at least have bitten him or something, just to even the score.

Except she'd never been a biter. Or a screamer. Or much of anything, really. She was just an ordinary woman, cautious by nature, without an ounce of drama queen in her. Her dad was enough of a drama queen, thank you very much, plus her job brought her in daily contact with enough drama to keep Broadway stocked with characters for ten years. That was maybe the biggest part of her job: keeping her head when everything was going to hell in a handbasket, and everyone else was having hysterical fits. An events planner had to be an expert at finding alternatives, making things work, and doing what had to be done.

"Caution" was practically her middle name. For goodness sake, before she bought her first car ten years ago, she'd researched resale values and repair rates for six months before taking the plunge— and it had taken Madelyn twice that long, a couple of years ago, to convince her that driving matching Jaguars would be a great business statement. She'd been right, of course; in the Buckhead area, status symbols mattered, and the Jaguars said that Premier was *the* events planning firm to hire if you wanted to make a splash. They'd bought the Jaguars used, and Jaclyn had approached the venture with her fingers crossed and her checkbook wincing. Two years later she had to admit that Madelyn had been right, overall, but both of their temperamental cars had seen time in repair shops.

It was *so* not like her to throw caution to the wind and jump into bed with a man she'd just met. She hadn't even slept with her ex until they'd been engaged. She'd been with her mother as Madelyn picked up the pieces of her heart after divorcing her dad, and subsequently watched Jacky make one bad choice after another when choosing who would join in the Stepmother Parade. To date, he'd been married a total of five times, divorced five times, and was probably actively looking for number six.

Being involved, even peripherally, in personal train wrecks like that had made her doubly cautious when it came to men, and even then her own marriage had had the life span of a soap bubble. How could she have been so wrong? She'd thought she and Steve would be married for a lifetime, and instead the attraction between them had fizzled in an embarrassingly short time. Now she doubted her own judgment when it came to men, to the point that the last time she'd had sex she'd . . . oh hell, she'd been married. She hadn't been with anyone since then. She wasn't carrying a torch for Steve. She wasn't a prude; at least, she didn't think she was. She'd been busy. Very busy.

There were a lot of reasons why she hadn't connected with any other men, most of them valid. She'd been careful. She'd been smart. It wasn't like her to be either impulsive or reckless.

Jumping into bed with Eric wasn't like her, but then it obviously *was,* since she had done it, and that was what alarmed her. Was she more like her father than she'd thought? The absolute last thing in the world she wanted was to become a slave to every whim that passed through her head, the way Jacky was. To him, *want* was the same as *need,* and he had few brakes on his behavior.

She loved him—it was difficult not to love

Jacky, because he wasn't at all mean-hearted and didn't intend to hurt people. He was charming, full of life, and completely irresponsible and focused on himself. He did hurt people, of course, but he didn't see it because he was always moving on to the next party, the next wife. Jaclyn's relationship with him was sporadic, and had been as long as she could remember; her security had come from Madelyn, who was the core constant in her life, who had stayed married to Jacky far longer than she should have and fought to maintain the same home and some semblance of stability in Jaclyn's life. Madelyn had finally thrown in the towel and filed for divorce when Jaclyn was thirteen, when Jacky's irresponsibility with money had threatened to drag them all down.

Jaclyn made a face in the mirror as she deftly twisted her heavy hair into a knot and shoved some long, stabilizing pins into place. Of course, Jacky being the half-assed father he was, and the divorce, had marked her. Everyone was marked by their experiences in life, so she wasn't special. She couldn't even say she'd had any un-usually traumatic events. But being Jacky's daughter had definitely made her wary and cautious, because he was exactly what she didn't want to be. Maybe she wouldn't have been like him anyway; maybe the wariness and caution were inborn, which made it possible for her to see him, love him, and not be bamboozled by him. Who knew?

All of which had nothing to do with the fact that she'd just had the first one-night stand of her life, and in retrospect, she didn't like the idea that she'd lost either her self-control or her mind. What would she do if he really did call her next week? Did she want a relationship? Was that even still on the board, or had she placed herself in the call-for-sex category?

Oh hell, of course she wanted to at least try for a real relationship with him. She'd never before had such an instant, compelling reaction to a man, and even though it scared the stuffing out of her, she wanted to see where it went. And if *he* thought she had been slotted into the call-for-sex category, well, she'd find out soon enough, and the sooner the better.

She took two deep breaths, squared her shoulders, then glanced at the clock and groaned. Introspection was a time-hog.

She grabbed a banana from the fruit bowl in the kitchen, poured the rest of the coffee into a to-go cup, and turned off all the appliances and lights before letting herself into the garage, locking the door behind her. A motion light in the garage came on, lighting her way to the car. Juggling her bag, coffee, and banana, she got into the car and locked the door before punching the garage door opener. Yep, "careful" was her middle name.

She backed smoothly out of the garage, and rain danced on her windshield. She braked, groaning in dismay. She was pretty sure rain hadn't been forecast, but here it was. No bride liked rain on her wedding day. Thankfully today's wedding wasn't an outside event . . . and that Madelyn was handling it. Still, was it an omen that it was raining on the first wedding of the week?

She hesitated for a moment, thinking of going back inside and changing her kitten-heeled sandals for something more substantial, but another glance at the time had her resolutely lowering the garage door and backing the rest of the way into the street. If her feet got wet, she'd live with it. She didn't have time to change.

It was still dark, the streetlights reflecting on the wet streets as she wound her way out of the residential area to the main road that would take her to Buckhead. Hopewell didn't have any industry; there were businesses, office buildings, doctors and dentists and restaurants, dry cleaners, things of that sort, but no honest-to-God industry involving factories. Hopewell was newer than Buckhead, didn't have the older stately mansions; instead, it had a sizable number of *new* stately mansions— not just the big McMansions, but actual estates, with large grounds, privacy walls, and gates at the end of the driveways.

Hopewell also had sections of what Jaclyn would term strictly middle-class housing, neighborhoods established before land prices soared. She had grown up in one of those houses; Madelyn had sold it only when Premier began taking up the lion's share of her time, and she couldn't handle the yard work and upkeep. Jaclyn hadn't said anything to her mother, but privately she had cried on the day the sale was final. The neat brick house had been her home, even if she had long since moved out. Now the town house was home in that it was where she went at the end of the day; it was where she relaxed, felt safe and comfortable. But deep in her heart it was just a town house, and if she had to move it wouldn't bother her one whit other than the aggravation of packing and unpacking.

Home was family, and Jaclyn wanted her own. How twisted was she, that she couldn't trust herself enough to let down her guard and actually let a man get emotionally close to her, when what she wanted most out of life required that closeness? Maybe she should consider therapy. Or maybe, because she didn't have her head in the sand and understood perfectly all the psychology behind her excessive caution, she should just kick herself in the ass and get on with life. Not only would that be faster, but she wouldn't have to pay herself.

Premier was housed in a stand-alone brick building that had once been a dentist's office, but she and Madelyn had liked it because the parking lot was spacious, in very good shape, and the landscaping was mature. They'd bought it in their fourth year of business, remodeling the interior to give it the look of a comfortable, upscale home that just happened to have two private offices. They had considered leasing space in a professional building, which would give them active security, but the cost had forced them to look at stand-alone buildings. Now they were both very happy with their choice, because the building was theirs and it actively reflected the sense of being solidly established, and of prestige, that the anonymous face of a professional building simply couldn't provide.

Because they were four women working alone, sometimes late at night—or early in the morning, as was the case today—they'd tried to make the building as safe as possible. There were sturdy doors and locks, monitored security, camera surveillance on the entrances, and the casement windows were all protected by some very thorny shrubbery. They had never had even a hint of trouble. The area was wonderful and, really, what idiot would break into an event planner establishment? Everything they did was paid for by check or credit card, so at any given time the only cash on the premises would be what they had in their wallets. A vending machine would be a better bet for a thief.

She pulled into her designated parking slot right beside the back door, and Madelyn's Jag pulled in not five seconds later. A pink umbrella bloomed like a giant exotic flower, then Madelyn got out of the car under its protective cap. Jaclyn mirrored her mother's actions, though her own umbrella was an ordinary black one. The rain wasn't heavy, but she didn't want to start the day with wet clothes and limp hair.

"I have protein smoothies," Madelyn said, then she leaned back inside to fetch the promised drinks.

"What flavor?"

"Don't look a gift smoothie in the mouth. Vanilla. I was out of strawberries."

"I have a banana I'll split with you. We can slice it into the smoothies, run them through the blender again."

"Deal."

She couldn't juggle everything at once, so Jaclyn got her briefcase and left the banana and coffee in the car for a second trip, then hurried to unlock the door. The security system began beeping and she set her briefcase on the small demilune table stationed in the short hallway, then coded in the number to disarm the system. Madelyn moved past her, carefully maneuvering the umbrella, her own briefcase, and the two smoothies.

Five minutes later they were sitting at the conference table with their jazzed-up smoothies, going over the wedding for that evening, making certain no detail had been forgotten. Madelyn had turned on the small television in the corner and they both breathed a sigh of relief when the local weather showed clearing by lunch. "Thank God," drawled Peach Reynolds as she breezed into the conference room in time to hear the weather prediction. She automatically started making a pot of coffee; she was one of those who drank coffee almost nonstop all day. "And while I'm giving thanks to the Good Lord, I'll throw in my heartfelt gratitude for air-conditioning, because the humidity is going to be unbearable. Are y'all drinking those god-awful smoothies again?"

Peach—whose real name was Georgia, of course—scorned anything that even remotely resembled healthy eating, evidenced by the chocolate-filled Krispy Kreme doughnut she'd brought in. She had a cloud of bright red hair, slanted green eyes, and fifteen or twenty extra pounds that put her just the other side of lush. It was evidently a body type that was very popular with men, because she never lacked for dates, though it was fair to say her exuberant personality also had something to do with that. Madelyn was more low-key, but barely. The two of them together could work a room in a way that would turn any politician green with envy.

"We are," said Madelyn. "But when you drop dead at the age of sixty from a heart attack caused by sky-high cholesterol, I promise I won't add insult to injury by toasting your poor stiff, cold body with a nutritious smoothie. Because you're my friend, I'll break out the good whiskey."

"Consider me comforted." Peach took a bite of her doughnut, delicately licking the chocolate that oozed out. "But I'm going to be cremated, so you'd better toast me before I'm toasted, if you want to keep to that stiff, cold idea."

"You are not."

"Are not what?"

"Going to be cremated. You've told me you want a lavish funeral with all your ex-lovers weeping over your beautiful body as you lie there in the casket, which, by the way, you said you wanted festooned with white lilies, though I think *festooning* is in poor taste for a funeral, with a bagpiper piping away and white horses pulling your gun-wagon thingie to the cemetery. You can't be beautiful in a casket *and* be cremated. They're kind of mutually exclusive."

"You don't get a gun carriage," Jaclyn said. "Heads of state get gun carriages. Think of the traffic nightmare. I'm pretty sure you'd have to have permission from the governor."

"Well, rain on my parade, why don't you?" Peach grumbled. "You'd think the one time a person could have everything she wanted was at her own damn funeral. At least play the songs I want, okay?"

"Sure," Madelyn agreed, "as long as it isn't 'You Picked a Fine Time to Leave Me, Lucille.'"

"Spoilsport. Okay, how about Floyd Cramer's 'Last Date'? Get it? Because it will be."

"You're sick. Just *sick*. You won't be here anyway, so what do you care? I'll give you a perfectly lovely funeral, in keeping with Premier's reputation and standards."

"You're turning my funeral into an event? I don't know whether to be flattered or pissed that you'd use my death to promote the business."

"Oh, honey, I promise you, your funeral *will* be an event. I'll just have to make sure it's a tasteful one."

"Speaking of taste . . . Jaclyn, sweetheart, you *do* know your Saturday wedding is a rolling disaster, don't you?"

Jaclyn looked up, her lips already twitching. "I began to get a glimmer of that when the bride insisted her eleven-month-old daughter, who isn't the groom's child by the way, be pulled down the aisle in a red wagon." She couldn't help laughing. The wedding was going to be hilarious, but as long as the couple was happy with the arrangements, her job was to make the wedding happen the way they wanted. Taste, or lack of it, wasn't her call to make. "Diedra is thanking her lucky stars we have so much booked this week, so she can take one of the Saturday rehearsals instead of doing the wedding."

"I'll be so glad when this week is over," Madelyn said, looking at the schedule on the board. Because they were so booked for the week, they weren't trying to slot in any appointments; they had their hands full, since six weddings also meant six rehearsals. She rubbed her hands together. "Our bank account, however, is very happy. None of the checks bounced."

"Glory hallelujah for that," Jaclyn said wryly. "Now, if I can just get through all of today's appointments with Carrie without anyone quitting, including me, the rest of the week will be smooth sailing in comparison."

"Quit if you have to," Madelyn said, her lips pressing together. "Don't take any bullshit from her. The amount we'd have to repay would be well worth getting rid of her."

Their contracts were prorated, so Premier got paid for the work they'd done to date. That protected them from being fired at the last minute and then refused payment because they hadn't completed the job. Several times some frugal, or fraudulent— depending on how you looked at it—brides and/or mothers had tried that. Once they'd learned they couldn't get the hefty fees repaid, every one of them had then decided that Premier's services were just fine, after all.

"If we can just get past that magic point where she thinks she can change her mind and still have time to get what she wants done, I think we'll be okay. Not happy, but okay."

Madelyn rolled her eyes. "We're already past that point."

"Not in her mind. I'm hoping she reaches it this afternoon. She isn't exactly reasonable, though," she added in the understatement of the year, and possibly the decade. She wondered if maybe she could get Eric to come stand behind her, with that big gun visible in his holster—

—and just like that, *boom*, he was front and center in her thoughts so sharply that for a moment she physically felt him inside her. A warm flush swept over her body, and her face got hot. Swiftly she looked down, hiding her expression. She should *not* be having thoughts like this with her mother sitting right there, for God's sake. She should be concentrating on the job and nothing else.

But how could she, really, just block him out as if the night hadn't happened? She couldn't compartmentalize her life like that.

He was way outside her experience, and until she got an emotional and mental handle on how explosively fast things had happened between them, of course she'd think about him—even when she was trying her best not to.

If she could just get through this week, she'd have time to think about him.

The weather cleared as promised, with a breeze chasing the rain to the east and a nice blue sky following. That afternoon, Jaclyn found herself smiling, just a little, even though she was on her way to meet with Carrie and the poor vendors. The next few days were going to be hectic, but so far things were going smoothly. Wedding number one was relatively small and Madelyn shouldn't have any trouble handling it on her own, unless there was an unforeseen problem. Unforeseen problems were par for the course, but they tried to be prepared for any contingency.

Lunch had been excellent, a take-out salad eaten at her desk. The phone hadn't rung for a good twenty minutes, so she'd had time to eat in peace.

And now the sky was a clear blue, traffic was light, and her body hummed in contentment, as it had all day.

"Don't think about him, don't think about him," she murmured to herself. She had to be on her toes for the next several days, until after the week's final wedding; if she let herself get distracted she'd make mistakes, overlook details. In five days this crush of work would be behind her and she could decide . . . whatever she decided. He might not call. She thought he would, but who knew? Maybe he was special—the possibility of which scared the crap out of her even though it also made her feel excited and happy and on the brink of something important. If he *did* call, and he *was* special— She was doing it again, thinking about him despite her best efforts.

But there was nothing like dealing with Carrie to bring her back to reality with a resounding thud.

The reception hall was built like a Greek temple, with columns and urns and ivy climbing the walls. The building was about ten years old, and judging by how long it took to get a booking, it had been a wonderful investment for the owners. Carrie had insisted that her wedding be here and nowhere else, and had even pushed back her wedding date when the date she'd selected had already been booked. That was one time she hadn't been able to throw a tantrum and get her way.

Because this was a weekday the spacious parking lot was far from full, but a few cars were parked near the side entrance. Jaclyn recognized Carrie's car, and her smile quickly faded. Carrie had the unique ability to affect time, making a minute seem like an hour, and an hour seem like an eternity in hell. There were times when Jaclyn had wondered what the poor groom saw in the woman he was marrying, but in Carrie's case she actually felt as if she should call the guy and tell him to run far and run fast.

As she grabbed her briefcase, slung her purse over her shoulder, and stepped out of the Jag, Jaclyn spotted Gretchen's car. Her heart dropped. Gretchen wasn't supposed to be here for another half hour; Jaclyn wouldn't schedule any vendor to meet with a bridezilla without someone from Premier present to smooth the way. She'd bet the Jag that Carrie had called the dressmaker and changed the time of their meeting. This could *not* be good.

Jaclyn picked up her pace as she strode toward the side entrance, hoping she wasn't too late. She'd taken six steps down the hallway when she found out she was much too late.

Gretchen turned a corner, all but running toward the parking lot and escape. Her face was red and she was clutching a short length of fabric in one hand. When she saw Jaclyn she skidded to a stop, her jaw clenching for a moment before she let loose.

"She could pay me a million dollars, and I wouldn't remake her bridesmaids' dresses. No amount of money is worth putting up with that bitch." Gretchen was short and plump, fiftyish and attractive, bottle blond and always nicely dressed. She was also normally easygoing and smiling, but not today. "The bridesmaids can be naked, for all I care."

Well, that was fairly definitive. Jaclyn took a deep breath. "What did she say?"

Gretchen blinked back tears. "Among other things, she said the quality of the work on the dresses is subpar, and I'm lucky she hasn't fired me. Because my work is so shoddy, she can't see why I won't make the new gowns in the next two weeks, because I can't possibly be that busy, not with so many *competent* seamstresses in the area." Gretchen's chin trembled, then she quickly firmed it. "She said she'd blackball me, that I'd never work on an important wedding again if I didn't do exactly as she ordered."

Jaclyn placed a calming hand on Gretchen's arm and said in a low voice. "You know better than that. Don't let her intimidate you. No one in her right mind will take a word she says seriously."

"I hope you're right." Gretchen gained control of herself. "We'll find out soon. No matter what, I'm out. Life's too short to deal with people like her."

Jaclyn had to agree, but she was going to do her best to hang in there. The groom's family was a prominent one; his mother came from an old Georgia family with money up the wazoo, and his father was in state politics. If she could get through the next month, she'd be golden.

Still, if Carrie ever attempted to hire Premier to plan an event again, they would be much too busy. Even if they were destitute and twiddling their thumbs, they'd be too busy.

She found Carrie sitting in the main reception hall, claiming a chair near the single table that was set up for her meetings. The rest of the large room was empty, cavernous and open. The stage at the far end of the room was dark, deserted. The hardwood floor had recently been cleaned and shined to a sparkle, but without the usual arrangement of chairs and tables, it looked a little sad. When everything was in place, the linen-covered tables and fragrant flower arrangements, the hot buffet and cakes, the flickering candlelight casting a magic spell while music flowed over the room, this became the perfect place for a wedding reception.

Right now it just looked empty, but for a crushed fabric sample that had been tossed to the floor, a few feet away from the bride-to-be.

"You're late," Carrie snapped without bothering to look at Jaclyn.

One more month . . .

"I'm five minutes early," Jaclyn said

calmly. "Did you change the time of the meeting with Gretchen and neglect to tell me?"

At that, Carrie flicked her hard gaze upward. "I strongly suggest that you steer your clients away from that unreasonable woman. In fact, I insist—"

Jaclyn placed her briefcase on the table. "I always recommend Gretchen highly, and I'll continue to do so."

"She's incompetent. Her work is shoddy."

"If I were you, I'd be very careful about making statements like that. She could sue you for damages, and despite your connections, she'd win. She's made dresses for some very important women in this town, in this state, and every one of them could come out on her side. And let me warn you: she has a lot of close friends in the same business. It's almost like a guild, and she's very well respected, especially in the Southeast. If you ever expect to have a gown custom made again, I'd suggest you let this one go. The bridesmaids' gowns have already been made, they're lovely, and now it's time to move on."

Carrie's jaw tightened and for a moment

Jaclyn thought she'd jump up and physically attack her. Carrie *really* didn't like not getting her way. Oh, the poor vendors who were still to come. If she could have warned them away, she would have, but this roller coaster was already going downhill; all she could do was hold on.

Chapter Six

Carrie stared stone-faced at the table before her, which was littered with the remnants of samples: cake samples, the remnants of shrimp and scallop kabobs, beef kabobs, lamb kabobs, meatball kabobs. *Meatballs.* As if she'd ever allow anything so low class at her wedding. They'd been good, as far as that went, but a meatball was still a meatball, no matter how fancy the spices or what kind of meat was used. It could have been an exotic blend of eel and emu, for all she cared; it would still have been a meatball.

"Forget the meatballs," she said curtly. "I

don't know what you were thinking, bringing them. This isn't some tacky middle-class wedding where half the women are wearing black hosiery with white shoes."

"The meatballs are my most requested item," replied the caterer, a thin, almost masculine-looking woman with short, iron gray hair and a stern face. "But they *are* the most expensive, because they're so difficult to make; most people opt for the more economical choices."

It was all Carrie could do to keep from slapping the bitch. Belatedly she sneaked a glance at the price sheet to make certain the woman wasn't lying to her, and it was right there in black on heavy cream paper: the meatballs were a third again more expensive than even the shrimp and scallop kabobs. And now she was stuck with the cheap choices, because there was no way she could back down; the only thing she could do was go with something even more expensive, in total, than the meatballs would have been.

"I want three different kinds: the scallops, the lamb, and the beef. That way my guests will have a *real* choice."

She wasn't worried about the money,

anyway; Sean's family was footing most of the bill, because no way could her own parents afford this kind of splash. They were contributing, of course; she refused to let her future mother-in-law think she was a freeloader. For the moment, they were on good terms, and Carrie intended to keep it that way for the time being. Later . . . who knew?

The caterer didn't comment on Carrie's choices, merely made notes, which irritated Carrie even more because the least the woman—and she used the term loosely—could do was say something like *Excellent choice.* Maybe she should tell the wedding planner to find a different caterer, but, really, Jaclyn was turning difficult about doing as she was told and she'd probably say something about all the really good caterers being booked months in advance.

She wanted to have *the* wedding of the year; she wanted to have the wedding that every other upcoming bride talked about, enviously, when planning her own wedding. It was frustrating that no one seemed to share her vision of something both stylish and exotic, outlandishly expensive but tasteful enough that no one made fun of her choices, and it was also damned frustrating that so many people seemed determined to let other people shine on the one day when only *she* was supposed to shine.

Take the bridesmaids' dresses. Yes, she'd deliberately chosen a style just tacky enough that none of them would come even close to being attractive when posing beside her, but not so tacky that any of them would rebel—well, except for that bitch Taite, but she'd thrown a tantrum because of something else entirely, completely unrelated to the wedding. She would be taken care of when the wedding was over and Carrie had more time; in fact, the first steps of Taite's comeuppance had already been taken, and Carrie couldn't be more pleased with the results.

She enjoyed the different reactions she got from people when they found out just what they were up against when dealing with her. Most people were spineless wimps; they simply folded when faced with her greater will, which was fine with her; they were less trouble to deal with. And they amused her, seeing how they got upset, how their feelings were hurt, how they'd scramble to keep from upsetting her again.

The truth was, Carrie was almost never upset, because that would mean she cared. And she didn't, at least not in any emotional way. She cared about the image she projected, she cared that things were done the way she wanted them done. She wanted what she wanted, when she wanted it, but while her behavior might be over-the-top, inside she was cool and calculating, watching every reaction, judging the best way to get her way.

If Sean's father won his election to the U.S. Senate, she was set for life. She had the money angle already taken care of, but an entrance to the D.C. social life was almost more than she could have hoped for. Once she was there, and entrenched, she might or might not keep Sean around, depending on the opportunities that came her way, but for right now he was just what she needed. And he was good-natured, which meant he was easy for her to manipulate.

Sean's mother, Fayre (pronounced "Fair," and wasn't that as pretentious as all hell?) Maywell Johnston Dennison, used all four names just often enough to remind people that she was from *the* Johnston and Maywell families, before marrying Douglas Dennison and working to help his political star rise through local and state governments to now reach the national level. Mrs. Dennison was a calm woman, but Carrie didn't underestimate her. She was the power behind the throne, the source of the money. Eventually Carrie would have to find a way to neutralize the woman, but for right now she was useful in other ways.

First, though, she had to get through all the annoyances this wedding was throwing at her. The table was too small for all the samples being presented; you'd think this place would be better prepared to accommodate her. The little table had gotten so crowded, she'd moved the wedding planner's briefcase a while back, shoving it under the table. That briefcase wasn't the only thing on the floor. Discarded ribbon and fabric samples had been dropped to the side, dismissed, unimportant. It wasn't as if *she* was going to clean up the mess.

Overall, she was unhappy with everything, but the dress situation ate at her. When she'd first visualized the colors, pink sashes on the gray dresses had seemed so cool and stylish, but now she thought pink was more froufrou than sophisticated, and the line of gray just seemed dull. Bishop Delaney, the floral designer, hadn't helped; he'd shrugged and said that his personal choice would have been dark gray dresses with bloodred flowers, but the pink sashes prevented that particular combination and now that the wretched dressmaker had simply *quit,* there was no way to get anyone else lined up in time to get the color of the sashes changed to teal, or even gray to match the dresses. Why couldn't he have said something about the gray and red combination at the very beginning? Now she was stuck with the pink, and that made her so angry she wanted to take scissors and slash something, preferably Wretched Gretchen, the seamstress, but if Jaclyn didn't fall in line soon she might make an acceptable substitute.

If she'd been in a better mood she might have enjoyed the spectacle of all these people gathered to try to please her, but the situation with the dresses had soured the day for her. She had to deal with the veil-maker and the pastry chef, choose the band's set list, and everyone was saying she had to make her selections now because time was running out and they had other obligations that would prevent them from doing so and so, blah blah blah, all these endless excuses for not doing things her way.

After the wedding, she'd start dropping comments about how incompetent they all had been. Let them see how they liked it when their business fell off. And the one she would talk the most about would be Premier. Everyone had said Premier had the most cachet of any event planner in the area, and of course their Buckhead location made them even more desirable, but Jaclyn Wilde had turned out to be a real pain in the ass, because she kept taking the side of the nitwits who said they couldn't do what Carrie wanted. Jaclyn was supposed to make it all happen, and not take any excuses; instead she'd been a complete failure at helping make this wedding the vision it should be.

The veil-maker, a short, plump Hispanic woman named Estefani, laid out her book with photographs of the headpieces, ranging from simple bands to ornate tiaras, along with fabric samples. Who knew there were so many options for veils, ranging from net to gossamer film that was so light it almost floated? "All of these are boring," she said pushing the book away. "Don't you have something with flair? Black, maybe?" Her wedding dress had a thin black ribbon running just under the bustline, so black wasn't completely out of the ballpark, but of course she'd never go with a black veil. Watching the woman's eyes round with horror, watching her try to control her expression, was amusing enough that she might let the idea run for a while, just to keep things stirred up, before settling on something more classic. She *wasn't* joking, however, about the tiaras. They all looked like beauty-pageant fare, and what she had in mind was more European royalty.

"Black?" Estefani said, her voice faltering. "With the white dress?"

"Yes, with the white dress," Carrie snarled, rejoicing inside because Estefani had risen to the bait. At least now she had a target. "Are all of you people so simpleminded that you can't see beyond what you've always done?"

To her surprise, Estefani's shoulders stiffened, and her brown eyes flashed. "I am not simpleminded. I have good taste."

"Meaning I don't?" Carrie demanded, hardening her tone and narrowing her eyes. Before she could launch into a more blistering attack, though, her cell phone rang. She glanced at the number display, intending to let the phone ring, but she saw it was Sean and she held up one finger for Estefani to wait. She took a deep breath, plastered a smile on her face, and answered in a sweet voice.

"Hi, honey."

Sean was cute, rich, and gullible. What more could a woman ask for in a husband? For now, she let him have his way in almost everything, but that would change after the wedding. Once she walked down the aisle, she'd be in the driver's seat. Actually, she already was; getting Sean to propose had been the first big step, but just yesterday she'd taken the second step, the money step. Things were working out just as she'd planned.

Sean was planning the honeymoon. It kept him busy, and out of her hair, and he was excited about being in charge and giving her the perfect honeymoon. Thank goodness he took her hints to heart. He was taking care of the last details today, and wanted her opinion. She simply agreed with everything he said, smiling the whole time because the smile was part of the persona she'd created to catch and keep Sean. Physically smiling changed the tone of her voice, kept it light and sweet.

She glanced up to find the wedding planner and the veil-maker staring at her as if she'd sprouted another head. Piss on 'em. Soon she wouldn't have any need of them. She listened to Sean's plans, laughed as if he were saying things that were either witty or amusing, told him how wonderful he was and how much she loved him, all the usual bullshit.

As she and Sean talked, she watched Jaclyn and Estefani move across the room, where they huddled with Bishop Delaney and Audrey Whisenant, the pastry chef. The caterer, Irena, stood off to the side making notes and didn't join them, but the reception hall manager—Melissa somebody—walked over to add her two cents' worth of nonsense. Carrie couldn't hear what they were saying; she had to concentrate on Sean, who kept rattling on even though he'd already covered the reasons why he'd called, but from the look Estefani threw at her Carrie knew they were talking about her. Jaclyn's tone was soothing, which meant she was probably telling them she'd deflect Carrie's complaints.

Cold rage bubbled through her veins at the idea of anyone thinking she could be handled, as if she were a difficult child. And Jaclyn, with her smooth skin and her smooth hair and the way she had of dressing as if she were really old money and embedded in the Buckhead social structure, instead of being nothing more than a wedding planner, made her even angrier. If it hadn't been for Jaclyn, things might have gone differently, but from the beginning she'd been an obstacle instead of a help . . . and now she was *talking* about Carrie, undermining her even more. That simply couldn't be allowed to happen.

"If the custom-made crystals hadn't already been ordered, I'd be out of here," Bishop Delaney told Jaclyn. "But I don't want to be hung out to dry on that expense, so I'll see it through. I won't ever take another job for the Dennisons, though."

"Thanks for sticking it out. I'm sorry the job has been such a disaster, for all of us." Jaclyn felt as if she'd been apologizing since she'd first walked through the door. Come to think of it, she *had.* So far Gretchen had been the only vendor to quit—though the bridesmaids' dresses were finished so she hadn't left the job in the lurch. Estefani might walk out at any moment, though. Her veils and headdresses were works of art and she was justifiably proud of them. Her schedule was packed; she wouldn't miss the income from this job at all. In fact, she could probably make two phone calls at the most and have an open slot filled. That was what Carrie didn't seem to realize, that she was dealing with top-flight vendors whose reputations were already made, and who didn't have to put up with her demands and insults.

"I've never before dealt with anyone this difficult," Melissa whispered. She'd been the manager of the reception hall for the past nine or ten years, so she had seen some doozies. If Carrie was difficult by her standards, that was saying something. She gave Jaclyn a sympathetic look.

"I will not let her say I am stupid," Estefani said fiercely. "It is she who is stupid. A black veil with a white dress! And my work is not boring."

"Don't let her upset you," Bishop drawled, taking care to keep his voice down. "She wouldn't know classic good taste if it bit her on the ass." He patted her on the arm. He was tall and muscled, with bleached blond hair and an exotic black goatee, an almost exact physical opposite from the short, grandmotherly Estefani. In their business they frequently ended up working together, so they had known each other for years. There seemed to be real affection between Bishop and Estefani; she was far more likely to listen to him than she was to anything Jaclyn could say to calm her.

Audrey Whisenant, the pastry chef, shrugged her muscled shoulders. She'd been an Olympic swimmer back in the day and still spent a lot of time in the water, but after winning a bronze medal she'd decided competition wasn't her thing. Instead, she explored another passion of hers—

baking. Her cakes were works of art, lighter and with a silkier texture than the average wedding cake. Unlike a lot of pastry chefs, she decorated her own cakes, too. "Now, if I can just get her to choose the flavors and fillings for the cakes. I have a couple of weeks leeway on these cakes, but I'd like to get the details nailed down because I'm going on vacation next week."

"Then let's see if we can move on you for now, and give things time to calm down between—"

Behind them, Carrie chirped a cheerful, "Bye, love you," to her poor unsuspecting groom, the sound followed almost immediately by a thud and crash as she swiped her arm across the table, sending Estefani's book flying, along with kabob skewers, cake samples, ribbons, brochures, a couple of ink pens, and Jaclyn's appointment book, all of which went skidding across the floor.

"Who do you think you are?" Carrie's voice was low but textured with venom as she stalked toward them. Melissa, Bishop, and Audrey faded back a little, but Jaclyn held her ground, figuring it was her job to stand between them and the advancing

demon. Estefani, though, narrowed her eyes and tensed her small dumpling of a body as if she was ready to put up her dukes. The mental image made Jaclyn's mouth quirk as she struggled not to smile.

"Audrey is going on vacation next week," Jaclyn said, hoping to deflect Carrie's attention. "There's some time to spare on the cakes, but if you can—"

The blow came out of nowhere. Carrie's palm cracked against her left cheek, sending her stumbling back. For a moment the shock and surprise were so great that Jaclyn seemed to disconnect from reality; the next thing she knew, she was standing with her hand pressed against her burning cheek and Bishop's muscular arms were holding her steady until she could regain her balance.

"You're *fired!*" Carrie spat at her. Her pretty face was twisted in rage, but her eyes were disturbingly cold and calm, as if two people inhabited the same body. "How dare you talk about me behind my back, undermine me with the people *I* choose to give my business to? From day one you've done everything you can to ruin my wedding, but this is the last straw. By the time

I'm finished, you'll be lucky if you can get a job planning a plumber's wedding. *No one* in Buckhead will ever use you again, and you know what that means. I want my money back, too, because you certainly haven't earned it!"

Jaclyn's head swam, but she stiffened her spine, forced the jelly out of her knees. Pride made her remove her hand from her face, as if the stinging had stopped. Her heart was racing so fast she could barely breathe. Her right hand curled into a fist; she could feel the muscles in her arm tensing of their own accord, as if she no longer had control over them, but Bishop saw the telltale sign and placed a warning hand on her wrist, at the same time putting another one on Estefani's shoulder. "Don't do it," he murmured, so low Carrie couldn't hear him. "The bitch would have you arrested for assault." Behind Carrie, Irena had shifted position so she was directly behind her, and the caterer looked ready to take her down.

He was right. Jaclyn took a deep breath. As things stood now, she was the one who had grounds for making any charges, if she chose to go that route. She wouldn't, so long as Carrie didn't escalate and hit someone else, but she should be smart and hold to her legal high ground. And, for Premier's sake, she would end this association as professionally as possible.

"I think all of the appointments should be rescheduled for another day," she said calmly, giving Bishop and Irena looks that said *Get Estefani out of here,* as well as *I'll be okay.*

"Who gives a fuck what you think?" Carrie asked viciously. "These people work for me, not you!"

Maybe so, but "these people" were moving to do exactly what Jaclyn had suggested, picking up the items scattered on the floor, replacing them on the table. Melissa picked up Jaclyn's appointment book and was brave enough to approach with it in her hand. "Thank you," Jaclyn said, taking the book. Melissa immediately backed away again, out of striking distance. As Carrie's hand moved as if she would slap the book from Jaclyn's grasp, she said sharply, "If you hit me again, I'll have you arrested. Is that plain? It'll make a great headline in the newspaper."

"I have some paperwork to do," Melissa

ventured, and Jaclyn gave her a brief nod, telling her that clearing the deck was the best thing she could do right now. Melissa wheeled and in short order had the room cleared, the vendors' tense but muted voices fading as they walked down the hallway.

The two women faced each other, both of them squared off and ready for battle.

It was probably the part about the newspaper, rather than being arrested, that made Carrie clench her jaw and keep her hand by her side. "Do you think any Atlanta cop would do anything to me, considering who I'm marrying?"

"Maybe not, but you aren't in Atlanta. You're in Hopewell, and I'm involved with one of the detectives, so you might not fare so well with him," Jaclyn said, seizing on Eric as a weapon even though he might dispute the "involved" part. "Regardless of that, if you hit me again I'm pretty sure I could hit you back and everyone here would testify that I was defending myself. Before you go that route, you should know that I take kickboxing, and I can wipe the floor with your ass."

Okay, so much for being professional.

The part about kickboxing was a lie, too, but damn if she didn't mean it about wiping the floor with Carrie's ass. She was so angry she was pretty sure she could do it. And whether it was the expression on her face or her threat, Carrie reevaluated her actions.

"As if I'd brawl with you like two bar sluts," she sneered. "You might as well leave. I'll expect my refund check in the mail within the week."

"I'll see to it immediately," Jaclyn said. "Though the amount will be prorated by the time I've spent on the job, most of which has been accomplished."

Carrie's face flushed an ugly red. "I want the full amount refunded. If you'd done your job, you wouldn't have been fired!"

"Read the contract you signed. I believe you might receive a thousand or so in refund." Considering how hefty Premier's fee had been, it wouldn't bother her at all to send Carrie a check for a thousand dollars. In fact, it would be downright satisfying.

"We'll see about that!" Carrie hissed. "My lawyer will be in contact."

"As soon as possible, please. And be certain to tell him there were five witnesses who saw you strike me. I'm sure he'll be thrilled with that." The adrenaline burning through her made her bare her teeth in a smile that probably looked more like a snarl. Jaclyn had never been in a fight in her life, at least not one that got physical, but she was almost hoping Carrie *would* take another swing at her because she'd never wanted anything as much in her life as she wanted to punch the bitch on the nose.

"If they want to keep their jobs, they'll be smart and not say anything," Carrie said, but her cold, watchful gaze was less certain.

Jaclyn snorted. "They could all walk away and have other jobs within the hour. Which is what I'll do," she added, "and there's no way it won't be with someone I like more. Have a happy wedding. Maybe someone will show up, other than the poor victim . . . uh, groom."

The childish shot didn't do anything to lessen her anger but it did make her feel better. She spun on her heel and stalked off. For whatever reason Carrie didn't yell anything else at her, so she even had the satisfaction of having the last word.

With every step she took the weight on her shoulders lessened. Free! The way it had happened was ugly, but she was released from the burden of dealing with Carrie ever again. From here on out, nothing that happened was her problem. By the time she reached her car she was beginning to think her throbbing cheek was worth the end result.

She unlocked the car and opened the door, standing there for a minute while some of the fierce afternoon heat dissipated from the interior. Taking out her cell phone, she called her mother. Madelyn answered quickly and brightly, obviously curious about how the afternoon had gone, but not curious enough to spend the afternoon at the reception hall, in the midst of the action.

"It's done?" Madelyn asked.

"Yep—in more ways than one."

Madelyn's voice immediately changed, taking on a wary tone. "What happened?"

"A lot. We're going to have to throw a lot of business to these vendors before they forgive us for Carrie Edwards. Gretchen quit. The others may, too. And, best of all, Carrie fired me." She didn't want to go into details right then, because her emotions were still running hot, her self-control was holding but was a tad shaky, and she wanted time to calm down before she told Madelyn exactly how it had all gone down.

"Hallelujah," Madelyn breathed. "Tell me all. Can you meet me at Claire's for coffee? I have almost an hour to kill before I meet the party for tonight's wedding."

A cup of coffee, and maybe one of Claire's fabulous blueberry muffins, would be a great way to wind down after a tense afternoon. "I can be there in less than ten minutes."

"I can be there in five. Tell me what you want and I'll have it waiting."

Jaclyn complied, ended the call, and got in her car. As she started the engine a silver sedan pulled into the parking slot to her right. A man stepped out of the car, and she stopped to look at him because she had to wonder if Carrie had scheduled any other meetings she didn't know about. Anything was possible. But she didn't recognize the gray-haired man who was wearing a well-cut gray suit, with a white shirt and a red tie; he was probably someone arriving to see Melissa about booking the hall. He glanced in her direction as he strode toward the side door, but his mind was definitely elsewhere.

She hoped he was lucky enough not to encounter Carrie. If he did, that was his tough luck.

It was *so* not her problem!

Chapter Seven

Jaclyn used the fairly brief drive to try to clear her mind and settle down, because Madelyn was going to be upset enough when she heard what had happened. She didn't want to add to her mother's agitation by being an emotional wreck; she wanted to be calm and cheerful about the outcome even if the way it had happened was enraging.

She deliberately didn't think about Carrie. Instead she imagined a nice, hot cup of coffee and a warm blueberry muffin. She didn't indulge in the muffins very often, so having one was a real treat, one she thought was well-deserved—though whether as consolation or reward was up in the air. Thinking of coffee made her think of Eric, and she wondered if he liked blueberry muffins, and if he did, would he stop at a chic establishment like Claire's to get one? Probably not; it wasn't at all a cop kind of place. Most of the customers were women, but the coffee was good and the baked goods were phenomenal, so maybe she could convert him. All day she'd very determinedly pushed away her thoughts of him, but now she gratefully seized on anything that would take her mind off what had just happened, and help her to calm down— though thinking about Eric made her feel agitated in an entirely different way.

She pulled off the busy street into the small parking lot and spotted her mother sitting in the shade at one of the outdoor tables, all of which sported huge umbrellas to shield the patrons from the sun. The small table held two cups of coffee and a couple of muffins; Madelyn was already pinching bites from one of them. Jaclyn got out of her car and unhurriedly walked through the wrought-iron gate; it could even be said that she sauntered, but it was the memory of Eric that put the slow sway into her hips.

God. Now she knew what the term "in heat" meant, which was *not* the kind of thought she wanted to be having right now. Maybe she should be thinking of the gorgeous knockout roses that were blooming in the small courtyard, or taking a dip in the community pool tonight—something calming and serene. Thinking of Eric was neither.

She sat down with a grateful sigh and smiled when she saw that Madelyn had even indulged and gotten the muffins with the glazing on top. Madelyn gave her a sudden sharp look, then jerked her sunglasses off and peered at Jaclyn's face. "What's wrong with your cheek?" she asked sharply. Jaclyn had so thoroughly succeeded in distracting herself that for a moment all she could do was give her mother a blank stare.

Then she realized her cheek must be red and said, "I can't believe I forgot. The bitch actually slapped me, and I'm so relieved and happy to be rid of her that it slipped my mind!"

"She *slapped* you?" Madelyn echoed in

an awful tone, her expression shifting into something so fierce as she half rose to her feet that Jaclyn put a calming hand on her mother's arm. "I'll have her guts for garters!"

"That's some nasty, mean, stinky garters you'd have," Jaclyn said, smiling. "Not that I'm happy she slapped me, but, damn, when you balance that against never having to see her again, the happy way outweighs the pissed off!"

"Maybe for you," Madelyn hissed, fully on her feet now. "We're going to press charges. Did you call the cops? Were there witnesses?"

"Mom, I handled it. I didn't call the cops, but there were five witnesses so we're covered legally if she tries to hurt Premier's reputation."

"I don't care about Premier!" Madelyn's eyes were slits of fury, and she was breathing hard. "That low-life poster child for skankhood slapped you, and I'll be damned if she gets away with it!"

"Mom," Jaclyn said again, her voice calm and patient. "I handled it. I told her I'd wipe the floor with her ass if she touched me again. I got our vendors out of there before any of them came to blows with her, though with Estefani it was a near thing. She may quit. I wouldn't blame any of them if they walked away. Would you stop huffing and puffing like a dragon, and sit down? We have something to celebrate!"

Madelyn sat, but she continued fuming. "I know someone who knows Fayre Dennison," she said. "I'll make certain word gets to her just what kind of vicious shitfaced fluffer her son is marrying."

Jaclyn's eyes went wide in shock that her mother—her *mother!*—knew what a fluffer was. Her mouth opened and closed, then opened again. "Mom!" she said weakly, which was the best she could do.

"What?" Madelyn growled.

"Fluffer?"

"Oh." A flush warmed her cheeks. She sniffed. "Well. Evidently you know what a fluffer is, too, so you can't say anything."

"I found out when I read it on a blog. How do *you* know what it is?"

"Oh, the same way," Madelyn said airily.

"Uh-huh," Jaclyn said. "Right."

"Don't go all Victorian on me when I've been ready to snatch that bitch bald-headed on your behalf, young lady."

"And I'm grateful for the hair-snatching sentiment, which has nothing to do with how you know what a fluffer is."

Madelyn gave her a stern glance. "I'm giving you the compliment of treating you like an adult. I imagine we've both done some personal fluffing, so let's just let the subject drop." She glanced at her wristwatch. "I want to give myself a cushion in case traffic is tied up, but I have another ten minutes or so. Do you have anything else to do, or are you finished for the day?"

"I'm finished. I have a ton of laundry to do, so I think I'll just go home. The stress of dealing with Carrie has worn me out. I need a couple of hours of HGTV, or maybe the History channel, to unwind."

"If anything else happens with that heifer, call me immediately. I don't want you dealing with her again. If she contacts Premier, I'll handle it."

"Fair enough," said Jaclyn. She'd held her temper and refrained from retaliating today, but she wasn't certain she could do it again. She doubted Carrie would contact them again, though, because she wouldn't want word of her behavior leaking out to the poor moron she was marrying. Sean Dennison seemed like a very sweet guy, and he probably wouldn't believe it, but from everything Jaclyn had heard, Sean's mother was a different kettle of fish. Fayre Dennison was a force to be reckoned with; Carrie wouldn't want to butt heads with her, especially not before she and Sean were married, or there might not be a wedding at all.

She and Madelyn parted company ten minutes later. For her part, Jaclyn felt much better. Listening to her mother rant about Carrie had given her back her sense of humor and perspective. Carrie was behind her now, nothing more than an ugly little speck of fly poop on her rearview mirror.

Funny how just getting Carrie out of her life made her feel much less pushed for time, even though Carrie's wedding wasn't one of this week's heavy load. Her schedule was still hectic, but her stress load had just been halved. Maybe she'd even have time for Eric after all. If just thinking about him had the power to push Carrie completely out of her mind, then at the very least she should muster the courage to find out if he was truly special or just another guy.

Maybe she'd call him. No, not yet. Uncertainly she bit her lip. Probably she should wait to see if he called her next week the way he'd said he would. And probably she should get over doubting herself and have a little fun. Eric didn't have to be the love of a lifetime, or even this year. She'd had sex with him last night without being in love with him, without any sort of commitment on either of their parts, and the world hadn't come to an end. Not that she intended to start sleeping around indiscriminately, which seemed kind of unsanitary, but she was overdue for a red-hot affair.

This could be a very interesting summer.

Melissa DeWitt looked up from the contracts on her desk, and for the fifth time in the past fifteen minutes she glanced out the window of the reception hall to see if Carrie Edwards's car was still there. It was. She heaved a sigh. Why wouldn't the woman just *leave*?

She couldn't see the entire parking lot, just one corner of it, less than a quarter of the large lot. Carrie had snagged a prime space in the shade. What a quandary she

must have faced when she'd arrived:
Should she choose the spot closest to the
door, or one of the few in the shade? Melissa was a little bit surprised she hadn't
been blasted by the bride because there
wasn't a spot that offered both. God knows
Carrie had complained about everything
else.

It had been a while since Melissa
had heard any noise at all from the reception area, but she'd been making—and
taking—a sudden spurt of phone calls, so
if there'd been any further fireworks she
might have missed them. She couldn't
imagine Jaclyn was still talking to the foul-
tempered witch, but why else would Carrie
still be here?

Melissa had thought she'd faint from
shock when Carrie had actually slapped
Jaclyn. Poor Jaclyn! Then she remembered the flash of fire in Jaclyn's eyes, and
the sentiment vanished. Poor Jaclyn, my
ass. If anyone could hold her own against
someone like Carrie Edwards, it was Jaclyn Wilde. Just because she was normally
calm and controlled, with the diplomacy of
an ambassador, didn't mean there wasn't
fire behind the facade. She wondered if

Carrie had any idea how close she'd come to getting decked. Jaclyn hadn't been about to return the slap, she'd been winding up for a full-strength fistfight.

But why was Carrie still here?

Melissa left her desk and stepped to the open doorway of her office, sticking her head into the hallway and straining to hear voices. Silence. Her office was on the other side of the building from the reception area, with a couple of other small meeting rooms and restrooms in between. All afternoon, since Carrie had first arrived, she'd heard the occasional raised voice. Usually there was a lot of laughter and good-natured joking, when these kinds of meetings were held here, but not today.

She didn't want to face Carrie Edwards alone, but she wanted to lock up and call it a day, and she couldn't very well do that if the bride-to-be was still in meetings. The only way to find out was to face Carrie. Since the woman had spent all day mowing down everyone in her way, Melissa wasn't at all anxious to place herself on that path.

Taking a deep breath, she steeled her spine. If the bitch wanted to get violent with her, she *would* hit back. She wasn't a violent woman—far from it. At the same time, she wasn't sure she had the kind of restraint Jaclyn had displayed. Not that Jaclyn had been meek. If looks could kill . . .

Melissa strained to hear something, anything, as she walked toward the reception area, but the building was completely silent. It was eerie, knowing Carrie was somewhere in the building but not knowing where. She peeked through the door of the reception hall, noted that the table there was still littered with samples and paperwork, and continued down the hallway to the side entrance she'd left unlocked for Carrie and her vendors.

Curiously she stepped outside, wondering if Carrie was standing out in the heat talking to someone else. No one was there. Carrie's car, and her own, were the only vehicles still in the parking lot.

She stepped back inside, frowning. Was Carrie in the ladies' room? Had she gotten a ride with someone else and just left her car in the lot to collect later? Why would she do that? Not that it was beyond the realm of possibility, but it would've been common courtesy to at least stop by the office and let her know everyone was gone, and that she was leaving her car there for a few hours while she went out for a drink with a friend, perhaps.

Carrie had never shown any common courtesy, though, to anyone. Not only that, it was doubtful she had any real friends. Given that, Melissa hoped Carrie was off with an *acquaintance* who passed as a friend, and not lurking in the restroom, priming herself for another confrontation. She seemed to thrive on them. Melissa did not thrive on confrontation. The idea of being Carrie's next target was enough to make her stomach clench in dread. She hadn't been present for all the meetings today, but she'd checked in often and had seen enough—more than enough.

She braced herself, just in case, and went into the reception hall to clean up the mess Carrie had left behind. The table was cluttered and there were even piles of fabric on the floor; she could see a bit of it though the long tablecloth blocked much of the view. Even if Carrie was still here she wasn't the type of person who cleaned up after herself.

As soon as she entered the room she caught a whiff of something unpleasant. She stopped, her head lifting and her nose wrinkling as she took a deeper sniff. Oh, dear. That smelled as if one of the toilets had overflowed. The restrooms were down the hallway, though, and she hadn't smelled anything when she'd passed them. The farther she walked into the reception hall, the stronger the odor became. Had a sewer line ruptured?

Her steps slowed, and she brought up her hand to cover her nose. Her heart began to race. Something was wrong. Something felt very wrong. The hairs on her arms lifted as chills roughened her skin. She moved forward another three steps, and her breath caught in her throat, strangling her.

That wasn't a pile of fabric on the floor behind the table, it was Carrie Edwards, staring back at her open-eyed and oddly blank through the fine net of the veil that had been draped over her face. Her blood pooled on the floor; kabob skewers—some still skewering shrimp and beef—stuck out of her body at odd angles.

Melissa vaguely heard a strange shrieking sound, and after a moment realized it was she who was making the noise. She had a reputation for being able to handle any crisis with aplomb, but other than a funeral, she'd never seen a real dead body before, and this was different from seeing one on television. Aplomb went out the window. Dear God! The smell, the con-gealing blood, the complete lifelessness of the woman on the floor, were all too gruesome and too real.

The end of a scream caught in her throat and she took a step back, her eyes still on the body. There was no reason to check for a pulse. She might never have seen a dead person before, but she didn't have any doubt Carrie was doornail dead. No way was she going to touch her.

Okay. Okay. What should she do? She couldn't just stand here and stare at a dead woman. Nor could she do what instinct said, which was lock the door, go home, and leave her lying there for someone else to handle. There *was* no one else to handle it.

She had to call someone—911. That's it. She should call 911.

She turned and ran for her office, the administrator in her abruptly taking charge.

There was an event planned for the weekend, a twenty-fifth high school reunion. Surely this wouldn't interfere with that; surely the police would have the mess cleaned up by then, and her nice, orderly reception hall would be in shining order again. She wasn't certain of that, though; even to the very end, Carrie Edwards had a gift for screwing up other people's lives.

And then another thought intruded. What if the murderer was still in the building? Watching her, maybe waiting around the next corner, armed with skewers and cake knives and floral sticks. Melissa faltered, then kicked off her high heels and picked up the pace, turning the corner and sliding like Tom Cruise across the floor into her office. She slammed the office door and locked it behind her, then glanced frantically around the small room to make sure she was truly alone before she lurched for the phone.

Chapter Eight

The hot, late-afternoon sun was shining directly into his eyes as Eric searched for enough room on the crowded street to park his car. The parking lot of the reception hall was a tangle of patrol cars, a medic truck, even a fire engine, though he couldn't imagine why the fire engine was there. All of them had flashing lights, adding to the visual chaos. Okay, the patrol cars in the streets needed their lights on, but why the hell didn't the rest of them turn them off? Across the street, news trucks were already parked, round satellite dishes blooming on their roofs. Eric found enough room to nose his car off the street and got out, nodding to a couple of patrolmen as he ducked under the crime scene tape.

Hopewell didn't have many murders; the town was mostly upscale, no gang activity, and even their drug cases tended more toward prescription drugs than meth or crack. That didn't mean the police department was inexperienced in handling murder cases, just that it wasn't an everyday occurrence. When he'd been on the Atlanta force, between the gangs and drugs and everything else thrown in, the violence had seemed unending. It had been like working in a war zone. Even better, with its tax base, Hopewell could afford to pay its police department well, meaning they had good people, good services, and good equipment, which in turn translated to a high solve-rate.

The lieutenant and sergeant were already there, which upped his level of alertness. He'd already spent time with the lieutenant that morning, because the media had seized on the foiled convenience store robbery as something out of the ordinary and had contacted the department wanting an interview with him. He'd declined, because who had time for that shit, but the lieutenant had deemed otherwise. In a brief meeting beforehand, Lieutenant Neille had given him a curious look and asked, "By the way, why didn't you use your weapon? Why throw something at him?"

"Paperwork," Eric had replied, earning an expression from Neille that was both understanding and admonishing. "Besides, I've played baseball since I was four; I knew I could hit him."

The reluctantly given interview hadn't gone quite as smoothly. The same question had been asked, and he'd given the same answer. Then the reporter had said, "The suspect is hospitalized with a concussion, which brings up the question of whether or not you could have thrown something that wasn't as heavy as a quart of oil."

"Sure," he'd replied. "But I wasn't standing in the soup aisle."

That remark had earned him a growled comment from Sergeant Garvey, something along the lines that one day his mouth was going to overload his ass and he'd end up in a lot of trouble. So what else was new?

Garvey moved to intercept him, his

expression grave. "The manager has identified the victim as Carrie Edwards, the fiancée of Sean Dennison, the son of State
Senator Douglas Dennison."

"Shit," Eric said. He hated high-profile
cases, because as often as not the family
caused problems and actually hindered
the investigation with their demands, not
to mention that the increased media attention also ate into their time. As luck would
have it, Franklin, the older, more experi-
enced detective who would likely have
drawn the case *because* it was high-
profile and he was more diplomatic—a
huge understatement—than Eric, was on
vacation at Disney World with his family.
Like it or not, this case was his.

"The victim's family is being notified, so
her name hasn't been released to the
media yet, " Sergeant Garvey continued
as they walked into the reception hall. The
crime scene guys were already at work,
taking pictures, combing the area for trace
evidence. Eric put his hands in his pockets and approached close enough that he
had a better view of the body, but not so
close that he got in the way. Garvey stayed
at his side.

The victim lay sprawled on her back in a pool of blood, one shoe on and one lying several feet away. A veil was draped across her face. Protruding from her body were several long, thin—

He blinked, to make sure he was seeing what he thought he was seeing.

"She's kabobed."

Behind him, stifled laughter escaped from a couple of the patrolmen who heard the remark. Garvey put on his long-suffering expression, but not before he had to control the grin that threatened to crack his face. "For God's sake, Wilder."

Eric squatted so he had a better view of the body, looking it over from head to toe, his sharp gaze noting every detail. "What else would you call it?"

"*Stabbed.* The term is *stabbed.* Remember that, especially when you're talking to her family or the media."

He grunted, continuing his visual. As far as he was concerned, "kabobed" was on the money. Metal skewers protruded from the corpse at different angles, and even from a distance he could tell that a couple of them had gone very deep, while others had barely punctured the skin. There were more puncture wounds than there were skewers; the killer had stabbed her repeatedly, maybe even using both hands, because of the difference in angles. The one that had apparently punctured her heart was buried damn near to the hilt, where a piece of blood-drenched meat dangled, along with what looked to be a pearl onion.

Too bad Franklin was on vacation. He thought he'd seen everything, but Eric would bet the farm this would be a new one on him.

Eric was very aware of the emotional wreckage this would cause. The dead weren't the only victims of a murder; the families suffered, long and deep. Carrie Edwards was—had been—a beautiful young woman, murdered as she was planning her wedding. She'd likely have parents, siblings, friends; she definitely had a fiancé who had yet to be notified. Someone, somewhere, loved her. But he'd learned long ago that if he took every case to heart he wouldn't be able to function, so he couldn't afford to be too empathetic, to let himself get sucked into the emotional pain and grief that surrounded a murder. All cops handled it with dark humor, the darker the better. For the family's sake, though, he'd remember to deep-six the kabob comments.

It was someone else's job to soothe the pain this woman's death would cause: a minister, a psychiatrist, a friend. His job was to find the killers and bring them to justice.

Food, ribbons, pictures of flowers and veils, and different brochures littered the area around the body. She'd struggled; the table she lay behind had been knocked askew, and her arms bore defense wounds. A briefcase lay on the floor. After the crime scene techs finished, he'd see what information the briefcase yielded, but he couldn't be so lucky that the killer had left such a huge identifying item at the scene. The victim's cell phone, which lay beside her, was more likely to point them in the right direction. It was an iPhone, so God only knew what they'd find on it.

Now that he knew the identity of the victim, he was aware of a small knot of tension easing from his stomach. He hadn't let himself consciously think of her, but when he'd heard "reception hall" he'd instinctively prepared himself for the possibility that

Jaclyn could be the victim. She was in the business, and she'd told him herself how crazy people got when they were planning weddings.

Maybe that was what had happened here. Someone had definitely gone crazy.

He rose to his feet; he'd seen all he could see for now. "Where's the manager?"

"One of the officers is taking her statement. She discovered the body, made the 911 call."

From the time the first patrol car arrived, an officer would have stayed with the woman, both to control the scene and to prevent her from making any calls. They didn't want her contacting the media, friends, or anyone else, because controlling the information that got out was as important as the physical scene.

"She was almost hysterical," Garvey said sourly. "She'd locked herself in the office, convinced a Freddy Krueger–like serial killer was hiding in a closet somewhere, ready to slice and dice her if she poked her nose out. An officer searched every room before she'd calm down, and she's still wound as tight as a yo-yo."

She could rest easy; this wasn't the

work of a serial killer. The veil placed over the face—after the victim's death, by the looks of it—suggested that the murder had been personal. The murderer had known the victim, probably very well. The multiple wounds were also the mark of someone in a rage, which wasn't the hallmark of murder by a stranger.

He got a quick briefing from the first-on-scene officer. The manager's name was Melissa DeWitt. She was much calmer now, though through the open door he could see that she was dabbing at her eyes with a tissue.

She might not be so calm if she knew that right now suspicion was resting most heavily on her. It was amazing how often the killer would "discover" the body, either figuring the police would assume he or she couldn't possibly have done it because otherwise why risk drawing so much attention, or thinking that would give a logical reason for any trace evidence left behind. Innocent or guilty, she was the starting point of the investigation.

When the briefing was finished, he went into the office, pad and pen in hand, ready to write down everything she said. "Mrs.

DeWitt, I'm Detective Wilder. Do you think you could answer some questions for me?"

"Yes, of course," she said. She closed her eyes for a moment, took a deep breath, then turned her head to look out of the window behind her. "That's Carrie's car," she said, pointing to a silver Toyota. "I was watching, waiting for her to leave so I could lock up. Everyone else had already gone, at least . . . I thought they had." She shuddered a little, but didn't appear to be losing control again.

"Everyone else? Can you give me their names? I need to know who all was here this afternoon."

The woman nodded. "Of course. Just give me a moment to clear my head. I swear, I can hardly think straight." She took another deep breath, and while she was occupied with calming herself, he visually inspected her. The attack would have left plenty of blood on the perp; she could easily have washed any blood from her skin before placing the 911 call, but he didn't see a speck of blood on her clothing—and she was wearing a white blouse. He'd have to see if she kept a change of clothing here at work.

"Carrie met with so many vendors," she finally said.

"Vendors?"

"You know—people who do work for the wedding. The caterer, the florist, they're all vendors. Some of them I know very well, others I know by first name and trade. Today they were all, well . . . unhappy. Carrie wasn't satisfied with anything anyone did. Time was getting short and they all needed decisions made, but she gave everyone the runaround. Anyway, Premier was handling the event, so Jaclyn Wilde will have everyone's contact information. You should talk to her."

Oh, shit. Everything inside Eric stilled, for a moment. There couldn't be two wedding planners with that name. "Jaclyn Wilde."

"Jaclyn Wilde, the wedding planner." Mrs. DeWitt frowned. "Well, she *was* the wedding planner, but Carrie fired her this afternoon. There was a horrible scene. Carrie actually slapped Jaclyn in the face, in front of several of the vendors. For a minute I thought there was going to be a brawl."

"Jaclyn . . . Ms. Wilde was fired this afternoon?" Double shit. And the victim had slapped her, too. Was she the kind of woman who might snap under those circumstances? He didn't know her nearly well enough to say. A memory came back to him: *She has the ability to turn the gentlest of people into raving lunatics.* Those were Jaclyn's own words, from just last night. And since Mrs. DeWitt had already told him that Carrie had been giving all the vendors a hard time, he'd bet his pension the "she" Jaclyn had been talking about was now lying dead, literally skewered, down the hall. Well, fuck.

"Excuse me for a minute."

"Sure," she said, reaching for her office phone. "I'll call my husband—"

"I'd appreciate it if you'd hold off on that," he said, giving the officer standing outside the door a glance that told him to continue controlling the outflow of information. "Even the smallest detail you might let slip while you're so upset could hinder the investigation. Ms. Edwards's family hasn't been notified yet, and it would be bad if they heard about this on television."

"Oh!" She snatched her hand away from the phone. "I understand."

Eric rose, closed his notebook, and

went in search of Sergeant Garvey, whom he found standing next to Lieutenant Neille. "Problem," he said briefly.

Both men gave him their full attention.

"Evidently there was a confrontation with the wedding planner this afternoon, and the victim not only struck the wedding planner, Jaclyn Wilde, in the face, but she fired her, too."

"And?" Garvey prompted.

"I know Jaclyn Wilde."

Lieutenant Neille frowned. "How well?"

"We're not involved, and I can't say I know her all that well, but . . ." Screw it, the truth wasn't pretty, but it was the truth. "One-night stand."

"When?"

"Last night."

Garvey's muttered curse was fouler than usual, but he followed the curse with a quiet, "Can you handle it?"

"Yes," Eric answered without hesitation. And he could. He wouldn't like it, he *didn't* like it, but he could do his job. Jaclyn Wilde was a . . . possibility, not a commitment.

Garvey glanced at Lieutenant Neille, who sighed as he scrubbed his hand across his jaw. "For now, proceed," said Neille. "If she

starts to look good for it, we'll put someone else on the case if you have any problem. And do it right, Wilder. If there's any
question, you'll have to look at her harder
and longer than you would otherwise, so
know that up front."

"I know." And he did. It wasn't as if
Hopewell was lousy with detectives. There
were six of them, two per shift. Franklin,
who worked the same shift as Eric, wouldn't
be back from Disney World until Sunday
night. No way would they call him back
from the happiest place on earth when
Eric said he could handle it. It was a measure of his superiors' trust in him that they
let him do this. If he said there wasn't a
conflict of interest, they believed him.

Now, if he could just convince himself.

Chapter Nine

Jaclyn heaved a sigh of relief when she entered the cool, quiet sanctuary of her town house. Now that she didn't have to put on a brave face for Madelyn, even more stress melted away and she actually felt kind of mellow—not completely calm, because there was still an inner core of anger that Carrie had slapped her and she'd had to take it instead of coldcocking the bitch, but calm enough that she could accept that what was done was done and she'd handled things the best way possible, even if the best way wasn't the most satis-fying way.

The stress had worn her out, though; she felt exhausted down to her bones, and the idea of a night at home doing nothing other than a few chores was just short of paradise. She stripped off the capri pants and sleeveless blouse she'd worn that day, gathered her dirty laundry, and dumped everything in the washer. Then she remade the bed with fresh sheets, and took the dirty ones to the laundry to wash later. After that she had nothing to do other than taking a shower and putting on her pajamas.

While she was in the shower she heard the phone ringing, but she didn't jump out and race to answer it; after the day she'd had, whoever it was could wait. She even took the time to wash her hair. After she'd blown her hair dry, dusted herself with fragrant powder, and put on her pajamas, she checked the phone for a message, but there wasn't one so she looked at Caller ID.

It was her father. She frowned. Jacky usually left a message when he called, even if it was nothing more than a "Hi, honey, haven't talked to you lately." Knowing her father, the fact that he hadn't left a message meant he wanted to talk to her about something, which probably meant he had a favor to ask.

There was no telling what he wanted. With Jacky, anything was possible. She dialed his number and he answered before the first ring completed. "Hi, baby," he said cheerfully. "How's my girl?"

"Tired. It was a rough day at work. I was in the shower when you called. What's up?"

"Why does anything have to be up? Can't I call just to talk to you?"

The slightly guilty-sounding indignation in his voice made her grin. Her father was good-natured, the life of any party, he truly loved her, charming as all hell, and completely irresponsible. She didn't doubt that he loved her, but neither did she doubt that, if he had to choose between saving her from drowning or saving himself, he'd weep huge tears at her funeral.

"You *could,*" she said, "but you didn't. So what's up?"

"Well . . . there is a little favor I need."

The little favor was usually money, because Jacky perpetually ran short. To him, buying an expensive bottle of champagne to celebrate anything was more important than paying his utility bills. Most of the time she refused, but sometimes she'd come through for him, if the amount wasn't too much and if the reason he wanted it made her smile. Once he'd wanted a hundred bucks to buy some little plastic ducks for a charity duck race, and she'd liked the idea so much she'd gone in with him to buy two hundred dollars' worth of little plastic duckies, and they'd attended the race together. None of their ducks had won, but they'd had a great time.

"How much, and for what?" she asked.

"It's not money," he quickly replied. "I'm doing okay. But I've met someone, and—"

"Good Lord, am I about to get stepmother number eleven?"

There was a short pause, then he said, *"Eleven?"* in a shocked tone. "Have I been married that many times? There was your mother, of course, then Brigitta, then Kristen, then . . ." His voice trailed off.

"Ariel," Jaclyn prompted. She wasn't surprised that he'd forgotten. Ariel had lasted two weeks—almost.

"Oh, yeah. I must have blocked her out. She was hell to live with. After her was . . . that was Tallie, wasn't it? That's just five. I don't remember anyone else."

"I was just teasing," she said. "Your total is five." He'd stayed married to Tallie longer than anyone had expected; in longevity, she'd placed second to Madelyn. The fact that "Tallie" was a nickname—short for "tallywhacker," which kind of gave an indication of her talents—explained the length of that particular marriage. Jaclyn knew the tale about the nickname was true, because Tallie herself had told her the meaning behind her name.

"I should know that," he mused. "I guess I was afraid I'd blanked out on a few."

"You might have picked up some Las Vegas barnacles I don't know about, but if you don't remember them either that would make you a bigamist. So far as I know, there have been five."

"I'm in the clear, then, because you know all of them."

He wasn't the least embarrassed by his marital misadventures. Jacky felt no need to excuse his behavior; to him, if he was having fun, then that was reason enough to do whatever he wanted.

"If you aren't about to get married, and you don't need money, then what's the favor?"

Another short pause. "I *have* met someone. I'm taking her out to dinner tomorrow
night, and I want to really impress her, so I
thought maybe you'd let me borrow your
Jag—"

"You thought wrong," Jaclyn said wryly,
not even letting him finish the sentence.
"No way."

"I promise I'd be careful—"

"No. Your idea of careful is actually closing the door when you get out of the car.
You'd either leave the keys in the ignition
and it would be stolen, or you'd wreck it, or
you'd have sex in it. *No.*"

"I wouldn't leave the keys in it," he pro-
tested. At least he was honest enough not
to deny the other two were possibilities.

"The answer is still no. If you want to go
on a date in a Jag, you'll have to rent one."

"In that case, I'll need a loan after all."

"No."

"Jaclyn, baby—"

He was stubborn. He kept her on the
phone for another twenty minutes, trying different angles of approach to the argument,
but she held firm. No, she didn't care that
his hot new date might turn out to be "the
one," if only he could sufficiently impress

her. No, she didn't think he might die heart-
broken from losing a great love. No, she
wouldn't do it even if he offered to have her
Jag completely cleaned and detailed before
he brought it back. She didn't doubt the offer, just that he would follow through on his
promise. By the time she finally got off the
phone with him, she was so exasperated
she was almost yelling as she shot down
every new proposal he threw at her.

Now she was well and truly exhausted. If
the phone rang again tonight, she'd be
damned if she answered it or returned any
calls—unless Madelyn called her, of course.

Or maybe Eric.

No, he wouldn't call. She knew he
wouldn't. Next week . . . maybe. She had
to hold to her wait-and-see decision.

The only thing that would soothe her
frazzled nerves was a couple of hours of
HGTV. She settled down to a string of several episodes of *House Hunters,* trying to
guess which house each person would
buy and getting the right answer most of
the time, though sometimes the choice
absolutely floored her.

She was immersed in the third episode
when her cell phone rang. The sound au-

tomatically made her tense, because she used her cell almost exclusively for work. Warily she picked it up and looked at the window. *Bishop Delaney?* Why on earth would he be calling? She clicked on the call.

"Hi, Bishop. Is something wrong?"

"There's been a murder at the reception hall," he said baldly. "I don't know who, but I thought, well, we *did* leave you there with Carnivore Edwards."

After a blank second during which she digested the news, she got a sick feeling in the pit of her stomach. "Oh my God. Do you think Melissa—" She couldn't complete the thought. It would be so horrible if Melissa had been attacked and murdered, though she was the most likely victim, considering the location. "Are you certain there was a murder?"

"That's what a friend of mine heard. He was driving home and tried to take that route, but the street was blocked off and he had to take a detour. He stopped and asked at the nearest service station, of course, and they told him they'd heard some woman had been killed."

"When? What time?" There might have

been a function held at the reception hall that night, though if there had been one scheduled Melissa hadn't mentioned it. You could never predict what might happen when a group of people got together. She hoped there *had* been an event held at the hall tonight, because that would drastically cut the odds that Melissa had been the one harmed.

"Haven't been able to find out. Details at eleven."

Jaclyn hadn't intended to stay up that long, but now she had to, to find out who had been murdered. She and Bishop spent a few minutes speculating on what might have happened, but that was unproductive because neither of them had any way of knowing. After they hung up she switched to each of the local network stations in turn, but none of them had anything showing other than regular programming, not even a news crawl at the bottom of the screen. Murder wasn't huge news in Atlanta unless someone important was involved, or the crime was particularly gruesome.

Her doorbell rang at nine forty-five. She was so on edge that she shot to her feet, her heartbeat hammering. *Who on earth—?*

She glanced down at herself, and grabbed a sweater from the entry closet to cover her obviously braless state, and pulled it on as she peeked through the peephole.

Eric?

He was undoubtedly one of the men standing on her stoop. In a flash the worst possible reason for his presence hit her like a blow a thousand times harder than Carrie Edwards's slap. Oh. My. God. *Madelyn.* Something had happened to her mother. *The murder—*

She fumbled with the lock, and jerked the door open. Her lips felt numb as she stared up at him. "Mom?" she asked in a thin, tight voice. "Is my mom okay?"

Eric and the other man glanced at each other. "As far as we know," he said, and she almost collapsed with relief, sagging against the door frame.

"This is Sergeant Garvey," he said, introducing the other man. "May we come in? We'd like to ask you some questions about Carrie Edwards."

She'd been so white when she'd jerked the door open that he'd thought she was about to faint. She still seemed shaky as she stepped back. *"Carrie?* I mean, yes, come in. So my mom—and it wasn't Melissa. Was it? Did Carrie kill Melissa?" She clenched her hands together almost as if she were praying, standing there in the small entry, her blue eyes huge in her pale, strained face.

She looked as freshly clean and unadorned and unabashedly sexy as she had the night before, Eric thought, though a sweater covered the tank top tonight. As he and Garvey stepped in he saw the open closet door in the entry, a coat hanger still swaying slightly, and knew she'd grabbed the sweater just before opening the door. Part of him regretted that, because he wanted to see her breasts again. Another part of him was glad she'd put on the sweater, because he sure as hell didn't want Garvey seeing them. Distantly he recognized that feeling possessive about her wasn't good, but that was something he'd deal with later.

Garvey's sharp gaze was taking in everything, from every detail of the stylish town house to Jaclyn herself. The sergeant had put in years on the detective level, in some rough places, before settling in Hopewell and moving up the ranks. As for Eric, given his previous involvement with Jaclyn, there wasn't any way he'd be allowed to question her by himself, which was fine with him. Whether she was guilty or innocent, Garvey was there as another set of eyes, another honed instinct, and as a witness that the job had been done right.

"Carrie Edwards was murdered this afternoon," he said. "How were you aware of this?"

"I wasn't," she said. "Not that it was Carrie, I mean. I got a phone call—" She waved a hand toward the living room, which was evidently meant to indicate a phone was in there somewhere, then took a deep breath. "I'm sorry. Let's sit down, please. Would you like some coffee? I can put on a pot of coffee."

"No, thanks," Eric said hastily, before Garvey could accept. He didn't want to deal with that swill again, not even a polite sip or two. They all sat down, and Jaclyn picked up the remote to turn off the television. He slipped his notebook out of his inside jacket pocket and made some notes.

"Who called you?" he asked, keeping his tone as conversational as possible.

"Bishop Delaney. He's the floral designer who's doing Carrie's wedding. *Was* doing it, anyway. He'd heard— A friend of his had called, told him a woman had been killed at the reception hall, so he called me."

"Why did he call you?"

"Because this afternoon he and the other vendors left me there alone with Carrie and he thought—*oh.*" The last word escaped her on a little gasp and she froze, her face going even whiter as she stared at him. She swallowed, her lips moving several times even though nothing else came out.

He watched her reach the inescapable conclusion, watched the expression in her eyes change from blank shock to a quick flash of anger, before going blank again. This time, though, the blankness was more of a deliberate shield.

"You know what happened this afternoon," she said flatly. "You think I killed her."

Chapter Ten

"We're questioning everyone," he replied in a smooth tone. "Why exactly did this Bishop Delaney call you?"

She didn't believe him. Oh, she believed they would *eventually* question everyone who had been at the reception hall that afternoon, but considering what had happened, she had to be at the top of their suspect list.

The sharp twist of pain in her chest both surprised and dismayed her. She didn't want to feel hurt. It was stupid. Intellectually, she knew that Eric was doing his job, knew she couldn't expect him to do anything else. They had no ties. They hadn't even dated. There was nothing between them other than a one-night stand.

But however sound and rational her intellect could be, emotionally she felt as if she'd been punched in the stomach. It wasn't any one thing, it was everything together: the shock and uneasiness over learning someone had been murdered at the reception hall, and thinking it might be Melissa, who was a friend even if she wasn't a close one; then there had been the visceral, unreasoning panic when she'd thought Eric had come to notify her that something had happened to Madelyn. Jaclyn thought of herself as a basically strong person, but in that moment the black terror had almost sent her to her knees. Just when she'd been pulling herself back from the edge of that, she'd been body-slammed by the realization that Eric, to whom she'd given more of herself in one night than she'd ever given to her husband, actually suspected she was a *murderer.*

She had barely been able to keep from hurling herself into his arms, seeking ref-

uge and comfort from the horrible moment
when she'd thought something had happened to her mother. She'd wanted to curl
up on his lap like a child, hide her face in
his broad shoulder, and let him close out
the world. What had she thought? That
one night together meant anything more
than sex? If so, he'd certainly disabused
her of that silliness. Instead of comfort
from him, she'd gotten an interrogation.
Boy, what a wake-up call.

She could barely breathe from the
weight pressing on her chest. Even realizing that the sense of betrayal she felt was
irrational didn't neutralize the hurt she felt.
For a mortifying second she thought she
might embarrass herself by bursting into
tears, but she swallowed hard and focused
on the other man, whose name she couldn't
remember. He was older than Eric, shorter,
graying hair, but there was breadth to his
shoulders and a direct alertness to his gaze.

"I'm sorry," she managed to say, though
her voice was still a little thin and shaky. "I
didn't catch your name."

"Garvey," he said. "Sergeant Randall
Garvey."

"Sergeant Garvey," she repeated, and

swallowed again. The weight on her chest loosened and she was able to suck in some much-needed air. Her head cleared a little. Eric had asked her the same question twice, and neither he nor Sergeant Garvey would like it if they had to ask it a third time. "Bishop—I think he was worried that something had happened to me. The afternoon meeting with Carrie was a disaster, and he and the other vendors left me alone with her, except for Melissa— Melissa DeWitt—but she was in her office."

"Why was he worried?"

"Why ask when you already know she slapped me?" Jaclyn flared, but she kept her gaze locked on Sergeant Garvey even though it was Eric who asked the question. It would be too weird to meet Garvey's eyes while she was talking to Eric, so instead she focused on his tie.

"We're just trying to find out what happened. Why did she slap you?"

"I'm not certain. She'd insulted Estefani Morales, the veil-maker, and Estefani was on the verge of quitting. The dressmaker had already quit, just before I got to the reception hall this afternoon. Carrie took a call from her fiancé, Sean Dennison, and while she was talking to him I tried to calm Estefani down. Bishop and I were talking to her, and I said we'd move on to the wedding cake and decide about the veil later. When Carrie got off the phone with Sean, she knocked everything off the table, came rushing over, and slapped me and told me I was fired." Automatically she put her hand to her cheek, though the sting was gone.

"I imagine handling the Dennison wedding paid you a hefty fee."

"It did, yes." She knew exactly where he was going with this, and thanked heaven that their standard contract had them, and her, covered.

"You'd have had to refund the money when you were fired?"

She was on solid ground here, and her voice gained a little confidence. "No. Our contract clearly states that in case the job is terminated, our fee will be prorated based on the amount of work done. Because Carrie's wedding is—was—so soon and I'd already overseen most of the event, I'm guessing that the amount we'd have had to refund was in the neighborhood of a thousand dollars. Everything was in place, except for the details she hadn't decided on yet. The proration clause is in there to prevent people from firing us at the last minute and refusing to pay anything. It's happened."

"The dressmaker is . . ."

"Gretchen Gibson. She'd finished the dresses, but yesterday Carrie decided she didn't like them, wanted to change them. I told her there probably wasn't time, not to mention the bridesmaids probably couldn't afford to have other dresses made, and Gretchen told her the same thing. Carrie doesn't—didn't—like being told 'no.'" She couldn't remember to use the past tense. Somehow she couldn't absorb that Carrie was really dead, that someone had murdered her. She'd been a nasty piece of work, but Jaclyn hadn't wished her any harm . . . nothing beyond wishing she'd fall on her face as she walked down the aisle, maybe. Or that someone would spill a glass of pink champagne on her head. That would be fun to see. But murder? No.

Eric was making notes; though she didn't look directly at him, she could see him in her peripheral vision. Lest Sergeant Garvey think she was staring at his chest, she moved her gaze down to his knees, then thought better of that and moved on to his feet. His shoes were scuffed on the toes.

"When Ms. Edwards slapped you, what did you do?"

"Nothing."

"Nothing?" He sounded skeptical. "Come on, Ms. Wilde, you had to have done something."

"I didn't hit her back, if that's what you mean," she told Garvey's shoes. Maybe it was time to focus on something else, because how long could she be expected to stare at someone's shoes? She shouldn't have turned off the television; if it were on, she could stare at the screen while she answered Eric's questions. She might not be able to focus on whether the buyer bought house number one, two, or three, but at least she wouldn't look as if she had a shoe fetish. "I wanted to. I wanted to punch her in the nose. But I didn't. Planning events is my livelihood, and punching a client wouldn't exactly be good advertising." Unless all potential clients knew Carrie, she thought, in which case punching her might be considered a plus. She didn't share that particular observation, though.

"But what exactly *did* you do?"

She took a deep breath, trying to organize her jumbled memories of the afternoon. She might as well tell them everything she could remember, even the things that didn't make her look good, because hearing them from her had to be better than hearing them from someone else, right? "Carrie threatened to ruin Premier's reputation; she said that no one would ever use us again. I really wanted to punch her then, but Bishop told me not to, that she'd have me arrested for assault if I did, and right then I was the one with the advantage because *she'd* hit *me.* So I didn't. I decided to be as professional as possible, under the circumstances. I got all of the vendors out of there, told them to reschedule, and told Carrie that if she hit me again I'd have her arrested." That particular memory burned, because it connected to Eric, and how she'd told Carrie she was involved with him and any complaint Carrie made wouldn't gain any traction. Evidently that was so not true.

She cleared her throat. "I also told her that I take kickboxing, and if she hit me again I'd wipe the floor with her ass. I don't. Take kickboxing, that is. Anyway, I figured the lie would stop her if she'd been about to take another swing at me." She simply couldn't stare at Garvey's shoes any longer. Desperately she looked at his left hand. Wedding ring in place. A few freckles on his thick fingers, maybe, but with just the lamps on she couldn't be certain.

"What happened then?"

"Um . . . she threatened to sue us to get all of her money back. I told her to go ahead, that she'd signed a contract *and* she'd hit me in front of five witnesses. She said the witnesses wouldn't say anything if they wanted to keep their jobs, and I told her they didn't need her job. Then I told her to have a happy wedding, that maybe someone would show up other than the poor fool who was marrying her, or words to that effect. Then I left."

"Who were the five witnesses?"

She gave them the names of the four vendors who'd been there, plus Melissa DeWitt.

"I thought you said Mrs. DeWitt was in her office."

"She was, at that time. After Carrie slapped me, I asked Melissa to let me handle things, so she said she had some phone calls to make and left. Then I got the vendors out of there, before they got drawn into a fight. Carrie and I had it out alone, then I left."

"What time was this?"

"I don't know exactly, but I called my mother—she's also my business partner in Premier," she said for Garvey's benefit, as Eric already knew that. "We met at Claire's for some coffee and a muffin, and I filled her in on what had happened. The time will be on my cell phone," she said, pointing to it. "Also the time that Bishop called me, if you're interested."

Evidently Eric was interested, because he picked up her phone, then paused and said, "May I?"

"Of course." She didn't have anything to hide, and they couldn't prove she'd killed Carrie for the simple reason that she hadn't. There was that pesky thing called circumstantial evidence, though, plus cause, and she had to admit she could be in some trouble there. She had to forget her hurt feelings and concentrate solely on the current situation, which was serious.

He flipped her phone open and ran through her call log, jotting down times and numbers. "Did anyone see you leave?" he asked in a casual tone as he closed the phone and placed it back on the table.

"A man drove up as I was leaving, but I don't know who he was."

There was a pause. "A man?"

"A gray-haired man. He was wearing a suit. That's really all I can tell you."

"Did you see his car?"

"Um . . . it was silver. A sedan. I didn't notice the make."

"Did he go inside?"

She thought about it for a moment. "Not really. He was walking toward the side door, but I didn't actually see him go inside."

"Did you go straight from the reception hall to Claire's?"

"Yes. Mom had some time before she had to be at the wedding we had scheduled tonight." Automatically Jaclyn checked the time, vaguely noticing how nice it was to look at something other than Garvey. "The reception should be over soon; she might check in to tell me how things went."

"What did you do after you left Claire's?"

"I came home. I had a pile of laundry to do."

"Did you see anyone, talk to anyone?"

"No, not until Bishop called to tell me someone had been murdered at the reception hall."

"Did you go back to the reception hall?"

"No, why would I?" she asked blankly.

"Your briefcase was found on the floor. Maybe you went back to retrieve it, found that Ms. Edwards was still there, and the two of you had another altercation."

"My br—" Jaclyn stopped, blinking in astonishment. How could she have forgotten her briefcase? Why hadn't she noticed it before now? Having it in her hand was as natural as having on clothes. She looked around, as if it might magically appear, but he was right: no briefcase.

She stared into the middle distance as she mentally reconstructed what had happened. "I'd put my briefcase on the table, but Carrie must have moved it. I'd taken my appointment book out, though, because I'd had a couple of calls from my assistant about scheduling, and it was on the table. When Carrie threw her temper tantrum and knocked everything off the table, Melissa picked up my appointment book and handed it to me before she went to her office. I had it in my hand when I left, so I never missed the briefcase."

Oh, God, the briefcase was bad news. It gave her a reason for going back, and she had no witnesses otherwise.

"What clothes were you wearing today?"

The question seemed to come out of nowhere. Surprised, Jaclyn almost looked at him before catching herself and instead focusing on the coffee table. It took her a minute to remember what she'd had on, and in that minute she realized that they already knew what she'd been wearing, that they had already interviewed Melissa and probably gotten a description of her clothes. A chill ran down her spine.

"Black capri pants, and a black top."

"May we see them?"

This wasn't good either. She bit her lip. "They're in the laundry."

"Laundry? You washed them?"

Suddenly she'd had enough, temper flaring and pushing out the shock and hurt. "That's what one does with dirty clothes," she said curtly. "Though maybe you don't know that." The instant the words left her mouth she knew she shouldn't have said them, shouldn't have made the conversation personal. She made an abrupt gesture. "Sorry, that was uncalled-for. The clothes are still in the washer, I haven't dried them yet."

"May we see them?"

"Sure. Knock yourself out."

She went with them to the small laundry room, watched as they removed her wet clothing and sorted out the capri pants and top. "Did you use bleach?" Eric asked.

"On *black* clothes? That would ruin them." He was asking her about *laundry*? He was a bachelor, so surely he did some laundry; he had to know about bleach.

"So you didn't use bleach?"

"No, of course not! Do they look gray now?"

"No, they don't." Was that amusement she heard in his voice? Maybe it was, maybe it wasn't, but she wanted to kick him anyway. "I'd like to take these clothes, if you don't mind. If you do mind, I can always get a warrant."

"Go ahead, take them," she said wearily. She minded, but she'd go along with anything to get this over. What she hadn't planned on was that they would take everything that had been in the washer, which put a serious dent in her wardrobe. She stood in mute shock as they took her clothing into custody. They were thorough, all right. Then she caught Eric eyeing the pile of sheets on the floor, and the thought that he might be getting some pleasure from remembering the night before sent a rush of anger through her that almost took off the top of her head.

"I'm sorry about the smell in here," she said sweetly. "A skunk must have peed on those sheets. I'll have to burn them, because no way do I want them now."

They were in the car before Garvey broke out in a broad grin. "Wilder, I hate to tell you this, but I don't think she's very happy with you right now."

Eric grunted. "I kind of noticed." Not only had she looked everywhere but at him, but the crack about the skunk and the sheets had been a dead giveaway.

"For what it's worth, I don't get the vibe off her. I think she's probably clean."

"I know." Her shock had been too profound; not even the best actress in the world could make herself go pale, or change the size of her pupils. Everything she'd said had jibed with what Mrs. DeWitt had told them, too. She had washed her clothes, but that in itself wasn't suspicious, and if there was any blood on them it would show up in examination. She hadn't used bleach, which would have destroyed trace evidence, but as she'd said, who used bleach on dark clothes?

She wouldn't have gone to meet her mother at Claire's if there had been blood on her clothing. She wasn't in the clear, though. She could have left Claire's, gone back to the reception hall to fetch her briefcase, and had another confrontation with Carrie Edwards, one that had ended with her stabbing Carrie with the kabob skewers.

Knowing her briefcase was there, though, would she have left it a second time? She struck him as too organized and together for that, but if she'd killed Carrie in a fit of rage she'd have been in shock at what she'd done, and her most likely response would have been to run.

The trouble with that scenario would be that it would have required Carrie to hang around the empty reception hall for about an hour, doing nothing and seeing no one.

Then there was the unknown man Jaclyn had seen arrive. Mrs. DeWitt hadn't mentioned anyone else being there, but she'd been in her office the whole time, so it was possible.

He concentrated on the myriad details they had to run down: the other vendors, two of whom had had their own problems with Ms. Edwards; the unknown man; the previous calls on Carrie's cell phone, logs to get from the cell carriers to make certain no calls had been deleted from the phone's memory. Jaclyn wasn't clear, but neither did he think she was guilty. As Garvey had said, the vibe just wasn't there. Until she was definitely cleared, though, he had to treat this as he would any other case.

She'd said she was going to burn the sheets, the ones they'd slept on. He'd recognized them, gold with white dots. She probably would, too, because she'd been fuming.

Fuck. She'd probably never speak to him again.

Chapter Eleven

Madelyn smiled across the room at the bride's mother, a sweet woman who'd been on pins and needles for the past two weeks and was now enjoying some liquid help in unwinding. Between them stretched a crowded dance floor where most of the recently fed friends and family danced to a live band—a good one, too. Everyone was dressed to the nines, and quite a few of them were more than a little tipsy. From her point of view, that was a mixed blessing. The good thing was, they were having a good time. The bad thing was, when people were tipsy, Things Could Happen that could result in people being injured, embarrassed, or arrested. At this point, though, it was out of her hands; all she could do was cross her fingers and hope everyone simply had a good time.

The wedding had gone off without a hitch, the bridal pictures had been taken, and the reception was in full swing. Thanks to Peach's makeup-wizard friend, the bridesmaid with the black eye looked as beautiful and unblemished as all the others. Currently the bridesmaids—all pretty blondes in sleek black satin—were posing for an informal photo, champagne glasses in hand. They were a striking contrast to the brunette bride in a cascade of white. Madelyn knew for certain at least one of the bridesmaids hadn't been a blonde before, but had bleached her hair at the bride's request. After all, the visual impact was important.

There was plenty of visual impact in the gown alone. For a relatively small wedding, the bride had gone all out with her gown. She could fit the groom *and* the best man under the full ballroom skirt, and no one would be the wiser, except maybe the devilish five-year-old ring-bearer, who had decided he had to see what was under that foaming, belling mountain of fabric. He had given everyone in the wedding party a good laugh, even the bride, who was both pretty and good-natured and had wanted to look like a princess for her wedding.

About two hundred guests had attended the ceremony, which had been held in a quaint chapel decked out in creamy-white flowers and flickering candles, giving it a dreamy quality that had charmed even her. She wasn't a romantic, marriage to Jacky Wilde had cured her of that, but sometimes one of the weddings would get to her. Maybe it had more to do with the bride and groom than the trappings, and this particular bride and groom were so besotted with each other it was difficult not to smile when you looked at them. She was happy for them that the wedding ceremony had been perfect.

The wedding party had then moved to a nearby hall that was all but impossible to book on a weekend without at least a six-month lead time; a year was better, for getting the exact date you wanted. Hence the midweek wedding, which was unusual, but if that was the only way the bride and groom could get the venue they wanted on short notice, it wasn't a bad way to go.

For the moment Madelyn's job here was done, so she could take a breather, but the operative term was "for the moment." Until the bride and groom actually left, her job wasn't finished. She had to make sure the departure went as planned, and then she'd be well and truly done for the night. One down, four more to go. If Peach was here they could have passed the time discussing the upcoming weddings and rehearsals, critiqued the food and fashions, and maybe gossiped a bit. This job hadn't required the efforts of two, though, and in a week when they were all working extra hours it didn't make sense to bring Peach into the mix tonight just for the company. For the next few days, they'd all be swamped.

She took a glass of champagne from a passing server, took a single sip, and made a circuit of the room. That single sip was all she'd allow herself, but she continued to carry the glass as she said hello to those she knew, and graciously accepted compliments from family members who were pleased with the way the wedding had gone. She made the time to speak to them all, because that was part of the game. Everyone here was a potential client—well, almost everyone, because she didn't think the ninety-two-year-old great-grandfather of the bride was likely to need Premier's services—and it was important to make a good impression without coming off like a snake oil salesman hawking her goods. She didn't press a single card into a single hand; those who were impressed would remember the name of the company that had handled the details of the event, and those who were either unimpressed or un-interested would just throw the card away. There was no telling how many trees she'd saved by not handing out business cards.

Sometimes it struck her how lucky she'd been that she and Jaclyn had somehow stumbled onto the perfect jobs for them both. Opening Premier with Jaclyn had certainly been the smartest decision she herself had ever made. She'd made some boneheaded ones—witness Jacky—but Premier had been a stroke of genius. She was her own boss, and she and Jaclyn had a wonderfully close relationship. Not every woman could work with her own child, she understood that, but the two of them had made it not only work, but work well. Peach and Diedra, added to the mix as their success had grown, had become like family. Well, Peach had been like family for a long time, but working together deepened the relationship.

For Madelyn, the long, sometimes hectic days usually helped distract her from the feeling that she was too young to have given up on men. Usually . . . but not always.

Marriages were like roller coasters. There were ups and downs, twists and turns, and sometimes they turned you on your head and made you puke. Being involved in weddings—which were like that exciting first moment when you climbed into the shiny little car and buckled in, ready for a fun ride, stomach full of butterflies—was maybe an odd choice for a woman whose own marriage had derailed, sailed off a cliff, crashed and burned. There were a lot of ways to describe being married to Jacky Wilde.

Her years with him had been quite a ride; there had been lots of ups, plenty of downs. If she'd known then what she knew now . . . she still would've married the bastard. He'd broken her heart, but there had

been some good times with him, especially at first. And above all else, he'd given
her Jaclyn.

She adored her daughter, loved her so
much not just because she was her child
but because she genuinely loved her as
a person. Even if they weren't related,
Madelyn thought Jaclyn would still be her
favorite person in the whole world. It de-
pressed her to think that her own marriage
made her daughter so cautious that she
might never let herself get lost in the almost
frightening ecstasy of a romantic relationship. It didn't help that Jaclyn's own marriage had ended so soon. Even worse,
there hadn't been any major drama in Jaclyn's divorce; they had both simply walked
away, as if they realized there was nothing
there worth fighting for.

And as for the example Jacky had set,
with his five marriages . . . well, the less
said about that, the better.

Madelyn wanted her child to know love,
to take a risk, to climb into the shiny car
at the starting gate not knowing where it
would take her, and it made her sad to
think that might never happen, that Jaclyn
might never truly fall in love. Falling in love

meant taking a leap of faith, it meant trusting someone else and letting them be important to you. So far, Jaclyn was very nimble at avoiding any emotional risk.

The caterer, a woman who worked Atlanta-area weddings often enough that she and Madelyn could call themselves well acquainted, walked up behind Madelyn and grabbed her arm. Madelyn jumped, startled both by the touch and by who had approached her. Shirley *never* left the kitchen during an event, so she could only imagine that there had been a kitchen catastrophe.

Shirley's expression was concerned. "Doesn't your daughter live in Hopewell?"

Madelyn's heart gave a little "thump" as she answered "Yes," her mother's instinct going on alert. It was obvious that something was wrong. Shirley's cheeks were red, her eyes bright. "Why?"

"There was a murder at the Hopewell reception hall," she said, lowering her voice to a forceful whisper. "You know, the big one?"

Madelyn went cold. She could barely force out one word: "Who?" Together she and Shirley moved toward the wall, away from the couple at the nearest white-tablecloth-covered table. What kind of event was taking place at the reception hall tonight? Her mind spun to the possibilities: Melissa, the manager? One of the vendors? Maybe someone she knew well? The victim could be anyone in their fairly small world. She said a silent prayer of thanks that Jaclyn had nothing scheduled, and had said she was going straight home; she should be safely there now, watching her beloved HGTV.

"I don't know," Shirley said. "But I heard that the parking lot was packed with emergency vehicles, and *somebody* is dead."

Knowing her daughter had come so close to a murder gave her chills, and she had a sudden urge to hear Jaclyn's voice. Not only that, but Jaclyn might have heard something, and have more details than Shirley could provide.

Madelyn gave a quick glance around the room, made sure no crises seemed to be brewing, then briskly headed for the ladies' room. As she walked she opened her small, rhinestone-encrusted evening bag, and reached inside for her phone. She'd silenced the ring for the wedding and reception, and as she flipped the phone open she saw that she had five missed calls.

None of them were from Jaclyn, and despite what logic was telling her, her heart began thumping hard at even the remote possibility that her daughter could be the victim. She stepped into the bathroom and began to dial.

Jaclyn answered on the first ring, as if she'd been waiting for the call. "Hello."

Her knees went a little weak as she heard Jaclyn's voice, though her tone sounded a little thin and tense. "Shirley just told me—"

"Mom! Have you heard—"

Their words tumbled over each other, and both stopped. Then Jaclyn blew out a breath and said, "You heard about what happened at the reception hall?"

"Shirley told me all she'd heard, which wasn't much. What do you know?"

"It was Carrie."

Madelyn blinked as multiple possibilities spun through her brain. "She killed someone? Can't say I'm surprised, the psychopathic little slut. Bless her heart."

"No, she didn't kill anyone. Someone killed *her.*"

Madelyn blinked again, trying to process

the news and come up with something to add. All that came out was, "I still can't say I'm surprised. She *was* a psychopathic little slut."

Jaclyn paused, waiting. When the usual phrase didn't follow, she said, "You didn't say 'bless her heart.'"

"God would know I didn't mean it. I'd rather be uncharitable than lie. Maybe. Okay, I'd rather lie. Bless her heart."

Jaclyn made a little sound that was half-laugh, half-hiccup, then she said raggedly, "The police have been here, asking questions. They know about Carrie slapping me. They think I did it."

A new horror seized Madelyn. *"What?"* The word was almost a shriek, and belatedly she glanced around to see if anyone else was in the bathroom. There was; beneath one of the stall doors she could see a pair of sensible black pumps; the wearer was being very still, not peeing or anything— well, she couldn't say for sure about the *anything*—obviously eavesdropping. "Hold on," she said. "Let me step outside."

Finding real privacy meant she had to thread her way through the crowd again, and step out into the humid night air. Even then she wasn't completely alone, because several smokers were standing around, the glowing ends of their cigarettes moving back and forth like red fireflies. She threw them a frustrated look, which of course they couldn't see, and walked several yards in the opposite direction. Only when their conversation became indistinct was she certain that anything she said would be just as indistinct to them.

"Okay," she finally said. "I'm alone. Are you serious? They actually questioned you about this? Are the cops in Hopewell absolute *morons*?"

"I was evidently the last one to see her alive," Jaclyn replied, her tone bleak.

"No, you weren't. The person who killed her was."

"Okay, the last one to see her that they know of. Throw in the fact that she slapped me, then fired me, and anyone could say I had motive."

"Considering her personality, probably half the Atlanta metro area had motive," Madelyn said fiercely. "Besides, when you left the reception hall, you met me at Claire's. I'm your alibi."

"Evidently coming up with an exact time

of death in real life isn't as easy as it is on television shows. Oh . . . even worse. I forgot my briefcase this afternoon, and left it at the reception hall. They found it there. I could have killed her either before meeting you, or after."

"But you *didn't.*"

"No, of course not. I'm not really worried," Jaclyn said, even though Madelyn could hear the thread of worry in her voice that said the exact opposite. "I didn't do it, so there can't be any evidence that says I did. It's just that, starting out, I'm the most likely suspect." She swallowed audibly. "They took my clothes."

"Your clothes?" Madelyn asked, trying to envision Jaclyn standing naked in her town house, without a stitch to wear.

"The clothes I wore today. I'd washed them, which doesn't look good, either. They took everything that was in the washing machine."

At least they hadn't taken *all* her clothes. Still, the action struck her as being rude and humiliating, and she knew her daughter needed her. "Let me see if I can't speed things up, get the happy couple on their way to forever together," she said. "Then

I'll be there lickety-split. Don't worry, sweetheart. I'll make sure this all gets straightened out."

Jaclyn hung up, comforted just by talking
to her mother. Hearing Madelyn's outrage
made her feel better, made her feel as if
this would all go away tomorrow. The police would find whoever had killed Carrie,
and tonight would be nothing more than a
nasty taste in her mouth.

The irrational thought occurred that
maybe she should call her dad. If anyone
would know some tricks about dealing with
the police, it would be Jacky.

Something was seriously wrong with
the world when she was considering asking her dad for advice. He'd probably have
her on the lam in Mexico before dawn.
Running away from trouble was Jacky's
stock-in-trade.

No, she'd stick right here, cooperate with
everything the police asked of her. Madelyn would support her through thick and
thin, and everyone else who had been at
the reception hall today would back up
everything she'd said. And when this was
over with, if Eric Wilder dared ask her out

again as if nothing had happened, she'd restrain the impulse to call him a low-lying, backstabbing, sewer-sucking son of a bitch—after all, he was only doing his job—and simply say she didn't think they suited each other. Taking the high road would make her feel better.

She burst into tears.

So much for feeling better.

Chapter Twelve

Eric was so tired he could practically feel his ass dragging on the pavement behind him as he trudged into H.P.D. Not only had it been a long day, but he hadn't gotten much sleep the night before. The *reason* he hadn't gotten much sleep had been a good one, but sleep-deprived was still sleep-deprived. He had a ton of evidence and paperwork to deal with before he could go home, so he doubted he'd be seeing his bed for another few hours, at least.

The victim's family had been notified. That was always the hardest part. In this case, because her fiancé's father was a state senator, he and Garvey had made two of the difficult visits. The victim's parents were devastated. They hadn't dissolved in a flood of tears and questions, but instead looked as if they'd been flattened, their reason for living suddenly taken away from them.

The fiancé, Sean Dennison, had been almost catatonic with shock. "But I talked to her," he kept saying. "It can't be her." They'd already known he'd called the victim because they'd checked the calls on her phone. He'd been at work when he called her, he said, something that could be easily verified in the morning, so if it was a lie, it was a stupid one. Not that Eric discounted stupid; he dealt with it every day. Criminals, by and large, weren't mental giants.

Eric had already made one trip back to H.P.D. to log in evidence, before going to interview Jaclyn, and now he had her wet clothing to deal with. He had the consent forms she'd signed, he had reports to write—hell, was it any wonder he'd decided to throw a can of oil at a robber instead of shooting at him? If he'd fired his weapon this morning, he'd *still* be filling out paperwork. Instead, he was free to work a case . . . and fill out paperwork. There wasn't any getting away from the damn forms and reports.

He took care of logging in the evidence and transferring it for testing, though in the case of Jaclyn's clothing he was pretty sure he wasn't proving guilt, more likely eliminating her as a viable suspect. As Garvey had said, she didn't have the vibe, didn't ring the internal alarm bells. They couldn't enter their gut feelings as evidence in court, though, so until she was solidly cleared he had to be extra careful in how he treated everything pertaining to her. Not only did every *i* have to be dotted, but he had to look at her longer and harder than he normally would have done, just to remove the possible taint of preferential treatment.

He couldn't even call her and say, "Hey, I don't think you did it, but I have to do this by the book and treat you like any other suspect." That in itself would be stepping over the line.

This wasn't the way he wanted it, but it was the way things had to be. After this case was closed, he'd try again with her. Maybe she wasn't the type to hold a grudge. Maybe she could be logical and not have drama all over the damn place. She didn't seem like the drama queen type, though; she was pretty cool and controlled. That gave him hope. It also gave him incentive to get this mess cleared up as fast as he could.

Out of sheer curiosity, he did a computer search on kabob skewers. There were bamboo skewers, stainless-steel skewers, decorative skewers, plain-jane skewers. This had to be a woman thing, because no man in his right mind would give a damn about cooking chunks of meat and vegetables on a stick. Okay, maybe a professional chef would, but as far as he was concerned it was damn silly.

He pushed away the report he was writing, leaned back in his chair, and propped his feet on top of the desk. Lacing his fingers behind his neck, he let his shoulder muscles relax as he closed his eyes and mentally processed everything he'd seen and heard tonight, putting things in order.

First and foremost, the homicide was almost certainly classified as second-degree murder rather than capital murder or even murder one. The choice of murder weapon—kabob skewers—suggested a lack of premeditation. Whoever had killed Carrie hadn't gone there with the intent to kill, because who could count on having kabob skewers conveniently at hand?

Any of the vendors who had been there, plus Jaclyn, plus Melissa DeWitt. They had all known the skewers were there. On the other hand, it would take someone conversant with homicide laws to make a crime look unpremeditated when it was actually capital murder, and generally a killer didn't think about lowering the level of the crime he'd be charged with so much as he thought about getting away with it, period. No, Carrie Edwards had been killed in the heat of the moment, with a weapon at hand, which in this case was kabob skewers. A skillful defense attorney might even make a credible argument that kabob skewers wouldn't normally be considered a deadly weapon, that it was an unfortunate accident that one of the skewers had slipped between Carrie's ribs and pierced her heart.

Carrie had been stabbed multiple times, with multiple skewers, as if the killer had simply started grabbing skewers and stabbing away. When one got stuck, or dropped, another one was at hand. That in turn suggested a frenzied rage. She hadn't been killed coldly, or calmly. And afterward her wedding veil had been draped over her face, a clear indication that the perp didn't want to see what had happened.

This was an acquaintance killing. Carrie had known her assailant.

The angles of the skewers might tell them something about the height of the attacker. Carrie had been—he checked his notes—five-foot-four. She'd been wearing shoes with three-inch heels, placing her at five-seven. He'd visually examined every skewer, and the skewers seemed to have been stuck in her at several different angles. She wouldn't have been standing there motionless, though, while someone skewered her—okay, bad pun, even though it was only in his head. She'd have been struggling, trying to get away, maybe trying to grapple with her assailant. That would skew—damn it, he couldn't avoid the word. It was as bad as paperwork, sticking to him like chewing gum on the bottom of his shoe.

"If you're gonna sleep, Wilder, why not go home?"

The voice was Garvey's. Without opening his eyes, Eric said, "Don't interrupt me while I'm detecting."

"Oh, is that what it's called now?"

He could feel Garvey settling on the edge of his desk, and he sighed as he gave in and opened his eyes, looking up at the slightly battered, slightly worn face of his sergeant. "Why are you still here?"

Garvey gave a thin smile. "Like you, I'm detecting. It feels good to actually be working a case instead of wading through paperwork, shuffling you guys around, and running interference when one of you screws up."

Eric could understand that. Even though his own ambition was to go as high as he could in the local police hierarchy—though he hadn't ruled out moving into a state or federal job—he could also see where he'd miss working the cases. If he went state or federal, he might be able to stay in investigations. That was in the future, though; the Edwards murder case was right now. "So, what are you detecting?"

"I'm visualizing the angles of penetration," Garvey began.

Eric snorted. "For God's sake, man, get your mind off sex and back on the case."

"Smart-ass," Garvey growled, before grinning in appreciation.

Eric took his feet off the top of the desk and sat up. "Funny thing; that's exactly what I was doing," he admitted. "From what I saw, the angles are all over the place: from the left, from the right, slanted up, slanted down. Some of them were dangling from fairly superficial wounds. She'd have been fighting, trying to run. Maybe she fell, and the perp came straight down with a skewer, and that's the one that got her heart. Unless the M.E. says the wounds only look as if they came from every direction, it's gonna be hard to guess at the perp's height."

He picked up a pen and quickly sketched one of the skewers. "These suckers are eighteen, nineteen inches long, stainless steel. They're big, but they'd be tricky to hold while you're stabbing someone with them. This little ring at the end is the only place to grip them, otherwise, when the point hit resistance, your hand would slide right down the skewer."

"Not the best weapon to choose if you want to kill someone. The perp didn't go there intending to kill her."

"Maybe, maybe not. We have seven people who knew the skewers were there: the wedding planner, the reception hall manager, the dressmaker, the florist, the veil-maker, the cake-maker, and the caterer. I haven't ruled out the butcher, the baker, and the candlestick maker, either." As Garvey rolled his eyes upward, Eric reminded himself to try going lighter on the smart-assness. He tried that a lot, usually without much success. "Anyway, three of those people had had disagreements with the victim just prior to the killing, but the other four may well have had run-ins with her in the past. The picture we're getting of her isn't warm and cozy; it's more like bitch-on-wheels, running down anyone who gets in her way."

"Nine times out of ten," Garvey said prosaically, "the perp is either family or friend. Maybe the groom realized his mistake and tried to break up with her."

"I wish it'd be that obvious, but I don't think he's good for it. He said he was at work when he called her, which is too easy to prove or disprove, and I think the M.E. is going to give us a t.o.d. that rules him out, unless he can teleport." He wouldn't say so out loud, but he hoped the time of death would rule out Jaclyn, too. The medical examiner's estimate of time of death wouldn't be down to the exact minute, the way it was on television shows—hell, practically nothing they did was the way it happened on television shows, except maybe breathing—but they could get a fairly narrow time frame.

The techs hadn't been able to lift any useable prints from the kabob skewers; as he'd noted, the skewers were too slender to really let anyone over the age of two get a good grip. Anyone grabbing the small wooden ring on the end would more likely hold the skewer with the ring pressing against his palm, rather than his fingertips, for striking power.

"What about the gray-haired man Ms. Wilde says she saw at the hall?"

"Neither of us thinks she's good for the perp, so if she's innocent, she'd have no reason to lie."

"Mrs. DeWitt didn't see anyone between the time she went into her office and when she found the body."

"Doesn't mean no one went in. She admitted the side door was unlocked. It may be that Ms. Wilde is actually the only witness who can tie the killer to the scene, unless we come up with some forensic evidence."

That could be complicated. He hadn't met the groom's father, the state senator, but he'd seen him in political ads; he was gray-haired. The victim's father was gray-haired. According to Mrs. DeWitt, there had been three other parties touring the reception hall earlier in the day, and two of them included an older man. He fully expected the crime scene techs to come up with a variety of stray gray hairs, and any of the multitude of people who'd been in the hall could have been in contact with someone gray-haired during the day and picked up a small hair. Wonderful.

Still, Jaclyn had said she'd seen a gray-haired man driving a gray, or silver, car. That gave him a little bit to go on, if nothing else panned out.

The problem with this case wasn't a shortage of suspects, but too damn many. Almost everyone who had dealt with the victim evidently had some kind of grudge against her.

Garvey yawned, then hauled his ass up

from the edge of Eric's desk. "We both need some sleep," he said, scrubbing a paw across his face and making a sandpaper sound. "My lovely bride is going to be pissed as hell at me, anyway. She wanted me to make sergeant so I wouldn't have any more of these late nights, and now here I am, doing them anyway."

Garvey always referred to his wife of fourteen years as his lovely bride, which sounded sweet, but Eric had met Garvey's wife and thought he probably called her that out of fear. She was a short, slightly plump, deceptively pleasant-faced woman who ran the Garvey household like a drill sergeant. Once Garvey had even bought a gag tag for his car that read "I LIVE WITH FEAR (but sometimes she lets me go fishing)." He'd bought it as a joke, but Mrs. Garvey had liked it and insisted he actually put it on his car. He'd endured a lot of teasing over that tag, which he'd been forced to keep until he'd traded cars and "accidentally" forgot to get the tag off his old car.

On the other hand, they'd been married for fourteen years, so maybe the trick to a successful marriage for a cop was to marry someone who could kick ass and take names. She had certainly kept Garvey straight.

Eric got up, too, because there wasn't a hell of a lot he could accomplish at this hour. "Give her a kiss for me," he said, figuring it wouldn't hurt to be on Mrs. Garvey's good side.

"Bullshit. Kiss her yourself, if you have the balls."

Chapter Thirteen

Jaclyn dragged herself out of bed early the next morning, watched a few minutes of the local news—no new developments in Carrie's murder, which meant no one had been arrested and this whole nightmare would dissolve like a soap bubble. Madelyn had stayed until after midnight, simultaneously trying to comfort her while at the same time hashing and rehashing everything that had been said and done at the reception hall that afternoon, which kind of canceled out the comforting part. But no matter what either of them thought, or how upset they were, the show—in this case, two wedding rehearsals that night, plus handling the details of the five weddings coming up over the next three days—must go on, meaning she had to get her butt out of bed and down to the office.

She was still worried about being questioned as a suspect in Carrie's murder; what sane person wouldn't be? But what could she do about it? She couldn't go out investigating, trying to find the real killer on her own, because she didn't know the first thing about investigating crimes; that was Eric's job, and the best thing she could do was pray that he was really, really good at it.

Coming to terms with the fact that he was doing his job by investigating *her* would take a while longer.

In fact, she might as well get over her hurt, get over him, and write him off. They'd spent the night together, but to men that was no big deal, and despite all her pep talks to herself about being cautious and not letting herself get too involved, the fact remained that she'd let herself expect too much. Now, no matter how she tried to reason herself out of how she felt, she didn't know if they'd be able to start over.

For that matter, he might not be interested in starting over. He might think that, if she was the type of person he could even momentarily suspect was a killer, then she wasn't the type of woman he wanted to get involved with. If so, she couldn't fault him for feeling that way, because it was how she'd feel.

She ate a few bites of cereal straight from the box, but the cornflakes tasted like sawdust and she made a face as she put the box back in the cabinet. Maybe she'd make do with coffee this morning. Her stomach, and her nerves, were too jittery for food.

The phone rang while she was getting dressed and she leaped for it, grabbing it up without even checking the caller ID.

"Hi, honey," came Jacky's cheerful voice.

Two calls in fewer than twelve hours? He must really, *really* want to impress his newest squeeze by borrowing her Jag. Sometimes months would go by without hearing from him; she would try to call him, of course, but all of her calls would go to voice mail, where she'd be told that his voice mail was full and she couldn't even leave a message. That was one of his favorite tricks for avoiding calls he didn't want to take.

"No, you can't use my car," she said. "And don't keep on at me about it, I can't handle it today."

"But it's such a little favor," he began wheedling, then something in her voice must have sparked his single, long-dormant parenting gene to life, because he paused. "What's wrong?"

Jaclyn inhaled. There wasn't any point in not telling him, and she really needed to finish dressing and get to the office. "The police questioned me last night, after I talked to you," she blurted, evidently so desperate for support she'd even turn to Jacky. "They suspect me of killing one of my clients."

"How stupid can they be?" he demanded instantly. "Of course you didn't."

That swift, unquestioning faith in her made tears swim in her eyes. "They aren't so sure about it. Thanks for not doubting me."

"Not for a second. Now, if they suspected *me*—" He stopped, as if realizing he'd been about to admit to something he might want to leave unsaid, then smoothly picked up the conversation again. "So, who got dead? Anyone I know?"

"Her name is—was—Carrie Edwards."

"Well, isn't that still her name, whether she's dead or not?"

"I guess . . . I mean, of course it's still her name, but she's a *was*, not an *is*." And this was a weird conversation to be having so early in the morning.

"Carrie Edwards, Carrie Edwards," Jacky mused. "I don't—Wait a minute. The state senator, the one who's running for Congress, Dennison . . . his son's fiancée was killed. Was she *your* client?"

"Yep. Until yesterday afternoon, anyway. She fired me before she was killed."

Jacky was silent a moment, then said, "Ouch."

"It was a pretty big coincidence."

"Don't worry about it," he said blithely. "The cops will get things straightened out."

Don't worry about it. There it was, Jacky Wilde's philosophy of life, which he applied to all situations no matter how dire. "I hope so. In the meantime, I'm worrying." She cast a glance at the clock; she couldn't stay on the phone much longer or she'd be late . . . at least, later than she wanted.

Being her own boss was great, but in a small firm like Premier it also meant she and Madelyn had to work long hours to make sure they prospered. "I'm sorry, I have to run. We have a really tight schedule this week and—"

"Wait, wait! Before you hang up, have you thought any more about loaning me the Jag?"

Jaclyn took the phone away from her ear and for several seconds stared at it in disbelief. Only when she heard him saying, "Hello? *Hello?*" did she put it back to her ear.

"No," she said firmly. "I haven't thought about it at all. I was more concerned with the fact that I might be arrested for murder than I was about you having a set of nice wheels to impress your latest floozie."

"Hey! There's no need to be disrespectful, young lady. Lola isn't a floozie."

"How old is she?"

"What difference does that make?" he asked evasively.

"Younger than I am?"

"I haven't asked."

"I'll take that as a yes. Not that it matters. Even if she was an appropriate age for you, I'd still say no. You go through cars the same way you go through money. I have one car. I need it."

"Not at night!"

"Jacky! At least half my work is at night! That's when a lot of people get married or have parties, you know. I'll be working every night for the rest of this week, and there's no way I can do without my car. But even if I wasn't working, the answer would still be no."

"Fine, if that's the way you're going to be about it," he said sulkily.

"It is."

His good-bye was curt. Jaclyn hung up, figuring she wouldn't hear from him for the next few months. Part of her was relieved, part of her was sad, and all of her was exasperated; the latter was pretty much her default setting when dealing with her father. She loved him, but she never relied on him. Her rose-colored glasses had been broken a long time ago and she saw him as he was, warts and all.

Funny how exasperation made her feel a little less worried about her precarious legal situation. No, she wasn't *less* worried, just not as focused on being worried. Jacky was good for that, at least.

She hurriedly finished dressing, grabbed her appointment book, then for a split second looked for her briefcase before memory slammed into her head. The cops had her briefcase. "Oh, no," she groaned, momentarily closing her eyes in dismay. She needed her briefcase; it held all the details of the rehearsals and weddings that were rushing at her like high tide. Surely she could get it back today . . . couldn't she? She couldn't think of any reason why she wouldn't be able to get it, because her briefcase didn't have anything to do with Carrie's murder, other than just lying there at the scene. Or would they consider it evidence? Maybe it was covered with Carrie's blood.

Crap. Crap, crap, *crap!*

Knowing it was her own fault—leaving her briefcase behind—didn't help the situation. She had Eric's card in her purse, with his private cell number written on the back. She hated to call him for anything, but maybe he'd say *No problem, the briefcase wasn't the murder weapon, you can pick it up at headquarters*. Maybe. Doubt-ful, but maybe. Because she was a sus-pect, she thought they'd probably keep the briefcase as proof she was there, as if they needed any more proof. Maybe the briefcase was circumstantial evidence, a reason for her to go back to the reception hall after meeting Madelyn.

She'd never know if she didn't try. A quick glance at the clock, though, told her that it might be too early to call. The fact that she didn't even know what hours he worked pointed out to her all over again how incredibly reckless she'd been to sleep with him on such short acquaintance.

Even if she couldn't retrieve the brief-case, she still had all of the information in physical files and on her computer at the office; it would be time-consuming to ac-cess all the files and pull the pertinent information out, but she could do it.

Frustrated, she made the drive to Pre-mier; the parking lot was empty, the build-ing dark, so she got her little bash-and-dash flashlight out of the console. Armed with the flashlight and her pepper spray, she un-locked the back door and let herself into the building. With the lights on and the door securely locked again, she put on a pot of coffee and began the daily routine of making a list of everything that had to be done that day. They had two wedding rehearsals that night; Madelyn was taking the pink one, and Jaclyn had the Bulldog one.

The Bulldog in question was, of course, the University of George's mascot, Uga. This wasn't the first football-themed wedding she'd done, and wouldn't be the last. They were, after all, in the South.

Diedra arrived next, surprising Jaclyn because her assistant was just twenty-four and had a very active social life, which meant she wasn't habitually an early riser. She was punctual, usually getting into the office at eight on the dot, but "early" seldom happened in Diedra's world.

She struggled in, carrying her purse, her briefcase, a venti Starbucks cup, and a large covered platter. When she saw her, Jaclyn leaped up from the worktable and hurried to take the platter before Diedra dropped it. It was surprisingly heavy, considering its size. "What's this?"

"Food. Double-deluxe brownies, to be exact, with fudge icing. Made by my own dainty hands, because I figured if there was anything a murder suspect needed, it was chocolate." Diedra set her cup of coffee down and shed her other burdens.

Jaclyn's mouth started watering as she set the platter on the table. "Double-deluxe?" She didn't know what that meant, but if it had to do with chocolate, it had to be good. Then she said, "How did you know?"

"Your mom called Peach, Peach called me. It's silly, thinking you'd have killed the bitch, though if you had I'd give you an iron-clad alibi, and you wouldn't even have to pay me." Diedra's dark brown eyes sparkled. "I shouldn't speak ill of the dead, but, damn, it's tough not to when you can't think of anything good to say."

"She can't have been all bad. She had family and friends who loved her. We only saw the demanding side, and, really, no one deserves to die just because they're demanding."

"And petty and spiteful," Diedra said drily. "Don't forget those parts."

"Okay, she was demanding, petty, and spiteful. She still didn't deserve to die." Jaclyn didn't know why she was defending Carrie; she hadn't liked her, was glad Carrie had fired her, and the only reasons she was upset about the murder were because of where it had happened, and because she herself was a suspect. She did feel sorry for Carrie's fiancé, but she'd have felt a lot sorrier for him if nothing had happened and he had actually married her.

"So, how did it happen? Was she shot? Clobbered over the head?"

Jaclyn paused, realized that last night neither Eric or Sergeant Garvey had said exactly how Carrie had been killed, and she'd been too rattled to ask. "I don't really know. I just assumed she was shot."

"You mean you didn't *ask*?" Diedra looked astounded, as if she couldn't believe Jaclyn's oversight.

"I didn't think about it. I was pretty upset when the detectives were interviewing me." The smell of the still-warm brownies was getting to her, bringing her appetite back with a vengeance. She lifted the aluminum foil and took a deep breath. "How early did you get up to make these?"

"Too damn early. I wouldn't have done it for anyone else."

"Well, thank God you came in early today of all days. One of the reasons the detectives were questioning me was that I left my briefcase at the reception hall, which means they have it and I don't."

Diedra looked taken aback. "You don't ever forget your briefcase."

"I did yesterday. I didn't even realize I'd left it until the detectives mentioned it. The time with Carrie was upsetting."

The question in Diedra's eyes made Jaclyn draw a deep breath. She hated to go into the sordid details, but Carrie had slapped her in front of so many witnesses there was no way to keep it quiet. "It was a disaster from start to finish," she said. "Gretchen quit, Estefani was about to quit, then Carrie slapped my face and fired me."

"Oh. My. God." Diedra's mouth dropped open. Appalled, she stared at Jaclyn.

"I'm embarrassed that I just *took* it, that I didn't hit her back," Jaclyn confessed. "On the other hand, I've never been in a fight. She might have mopped the floor with me. But Bishop said she'd sue me, us, if I hit her, so I didn't. I kept the legal and moral high ground, but, damn, I didn't like doing it."

"You were smart. She probably slapped you *hoping* she could get you to do something she could sue Premier for. I've met a few people like her before. They're always pushing, always stirring up trouble and seeing how far they can go. It's like they get off on it."

That description summed up Carrie pretty well, Jaclyn thought. "Anyway, all I could think was to get the vendors out of there before she slapped one of them, too. Estefani was a little volcano, threatening to blow. I could just see the whole thing turning into a brawl that made the papers. Carrie demanded a refund, though, and I reminded her that the contract she'd signed stated any refunds were prorated. She didn't like that, but there wasn't anything she could do about it. Then I left. Melissa was in her office so she didn't see me leave. A man drove up as I was getting in my car and he saw me, but I don't know who he was so I don't know how to find him, and he might have been the one who killed her, anyway."

Diedra gasped. *"You saw the killer?"*

"I saw a man. He *could* have killed her. I don't know that he did or didn't." Neither Eric nor Sergeant Garvey had seemed very impressed by her tale of a gray-haired man, and if Melissa hadn't seen him, there was no way to prove he'd been there at all. After all, Jaclyn thought, she hadn't actually seen him enter the building, either. Melissa might have already locked the front door, if she hadn't had any other appointments coming in that day. The man might have gone around to the front, tried the door, then left.

"Did he see you?"

"He parked right beside me. I don't know how he could have missed seeing me."

Maybe Diedra watched too many crime shows on television, but her dark eyes got wide again. "If he's the one who killed Carrie," she said sharply, "then you're the only one who can place him at the scene. He knows you saw him. You have to go into hiding!"

Chapter Fourteen

Going into hiding wasn't an option—at least not this week, with their schedule so packed, not to mention she was pretty sure the Hopewell PD wouldn't look kindly on her disappearing. Besides, how could the man she'd seen have had any idea who she was? For all he knew, she was someone there to inspect the hall with an eye toward booking it. And that was assuming the gray-haired man had killed Carrie, that he'd have any interest in her at all.

Still, the very idea was unsettling. She took solace in one of the brownies—there really was something comforting about chocolate—as she began going through her files and pulling out the details she needed for her working list for the day. Something in her balked at the idea of calling Eric for a favor; she'd rather go to the extra trouble of reassembling her file. Diedra helped her, combing through the computer for salient details, printing out photographs, digging out phone numbers.

Madelyn and Peach arrived within five minutes of each other, and each new arrival necessitated a rehashing of yesterday's disastrous meeting, Carrie's murder, speculation on who could have done it—the list was long and varied—as well as going over and over all the questions the police had asked. All of this was punctuated by expressions of outrage, concern, and support, and all of it took up time. So did their repeated raids on the brownies, but, damn, they were good.

Jaclyn was in her office on the phone to the restaurant where the post-rehearsal dinner was being held that night, confirming the reservation, when she heard the discreet chime of the security system that signaled the opening of the front door. A second later Diedra said, "Good morning, may I help you?"

"I'm Detective Wilder. Is Madelyn Wilde in?" a man asked, and Jaclyn went rigid. What was he doing here? Oh, right: asking more questions. Just hearing him speak made the bottom drop out of her stomach. She knew that voice, in ways she wished she didn't. She'd first heard it fewer than forty-eight hours ago, but the fabric of it was ingrained on her consciousness. She'd heard him casually making small talk; she'd heard the deeper, rougher tones as they had sex; she'd heard him flat and dispassionate as he grilled her on whether or not she'd committed murder.

Instantly she was on her feet, then hesitated. Her instincts recognized him as a threat, but, realistically, what could she do? Deny him access to her mother? No way; he was a cop. If Madelyn refused to talk to him because she wanted to defend Jaclyn, that would only result in her mother being taken to police headquarters to answer questions there, and Jaclyn definitely didn't want that.

Her only recourse, then, was to ignore him. That was the best-case scenario, if he and Madelyn would allow it. If Madelyn kicked up, Jaclyn would have to convince her mother to cooperate and answer all his questions. Anything else was up to Eric. She hoped he didn't have any more questions for her, but if he did, she'd have to answer them as calmly as possible.

She was damned, though, if she'd go to the door, or even acknowledge his presence unless she was forced to; she sat back down, recovered herself enough to say "thank you" to the restaurant manager, and hang up while she checked that little item off her list. Then she very determinedly didn't raise her head or even glance in the direction of the doorway.

Except she felt exposed, as if she'd been tossed naked into the middle of I-285. Before she could stop herself, she got up, leaped for the door, and slammed it shut.

The loud crack of the slamming door resounded through the office. Thoughtfully Eric stared at the glossy wooden panels. All he'd seen was a slim arm reaching for the edge of the door, but he didn't have a second's doubt whose office that was:

Jaclyn's. She was definitely pissed, and she definitely didn't want to see him.

He looked back at the pretty young mixed-race woman who was now glaring at him, all welcome wiped from her expression.

No doubt about it, he was in an enemy camp.

The Premier office didn't look like an armed camp; it was feminine without being froufrou, more Old World traditional than anything else, with heavy curtains at the windows, rich-looking furniture, and a sense of permanency, as if it had been there since the *Mayflower* landed. Having been inside Jaclyn's town house he could see some of her taste here in the office, in some of the pieces of furniture, in the artwork and flower arrangements. Even the desk of the young woman wasn't a real desk, at least not a desk like the battered metal thing he had, but looked like an ornate table that just happened to have a sleek computer monitor on it.

The slamming door brought two more women into view, both of them middle-aged and attractive, though in different ways.

One was shorter, rounder, with bright green eyes and pouffy red hair, and a sparkle in her eyes that said "good times had here." She was obviously not Jaclyn's mother, while the other woman just as obviously was, not in coloring—her hair was blond, though probably a shade found in a bottle, and while her eyes were blue they weren't the vivid Black Irish blue of Jaclyn's eyes— but in facial structure, with the same chiseled cheekbones, slightly squared-off chin, and the softly full shape of her mouth. Looking at Madelyn Wilde gave him a preview of what Jaclyn would look like in twenty-five or thirty years, and it was good.

Mentally he shook himself. What Madelyn Wilde looked like now, and how Jaclyn looked years from now, had nothing to do with him. "Madelyn Wilde?" he asked politely, even though he knew exactly who she was. He flashed his badge again. "Detective Eric Wilder. May I speak with you, please?"

She coldly eyed him, her pretty face taking on a belligerent expression. "What police department are you with?" she asked, though he thought she already knew damn good and well where he worked.

"Hopewell," he replied.

"Out of your jurisdiction, aren't you?"

He was willing to cut her a lot of slack, because neither he nor Garvey thought Jaclyn was their perp and this interview was just more *i* dotting and *t* crossing, but he wasn't willing to let her challenge him on his authority. "Yes, ma'am, I am. I'm not here to arrest anyone, though, just ask a few questions. If you aren't willing, I suppose I could make a call and get a couple of Atlanta squad cars here, if that would make you feel better—or invite you to visit me at Hopewell's police department, whichever you'd prefer."

Before she could answer the closed door was jerked open and Jaclyn stood there, her eyes blazing like blue fire in her white, angry face. "You leave my mother alone," she said in a fierce, stifled tone, as if she was so angry she could barely speak.

Now, wasn't that interesting? he thought, eyeing her while carefully keeping his expression blank so she couldn't see his sharp appreciation. Jaclyn Wilde in a temper was pretty damn impressive, not only because of the vividness of her eyes but because she was normally so cool and controlled. Seeing her lose control wasn't as good as having sex with her, but it sure reminded him of it, and made him think he might want to make her lose her temper more often. Not today, though; he had to keep his focus on the case, because the sooner he could rule her out as a suspect, the better.

"What happens is entirely up to Mrs. Wilde," he said in a flat, neutral tone. "I don't care where the interview takes place."

But there *would* be an interview, and his voice made that plain.

Madelyn hurried to her daughter and placed a hand on her arm. "It's okay," she said, upset in turn because Jaclyn was so upset. "Don't do anything to get yourself in trouble. It's just a few questions."

The four women couldn't have been more different in style and attitude, but he got the feeling they would walk through fire for one another. They would circle the wagons in any time of trouble, and he imagined if he wasn't a cop the four of them would even now be pushing him out the door. Of course, if he wasn't a cop he wouldn't be here to question one of them in the first place. This was a kind of good thing/bad thing from his point of view: it was good that he got to push Jaclyn's buttons and watch her flare up, but bad that he had to keep her at a distance right now.

Tension crackled in the air, and if the proverbial looks could kill, he would already be assuming room temperature. He represented a threat and they were mad as hell about it. Maybe Jaclyn had cried on their collective shoulders about what a dickhead he was for questioning her, taking her clothes—in other words, treating her like a suspect, which technically she was. Women tended to close ranks around one of their own anyway, and these ranks had definitely closed.

It made him wonder how they, both collectively and individually, had responded when they learned Carrie had slapped Jaclyn. Carrie's murder had all the signs of something that happened in the heat of the moment, in an argument that escalated way out of hand. If that were so, then maybe he should take a long hard look at Madelyn Wilde herself, because he could see a mother defending her daughter.

"This way," Madelyn said in a clipped tone, and without looking at him led the way down the hall to her office, her heels clipping on the runner that protected the glossy hardwood floors. Eric followed her, not allowing himself even a glance at Jaclyn as he walked by. Anger he could handle; hell, seeing her like that had kind of turned him on, but then everything about her had turned him on from the beginning. What he didn't want to see in her eyes was hate, and he thought she probably hated him right about now.

Madelyn entered a room on the right at the end of the hall. Eric followed her, closed the door behind him, and took a moment to look around. It was a very feminine room, with fringed lamps and ornately framed artwork, and chairs sized for women. "Please," she said, indicating one of those chairs as she took her own seat behind her desk. "Sit down."

Eric eyed the chairs, then chose one and cautiously lowered his weight onto it. He breathed a sigh of relief; it was sturdier than it looked, though lower than he liked. He felt as if his knees were about chest high, so he compensated by stretching his legs out some. He looked up to find Madelyn eyeing him with grim satisfaction, as if she knew how awkward he found the low-sitting chair.

He took out his pen and notebook, flipping through it until he found the pages where he'd jotted down the details of his interview with Jaclyn the night before. "Thank you for agreeing to talk to me," he said politely, hoping to calm some of the troubled waters.

She snorted. It was a ladylike snort, but still a snort. "I don't believe I had much choice, Detective."

"Only in the location, ma'am."

"All right, we're talking. Ask your questions."

He leaned back and crossed his ankle on his knee, taking a relaxed position, his body language saying that he was the one in authority even though she was the one who was sitting behind the desk. "Why don't you take me through what you were doing yesterday afternoon?"

"From when to when?" she asked.

"Say three o'clock on." The M.E. had put Carrie's death later than that, but he didn't say so.

She reached to the side of her desk and flipped open an appointment book. Then she got her BlackBerry from her purse, thumbed through the calls, and began her recital, leading him through every appointment, every meeting, every phone call. She got to the phone call she'd received from Jaclyn, and the time she read off matched exactly the time that had been on Jaclyn's phone. She handed him the BlackBerry for verification; he duly noted the time and gave the phone back.

"You're very organized," he said.

She sniffed. "I'm an events planner. Organization is what I do. Every detail has to be controlled and overseen."

"So I see. What did you do after talking with your daughter?"

"Then I drove to Claire's, ordered our muffins, and was waiting at one of the tables when Jaclyn got there."

"Do you have the receipt?"

"No. Do you have the receipt from your lunch yesterday? But I put it on my credit card, so there's a record, if it becomes an issue."

"What did you do then?"

"We sat and talked. I had a wedding to do last night, and I didn't have time to go home and relax."

"What did Jaclyn tell you?"

"She told me that Carrie slapped her, if that's what you're asking," Madelyn said sharply. "Carrie was a bitch. I regret the day I took her booking. She was hands down the worst client Premier has ever had, and it wasn't even because of her un-reasonable demands. A lot of brides are demanding, and a lot of them are unrea-sonable, but they're under stress, so when they freak out it's understandable. What made Carrie stand out was how *mean* she was. She enjoyed causing everyone a lot of extra trouble. She enjoyed insulting people and keeping them upset."

"What did you do when Jaclyn told you Carrie had struck her?"

"I didn't actually *do* anything, because Jaclyn wouldn't let me. She's very level-headed. What I *wanted* to do was hunt down the bullying little low-life heifer and beat the sh— *snot* out of her."

"But you didn't?"

"No, Jaclyn pointed out that Premier had the legal high ground, and best of all, Carrie had fired us. We were free of her."

"What about the fee she'd paid?" he asked, even though he knew the answer.

The trick was to keep asking the same questions over and over, to see if you got the same answers. If you didn't, that was a clue to where to look, where to keep picking.

"She wouldn't have gotten much money back. Our contracts state that, in case of termination, our fees are prorated according to the amount of work the agency has done. With Carrie's wedding, the vast majority of planning and arrangements had already been made."

That jibed exactly with what Jaclyn had told him, but she and her mother had obviously talked, so it was possible they'd gone over that detail and rehearsed what to say. "May I see a copy of the contract?" he asked.

"Certainly."

Madelyn opened a drawer, flicked through the files, and withdrew a moss green folder. "Here it is." She placed the file on the desk and slid it across to him. Eric leaned forward and took the file, opened it. He leafed through the thick stack of paperwork until he found the contract. Finding the pertinent clause took only a few seconds, and it was exactly as they'd said. Carrie Edwards had signed it, and it was dated more than a year before.

"Damn," he said without thinking. "It takes *that* long to plan a wedding?" Then he caught himself and looked up. "Sorry."

She waved away the apology. "Do you want a copy of the contract?"

"If you don't mind." He didn't know that he'd need it, but having a copy was one more *i* dotted.

She took the contract, opened a closet door to reveal a small printer, and copied every page. He waited in silence. When she was finished she neatly stacked the pages, stapled them together in one corner, and handed them to him before repeating the sequence with the original contract and returning it to its file folder, which she then replaced in the file drawer.

He'd bet his badge that if any of these four women ever killed anyone, the murder would be carefully researched, planned, and meticulously orchestrated. There wouldn't be any detail left to chance, nothing done in the heat of the moment, no messy clues left behind. They'd probably get away with the crime, too, he thought, torn between amusement and irritation, because the cop in him didn't like the idea of anyone getting away with anything on his watch.

"What time did you leave Claire's?"

"Five-fifteen."

"Exactly?" he asked, less than pleased that she'd come back with such a specific answer. In his experience, people might know about when they did something, but not down to the minute.

"Exactly," Madelyn said firmly. "I'm a clock-watcher. We all are. I told you, I had a wedding to oversee last night. I had to be there well in advance."

"Where was the wedding?"

She told him, and he knew from experience the drive would have taken her at least forty-five minutes. Not only that, it was in the opposite direction from Hopewell. "What time did you arrive?"

"Six oh two. And, yes, there were a number of vendors already at the church, as well as most of the wedding party, so there are people who can verify the time. Would you like a list of their names?"

"Please," he said politely, and took notes as she consulted her own notes and rattled off names, as well as phone numbers. God, these women were so organized it was scary. Madelyn hadn't been on his short list of suspects but she'd definitely been a possibility, but this pretty much ruled her out. If she'd arrived at the church when she said she had, there was no way she could have driven to Hopewell, killed Carrie, then made the drive to the church, not to mention she'd have had to go home and change clothes, too.

She'd given Jaclyn a pretty good alibi, too. The t.o.d. time frame the medical examiner had given them put Carrie's death pretty close to the time Jaclyn had left her—but if Jaclyn had killed her and then calmly went to have a muffin with her mother at a public restaurant, she'd have been covered with blood.

Carrie's murder had been messy. Whoever had killed her had walked—or run—away from the scene bloody and enraged, likely in a panic. He'd play this by the book and wait for word that no blood had been found on Jaclyn's clothes, but he was pretty sure none of these women ever panicked. No matter how he played the scene in his mind, he just couldn't see Jaclyn Wilde losing her cool and killing Carrie Edwards in a rage. He could see her a lot of ways, not least of which was beneath him, naked and flushed, but not as a killer—and he shouldn't be thinking about her naked, either, not until she was officially off the suspect list.

The problem was, though he could make his actions objective, his mind kept going back to the night they'd spent together, and he didn't feel objective about that at all.

On the good side, he was one step closer to clearing Jaclyn. On the bad side, he was back to square one in finding Carrie's killer, with a victim almost no one liked, and ass-deep in potential suspects.

There wasn't anything more he could find out from Madelyn. She was clear, and she'd provided a damn good alibi for Jaclyn, though until he got the report back on Jaclyn's clothes he couldn't say anything. He'd be better off spending his time chasing down the other possibilities. He studied his notes for a moment, trying to think of any angle he might have missed, but everything was pretty straightforward. Finally he flipped his notebook shut and rose to his feet. "Thank you for answering my questions, Mrs. Wilde. I'll be in touch."

Again, she made that disgusted little

snorting sound. It was almost like a feminine grunt.

The two other women were still in the outer office, their expressions closed and hostile. Jaclyn's door was firmly closed again. Eric said good-bye to the two women, smiling warmly at them just to tweak them; the older redhead narrowed her eyes and pressed her lips together.

Soon enough he'd have Jaclyn cleared, but by then it might well be too late, might have been too late since last night when he'd questioned her. As he got into his car he remembered the skunk comment, and inwardly winced. Like the two women who had just glared at his back as he went out the door, he figured Jaclyn was going to carry this grudge for a long time.

A thought occurred to him: Had Jaclyn told her mother that they'd spent the night together?

Naw.

For one thing, she wasn't the kiss-and-tell type. For another, Madelyn hadn't tried to gut him.

Chapter Fifteen

When Jaclyn heard Madelyn's voice out-side her door, with Peach and Diedra's voices running over each other as they asked simultaneous questions, she paused for a moment to listen harder. Not hearing Eric's much deeper voice, she huffed out a quick breath of relief and jerked her door open, though she took a quick look around to make sure he was gone before she asked, "What happened?"

"He asked questions about what I was doing yesterday afternoon, and took a lot of notes," Madelyn replied. "I think he was making certain I didn't kill Carrie, but there was no way. After we had muffins at Claire's, I didn't have time to go back and do the deed, then get to the wedding."

"You had muffins at Claire's?" Peach asked.

"Yesterday afternoon, after Carrie fired us," Jaclyn said.

"Well," Diedra humphed. "Number one: you *could* have bought enough muffins for us to have today. I'm just saying. Number two: more than likely, he was verifying that you were where you said you were. Madelyn is your alibi."

"Maybe," Jaclyn said unhappily. She should have known he'd have to question Madelyn. If she'd thought of it beforehand she might have been better prepared for the shock. Instead, sudden rage had roared through her like a wildfire, and she was left feeling shaky in the aftermath.

"I don't know," Madelyn added. "He asked what I did from three o'clock yesterday afternoon until I got to the wedding, so—" She lifted her shoulder in a "who knows" gesture. "Did anyone get a newspaper this morning? The news on television didn't give many details. Maybe the newspaper will tell us what time they think the murder happened."

No one had. "I'll go get one," said Diedra. She grabbed her bag and car keys, and hurried out the door.

"I need more coffee," Peach said. "And another brownie." She turned and headed toward the kitchen area.

"Why?" Madelyn demanded as she followed. "*You* weren't questioned."

Thinking she needed to soothe her jangled nerves with chocolate more than she needed to worry about the empty calories, Jaclyn decided to join them. She was in time to hear Peach say, "I'm consoling myself *because* I wasn't questioned."

"What?"

"Lord have mercy, Madelyn, are you dead from the waist down?" As Jaclyn came through the door, Peach shot her a guilty look. "Sorry, honey. But you *do* know your mother has a love life—"

"Peach!" Madelyn said in a threatening tone.

"Actually, I do." Jaclyn poured herself some coffee and got another brownie from the tray.

"See, you don't have to act as if you're the Mother Superior in a convent." Peach gave Madelyn an "I told you so" look and took a bite of her brownie. "As I was saying, that man just oozed testosterone. The chemical reaction almost made me go into heat—and I was *mad* at him, so just imagine what would've happened if I hadn't been!"

Jaclyn almost choked on a sip of coffee.

"I'm a good twenty years older than the detective, and so are you, Peach Reynolds. I didn't notice his testosterone and you shouldn't have, either."

"Older women can go after younger men now. Personally, I've never thought there was anything wrong with it. Old codgers go after young airheads all the time, so why can't women of our age have a little fun every now and then? It actually makes sense, because we don't have to worry about getting pregnant. Celibacy should be for the young and stupid, not the mature and wise."

Run or stand her ground? Spill the beans about knowing Eric—though *not* about sleeping with him—or keep quiet? Jaclyn had no idea what to do, but she did know she didn't want to listen to her mother and a woman who was like an aunt to her talk about Eric's testosterone level. "Uh . . ." she began, not knowing exactly what she was going to say, but it didn't matter; she might as well not have made a sound, for all the attention they paid her.

Madelyn planted her hands on her hips. "I have news for you. By the time you're mature and wise, it's too late to be celibate. Talk about shutting the barn door after the horse is already out!"

"That's the whole point! Wise and mature women shouldn't be celibate; we should go for the gusto, which in this case is younger men."

"That man is investigating my daughter for murder! Are you out of your mind? I don't care if he's the gusto, or the goulash, or the crème brûlée—I didn't like him!"

"There is that," Peach agreed after a moment. "I didn't like him, either, on a personal basis. But on an impersonal basis, tall, dark, and rugged does it for me every time."

Jaclyn put the brownie down on a paper towel, thinking that she'd choke if she tried to eat it just now. She didn't know who

would be more embarrassed, herself or
Madelyn and Peach, if she told them now
that she'd had a . . . a *thing* with Eric. That
was all it was—just a thing—because one
night did not a relationship make. But even
a thing was too much to talk about in light
of everything they'd just said. Not that it
mattered, because the "thing" was over
and nothing else was going to happen between them, assuming he didn't end up
arresting her for Carrie's murder on circumstantial evidence alone.

She couldn't say anything now, because
that would be making too big a deal over it,
when it wasn't. Being investigated for murder, on the other hand, was definitely a big
deal. She should forget the thing with Eric
and deal with the most important issue,
though she had no idea how she could be
proactive in this situation.

"I can't do anything except work," she
said aloud, drawing her mother's and
Peach's attention from their argument.

Both of them looked at her. "What?"

"This whole situation. It's out of my control. I don't like it, but I have to step back
and concentrate on what *is* in my control,
which is work. But . . . oh, *damn,* when he

was here I could have asked him about getting my briefcase, and instead I blew up at him and then hid in my office like a scared little kid!" She smacked herself on the forehead.

"I thought you and Diedra had already re-created the file," Peach said.

"For the Bulldog rehearsal and wedding, yes, because that was the most immediate, but now we'll have to do the others, too."

Madelyn pinched off a corner of her brownie, chewed it. "That's an annoyance, but we can handle it. We have all the information on everything; it's just a matter of pulling it all together in one neat list."

"I know, but it's time we could spend doing other things."

"Like eating brownies," said Peach, smiling at her. "Honey, I know this is stressful, but it'll be over soon and everything will work out. You didn't kill her, therefore they can't prove that you did."

"Circumstantial evidence—"

"Will apply to a lot of people, all of whom had a grudge against Carrie. I'm assuming they took your clothes because they were looking for blood. You didn't kill her, so there won't be any blood. As soon as they run all their tests and get the reports back, you'll be in the clear."

"Is that the way it happens on *CSI*?"

"Well, all the guys I date love *CSI,* so I end up watching a lot of it. On the show, the most obvious suspect is never the one who did the deed, so that's a comfort. But *CSI* aside, common sense says they're looking for blood; that's the only reason they'd have taken your clothes. Hey, sweetie, did they maybe swab your hands or something last night, looking for gunshot residue?"

"No, why?"

"Then that means she wasn't shot. If she had been, they'd have done that."

Evidently her assumption that Carrie had been shot was wrong, Jaclyn thought. She was conditioned by the news to assume every murder was committed with a gun. Probably when gangs were involved they mostly were, but how about other types of murders?

"There are a lot of other ways to kill someone," said Madelyn, giving the idea some thought. "Strangling, conking her on the head, stabbing, pushing her and she falls and hits her head on something, though I'd say that's an accident. Um, there's poison, but then they'd be looking at either Irena or Audrey, because they brought food samples, right? Forget poison, then."

They could probably go on for quite a while listing possible ways Carrie had been done in, and Jaclyn thought she could probably come up with some entertaining possibilities herself, but she had things to do. She glanced at her watch, wondering how much longer Diedra would be gone. "I need to pick up some dry-cleaning before my appointment in Dunwoody. If the newspaper says anything interesting, call me."

She fetched her purse and appointment book from her office, as well as the file folder with the new list she and Diedra had assembled—drat, she needed her briefcase—and let herself out the back door.

Eric was leaning against her car, ankles and arms crossed, waiting.

Jaclyn skidded to a halt, her kitten heels sliding a little on the concrete pad. An almost uncontrollable surge of panic, combined with anger, made the bottom drop out of her stomach and her hair feel as if it were lifting away from her scalp. She almost bolted back inside—her hand was already on the doorknob—but that would be cowardly, and she was still annoyed with herself for not punching Carrie when she had the chance, so she forced herself to stand her ground.

He straightened away from the Jag and closed the short distance between them.

There wasn't a thing wrong with cowardice, she thought, and started to shove the door open. If he had anything to say to her, she wanted witnesses.

"I thought I should probably tell you not to leave town," he said in that flat, cold cop tone, his hazel eyes narrowed.

Not leave town? She was already out of town, because she was in Atlanta instead of Hopewell. "What constitutes 'town'? Hopewell, or the greater Atlanta area? I was just on my way to Dunwoody for an appointment. Is that out of town?"

A faintly impatient expression crossed his face. "Dunwoody is fine. Don't leave the *area*. Don't go to the Bahamas for a vacation."

Now that she'd had a second to think, she wondered what the heck he was doing there. She looked at his car, parked next to hers. If he had something to say to her, why hadn't he come back inside? For that matter, why hadn't he called her? He had the number of Premier, and he knew she was there. He also had her cell number. He'd been leaning against her car as if prepared to wait for however long it took her to come out, but for all he knew she would be in the office all day.

One thing was for certain: he hadn't been there when Diedra left, because she'd have called in an alert. So he'd left, then returned.

"What are you doing out here?" she asked suspiciously, though she didn't want to talk to him more than she had to. Something fishy was going on, and she wanted to know what it was. "Were you about to search my car?"

"Can't do that without a search warrant," he said calmly.

"Maybe you were about to do it *without* a search warrant." She could feel her jaw set as she glared up at him.

"No, ma'am. I'm doing this by the book."

"You were leaning against *my* car, so if you weren't about to do an illegal search, what the hell *were* you doing?" she asked sharply. She could hear the hostility in her voice—she, who made it a practice to stay cool and calm, but she didn't care.

"Waiting for you."

"For what reason? Why didn't you come inside and say whatever you want to say? For that matter, why come back at all? You could have called."

"I thought I might get some runaround about you not being available if I called."

She jerked her head up, anger glittering in her eyes. "I've cooperated completely. So has my mother. I haven't given you any reason to think you might get the runaround."

"Yes, ma'am, you have cooperated," he said in a bland voice. "I appreciate it, too."

The way he kept calling her "ma'am" was setting her teeth on edge, and he knew it. "Then your excuse doesn't hold water, Detective."

"I wanted to make certain you got my message."

"I got it, loud and clear," she said tersely. She looked at his car, parked beside hers, and a couple of questions came to mind. "How did you know which car is mine?" After all, she and Madelyn drove identical Jags.

"I ran the license plate."

Great. She didn't like the idea of her name being sent all over law enforcement land, but there was nothing she could do about it. The fact that she was a suspect in a murder case probably wasn't a state secret, either. Without commenting, she moved on to the second question: "How did you know I'd be coming out?" Surely he hadn't been intending to lean against her car, waiting for her, until she went out for lunch. She thought she knew the answer, but she wanted to make certain.

"I have your briefcase, remember? I've read everything in it. I know what your schedule is, so I figured you'd be leaving for your appointment in Dunwoody pretty soon."

Just as she'd thought. She clenched her teeth. She hated to ask him for *anything,* but this was the perfect opportunity. "May I have my briefcase back?" Before he could refuse, she tacked on, "Or keep the briefcase and let me have the contents. I need my files. Failing that, could you have someone just *copy* the files for me?"

"The briefcase is evidence recovered at a crime scene," he said, which she took for a big fat No. Then he continued, "I don't see any reason why copies of the contents can't be made for you. I'll check with the lieutenant. If he gives the okay, I'll make sure you get them."

Crap, now she had to thank him. The words were like sawdust in her mouth, but she got them out. "Thank you."

"You're welcome."

God, talking to him was like ripping a bandage off a wound that had just that moment stopped bleeding. She would not let him get to her like this. She would get angry, but she refused to let him hurt her, refused to let him mean that much to her.

Too late, a little voice whispered in the back of her mind. She should have listened to that little voice the night before last when she'd invited Eric over, but instead she'd shoved it aside. She should have listened then, but she still didn't want to listen now. She wanted both the little voice and Eric to just go away. She could deal; she *would* deal. It might take some time, but she'd do it.

"Is there anything else?" she asked, her voice stiff.

"No, that's all for now."

Keeping her expression as blank as possible, she edged past him to her car, got in, and drove away without looking back.

That had gone well, Eric thought sourly as he got back in his car. He'd known she wouldn't like being told not to leave the area, but he'd done it because she was a person of interest and that was what he was supposed to do. He'd followed the book; he'd played by the rules. He hadn't given her any indication of special consideration, hadn't offered to do her any favors, not even a tiny one. As his reward, she'd looked at him as if he were a slug she'd just stepped on, and she needed to wipe the slime off the bottom of her fancy shoe.

It especially pissed him off because he was doing everything he could to get her removed from their suspect list, and if he didn't play by the rules, he'd be removed from the case. Any of the other detectives on the force would do their best to solve the case, and they were good guys, but they didn't have the extra motivation he did.

He'd been up late the previous night, and he'd gotten an early start today. He hadn't even been in to headquarters yet because he'd wanted to interview Madelyn Wilde and get that over with. The fact that she was so organized helped; he doubted she took a piss break without making a little note of it in her schedule—coded, of course, so no one glancing at her paperwork would know she'd actually had to stop and take a leak. She was a solid alibi. Unless the lab report came back saying Jaclyn's black outfit had been covered with Carrie Edwards's blood, which he sure as hell didn't expect, then Jaclyn was well on the way to being cleared.

Not that she appeared to give a shit. She was so pissed at him she wasn't even going to give him the benefit of the doubt.

But, damn, he liked the way she looked with fire in her eyes. The cool lady could be pushed out of control, and he bet that would be a lot of fun. He'd broken through that control in bed, he'd had her digging her fingernails into his back and biting her pillow to keep from screaming, but he liked knowing he could get to her out of bed, too. It was kind of the same thing as the fact that she made lousy coffee. He felt a little bit of the princess and the pauper with her, even though she hadn't said or done anything to suggest she felt the same. Maybe he was a little insecure.

He thought about that for a split second, then shook his head. Nah. He just wanted to know if he could roll and tumble with her, without her freaking out if her hair got messed up, or if she'd break down in tears if he so much as raised his voice. From what he'd seen this morning, he had no worries on that score—assuming she'd ever give him the chance to roll and tumble with her.

First things first: clear her of suspicion, then work on getting back in her good graces.

With an eye toward the first require-ment, the next stop on his list was Gretchen Gibson's dressmaking shop, El-egant Stitches, which was in a small, fairly exclusive shopping area, built in a U shape around a center fountain, with parking on all three sides. The shop was situated on the left leg of the U. Because of the rela-tively early hour—before nine—there were no cars in the parking lot, but he checked the rear of the building and a Honda Civic was parked just outside the back door of Elegant Stitches.

He went to the front and firmly rapped on

the glass. After about ten seconds a short, plump, middle-aged blonde appeared and pointed at the "Closed" sign. Eric pulled his wallet out and flipped it open to show his badge. The woman's mouth made an O of surprise, then she held up one finger and disappeared toward the back of the shop. She reappeared almost instantly, a key ring in her hand. He waited while she unlocked the deadbolt and threw the chain, then opened the door.

"Gretchen Gibson?"

"Yes," she said warily. "May I help you?"

"I'm Detective Eric Wilder. May I come in?"

"Yes. Yes, of course." She stepped back, opening the door wider. He stepped through, and she firmly closed the door and locked it again. "This is about Carrie Edwards, isn't it?"

"I'd like to ask you a few questions about Ms. Edwards, if you don't mind," he said, keeping his tone easy and low-key. A big part of being a detective was getting people to talk, and they were more likely to talk if they felt comfortable with him. He was about a foot taller than Gretchen Gibson, so she might already feel intimidated.

He couldn't do anything about his size, but he could make a conscious effort to come across as a nice guy.

"I read in the paper that she was killed yesterday afternoon," she said. "Well, and a couple of friends called me last night to tell me, too." She heaved a sigh, then squared her plump shoulders. "I guess you know about the argument we had."

"I gather she was a difficult client."

Her face turned red. "Difficult? That's like saying Charles Manson is a little disturbed. She was a mean, vicious bitch, and I don't mind saying it."

"Tell me what happened," Eric invited.

Gretchen Gibson pressed her lips together. "I have a pot of fresh coffee in the back. Would you like some? Let's go to my office and sit down, and I'll tell you what it was like dealing with Carrie Edwards."

Eric left the shop half an hour later with a few pages of notes, and another person of interest crossed off his list. Carrie Edwards had still been very much alive when the dressmaker had left the reception hall, and she'd been here taking measurements and discussing a wedding gown with a new client when Carrie had been killed.

Gretchen Gibson had filled his ears. If he went by what she said, the list of people who would have liked to kill Carrie Edwards far outnumbered the people who wouldn't. The maid of honor had even quit the wedding party, after a screaming argument with Carrie.

With most victims, he'd find one or two people who wanted to do them harm. With Carrie Edwards, he could practically fill a football stadium.

Chapter Sixteen

On the way in to headquarters, Eric hit the McDonald's drive-through window for another cup of coffee. The coffee Mrs. Gibson had offered him had been regular coffee, not one of those flavored ones, but so weak he could see the bottom of the cup through the liquid. He needed caffeine. Mickey D made good coffee, and he didn't want to risk another convenience store. A drive-through had to be as uneventful as possible, right?

The cashier, a gangly teenage girl who looked about six feet tall, slid the window open. "Cream or sugar?" she asked, then widened her already slightly protruding eyes and rolled them twice toward the direction of the counter before mouthing *Call the cops.*

"No, just black," he replied as he gave the interior of the restaurant a quick survey. Everyone behind the counter was standing stiffly, instead of dodging around filling orders as they usually did. He couldn't see many of the customers, but the ones he could see were doing the same thing: standing still.

No fucking way. Not again. What were the odds?

"Shit on a fucking stick," he muttered, fighting the urge to beat his head on the steering wheel. All he wanted was a cup of coffee, but some dickhead was in the process of robbing the place. What was wrong with the universe that he couldn't just get some coffee and drink it in peace?

He couldn't see the robber, but had a real good guess at the dickhead's location; he was actually standing close to the side door that would open almost in front of Eric's car. What he also couldn't see was whether or not the robber was maybe holding a weapon to a little kid's head, or something.

Swiftly he looked around. Yeah, there it was, parked to his right: a beater with the engine still running, exhaust pouring from the tailpipe. No driver, so that meant this stupid shit was on his own.

The google-eyed girl handed the coffee out to him. He gave her a brief nod, pretended to take a sip of the coffee, then said loudly, "This coffee is old. Could you make a fresh pot, please?"

She gave him an agonized look. He said, "Look, if you think it's too much trouble to make some fresh coffee, then let me speak to the manager." As he was talking he flipped open his wallet, let her get a quick flash of his badge. She took a deep breath, gave a nod as brief as his, then said, "Yes, sir. It'll take a minute, though."

"I don't mind."

Shit. Now what? His car was too close to the building for him to squeeze out through the driver's-side door. Moving as fast as possible, he put the transmission in park, put the cup in the cup holder, released his seat belt, and jacked himself over the passenger seat and out the door, grabbing the coffee cup from the holder as he went out. He didn't have a second to waste. Shit could go down fast, and people could get hurt. The last thing he wanted was to start a shooting spree in a crowded fast-food restaurant.

He jerked the plastic top off the coffee cup, rounded the front of the car, and was pulling his weapon from his holster when he all but collided with a thick-necked bozo who came barreling out of the door with a money bag in one hand and a pistol in the other. The bozo roared, "*Move,* fucker!" and jabbed the pistol in Eric's direction.

With his left hand Eric threw the hot coffee in the bozo's face, cup and all. Bozo bellowed, automatically raising both hands to his face; he was so close, less than half a step away, that his pistol almost hit Eric in the nose as he swung it up. Eric shot out his left hand and caught the guy's wrist, giving it a savage twist. The bozo squealed like a little schoolgirl, his voice rising high with panic, and dropped the pistol, which went skidding across the pavement with a speed and sound that made Eric stop and stare at the weapon in disbelief. A heavy pistol wouldn't skid like that, wouldn't make that sound. Only something lightweight, and made of plastic—

A fucking *water pistol*?

"That does it!" he snapped as he whirled Bozo around and slammed him facedown on the hood on the car, dragging out his cuffs and snapping them on before the guy could stop whining about being burned. He felt as if steam were boiling from the top of his head, he was so angry. "I'm not stopping for fucking coffee ever again!"

Behind him, the crowd that had spilled out of the McDonald's began applauding.

"Hey, Wilder, are you *paying* these dickheads to rob places so you can play hero?"

The jibe was lobbed at him as soon as he showed his face in the bullpen. He growled under his breath as he wove his way to his battered desk. Garvey walked over, grinning. Hell, everyone around him was grinning. "That kid they interviewed did a great job," he said. "Of course, they had to bleep the part about what kind of coffee you're never stopping for again, but if you're any kind of lip-reader you can tell what the kid was saying. By the way, the lieutenant wants to see you."

"Now?"

"Wouldn't hurt."

"Fucking great," Eric muttered, but took himself upstairs. How was he supposed to have stopped one of the local TV stations from interviewing the restaurant's customers? He supposed he could have slapped a hand over the kid's mouth and told him to keep quiet, but at the same time he hadn't realized how many of the customers had heard him ranting about his coffee. Wouldn't you know it, the reporter had picked one of the kids with bright eyes and big ears who was all but dancing with excitement at being on television. Why couldn't they have gone for some shy kid who was scared to death, hiding his face against his mama's arm?

It had been all over the noon news. *"Whoosh!"* the kid had said, imitating the motion Eric had made in tossing the coffee in the bozo's face. A big grin had lit the kid's face like it was Christmas. "Then he took the gun away from the robber and threw him down on the car, *wham,* like this—" He imitated that motion, too. "And said he was never stopping for fucking coffee again!"

They'd bleeped the "fucking," but Garvey was right, there wasn't any doubt about exactly what the kid had said.

He knocked on Lieutenant Neille's door and pushed it open at the muffled "come in." "You wanted to see me?" He sounded grumpy to his own ears, but he didn't care.

"Sit down." Neille leaned back in his black leather chair, a perplexed look on his face. "Wilder, do you have any objection to making an apprehension using normal methods?"

Eric dropped into one of the visitors' chairs. "There was a restaurant full of people. I didn't want any bullets flying around." That should have been self-explanatory.

"I don't know if you could get any luckier, considering the guy didn't have a real gun. If you'd shot him, the media would be raising hell."

"If I were lucky, I wouldn't keep walking into situations like this," he said irritably.

"As it is, the mayor's office has called, I've already had five requests for interviews with you, and a charity group wants to know if you'll be one of the bachelors auctioned off—"

"*Hell,* no!" Eric barked, then caught himself. "Sorry, sir."

Neille grinned. "I didn't think so. I refused on your behalf." Still grinning, he looped his arms behind his head. "I don't know if I can get you out of the interviews, though. This is two days in a row you've brought the bad guy down in an unconventional way, and the mayor thinks this will be great publicity."

"Except I don't have time for publicity." He scrubbed his hand over his face. "I'm investigating a murder, I have suspects practically falling out of the trees but none of them look all that good for the job, and this circus has already taken up most of the morning."

"Understood. I'll do what I can to stall, and maybe something else will happen to take the spotlight off your smiling face and turn it on someone else. But if the mayor says you do the interviews, then you do the interviews."

"Yes, sir." Frustrated, Eric got to his feet and returned downstairs to his desk, and the mountain of paperwork that was waiting for him. It didn't help that grins followed him every step of the way. Of all the days for a huge time-suck to happen, when he had more to wade through than he could handle.

He glared at the thick stack of reports and paperwork on his desk. That was something about television cop shows that really griped him: they never showed the mountain of paperwork real cops had to wade through on every case, every day. Reports had to be written and filed, requests written and filed, every shred of evidence accounted for every step of the way.

He dropped into his chair, and began flipping through the reports to see what he wanted to read first. He knew the report on Jaclyn's clothes wouldn't be back yet; he'd just logged them in last night, so the lab techs probably hadn't even started yet. The clothes had been wet, and they'd have to air dry before they could be tested.

There was a preliminary report on the trace evidence the crime techs had turned up. No analysis yet; that took time. But just knowing what was there would usually point him in the right direction. It might take him awhile to weed out what was important from what wasn't, but this was a start.

He pulled the report out of the manila envelope and began to read. The first thing he noticed was that there was hair—a lot of it, in just about every color he thought human hair came in, though there were a couple of hot pink ones that threw him.

Garvey dropped into the chair beside Eric's desk. He glanced up at the sergeant. "Have you seen this?"

"Yeah."

"Gray hair."

"No telling where it came from, though. It's a public place."

Which enormously compounded their problem, but then again, maybe not. Sometimes when you started digging into something that looked complicated, at the end of the day you found that the answer was simple, after all.

"I interviewed Jaclyn Wilde's mother this morning. She's so organized she makes a Swiss bank look fucked-up. Every minute is accounted for. She and Jaclyn had a muffin at Claire's yesterday afternoon, and the time frame means that if Jaclyn is our killer, then she calmly left the scene and went straight to have an afternoon snackie with mom."

"Which she wouldn't have done if she'd had blood all over her."

"Right."

"I didn't think she was good for it, anyway. We can't completely write her off yet, but I think we'd be wasting our time to keep looking at her."

Eric was relieved to hear his sergeant say that. For the most part Garvey let them follow their instincts, knowing he had some good men under him, but it was nice to have his approval to change their focus.

Because of the medical examiner's estimated time of death for Carrie Edwards, and Jaclyn's statement about a gray-haired man arriving at the reception hall just as she was leaving, they had to look hard at the gray-haired men in the victim's life. They'd have to do some digging, but the two most obvious, as he'd previously noted, were her father and her fiancé's father. It was a sad fact that whenever a woman was killed, it was usually a man close to her who did the killing.

"She was so beautiful," said Corene Edwards, her voice thin and so ineffably sad that Eric wondered if she'd ever recover from the death of her daughter. How did anyone recover from that? He knew people did, he knew they were usually much stronger than even they themselves expected, but in the moment they were broken and seemed beyond repair.

"Yes, she was," he agreed gently. Carrie Edwards might not have been pretty in personality, but she'd been their child. He and Garvey sat side by side in the Edwardses' living room. The house was an eighties-style brick, but the yard was meticulously maintained and the interior, though dated, was spotless. The doors had been raised on the garage when he and Garvey arrived. There were two vehicles parked side by side: a red Ford, and a blue Ford pickup. Other cars choked the driveway—one of them gray, and he'd duly noted down the tag number and run it before they even went inside, to find it belonged to an eighty-three-year-old woman—and several friends and family were in the house with the bereaved couple, offering what solace their company would bring, fielding phone calls, answering the door to accept so many offerings of food that the dining room table, which Eric could see through the open archway behind them, looked as if it would collapse under the weight. The eighty-three-year-old woman turned out to be Corene's aunt, and she was all of five feet tall and as wispy as smoke. No way was she the killer.

An authoritative woman who introduced herself as the next-door neighbor had taken charge of the others in the house, shepherding them toward the kitchen in the back, so the Edwardses could have some privacy with the detectives.

Carrie's father, Howard, sat beside his wife, his head down. The two were holding hands, as if only the other's support kept each of them upright. They both seemed to have aged years since he'd notified them the night before of Carrie's death. Howard wasn't gray-haired so much as silver-haired, a thin, long-limbed man with the long, graceful hands of a piano player.

"Do you know who did this to our baby?" he asked, his voice trembling as he got to the last word, and tears began sliding soundlessly down his face.

"Not yet," Eric said. "We're hoping you might know something that will help us catch her killer. Did she tell you anything about what she had scheduled yesterday afternoon, after meeting with the vendors at the reception hall?"

"No," Corene said. Her eyes were swollen, but her face was completely pale, as if she'd cried so much her complexion had moved beyond the ability to turn red and blotchy. "I know she wasn't happy with her gown. I don't know why; I thought she looked like a princess in it. But Carrie was so particular about things. She wanted her wedding to be perfect. She was marrying the perfect man, she said, so everything else had to be perfect."

She sounded like the pain in the ass everyone had said she was, but Eric kept that opinion to himself.

"She was going to eat dinner with us tonight," Howard said. "It's Thursday. She eats dinner with us every Thursday night." The thought that they'd never have those Thursday-night dinners with her again made his thin chest heave.

"Had she mentioned anyone she might have had an argument with, someone who might have held a grudge?"

"I don't know," said Corene listlessly. "All Carrie said was that people were giving her trouble, but that she'd take care of them. She talked a lot about how she wanted everything to look."

"The dressmaker, Gretchen Gibson, mentioned something about an argument with a bridesmaid?"

"Taite Boyne. Yes, she's Carrie's best friend. Carrie said she'd handle it, so I assume she did. They've been friends forever."

"Ms. Boyne dropped out of the wedding party. Didn't that put pressure on Carrie to find another maid of honor?"

"Oh, no, she simply called someone else. She told me that Taite couldn't afford the dress, that was why she dropped out, and she was embarrassed because of her money problems."

That wasn't the tale Mrs. Gibson had told him, having witnessed the vicious argument between the two young women, but Eric didn't contradict Mrs. Edwards. His job was to keep people talking, not antagonize them to the point where they wouldn't talk to him at all.

"Did Carrie seem worried about anything?"

"My goodness, no. She was on top of

the world. She was more and more excited about the wedding every time we saw her. She said it was going to be big, the biggest wedding of the year, and everyone would talk about it and imitate it. She really liked that idea, that people would imitate what she did. She thought the wedding might even be featured in some magazines."

"Was she getting along okay with her fiancé and his family?"

Howard's head came up, and his spine stiffened a little. "You think Sean might have done this?" Life came back into his eyes, in the form of growing anger. It was easy to see he wanted, needed, someone he could blame for the pain he was feeling.

"No, not at all," Eric said, and that was true as far as it went. Sean Dennison had talked on his cell phone to Carrie right before she died; he'd been at work at the time, and had remained there for more than an hour after her estimated time of death—an easily verified, solid-as-stone alibi. "But any investigation starts with the nucleus of people around the victim, then you find out who they knew, moving out in widening circles. Does that make sense?" It was kind of bullshit, but at the same time kind of true. It's just that they seldom had to look further than the nucleus.

Howard's shoulders slumped again. "As far as I know, she didn't have any trouble with any of his family. I don't really know any of Sean's friends. We've met his parents, of course, but we've seen them just twice."

"They seem like nice people," Corene offered, then her voice faded away and she kind of checked out, sitting motionless and staring at the floor.

"Thank you for your time," Eric said gently. They had no information to offer, and they were so numb with grief that asking them any more questions would be abusive. "I'll be in touch."

He and Garvey walked out to the car. Garvey put his hands in his pockets, jingled his change. "Nothing there."

"No. Maybe we'll have better luck with the Dennisons."

The Dennisons lived in Buckhead, which meant they were out of their jurisdiction, again, but Eric had called beforehand and requested an interview, and both Senator and Mrs. Dennison were supposed to be there. He'd kept the request general, because if the senator was involved in any way Eric didn't want to tip him off ahead of time.

The Dennison family money, actually Mrs. Dennison's family money, was evidenced by the massive gated entrance, with no house in sight behind the high rock wall. There was a keypad on the left, as well as a security camera. Eric lowered his window to press the alert button beside the keypad. A woman's brisk voice came clearly over the speaker: "Yes."

"Sergeant Garvey and Detective Wilder to see Senator and Mrs. Dennison."

There was a delay while their names were evidently checked against a list, then the gate began to swing open. Eric exchanged a glance with Garvey, then drove through the entrance; he watched in his rearview mirror as the gate smoothly closed behind them.

The stamped concrete drive curved to the right, through a thick stand of various species of mature shade trees. Once they were past the trees the house came into view, set back to the left, among more trees. It was like looking at something from a travel catalog. The massive house, crafted of golden stone, was three stories tall, with balconies and porticos and a five-car attached garage. All of the garage doors were lowered, so he couldn't see the vehicles. Garvey grunted, and took out his cell. They didn't have to see the cars, though it would have been nice to actually eyeball them. Records from the DMV would tell them exactly what vehicles were in the senator's name.

Eric parked in front, and together they walked up to the double front doors, which were easily ten feet tall. He pressed his finger to the doorbell, and even from outside heard the reverberation of a bass gong on the other side of the doors. "What is this, a temple?" he muttered.

"Only if you're Indiana Jones," Garvey replied.

Because he hated being kept waiting on a step, Eric watched the second hand of his watch sweep around. When it hit fifteen, he lifted his finger to gong the house again, but before he could the left-side door was opened by a woman of indeterminate age, dressed in the most severe business suit he'd ever seen. "I'm Nora

Franks, Mrs. Dennison's assistant," she said with as much emotion as an eggplant. "Please come in."

They stepped inside. Eric eyed the woman with more than a little wariness. Nora Franks, his ass; he'd bet her last name was Danvers, and Rebecca's ghost was flitting around somewhere, except he couldn't remember if Rebecca had been a ghost or not. He'd read the damn book under protest, to pass his high school literature class, and he'd hated every minute of it. Maybe he had the details confused with *Macbeth,* or something.

"This way." She led them across a marble-tiled floor, the heels of her sensible pumps clipping on the stone. A double-barreled grand staircase curved up on both the left and the right, meeting in a landing and merging to make the final five steps up to the second floor. A crystal chandelier at least as tall as he was hung like a giant faceted tear in the middle of the foyer, under which an inlaid table was precisely centered. The table held an enormous bouquet of fresh-cut flowers. He recognized the hydrangeas, because his mother had some, but he had no idea what the other flowers were. They smelled good, though.

Mrs. Danvers—shit, Mrs. *Franks,* and he'd better remember that or he'd slip up and call her the wrong name—paused beside a closed door on the left, and gave a light tap on the wooden panel. She had her head tilted close to the door; Eric didn't hear the answer but she must have, because she opened the door.

"Ma'am, Senator . . . Sergeant Garvey and Detective Wilder." Then she stepped back, gave both of them a brief nod as they moved into the room, and closed the door behind him. They hadn't introduced themselves, Eric thought, so she must have been the woman who they'd talked to over the intercom.

The room they were in was a library, the walls dominated by floor-to-ceiling built-in shelves that were crammed with books of all sizes. Unlike some libraries, this one looked as if the contents were actually read. For one thing, the books weren't arranged by size or color. Paperbacks were shoved in among hardbacks. Some were stacked on top of each other, some of them were spine out. Knickknacks dotted the shelves, too: candid photographs, pieces that looked like expensive sculpture mixed with what had to be cheap memorabilia from vacations, like the starfish that was propped against a stack of books.

He liked the room, Eric thought, and that surprised him, because he hadn't expected to like anything about the Dennisons. He could keep an open mind about whether or not either of them struck him as being a good bet for their killer, but that had nothing to do with whether or not he personally liked anything.

But the woman who put aside her book and rose from a deep, rich brown leather chair where she'd been sitting with her feet curled under her . . . he liked her immediately.

"I'm Fayre Dennison," she said in a straightforward manner, coming to them and holding out her hand. They each shook it briefly; Eric even liked that about her, the way she gripped firmly instead of extending a cold limp fish of a hand. She wasn't a big woman, no more than average height, and slim in a lithe, athletic way that said she burned off calories in activity, not by restricting herself to a lettuce leaf every day.

She was striking. If Douglas Dennison had set out to get himself a wife who would be an asset in politics, he couldn't have done any better if he'd had her designed. Fayre Dennison had shoulder-length platinum hair pulled straight back and caught in a black clasp at the nape of her neck. The style wasn't softened by bangs or stray wisps, but her face didn't need any softening; it was what it was, strong-boned but very feminine, with a faint cleft in her chin, straight dark brows, and eyes so dark they looked black against the whiteness of her hair. Her voice was brisk, her gaze both friendly and shrewd. She was casually dressed in white pants, a black top, and black flats, but on her the outfit looked like a million bucks. At a guess, Eric put her age at close to sixty, but that was more because of the authority that sat so easily on her slim shoulders than any wrinkles in her skin, which were few.

Behind her, Senator Dennison was also on his feet. Unlike some people who didn't resemble their photos very much at all, Senator Dennison photographed well and looked the same in person. He was about half a foot taller than his wife, with a trim, athletic build, his shoulders still wide with muscle. His skin was tanned, and it looked like a real tan and not something that had been sprayed on. He had dark hair that had gone mostly gray, an easy smile, and friendly blue eyes. He was less casually dressed than his wife, still in his dress pants and shirt, but he'd removed his jacket and tie, rolled up his sleeves.

Without appearing to, Eric paid sharp attention to the senator. On the surface, he was one of those immediately likable men—affable, intelligent, but with drive to him. He hadn't been content to live off his wife's money, but had started his own business and made a success of it before going into politics and being successful there, too.

They both looked relaxed, but he could see the tension in them. Their son's fiancée had been murdered. At the moment they were on the sidelines, but all too soon they would be called front and center; they'd have to be in the public eye, answer questions from the press, comfort their son, do what they could to support the bereaved couple who in another month would have been Sean's in-laws. They were in the eye of the hurricane now and they were taking advantage of the relative quiet, because it wouldn't last long.

"Please sit down," Fayre said, indicating an oversized leather sofa that was made to accommodate men. "Would you like anything to drink? I know alcohol's out, but there's coffee, iced tea, or soft drinks." Both of the Dennisons had a glass of white wine beside them.

"No, thank you, ma'am," said Eric as they sat. The plush leather enveloped his ass with just the right amount of support, inviting him to sink back. He didn't, sitting forward with his notebook on his knee.

She looked at him and a slow grin lit her face. "That's right. I caught the noon news. You're giving up coffee forever."

Garvey made a stifled snorting sound, and Eric felt his face getting hot. "Ma'am, I apologize," he said.

"Don't you dare apologize. That brought some humor into the day, the only little bit we've had since we got the news last night about Carrie. That little boy was a charmer, but I thank my lucky stars he's some other woman's problem and not mine because he looks like a handful. You did a remarkably brave thing, so I think you're entitled to use a few cuss words if you want."

"Not so brave." He tugged at his collar, feeling the heat run down his neck. "The guy was armed with a squirt gun."

"But you didn't know that. You thought it was a real gun."

"Yes, ma'am."

"I missed the news," said the senator, looking at each of them in turn. "What are you talking about?"

"I'll tell you later. It'll probably be on tonight, too, and you can see it."

"Must be X-rated, then," the senator observed, smiling a little. "Okay, I can wait."

"Now," she said briskly, looking from Eric to Garvey. "I suppose you're here to ask us if either of us killed Carrie."

"Fayre!" the senator said, shocked.

"Yes, ma'am," Eric said, going on instinct. Bullshit wouldn't work with her, and he'd bet she had an inborn lie detector. "It's standard."

"I know; look at the family first. For my part, I didn't like her, but I got along with her, for Sean's sake."

"I thought you liked her!" the senator said, going from shock to puzzlement so fast he was in danger of getting whiplash.

"Liked her, no. But as long as Sean was happy, I was okay with him marrying her. Carrie and I had a silent understanding. As long as she didn't try running any power plays on me, and made Sean happy, we were good. She signed the prenup agreement without any fuss, so maybe she really loved Sean and wasn't just using him."

"What made you think she might be using him?" Garvey asked. Normally he stayed in the background and let Eric do the questioning, but Fayre Dennison had a way about her that drew people out. Eric couldn't quite put his finger on what it was, but he could almost forget why he was here, his job overshadowed by the simple act of conversing with her.

Charisma. That was it. Fayre Dennison had charisma, the kind that pulled people to her and then pried them out of their shells. Talking to her felt like being a kid again and opening Christmas presents.

Shit. He was crushing on her like a teenager, and she was the same age as his mom. Today must be his day for meeting attractive older women: first Madelyn Wilde, and now Fayre Dennison. One was very different from the other, but both were people he instinctively liked and wanted to spend more time around—and Jaclyn's mom hadn't been trying to charm him at all, she'd been too pissed.

"Gut feeling," Fayre replied after a brief consideration. "Carrie was a user. She didn't try to pull anything with me, and she was always sweet with Sean, but I saw how she acted with other people. There wasn't anything definite, but I always got the feeling she was reminding herself to be nice. If we were at a restaurant, for example. If the least little thing wasn't exactly how she wanted it, for a second she'd get this incredibly cold, mean expression, then she'd kind of catch herself and she'd put on this smile so sweet it made my teeth hurt."

"You said there was a prenup?"

"Yes. We worked hard to make certain Sean didn't grow up a spoiled brat like so many other kids in his position did. He wasn't given a job, he had to go out and get one on his own, and he's responsible for his own bills. We're lucky in that he's a genuinely nice person. His one fault, if you want to call it a fault, is that he tends to see the good in people." She gave a small smile that was full of pride. "But he's smart, and we're smart, and we took the family money out of the equation. Carrie signed a prenup giving up all rights to any money he inherited. That's all. Anything he made on his own, we thought that was his decision to make if he included provisions regarding that. He didn't. And, as I said, Carrie didn't question any of it, just signed the agreement."

"Maybe she loved him."

"Maybe," said Fayre. "Anything's possible." Her tone of voice said she didn't truly think so, but Carrie was dead so she was willing to give her the benefit of the doubt.

"Do you know of anyone Carrie wasn't getting along with, someone she may have argued with and it got out of hand?"

"Carrie argued with everyone—except us, and Sean," said the senator. He breathed out a sigh. "I admit I was worried about Sean marrying her, but she was always— It was as if he brought out the best in her, if you know what I mean. She was never that way when she was with him."

"Any particular argument that stands out?"

"Only the one with Taite Boyne," Fayre said. "They were best friends. Taite was supposed to be the maid of honor in the wedding, but the way I understand it, she and Carrie got into a huge argument and Taite quit the wedding party." The tone of her voice told them that the maid of honor quitting the wedding party was a disaster on the same level with the church burning down.

That was twice the erstwhile maid of honor had been mentioned. The problem with that was, she obviously wasn't a gray-haired man, and no one had placed her at the reception hall.

"I think they made up," the senator put in, then shrugged. "I'm not sure. I heard Sean and Carrie talking about it, and that's the impression I got."

"Maybe." Fayre shrugged, too. "There was so much endless drama attached to the wedding preparations that after a while I stopped listening." She wouldn't have had any problems with anything she planned; she'd make the decisions, stick to them, let professionals handle the details, and if there were any problems she'd improvise, all without breaking a sweat.

"I have to ask," said Eric. "Where were you yesterday, between the hours of three and six p.m.?"

She wasn't insulted by the question at all. In fact, she gave him an understanding look. "I was here, with the four other members of the Crystalle Ball planning committee, doing what we do best: planning. I believe Sydney Phillips was the last person to leave, at . . . oh, I think around five-thirty. And of course Nora—Mrs. Franks—was here."

"I was at work," added the senator. "I had to stay a little later than usual. I left the office about five-fifteen, arrived home about . . . what? Six o'clock? A little before that, I think."

As alibis went, they were solid, providing they checked out. Eric got the names of Mrs. Dennison's fellow committee members, and the pertinent information from the senator, but they would be so easily verified that lying would have been a waste of time, which left him with nowhere to go on the gray-haired man Jaclyn had seen.

He and Garvey got up, and the senator stood also. "I'll see you to the door," he said. As they walked across the marble foyer he asked, "Do you have any idea when Carrie's body will be released to her parents?"

"Probably tomorrow," Garvey answered.

The senator nodded, looked thoughtful. "Then the arrangements would be made tomorrow afternoon; Fayre and I will clear time to be with Sean and Carrie's parents, maybe help them make some of the decisions. Sean is devastated. He's here, in fact, asleep upstairs. He couldn't sleep at all last night, but finally he was so tired he couldn't stay on his feet." He opened the door, walked outside with them.

That was where he halted, put his hands in his pockets, and looked down.

Something about the way the senator was standing, a look of guilt shadowing his face, brought Eric to a halt, too. Garvey looked around, stopped. The three men stood in a loose circle.

"I have to admit to something I don't like saying," the senator said heavily.

Eric waited, studying every flicker of expression the senator gave.

"I wasn't at work," he admitted, keeping his voice low.

Without wasting more than a second's thought, Eric could tell where this was heading. "Do you want to tell us where you really were?"

"With my— Look, I have a girlfriend. I was with her."

Bingo! He'd been right. What kind of fucking fool would cheat on a woman like Fayre Dennison? Eric wondered. Oh, right—a fucking fool, that's what kind. He didn't say what he was thinking, just said, "We'll need her name and address, her phone number."

The senator nodded. "I left work early so I could be with her. She was able to get some free time from her own job, so we took the opportunity to be together."

"Her name?" Eric prodded.

The senator looked miserable. "I— Never mind, I'm not going to make excuses. It's Taite Boyne."

The erstwhile maid of honor, Eric thought. Well, well. Things were getting interesting.

Chapter Seventeen

"You up for another interview?" Garvey asked as soon as they were in the car. He was already dialing Taite Boyne's number.

"Sure." It was after five o'clock, the hot afternoon sun scorching everything it touched, but police work wasn't a nine-to-five job. Hell, it wasn't even eight-to-five. If he was lucky, on any given day it was more like seven-to-six. He cranked the air-conditioning on high.

After a minute Garvey disconnected, unnecessarily said "No answer," and dialed the other number Senator Dennison had given them. Another minute and he said, "Ms. Boyne, this is Detective Eric Wilder with the Hopewell Police Department."

"Gee, thanks," Eric muttered, but, yeah, this was his case and the sarge would let him handle it.

"I'd like to get some information from you regarding Carrie Edwards," Garvey smoothly continued. "Please call me at . . ." He paused, thinking, then rattled off Eric's cell phone number.

The exclusive boutique where Taite Boyne worked as a buyer would already be closed, though he wasn't sure how much time a buyer would actually spend in the store she bought for. She wasn't answering her cell phone, and if she was at home she wasn't answering that phone, either, so it looked as if they were done for the day, unless Ms. Boyne returned the call pretty soon. He didn't expect that to happen.

Neither did Garvey, because he yawned and said, "My blushing bride will be glad if I make it home at a decent hour tonight."

"You mean you'll be glad if you make it home at a decent hour, so your blushing bride won't cut your nuts off and feed them to you."

"There's that," Garvey agreed, smiling a little as he always did when he mentioned his wife. "Nut stew is a little chewy." Eric might not envy the sergeant his wife—*God, no!*—but he envied the relationship. He hoped some day he found a woman he was still smiling about when they were years into the marriage, which made him think about Jaclyn, because that relationship had taken a shot to the heart before it could even get off the ground—not that he was thinking marriage or anything like that, God forbid. It was just that he'd really thought they clicked.

"I don't understand jerk wads like the senator," he said, because that thought led naturally to the couple they'd just left behind. "How can any man be stupid enough to cheat on a woman like that?"

"I was thinking the same thing. Smart, good-looking, nice, rich—what more could a man want?"

There was no way they could know what went on between two people in private, but on the surface of the thing, Eric thought the senator was a piece of shit. Maybe it had something to do with him being in politics in general, because it seemed as if so many politicians cheated on their spouses, but he'd instantly liked Mrs. Dennison so much that cheating on her threw the senator straight into the realm of cosmically stupid.

When they got back to the Hopewell P.D., they trudged in to check messages and see what reports were in. The bullpen wasn't exactly humming like a beehive, but it was still busy, and at least half the people in there had something to say about the morning's coffee incident. Ha ha. Thinking of coffee reminded him of Jaclyn. Eric remembered that he'd promised her he'd have the contents of her briefcase copied for her, and mentally smacked himself on the forehead.

While Garvey went to his desk, Eric called a clerk in Evidence who owed him a favor, and was just thumbing through his messages when Garvey called him over.

"Got something interesting from DMV," Garvey said. "Guess who owns a silver Mercedes."

Mercedes was a big clue. "The senator," Eric said. "No shit?"

"No shit. This case just got a whole lot stickier." A rich politician was about as sticky as it could get, and they both knew it.

"And turned our potential number one suspect into our potential number one witness." Which wasn't also without problems. Now that they had a direction, they could show Jaclyn photographs of various gray-haired men, with the senator's included, to see if she could identify him, but that was one of the aforementioned problems. He was a state senator who was running for Congress; his political ads were all over television. She could easily "recognize" him from those ads. Eric wanted to make an arrest, but above and beyond that he didn't want to make the *wrong* arrest.

Right now they didn't have enough evidence to get a search warrant of the car, and he'd really, really like to have one. But they didn't have enough to get a judge to even listen to them, plus the senator had an alibi in his girlfriend. They had a direction, and they'd keep chipping away. Alibis could be rattled. For that matter, if it got out that the senator had a girlfriend, Fayre Dennison might step in and do her own rattling.

"I think you need to talk to Jaclyn Wilde again," said Garvey. "See if you can get a more detailed description of the man she saw."

Eric thought of the detailed schedule that had been in her briefcase. For the remainder of this week, at least, he knew exactly where she was going and when she'd get there. Being organized was a wonderful thing.

"I'm on my way," he said.

As he turned away, Garvey said, "Wilder."

Eric stopped and looked around, eyebrows raised in question.

"Tomorrow morning, if you think about stopping to get a cup of coffee . . . don't."

There had been times when Madelyn had overseen an event feeling so ill she could barely hold her head up, but if she needed to be there, she'd made the effort. Through headaches, menstrual cramps (those were finally, completely in her past, thank God), and stomach viruses, she'd been there, though with the last she'd always wondered how grateful the bride would be if she came down with the virus during her honeymoon. She'd always done her best to limit direct contact when she'd been sick, but if no one else had been available to take her place, she'd done her job. She felt pretty much the same that

night, approaching the rehearsal with a
"damn the torpedoes, full speed ahead" attitude. What choice did she have? Just because Carrie Edwards had gotten herself
killed, that didn't mean time stopped for
other brides. Life went on. Premier went on.

She had to steel herself to face the rehearsal tonight, and the wedding tomorrow,
with a smiling face. No one wanted an
event planner with the face of Doom, but,
damn, with the mood she was in, this was
going to be tough.

The bride, who was really a sweet
young woman, had an almost pathologi-
cal love of the color pink that had turned
the wedding into an explosion of bubblegum. Pink flowers, pink invitations, and
miles of pink ribbon. There were pink
bridesmaids' dresses, pink candles, and
even the groomsmen's cummerbunds
were pink. The wedding cake was straw-
berry, with pink icing. At least the cake was
decorated with white roses instead of
pink—someone had pointed out that pink
roses would get lost against the pink icing,
so the bride had given in on that detail.

Even the rehearsal wasn't safe. The
bride wore a pink dress, and the groom

sported a matching tie. Each and every bridesmaid was wearing some shade of the color, though tonight they didn't match. Their pretty—and colorful—dresses ran the gamut from pastel to hot pink to raspberry. The bride's mother was wearing a lovely champagne suit, and carrying an oversized bright pink purse. There were big pink flowers on the groom's mother's long, flowing skirt.

There was even a touch of pale pink on Peach's flower-print blouse.

Wearing a sharp teal suit, Madelyn felt like a fish swimming in a sea of pink. It wasn't just the color of her clothing that set her apart, it was the mounting anger and frustration she didn't dare let out. She wouldn't ruin this special event for any of them, not for anything in the world.

If this wasn't just like Carrie Edwards, she thought resentfully. Why couldn't the woman have gotten herself murdered on a week when they didn't have an insane number of weddings to handle? She'd be a cross to bear to the bitter end.

Peach leaned over and whispered to Madelyn, "I think I'm going to puke."

Madelyn glanced meaningfully at the pink on Peach's blouse and gave her friend a warning glare, but the glare didn't last. Her sense of humor recovered a little at Peach's priceless expression, as she attempted to conceal her horror from the wedding party which, to be honest, wasn't paying a bit of attention to either of them. They stood well to the side, watching the rehearsal, and no one had heard the whispered comment.

"It was an accident," Peach whispered, picking surreptitiously at a tiny pink flower on her sleeve. "Unless I had a psychic moment, or something. I mean, I knew the *wedding* was pink, but the rehearsal, too?"

There was some confusion about when the ring-bearer, age five, should go down the aisle. The flower girl, age three, was adamant that she should go first, because she was a "gwill," and "gwills always go fust!" Madelyn stepped in and explained to the silky-haired little demon that the really important people went last, and that's why the bride was the last one in the parade down the aisle. The little girl looked thoughtful, then decided she didn't want to be in the stupid parade anyway.

Okay, this was going to be fun.

The bubblegum wedding was nowhere close to being the most horrendous event

Premier had ever taken on; in fact, it wasn't even in the top ten. If she'd been in a better mood, Madelyn might even have found the excess of pink innocently charming, because after all their job was to give the bride what she wanted, to make her day special and, fingers crossed, trouble-free. This particular bride had wanted pink, and lots of it, so they'd given it to her. From fabrics to flowers to cakes and napkins and tablecloths and bridesmaids' gifts, Premier had delivered. There were so many different shades of pink, making sure everything coordinated had taken some time and research. Maybe damn near everything in sight tomorrow would be pink, but by God every single scrap would be well-coordinated. Clashing shades were not allowed. The effect didn't look bad; it was even pretty, if she'd been in the mood for pink.

Aside from the profusion of one color, getting this particular wedding put together had been a breeze. Both families were nice, everyone was friendly, and there wasn't a drama queen in the bunch, except for the flower girl. The bride and groom were obviously very much in love. They were lovely, pleasant young people who looked at each other with stars in their eyes. If it would help all their weddings go this smoothly, Madelyn would gladly invest in a pink wardrobe of her own. Maybe matching pink suits for everyone at Premier. Pink business cards. Hot pink Jags. Jaclyn would be horrified at the very idea.

For the first time in this very long day, Madelyn felt a hint of a real smile briefly touch her lips.

When the rehearsal was successfully over and the flower girl convinced that she'd be the star of the show if she agreed to go down the aisle ahead of the bride, the bride's mother very graciously invited Peach and Madelyn to dinner, which was being held at one of the finest seafood restaurants on this side of town. On another night she might have been tempted, but it had been a very long day. To be honest, she was tired of being "on," tired of pretending that everything was all right when nothing was all right. Madelyn smiled and declined the invitation, and reaffirmed the time for their meeting at the church tomorrow evening.

In the parking lot, Peach followed Madelyn to her car, instead of heading for her own. "How's Jaclyn doing? Really. I don't want a generic and halfhearted 'fine' as an answer. She seems to be holding up very well, but since you're her mother I figure you'd know if she's putting on a show or if she's really as calm as she's acting."

"She's handling it better than I would be, if I were in her shoes." Madelyn tried very hard to separate business from her worry about her daughter, but the worry was never absent. As the day had passed, that worry had been buried under a mounting anger. Anger was easier than worry; she could handle anger. Now, if she could just settle on one person with whom to be angry, but there were so many targets she couldn't pick just one.

Should she be mad at Carrie Edwards, for being a supreme bitch and bringing this upon them all? Or should her target be Detective Eric Wilder, who had the absolute gall to treat Jaclyn like a criminal? At the moment it was easier to just be mad at everyone and everything.

"The murder itself is bad enough," she growled, "but it chaps my butt that anyone could think, even for a minute, that she could do something like that. I swear, if I could get that Eric Wilder alone in a room—"

"I know what I'd want to do with him if I had him in a room to myself," Peach muttered, then she breathed a warm hum before she caught herself, and quickly added, "He needs a good spanking." She stopped, pursed her lips. "Well, that didn't come out sounding the way I meant it."

Madelyn sighed. "Actually, it probably did. How can a trained detective be so blind? Jaclyn isn't capable—"

Peach's voice was unusually serious as she said, "I don't know about that. Aren't we all capable, somewhere deep down? With the proper opportunity and the right motivation? . . . Not that I think Jaclyn killed Carrie Edwards," she added quickly. "Not for one second. But in the right circumstances, to protect someone you love, don't you think you might be able to kill someone? I know I could. Maybe whoever killed Carrie is someone no one thinks is capable of such violence."

"I suppose," Madelyn said softly. Peach was trying to be reasonable, when Madelyn didn't want to be reasonable. She was a mother, and her child was being threatened. Her anger flared to life again. "I can tell you this much: if Jaclyn had decided to kill Carrie Edwards, she would've done it in a way that didn't draw attention to herself. She's too smart to murder the woman right after being slapped and fired in front of a handful of reliable witnesses." If Jaclyn had decided to kill Carrie Edwards—not that she would've done it, but in theory—the body never would've been found. Madelyn didn't have a second's doubt about that, because she and her daughter were so much alike, and that's what she would have done.

Cars were pulling out of the parking lot now, as the wedding party made their way from the church to the rehearsal dinner. She and Peach waved to them all, smiling and calling cheerful good-byes.

Madelyn very much wanted to talk to Jaclyn, if for no other reason than to tell her daughter that she was here for her, to ask, again, if there was anything she needed. But the rehearsal Jaclyn was handling had started an hour later than the bubblegum rehearsal, so now wasn't the time to call. She had to wait for Jaclyn to call her.

With murder and suspicion in the air,

and undirected anger building rapidly, Madelyn wasn't anxious to be alone. She tilted her head at her friend. "Do you have plans for dinner?"

"Does Lean Cuisine count?" Peach asked wryly.

"No, it doesn't. I have some lasagna in the freezer. Come home with me and I'll crank up the microwave and open a bottle of red wine. We can kick off our shoes and relax for a while. You still haven't told me all the details of last weekend's date, and to be honest, I could stand to be distracted for a while."

Peach sighed. "You silver-tongued devil, you had me at lasagna."

Madelyn had hopes that Peach's company and a couple glasses of wine would help to ease her toward a decent night's sleep, but it was likely a hopeless cause. Until her baby was in the clear, she wouldn't rest easy.

This wasn't the first Bulldog wedding Premier had ever directed, but Jaclyn couldn't help noticing that the participants of this one were more rabid fans than most, and that was saying something. It was the middle of summer, and for the rehearsal the groom and groomsmen were in the jerseys of their favorite football team. She was a bit surprised that someone hadn't suggested—thank   goodness—passing the rings down the aisle by way of a spiraling football festooned with red and black ribbon. She might've had to put her foot down. In her experience, throwing anything at a wedding wasn't a good idea.

In the South, college football was practically a religion, yet she was still surprised when the bride requested a team theme. It was Premier's job to give the bride what she wanted, but finding the exact shade of Georgia Bulldog red fabric, ribbon, and flowers was a bitch.

And Diedra had been forbidden to mention, at any point during the planning or execution of the wedding, that she was a die-hard Georgia Tech fan. Wedding planners had been fired for less. Jaclyn had been to more than one event-planner convention where discussions centered around the dicey subject of college football and how to deal with the intense rivalries and loyalties. In Alabama, for instance, no one with any sense scheduled a wedding on the same day Au-

burn and Alabama played, because no one
would attend the wedding other than family
members, and most of them would be
pissed at missing the game, which wouldn't
make for a happy time.

Diedra would be with her tomorrow
night, for the wedding, but one representa-
tive was enough for the rehearsal unless
Diedra had just wanted to be here, which
she hadn't. Nevertheless, Jaclyn could have
easily begged off—she *was* the boss—and
let Diedra handle tonight's chores, but she
wanted to stay busy. No, she needed to
stay busy with something, anything, other
than thoughts of dead brides and annoying
cops.

No, she wasn't going to think about the
annoying cop. That horse was dead, and
she was getting frustrated because she
couldn't seem to stop kicking it. Being angry was okay. Being angry was probably
healthy. Being *hurt* was silly and unreasonable, two words she didn't like when applied to herself. All day she'd been telling
herself to just get over it, with limited success. Hell, how about no success?

Her attention was yanked back to the
rehearsal when the groom barked, a

distinctive Bulldog woof of pleasure, excitement, and gratification. Jaclyn fought to keep her face still, her expression bland. Was this the groom's normal way of expressing joy? Did he bark during sex? The mind boggled. The good thing was, the bride laughed; the bad thing was, several other men barked in response.

It was going to be a long night. Jaclyn simply wasn't in the mood for barking.

Two of the younger children, the bride's niece and nephew, were entertaining themselves by running up and down the aisle, playing some game only they could understand, but it involved a lot of shrieking and giggling, which blended nicely with the barking. Because the mindless activity kept them busy, and they weren't too loud—too loud being subjective—everyone let them have their fun. The family was accustomed to the chaos. Even Jaclyn had tuned them out, as she instructed the wedding party and then stood back to watch the rehearsal. If the processional had to dodge around the youngsters, no one seemed to mind. The mood of the evening was boisterous and happy.

She supposed it was too much to ask

that the evening continue without some sort of disaster. The little boy—four years old or so, Jaclyn would guess—rounded the end of a pew at a dead run, tripped and fell forward, landing facedown in the center of the side aisle just in front of her. For a long, heart-stopping minute, he didn't make a sound.

Her heart in her mouth, she hurried to the little boy to assess the damage. Good Lord, was he unconscious? That fear was banished when he abruptly began to wail, a sound that grew in volume and pitch until it resembled a steam whistle. She knelt beside him, touched his back, which if anything sent his screams into a dimension she couldn't quantify. Everyone began hurrying toward them, while the recorded music continued to play.

"Come on, sweetie, let's sit up and see where you banged your head," she said, hoping there wasn't any blood. She wasn't overly squeamish, but— Bracing herself, she helped him to roll over and sit up, then she literally breathed a huge sigh of relief when she got a look at his face. There was a lot of tears and snot, but no blood.

"You're going to be just fine," Jaclyn said

gently, brushing his hair back to see if there was a knot on his forehead.

Upon hearing her voice, and realizing that it was not his mother or grandmother who had come to his rescue but was instead a stranger, the kid squalled even louder.

Did she really want one or two of these? Jaclyn thought as she rose to her feet and backed away to allow the mother, who was very calm given the volume of the scream, to take her place. There were no small children in Jaclyn's life; she had no brothers or sisters and so no nieces or nephews. If this was what she had to look forward to, maybe she was better off getting a gerbil. Or a fish.

Which was a very sad thought. Screams or not, that wasn't the way she wanted to live the rest of her life.

The mother checked the child's mouth, nose, and head, as if she'd completed this particular check a thousand times, and maybe she had. She pulled a tissue out of her pocket and wiped away the snot. The kid kept screaming, to which his mother responded with a gentling shush. She didn't seem to be worried, so Jaclyn figured she could stop worrying herself.

And then a familiar voice behind Jaclyn said, "What are y'all doing, skinning that kid alive?"

She went rigid, and the hair on the back of her neck lifted in horror. Oh my God, what was *he* doing here? If he questioned her in front of clients, if he was here to actually arrest her, she'd . . . she'd *kill* him, and then he'd have a real reason to slap on the cuffs.

Instead of grabbing her hands and cuffing her, he brushed by her, crowding so close in the aisle she had to step back and even then she could smell him, momentarily feel his warmth. He crouched down beside the screeching little boy, brushed back his jacket so that his big black gun was visible along with the badge clipped to his belt, and ruffled the kid's hair with his big hand. "Looks like you had a spill."

The kid momentarily stopped screaming, distracted by this big man he didn't know. He saw the gun and the badge, and his eyes got big. He gave a big sniff and nodded his head. His mother shot an assessing look at Eric, then made a lightning decision and stood, stepping back out of the way. She was just a mother; how could she hope to compete with the enticement of a real gun and a shiny badge?

"Is that real?" the kid asked, pointing at the gun.

"Sure is. The badge is real, too."

"Bad boys, bad boys," the kid started singing. Not bad. He could carry a tune, even if he was only four. His lip started trembling and tears welled in his eyes again.

"You come for *me*?" he asked in an anguished tone. His mother clamped her hand over her mouth to keep from laughing out loud.

"No, I only come for bad boys, and from what I can tell, you're one of the good ones." Eric ruffled his hair again. "Brave, too. Looks like you're gonna have a lump on your noggin. If you're going to play rough, you have to learn how to protect yourself."

"But how?"

Eric stood up, but put his hand on the kid's little shoulder. "Let me think about this." Then he said in a voice loud enough for everyone to hear. "I see you've got some football fans in your family."

Some of the men barked on cue. The kid nodded, and together he and Eric looked to the altar where half a dozen men stood around, waiting for the rehearsal to resume. "I'll bet you one of them would be happy to buy you a helmet just your size, so the next time you take a header you'll be protected. Are you going to be a football player when you get bigger?"

The boy nodded enthusiastically.

"Yeah, I can see that," Eric said. "You're tough. I bet you could play running back, because that's a tough position."

"Quarterback!" the kid said indignantly.

"You're kidding? You're going to play quarterback? Man, that's *really* tough. You definitely need a helmet for that."

The little chest was puffed up with pride, the tears gone, the lower lip steady. One moment he was screeching as if he'd been scalded, and the next, all was well.

She was *not* going to thank him. Yes, Eric had provided a distraction when one was needed, but it wasn't as if anything dire had been going on.

The groom promised to buy the kid a football helmet, and said he could wear it to the wedding tomorrow night. That wasn't exactly the picture Jaclyn had of an elegant wedding, but it wasn't her wedding, it was theirs. If they were happy, that was all that mattered. She'd get all the kids football helmets if that was what they wanted.

"Is something wrong?" the mother of the bride warily asked Eric.

"No, everything's fine. I'm a friend of Jaclyn's."

Oh, really? Jaclyn clenched her jaw against the retort that bubbled up. The M.O.B. glanced from Jaclyn to Eric, smiled a little, and left them alone.

The wedding party returned its attention to the matter at hand, the rehearsal. They were already running late, because they'd been having too much fun, and they weren't going to make it to the restaurant in time for their reservations if they didn't pick up the pace a lot.

Jaclyn moved forward a little, got everyone lined up in the correct order, and picked up where they'd left off. She felt Eric move closer, standing right at her back like a rock. She got an itch between her shoulder blades, as if he had drawn his pistol and held it pointed at her. A nightmarish vision swam in front of her eyes: Was he going to question her here? Or worse, arrest her in front of her clients?

But he just stood there, cool and calm, watching the rehearsal. The minister had everything well in hand, at the moment, so there was nothing more for Jaclyn to do but be present in case she was needed. The previously rambunctious children had, at their mother's insistence, taken seats on the second pew, where they sat whispering and swinging their legs.

Finally, she couldn't stand it any longer. "What are you doing here?" she whispered, fiercely resentful.

"I heard a cry for help and was duty-bound to investigate. Serve and protect, that's the deal."

That wasn't what she'd meant and he knew it.

He didn't haul out the handcuffs or his little notebook, so she relaxed a little. If he wanted to ask her more questions, it looked as if he intended to wait for the rehearsal to be over, so he wasn't going to embarrass her. If he'd come to arrest her, he wouldn't be waiting. Probably.

Dammit, she hadn't done anything wrong, she thought bitterly, but she was paying a price anyway! Yes, if anyone asked her she'd have to say the world was

LINDA HOWARD

a better place without Carrie Edwards in it, but that didn't mean she was a murderer. And right now she'd love to have Carrie back for just a few minutes, so she could give her a real piece of her mind and tell her everything she'd thought but held back during the long months of dealing with her.

When the rehearsal was over, she walked away from Eric without looking back or saying a word. She said her good-byes to the bride and the bride's mother, and reminded everyone of the time they'd be meeting tomorrow night. She'd already made her excuses for skipping the rehearsal dinner, and the way the bride and her friends were staring at Eric, they probably thought he was the real reason for skipping the meal.

As if.

As members of the wedding party started to leave, Jaclyn turned to see if Eric was standing there twirling his cuffs like the villain in a Saturday-morning cartoon. He wasn't there. Shocked, she looked around, but didn't see him anywhere. For a stupid, giddy moment she was hit with mixed relief and disappointment. She pushed the disappointment away and concentrated on the relief, but that still left the question of why he'd been there at all.

She was the last to leave, except for the minister, who locked the big sanctuary doors behind her. He would let himself out through the back door, where he was parked, after he'd made certain the church was buttoned down for the night. She paused at the top of the steps, taking a quick look around.

There were still a few cars in the parking lot, others just now pulling onto the street. The happy couple was getting into his red pickup truck, which came complete with Bulldog stickers and flags. No surprise there, she thought. A few parking spaces away sat one bridesmaid's Toyota; she was taking a moment to refresh her lipstick, while another bridesmaid, sitting in the passenger seat, chattered away. These were happy people, Jaclyn thought, and lucky people. So what if they took their football obsession a bit too far? In the scheme of things, that was nothing. What mattered was that they enjoyed their lives, they didn't hurt anyone else, and tomorrow they were going to have one great big party.

The minister's car was still there, of course, and her Jag—and Eric's car was parked right beside her's, but he wasn't in it. No, he was leaning against her Jag, easy as you please, just as he'd been that morning, a bunch of papers rolled up in his hand.

Jaclyn took a deep breath and walked toward her car, her spine straight and her heart pounding. She'd love to tell him off, to rip into him and vent all the frustration and anger that had been eating at her all day, but she couldn't. He wasn't just Eric Wilder, one-night stand gone wrong; he was *Detective* Eric Wilder, and ripping into him might land her in jail.

At any other time, the satisfaction might be worth the risk, but not this week; her schedule was just too hectic.

She stopped in front of him, her key in hand. "Do you have more questions for me, Detective?"

He sighed, maybe because she'd called him "Detective," maybe because he was as tired as she was. "Yes, I do. The gray-haired man you saw going into the reception hall yesterday afternoon: Can you give me any more details about him? The make of car? Anything?"

"No," she said briefly. "Gray-haired man, silver car. That's it. I was having a bad day and my mind wasn't on scanning people in the parking lot. There's really no reason to harass me while I'm working, Detective. I have your number, and if I remember anything new I'll call and let you know."

"I'm not harassing you."

"That's a matter of opinion." She jingled her keys as a hint, but he remained where he was, solidly blocking her from getting into the car. He'd probably chosen that position on purpose. Instead of trying to force him out of the way—yeah, like she'd have any luck trying that—or looking desperate by opening the passenger door and inelegantly climbing over the console, she stood her ground.

Damn him. Looking at him, she couldn't help but be yanked back to the other night, when he'd made her feel better than she'd felt in years, when he'd made her laugh, made her cry out, made her forget everything except being a woman. He'd been a night of escape, a momentary slip, and yet right now she'd give anything to have him tell her that he knew she couldn't have killed Carrie or anyone else, that he believed in her and would fight for her.

Yeah, right. She was wasting her time there.

After a moment of silence, he said, "I have those copies you asked for."

"Oh."

Well, damn him, how dare he do something nice for her when she had a good mad worked up against him? "Oh" wasn't good enough; now she had to thank him. Again.

"Thank you," she said stiffly, taking the roll of papers he held out to her.

"I'll need you to come in tomorrow and look at some photographs—"

Tomorrow? She was so horrified, thinking of everything they had going on tomorrow—it would be their busiest, most hectic, absolutely insane day—that for a moment her mind went blank and all she could hear was a sort of white noise. Then she felt her mouth move, and what came out of it was: "Look, Studly Do-Right, either arrest me or leave me alone!"

Chapter Eighteen

"What did you call me?" he asked, his tone stifled.

Jaclyn covered her mouth with her fingers. Oh, God, surely she hadn't said that out loud! Surely this was a nightmare and she'd wake up in a few minutes nice and snug in her bed, instead of standing with Eric Wilder in an almost deserted parking lot lit only by the stark, weird tones of the sodium vampire security lights, which was nightmare inducing if she'd ever seen anything that was.

"Studly Do-Right?" he repeated.

Why couldn't the pavement just open up and swallow her whole? Why couldn't she have been struck mute before she opened her mouth? Why couldn't Eric Wilder have stayed at least sixty miles away from her and never bumped into her in city hall?

"You can be arrested for hostile acts toward a law enforcement officer," he said, still in that stifled tone, as if he could barely speak.

"Then why don't you arrest me?" she flared, goaded beyond control. She was so angry that she stuck out her hands, wrists together, daring him. "Why don't you cuff me and drag me to jail right now, huh? *Huh*? Go ahead! Charge me with the heinous crime of calling you Studly Do-Right, and let's see you get laughed out of court, Mr. High and Mighty Law Enforcement Officer!" Some moronic woman she didn't know had taken charge of her body, and her mouth. The same moron thrust her shoulder into the detective, pushing him back. "Go ahead! Arrest me!" Then she lowered her shoulder again and gave him one more shove, just for good measure.

"Jaclyn," he said, sounding as if he were strangling. Then he began howling. Literally. Well, not actually baying at the moon or barking like the Georgia fans, but bent over at the waist, red in the face, howling with laughter.

If she could be sure he wouldn't charge her with assault, she'd have punted him into next week. "Go away!" she shouted. "I regret ever meeting you! I hope you get scurvy and your teeth fall out! I hope you get rickets! I hope you get *beriberi*!"

"You don't even know what beriberi is," he managed to say, before going off again.

"It's a dread disease that turns you into a stupid jerk *man*!" She couldn't remember ever being so beside herself with rage before, and it was all the worse for being so impotent. She couldn't pick him up and hurl him through a plate-glass window, which would have been hugely satisfying. She couldn't shoot him or stab him, because she didn't have any shooting or stabbing weapons. She couldn't kick him, because she was wearing open-toed pumps and she'd only hurt herself. She couldn't even hit him with the rolled-up papers, because that wouldn't do any more damage than swatting a fly. All she could do was yell at him with the mouth that was still under the control of the moron woman she didn't know.

"Miss Wilde?" the minister asked hesitantly from several yards away, having left the church by the side door and witnessed her pitching a hissy fit. "Are you all right?"

"No, I'm not all right!" She stomped her foot, threw her keys on the ground, and would have jumped up and down on them with both feet but at the last second destroying her remote struck her as self-defeating, so she clenched every muscle in her body and screamed a wordless sound of fury.

Eric was laughing so hard he had to lean against her car for support, his hands braced on his knees. Still whooping, he recovered enough to bend a little farther to pick up her keys, but it took him three tries to actually grab them.

"Is there anything I can do to help?" the minister persisted. He was visibly perturbed, perhaps because he thought there was some threat to her, but more than likely because the ladylike Jaclyn Wilder had turned into a raving maniac in front of his very eyes.

"Yes!" she roared, and pointed at Eric. "Punch him in the nose! Punch him as hard as you can, and then I'll feel better."

"I can't do that," said the minister, aghast.

"Then *don't volunteer!*" She snatched her keys out of Eric's hand and hit the remote to unlock the door. Some glimmer of sanity was returning to her rage-fogged mind, and it struck her that the best thing she could do was get out of there before she really did end up arrested for something, probably disturbing the peace, because she'd certainly done that.

Choking and wheezing with laughter, Eric slapped a hand against her car door and prevented her from opening it. "Jaclyn . . . stop," he managed to say, his shoulders heaving.

She pushed her face close up to his and snarled, *"Make me."*

"Oh, God." He sucked in a huge, shuddering breath, looked at the minister, and said, "Sorry, padre."

"It's okay," said the minister, smiling a little. "I think I understand."

"She'll see you tomorrow, and she'll be so calm you'll think you dreamed this."

"I doubt that, but I'll give it a try. Now, young man, is she going to be all right if I leave her with you?"

"*She* will be. I'm not so sure I'll survive." He began snickering again.

"Stop giggling," Jaclyn snapped. The presence of a third party had given her time to catch her breath, a little, though it hadn't done a lot to ease her temper. She *never* lost her temper like this, but she couldn't think of anyone who had ever made her so angry before. Even when Carrie had slapped her, she hadn't thrown a full-scale tantrum.

Eric scrubbed his hand over his face. "Cops don't giggle. I'm a cop, therefore I don't giggle." He was teary-eyed, red-faced, and breathless from laughing so hard. The minister gave them a warm smile—what was up with *him*?—and walked back to his car, leaving them alone.

In the deep well of silence that followed, Jaclyn could hear herself breathing hard, too. The unreality of the past five minutes seized her as the cool voice of reason began to make itself heard again. She *never* acted like that, especially not in public. The way she felt went beyond mere embarrassment; a mixture of horror and sheer mortification froze her in place. She'd been out of control, acting like a child, and she hadn't been able to stop.

A buzzing in her ears warned her that she needed to breathe, though she honestly would prefer not to; she'd rather just drop unconscious to the ground and lay there until Eric left. The problem with that was, he wouldn't leave. He'd stay with her, maybe take off his jacket and put it under her head, call 911, things like that. As uncomfortable as remaining conscious was, it was probably her best option. She gulped in a breath of air. "I'm sorry," she forced herself to say. She had to clear her throat before she could get the words out. Even then her voice was hoarse and kind of hollow; she didn't sound like herself at all.

"That's okay," he said lazily, settling his ass against her car again.

A simple "sorry" wasn't good enough, she thought fuzzily, not after everything she'd said and done. Her face burned, and her voice took on a ragged edge in addition to the hoarseness as she said, "No, it isn't okay. The way I acted was appalling. I embarrassed you—"

"I wasn't embarrassed. I was entertained.

That was one of the best hissy fits I've ever seen. For sheer inventiveness, it even tops the time my mom dumped a canister of flour on top of my dad's head. Mom is more into action. She never would have thought of beriberi." He crossed his arms and smiled at her; for an instant she was caught in the same tractor beam of chemistry or hormones or pure insanity that had gripped her the first time she'd seen him. She could feel it start dragging her in, which horrified her almost as much as her loss of control. She had to tear her gaze away from his before she could resume her apology.

Doggedly she plowed on. "Well, I embarrassed myself. I'm truly, deeply sorry."

"Jaclyn." His deep voice flowed over her. "I understand that you're under a lot of stress. I'm sorry to add to it, but I do need you to look at some photographs."

He only thought he knew what her stress level was. "I have a wedding *and* a rehearsal tomorrow, and I personally have to handle both because Mom has a wedding and a rehearsal, too. We'll be running from one place to another all day long. I know you can force me to look at photographs instead, I understand that—"

"Murder trumps weddings," he pointed out.

"Making a living is pretty high on the list, too," she snapped, feeling her self-control begin to fray again. "Besides, I couldn't identify the man I saw if he were standing next to me."

"You don't know until you try," he said, straightening from her car and reaching to open the door for her. "Go on home now, and decompress. I'll be in touch."

She got in the car, still clutching the roll of papers. From those parting words, she thought she could safely assume he was going to completely wreck her schedule for the next day.

Bright and early the next morning, Friday, Eric made it to work without getting involved in any robberies that ate up half his day. The solution was simple: he made coffee at home, scouted around and found an old thermos, and brought his own coffee. When even a McDonald's drive-through wasn't safe for his coffee hit, it was time to come up with another way of doing things. He'd make his own damn coffee from now on. God knows he wasn't having any luck getting good coffee any other way.

The first thing he saw when he approached his desk was a manila folder that hadn't been there the afternoon before when he and Garvey had come in, but it was there now, on top of the stack. No one was in the lab at this hour, so someone must have placed the paperwork on his desk last night.

That was what he'd been waiting for. Maybe he should've swung by the office after he'd left Jaclyn, but he'd been in an irritable, pissy mood after watching her drive out of the church parking lot, and he'd headed straight home so he could lie in bed and not sleep for a few hours.

The pissiness wasn't because of her temper tantrum, but rather because he'd been hamstrung by the case and couldn't do anything about her tantrum—and he'd really, really wanted to. Man, how he'd wanted to. He'd had to fight to keep from simply grabbing her, kissing her until they both fell down, and then he'd kiss her some more. God, who knew a temper tantrum could turn him on so much? It wasn't the tantrum itself; it was *Jaclyn*—losing her ladylike cool. Even then . . . she really hadn't.

She hadn't used a single cuss word. She'd stomped her feet, thrown her keys down, yelled some inventive and amusing . . . hell, he couldn't even call them insults, because saying she hoped he got beriberi wasn't an insult, it was more of a complete lack of good wishes. She'd jammed her shoulder into him—twice—and though technically he could have charged her for that he'd have felt like a fool if he had, because he outweighed her by at least eighty pounds, maybe even a hundred. But she hadn't poked him, hadn't hit him, hadn't tried to bite him. It was as if she had no idea how to physically attack someone, even though she'd admitted being an inch away from punching Carrie Edwards, but that was different because she'd been physically attacked first.

Making Jaclyn Wilde lose control was fast becoming his favorite thing in the world to do.

So he'd gone home and not slept while he was thinking about sliding into her, her pussy all wet and slick and swollen, those fuck-me legs wrapped around him, her head tilted back and all but screaming as she came—yeah, that was a good way to not sleep, the best, but he'd paid for it because now he was tired and the day had just begun. Finally he'd tried to get some shut-eye by using the oldest method known to the male persuasion, Mrs. Thumb and her Four Sisters, but while jacking off had relieved some pressure it was a far cry from being as satisfying as coming inside Jaclyn.

He dropped heavily into his chair and picked up the folder, wrenching his mind from the X-rated fantasies that kept popping into his head.

He knew what he'd find inside the folder, and still he hesitated for a split second before opening it. The tests would clear Jaclyn; if he'd had any doubt at all about that, last night would have cured him of it. His gut *and* his brain told him that she couldn't have killed Carrie Edwards, so the hesitation worried him.

Maybe he was too certain. Maybe he'd broken his own rule and let his emotions cloud his mind. Maybe—oh, shit!—maybe she'd sneaked in under his guard and he was more than halfway to falling in love with her, like some stupid kid getting a crush in the matter of a few minutes. He was too old and too smart to let one night of great sex affect his thinking . . . well, maybe not all that smart, since like it or not, he *was* affected.

He couldn't be falling for her like that. He wasn't ready to give up the single life. He *liked* being single.

But . . . damn. Jaclyn. Long legs, classy, surprisingly funny in an off-the-wall kind of way that he never would have expected. Could he just walk away, give her up, not even try for something more?

Fuck, no. He was going after her with every ounce of determination he had, and as his mother would attest, when he set his mind to do something then, come hell or high water, he'd do it. He had a mountain to climb in convincing her to give him a chance, but he liked a challenge. And maybe the mountain wasn't that high; he figured if she truly didn't give a damn, she wouldn't get so hot under the collar at him.

Deeply satisfied with his decision, he poured some coffee from the thermos into his cup, took a sip, then flipped the file open, leaned back, and began to read.

On television a person could walk into a room and start shedding telling skin cells that would conclusively tie them to the crime, but in real life it wasn't so easy. The first page of the report recorded greater detail on the trace evidence that had been collected at the scene. The crime techs had found numerous carpet fibers that had clung to people's shoes and been transferred to the reception hall floor. They'd also found dirt, grass, unidentified fibers, and hair . . . lots and lots of hair, a shitload of hair, from animals as well as humans. Evidently people had been sneaking their Fluffys and Fidos into receptions, which didn't surprise him in the least. Cat and dog hair was to be expected. It was when the hair came from goats and other livestock that he began to go a little cross-eyed at the possible scenarios.

The gray hairs collected had come from seven different heads, according to the lab, which was really a surprisingly low number. Hundreds of people were in and out of that room on a regular basis, and while it was cleaned in between each event, a hair here and there wasn't something a janitorial crew would notice. Not a single one of the gray hairs had a follicle attached, which meant that even if they had a sample to compare it to, a DNA match was out.

There were several pages in the report, and after scanning the first Eric started flipping through, searching for that one specific bit of evidence—or lack thereof— that he was most interested in. Four pages in, he found it.

No blood had been found on the clothes Jaclyn had worn Wednesday.

A rush of relief filled him. Eric didn't think he could have felt any more relieved if the evidence had cleared *him* of suspicion of murder. When Sergeant Garvey and Lieutenant Neille got in they'd talk this over, but this pretty much took Jaclyn off the list of suspects, the way they'd thought it would. He'd give her the good news—

Whoa. Wait a minute.

She'd be glad to hear it, but she sure as hell wouldn't be doing any celebrating with him. Instead, she'd probably let him have it with both barrels for doubting her in the first place. He hadn't doubted her, but she wasn't going to see it that way. She'd treat him to an I-told-you-so rebuke combined with a royal ass-chewing.

Besides, if Jaclyn was no longer a suspect he'd have a tougher time seeing her. She wouldn't play nice—not that she'd played very nice last night, but that had been so much fun he didn't mind. She could, and likely would, make his life hell. There were only so many photographs he could produce for her to look at.

And then she'd order him to leave her alone, and he'd have no choice but to do it. She could even demand that if she was required for any further investigation someone other than he do the questioning, which meant Garvey would be the one handling her from here on out, or maybe Franklin, when he got back from vacation.

Nope. Not going to happen.

A slow grin curved his mouth. There wasn't any need to share this particular news with her right now. This was something that could wait for a couple of days, until she was past being furious with him. In the meantime, he'd be working to get back in her good graces.

He finished reading through the report, which was very thorough but not particularly helpful. Too many people had tromped and danced through that room. Besides, if

it came down to it, any suspect could probably explain away his or her presence in
the reception hall; after all, it was a public
venue. There was no skin under the victim's fingernails, no damning evidence on
the body, so essentially he was back to
square one. Ruling Jaclyn out as a suspect
was the only significant result of the report.

But then there was the gray-haired man,
driving a silver car, who might or might not
be Senator Dennison. Even if Jaclyn picked
his picture out of a stack, any good attorney could say she recognized him because
his face was all over television these days,
in his political ads.

It was blood that would give him the killer,
one way or another. The murderer had made
a mess of Carrie, and hadn't walked away
in pristine clothes. Whether her killer had
been an enraged vendor, a secret lover,
the senator, a pissed-off bloodthirsty bridesmaid, or someone as yet unidentified, blood
evidence would tell the tale. Even if the killer
had disposed of the clothes he'd been wearing at the time of the murder, odds were that
no matter how well he cleaned his car some
blood evidence would remain—maybe just
a single smudge on the carpet where he'd

stepped on a drop of blood—something would show up.

Say the senator was their guy; Eric's gut was sending out alarm signals on the senator, maybe because he was a cheating shit, but Eric was going to be looking hard at anything out of the way. If Senator Dennison decided to trade cars, well, that would be damn suspicious, so he bet the senator might start driving one of the other cars sitting in that five-car garage but he wouldn't be getting rid of the silver car. In that case, the blood evidence was still out there, just waiting to be discovered.

He didn't have anywhere near enough to convince a judge to give him a search warrant for a state senator's car, though. As for clothing . . . almost two days had gone by. The killer had had plenty of time to dispose of that evidence, maybe by burning it, maybe taking it out in the country and burying it, or by simply sponging away the visible blood and giving the garments to some homeless shelter. Finding the clothes now would take a huge stroke of luck. The car was his best bet. All he had to do was build a case.

Garvey sauntered in and headed for the

coffeepot. "No adventures in buying coffee this morning?" he asked.

"I brought my own."

"Smart move, the way your luck has been going. I can't believe you beat me in today," the sergeant said as he poured coffee into his favorite mug.

"Lots to do," Eric said. "Lab reports are in." He waved the manila folder.

"Break it down for me." Garvey half-sat on the edge of Eric's desk and took a long sip of the coffee.

"No blood on Jaclyn Wilde's clothes."

Garvey grimaced, and frowned down into his cup. "This shit's left over from the nightshift, isn't it?"

"Yep. Want some of mine?"

"Yeah." He went into the break room and poured the offending swill down the drain, then returned and filled up from Eric's thermos. "Okay, so we call in the senator's girlfriend and see what we can get from her."

"I'm on it."

In spite of herself Jaclyn had gotten a few hours of deep sleep last night. Pitching full-blown temper tantrums was exhausting.

Well, not completely full-blown; at least she hadn't thrown herself on the ground and started drumming her heels, or spitting. But whereas a real tantrum-thrower would have considered her's only a halfhearted tantrum, for her it had been an all-out effort. She'd gone to sleep as soon as she tumbled into bed. She didn't feel exactly well-rested, but at least she wasn't dead on her feet.

They were halfway through. This was Friday; if they could make it through today and tomorrow without any major blowups, they'd be on the downhill side of this marriage marathon. They did have the one big wedding on Sunday, an all-out affair, but she and Madelyn were both working it, and Peach and Diedra were available, so they had plenty of womanpower on hand.

Once again she'd rushed out without eating breakfast. Maybe there'd be some brownies left from yesterday, she thought as she drove to work. She needed more of that chocolate. A brownie and a cup of coffee would be perfect.

She wheeled into Premier's parking lot, and blinked in surprise. Even though she was early, everyone else was already in, which was unusual.

Diedra met Jaclyn in the hallway. Her eyes positively sparkled. "Did you hear?" she asked, excitement in her voice.

"Hear what?"

Diedra lowered her voice, as though it mattered if anyone in the office overheard them. After all, it was just the four of them. "How Carrie was murdered."

Jaclyn's stomach did a sick flip. Did she want to know the details? Dead was dead, and how Carrie got that way didn't seem all that pertinent. Still, since she was smack dab in the middle of this investigation, she was curious. "I haven't heard anything. What have you heard?"

"She was skewered."

Oh, ick! Jaclyn's first thought was that a knife was way messier than a gun. A knife was up close and personal. No wonder Eric had been looking for blood on her clothing!

"*Literally* skewered," Diedra continued. "Like, with the kabob skewers that were lying on the table. Not just once, either, but lots of times. Melissa DeWitt found the body. She told her friend Sharon and swore her to secrecy, because she really isn't supposed to talk about it, but Sharon told Gretchen, Gretchen told Bishop Delaney,

and you know once Bishop knows *everyone* knows."

Kabob skewers? Double ick! There had
been a lot of skewers there, and now she
had the image of Carrie with kabob skewers sticking every which way out of her
body, and that was just gross.

Peach joined them, a china cup of
steaming coffee in her hand. "Makes you
wonder why they didn't immediately question the caterer. Surely the police consider
the weapon when making their list of suspects."

"So, if she'd had a glob of fondant icing
shoved down her throat, they'd go directly
to the cake decorator," Diedra said, looking thoughtful.

"Exactly," Peach responded. "And if there
were a hundred floral picks driven into appropriately vulnerable areas, a florist."

"Choked with a length of white satin, the
seamstress."

"Meatballs in each nostril and shoved
into her mouth, caterer again. I'm thinking
the caterer is looking better and better for
this," Peach said.

"How about a little bride and groom
shoved—"

"Y'all stop it!" Jaclyn said, but she couldn't help laughing. "That's terrible. Carrie might have been—well, *Carrie*—but she's dead."

"I like her better that way, too," said Diedra. "Just saying."

"It's not like there weren't plenty of vendors who wanted her that way," Peach said with a smile. "Maybe most of them just wished the deed done, but one of them might've actually done it."

"Not with fondant or floral picks, thank goodness." Jaclyn headed toward her mother's office, trying to dismiss the idea that someone she knew well, someone she worked with, might've skewered a difficult bride. "Y'all do know there's an old saying about not speaking ill of the dead," she called back.

Diedra responded quickly. "There's also an old saying that says honesty is the best policy. In this instance, the two old sayings don't work well together."

And wasn't that the truth.

Taite Boyne was annoyed as hell that the Hopewell Police Department wanted to interview her, but it wasn't as if she hadn't been expecting the call. Doug had called her in a panic, but she'd calmed him down, told him she'd handle things. She had better things to do with her time, but for now, she'd play nice. After all, it was in her best interests not to piss off the investigators.

Detective Eric Wilder had called both her cell and her home phone the night before, but she hadn't answered because she'd needed time to think things through, to get herself into the proper frame of mind. When he'd called early that morning, she had finally been ready to answer, and they'd arranged a time to meet. She'd suggested her home instead of work, because she didn't want cops in and out of the boutique where she worked as a buyer. It was the perfect job, because she made her own hours and was often out of town. That left plenty of time for the senator, and he took a lot of time.

When the doorbell rang, she was ready. This was a bit like being in a play, she thought. Get into the role, practice your expressions and tone of voice, immerse yourself in the character. A lot was riding on how well she balanced several different things.

She answered the door of the twenty-eight-hundred-square-foot lake house Doug had bought for her. The lake was a private one, with only eight building sites around it, and three of the sites were still unsold. The acreage was sufficient that her neighbors weren't close enough to see who came and went, plus Doug always simply pulled into the three-car garage and got out of his car there. It wasn't as if he was ever out-side doing yard work. The house was in her name, the utility bills were in her name, and she paid for everything from her check-ing account. A nosy reporter would have to dig very deep, or get very lucky, to connect Doug to any of this.

All of this was in jeopardy now, because Carrie had been a greedy bitch.

Her expression was calm but sad as she led the two cops—Wilder and Garvey—into the den. From the den you could see the sparkling pool through the double French doors, and fifty yards beyond the pool, there was the lake, the blueness of the cloudless sky reflected on the surface. She saw them looking around, noting every detail—one of which was a photo-graph she'd dug out of the back of the closet, one of her and Carrie with their heads together, laughing. In any play, the props on the set mattered because they set the mood. The mood she was going for was bereaved but not hysterical.

"Would you like some coffee, or iced tea?" she asked as they sat.

"No, thank you," said Wilder, answering for the both of them. Thank God they didn't want anything; the sooner they got this over with, the sooner they'd be out of here. In the back of her mind she coolly noted that he looked like someone she wouldn't mind getting to know better, back in the days before Doug. He would have been a fun time, but she wouldn't risk what she had now just to have a hot roll in the hay.

She took the chair facing the sofa where they'd both sat down. She'd chosen her costume for effect: a snug, but not too snug, knee-length black skirt, and a crisply tailored white blouse. She'd also gone easy on the makeup; she didn't exactly look wan, but neither did she look festive. She had even used just a touch of eyeshadow to put faint bruises under her eyes. Because she was a buyer she had to always look sharp, so she hadn't gone for dowdy, just restrained. Her four-inch heels were sharp and stylish, the type a sophisticated buyer would wear for work, and she really was going to work as soon as they left. A little touch of reality was always handy.

"Thank you for speaking to us, Ms. Boyne," Detective Wilder said. "We're investigating Carrie Edwards's murder. What can you tell us about her?"

Well, that was an open-ended question. Taite supposed it was designed to get her talking, maybe saying more than she intended.

"We were best friends," she said simply, and let her voice wobble a little on the last word. It was a nice touch.

For a few minutes he asked her meaningless questions: How long had she known Carrie, where had they met, when was the last time she'd seen her, blah, blah blah. She answered with complete honesty, because she knew he'd check out every detail. Why lie about something when you didn't need to? If you kept to the truth whenever possible, that made people more inclined to believe you when you had to lie.

"Where were you on Wednesday afternoon, between three and six?"

"Here."

"Alone?"

She took a deep breath, let it out. "No." She looked down at her hands, clasped her fingers together. "Doug—Senator Dennison—was here. I got back in town the day before from a two-week trip to London, and he left work early so we could have some time together."

"He didn't come over the day you got home?"

"No. I was too jet-lagged."

That, too, was true, at least as far as the jet lag went. And she *had* been in London.

"What time did he get here?"

Taite rubbed her forehead, trying to remember the automatic tells for lying, so she didn't give any of them. Was it looking to the left, or the right? She couldn't remember, so she closed her eyes as if she could see the answer on the inside of her eyelids. "He got here . . . just after three."

"What time did he leave?"

"He was here for almost three hours so . . . about six."

"Are you sure about the time?"

She met his hard gaze, keeping hers direct. "We're clock-watchers, Detective. We have to be." Let him make of that what he wanted; she wasn't about to apologize or act embarrassed, because she wasn't.

Finally, Wilder got to the meat of the interview, the question she'd known was coming. "I understand you and Carrie had a falling-out not too long ago."

She sighed. "Not really."

"You didn't? You were supposed to be her maid of honor, but you dropped out of the wedding party."

"I . . . we—" She stopped, took a deep breath. "Carrie was the one who introduced me to Doug, at a fund-raiser for his new campaign. We didn't intend for— Well, I wasn't looking to get involved and neither was he, but things happened."

"And Carrie found out."

Taite looked up, a faintly surprised expression in place. "She knew about it from the beginning."

The two cops exchanged quick glances. "What was the argument about?"

"It wasn't a real argument. When Carrie asked me to be her maid of honor, I had no idea who Doug was or anything about him. But when we got involved, well, I thought it would be . . . awkward, if I was there when she married his son, and he was there with his wife. I just didn't want to do it. But if I quit without a good reason it would look funny, so Carrie and I staged the argument."

"She approved of your arrangement with the senator?"

"Not really. She worried about me. She said the other woman never ended up in a good place, and she might be right." She took a quick breath. "That's a chance I'm willing to take." Whether or not Doug ever left his wife, Taite figured she'd come out of things just fine. If news of the affair got out, and the rich bitch Mrs. Dennison tossed her cheating husband out on his ass, Doug's career would probably survive. You couldn't throw a stone in D.C. without hitting a politician who'd been unfaithful to his wife; when they were caught they'd lie low for a while, then pick up where they'd left off.

If Doug ended up divorced . . . Taite knew she'd make a great senator's wife. If he didn't, well, the life she had now wasn't bad. No matter what, she was hanging on to Douglas with everything in her. He was her ticket to a better life and she meant to keep him.

"Carrie and I were best friends," she

said, and managed to blink up a teary-eyed
look. Really crying was beyond her, but
that would have been a bit much, anyway.
"We stayed friends. She was here visiting
just last week. She'd been getting some
grief about the details of the wedding, and
she needed to decompress. Oh, I know
she could sometimes be a pain in the ass,
but she was a good friend to me. I'm going
to miss her." There. A little bit of truth mixed
in with a few very big lies. Couldn't get any
better than that.

When they got back to the department
Eric sat back in his chair, his hands looped
behind his head as he stared at the ceil-
ing. Every detail of the case was spinning
in his brain. His desk was littered with reports and notes, but everything there was
also in his head, and that was where things
would finally come together.

Every witness should be as good as
wedding vendors. Each and every one of
them who had been at the reception hall
on Wednesday afternoon had told the same
story. Eyewitnesses were remarkably un-
reliable, but these were people who were
trained to pay attention to detail, to what

was going on around them. Their stories had all matched—not exactly, but in all the major areas. If every detail had been the same, he'd have known they'd gotten together and agreed on what they were going to say.

They each told the story of the confrontation between Jaclyn and Carrie Edwards in their own way, with subtle differences in wording and the progression of events. But their recall of the events was close enough, and consistent enough, for him to believe them.

On the surface, Jaclyn had the best motive, but none of the evidence supported it. She simply wasn't a viable suspect, thank God.

The senator, now . . . he looked good for it, but his girlfriend had solidly alibied him. Unless they could get some physical evidence from his car, which wasn't likely considering he *was* alibied, they had zilch.

Taite Boyne was the one he couldn't quite figure out. According to several witnesses, she and Carrie had had a falling out. Falling out, hell, they'd had a spectacular, very believable blowup, and unless they were both very good actresses, that would have been hard to pull off and make it look credible. If Taite was that good of an actress, that threw her little perfor-mance today into question.

She'd cried a little, and expressed what seemed to be genuine dismay. She hadn't gone overboard with it, and she hadn't even pretended to be embarrassed by her affair with the senator. He had her pegged as a pretty tough cookie.

It was the fight she'd had with Carrie that didn't pan out. It just didn't feel right. So, it was okay to screw the senator's brains out a couple times a week, but not to stand by while he and his wife watched their son get married? It didn't wash.

Garvey walked over, ever-present coffee cup in his hand, and propped himself against the side of Eric's desk. "Interesting. Only one person has good things to say about Carrie, and she just *happens* to be banging the soon-to-be father-in-law at the time of the murder. Sounds like we have the making of our own daytime drama. All we need is an evil twin and an illegiti-mate baby. Stay tuned."

Eric smiled. "What we have here is one colossal clusterfuck."

"So, what else is new?" Garvey said, then he added, with more than a touch of genuine emotion, "Man, I love my job. Maybe Franklin will stay gone another week. I'm enjoying the hell out of this."

Normally, Eric was right there with Garvey: he loved being a cop. They had all the pieces of a puzzle jumbled before them, and it was their job to make a picture from the mess. They'd do it this time, too. Somewhere, someone had made a mistake. All he had to do was find out who, and what.

He yawned, glanced out the window at the afternoon sun. He pushed back and stood. He and Garvey had already had a long day, because they'd both come in so early. It was late in the afternoon, and no one would blame them if they knocked off now. The last few hours had been filled with interviews, paperwork, lab requests, and reports. He was beat, but he had one more stop before he could call the day done.

And this time, he was going alone.

Chapter Nineteen

Some marriages you just knew weren't going to last.

Jaclyn took a deep breath, then exhaled slowly, trying to keep her expression as neutral as possible. Photos of this particular event would never make it into the pamphlets all of them at Premier sometimes used to sell their services to potential clients. Never. In fact, she hoped with all her heart that no one ever knew they were involved.

This wasn't the sort of event that usually called for an event planner, but the groom's mother, horrified by the bride's plans, had hired Premier in a last-ditch attempt to salvage some dignity for the occasion. Jaclyn realized now that she shouldn't have taken it on, not when they were already so busy, but the poor woman had been desperate— and with good reason. The awful truth was, Jaclyn didn't think there was anything she could do that would really help, so the woman was out the money and the wedding was still going to be a disaster, which was only fitting in a bad-karma kind of way, because she'd bet everything she owned that the marriage would be just as bad.

There were two weddings and another rehearsal taking place tonight. Tonight was the crescendo of their frantic pace, and if they could get through this then tomorrow would be fractionally easier, with two weddings and just one rehearsal. Sunday, thank God, was the last of the six weddings, and after that they would be back on a more sane—or was it merely less *in*sane—schedule, and if Madelyn ever, *ever* again booked this many weddings this close together, Jaclyn promised herself she was going on vacation and not coming back until they were all over with.

Normally Jaclyn would have been at one of the weddings while Peach and Diedra handled the rehearsals. Instead, she was here because she was the only one at Premier who could face the bride's family without either losing her temper or laughing out loud. This rehearsal and tomorrow's wedding were all hers, like it or not. Thank goodness the family had agreed to hold their rehearsal at a slightly earlier hour than usual, so Jaclyn could go straight from here to the Bulldog wedding, where Diedra was already hard at work. Between them, Madelyn and Peach were handling the other rehearsal—the one they had started calling "Family Drama"—and the Pink wedding in much the same way.

This wedding was pretty much a lost cause, but Jaclyn had managed to talk the bride out of a wedding cake with a NASCAR theme. That was one point for their side, though even now the bride kept insisting how cute it would be to have the little bride and groom figures climbing out of a decal-covered model car, which she insisted was just like Dale Junior's. Jaclyn wasn't a race fan, but at least she knew who Dale Junior was, and she was pretty sure his car wasn't bright blue. Evidently it was the decals that counted.

She'd also convinced the bride's mother that using her multicolored Christmas lights ("But they flash!") to decorate the barn where the wedding would be held tomorrow wasn't entirely appropriate. She'd rearranged some of the music, so at least the bride would walk down the "aisle" to the wedding march instead of Willie Nelson or Brad Paisley. Willie and Brad would still make their appearances, just not during the bride's walk to glory. Tomorrow there would be real flowers, not the plastic ones the bride had originally planned to use because she said they'd never die and she could use them in her new home—either that or use them to make the flower arrangements for Decoration Day at the cemetery where her daddy was buried. The flowers hadn't even been decent silk flowers; they were literally plastic, and came in all colors—few of which had ever graced an actual living bloom.

If she hadn't been shell-shocked, Jaclyn thought a little hysterically, she would have seen right away what a perfect match the plastic flowers had been for the blinking Christmas lights. It wasn't as if she had anything against Christmas lights; she actually loved them . . . at Christmas. She didn't love plastic flowers any time.

Fortunately there was no proper lighting at the barn for the rehearsal to take place there so late in the afternoon, so the rehearsal and reception were being held at a restaurant/bar that was owned by the "minister." Unfortunately, that restaurant was Porky's BBQ, and there were signs scattered about that bragged about the food. Most prominent was the proud claim: "You'll love our butts." Second place went to "Best butts in town."

She wasn't certain the minister was really a minister, but at this point that was the least of her worries. It would be a blessing in disguise for the groom if the marriage wasn't legal, so she kept her mouth shut about the minister.

A makeshift altar had been set up under a neon Budweiser sign, which had been glowing brightly until Jaclyn had insisted that it be turned off. If she could have come up with a way to take it down she'd have done so, but like the "butts" signs, it was attached to the rough plank paneling. Multicolored plastic flowers—almost certainly the ones Jaclyn had banned from the wedding—had been used to decorate the table beneath the now-dark neon sign. The flowers clashed horribly with the plastic red-and-white-checkered tablecloths that covered the tables. Some of the tables were round, some of them were square, but all of the tablecloths were square.

The tablecloths, plastic or not, weren't that bad. It was a theme she could have worked with, given the time, money, and, most important, permission. White daisies, red and white plates and glasses, and she'd have had an elegant picnic theme. Instead, the best she could do was, whenever possible, stave off disaster.

Unfortunately, she didn't think it was possible.

The groom's mother, a middle-aged widow, was very pale, but she did her best to smile. It was a wavering, uncertain smile, and Jaclyn was almost certain the poor woman's teeth were clenched. She could sympathize. She'd never seen so many mullets in one room. The dress for this event was supercasual—only Jaclyn and the groom's mother and sisters were dressed in a way that she would consider appropriate, which basically meant they weren't wearing jeans and T-shirts with slogans on them. And the minister—she was almost certain he'd come by the title via the Internet—well, all she could do was hope that tomorrow he'd clean himself up a little, maybe even put on a tie. He was a big man with a handlebar mustache and a red bandanna tied over his bald head, and tonight he wore faded jeans and a Harley tee with the sleeves ripped out, which revealed his colorful tattoos from shoulder to wrist, on both arms.

On the other hand, if she could ever say with absolute certainty that her services were needed, that time was now and the place was here. No one knew who was supposed to stand where, or what the proper progression of events should be. Maybe the bride's mother would be seated to a Brad Paisley song about checking you for ticks, but she would, by golly, be seated at the right time, and in the right place.

That was if everything went as planned

tomorrow. If neither the bride nor her mother got arrested tonight. If the minister wasn't killed by a rival motorcycle gang.

That was a lot of ifs, and she thought their chances of making it through were low.

First, she had to get through tonight.

The Christmas lights Jaclyn had gently banned from the wedding ceremony had been broken out for tonight. They hung everywhere, cheerful and random and occasionally tangled, and completely wrong. At least she'd been able to dissuade the bride's friends from outlining everything in sight, from the beer spigot behind the bar to the loaf of bread sitting on the long counter, with the twinkling, brightly colored lights.

The disastrous rehearsal was bizarre enough to take her mind off Carrie Edwards and Eric Wilder for a while. Well, to be honest, she didn't think about Carrie as much as she did Eric, and that was kind of sad. It wasn't sad enough to make her dwell on the woman, though.

But Eric . . . he was the most maddening man she'd ever met. The more she tried not to think about him, the more stubbornly he lodged himself front and center in her brain. Because of him she'd made a spectacle of herself, and how she'd face the minister tonight at the Bulldog wedding, she had no idea. Maybe she'd pretend she'd been in a fugue state, and didn't remember anything that had happened.

But she was able to banish Eric while she oversaw the rehearsal, which was much like corralling wild pigs and putting bows on their tails. The bows didn't help, and the pigs were fractious. The rehearsal went relatively well; a touch of color began creeping back into the groom's mother's face—until the minister let out a whoop and directed everyone to the bar for hot wings and beer, to be followed by banana pudding and brownies.

All of the color immediately left the woman's face again. Jaclyn had seen the spread earlier, and had noted with horror the cans of icing sitting by the brownies and the brightly colored sprinkles on both desserts. Her client had tried—she'd tried very hard—to put together a proper rehearsal dinner. That should've been the one aspect of the wedding where she had some control. But the happy couple had insisted that it didn't make any sense to go elsewhere when there was great food right here, and they already had the place to themselves for the night. Basically, the groom's mother had been bulldozed.

Jaclyn even heard her whisper to one of her daughters that maybe her son had been switched with someone else's baby at the hospital, because she could *not* have given birth to a man who would do this to her.

The bride's mulleted brother sidled up next to Jaclyn, gave her a come-on smile and a nod of his head. With a knowing look he said, "I can't believe a pretty thing like you is here all alone. A woman like you should never be without a date."

"I'm working," Jaclyn said coolly.

The kid, and he couldn't be more than twenty-one or twenty-two, didn't take the hint. He moved in closer, invading her personal space with the smell of fresh beer and stale breath. Oh, good lord, she just caught a flash of rotten teeth. He shouldn't smile. He *really* shouldn't smile. Jaclyn took a step away. Swear to God, if he touched her she'd flatten him. She'd had just about all she could take in the past two days, and if he was the one who pushed her over the edge she wouldn't hesitate to push back, not this time.

Yeah, *that* would look good, when she was suspected of murdering Carrie Edwards. Some things, though, were just worth the price you had to pay.

"Let me give you a ride home, sweet thing."

She gave the mullet-head a quick but decisive "not interested," and turned away.

Her job here was done, thank God. If she could just make it to her car unmolested, she still had the Bulldog wedding—which would probably come complete with the ring-bearer wearing a football helmet, thanks to Eric—to get through, but Diedra would be there to help. Tomorrow was going to be a very long day, and eventually she needed to get home, to lie down in her bed and pull the cover over her head. Just as she was about to say good-bye to the woman who'd hired her, the door to the restaurant opened. The bride's mother snapped in her grating smoker's voice, "This is a private party. Can't you read the 'closed' sign, moron?"

Everyone turned, and Jaclyn's eyes

widened with horror as she recognized the tall, muscled man whose piercing gaze swept the interior of the barbecue joint. Eric gave the mother of the bride an icy stare as he flashed his badge. "That's *Detective* Moron."

The entire room went silent. For the first time all night, you could've heard a pin drop. Then the bride's mother said, in a resigned voice. "Sorry about the moron bit. Come on in." The "I guess" was unspoken.

A couple of the guests looked truly alarmed, and Jaclyn wondered how many of them thought the cop was here for them. Probably on just about any other night, they'd have been right, but tonight they were safe. Detective Wilder had come for her.

She stalked toward him, chin high, eyes flashing. This was twice he'd interrupted her while she was working. Once was one time too many, and twice was enraging.

"I have a couple more questions," he said as she came close. Behind her the party resumed, though the guests were more subdued than before and several pairs of eyes were focused on the newcomer. That was a two-way street. Eric didn't look directly at her, but kept his gaze on the room behind her.

"It can't wait?" she asked in a tight voice only he could hear.

"No, I need to talk to you tonight." He glanced around the room, smirked, and said, "Nice work, by the way. I particularly like the Christmas lights. Jazzes things up."

"Bite me."

His gaze switched to her face, narrowed with sharp focus. "Any time, sweetheart," he said. "Anywhere."

She went white and fell back a step. No. After switching himself off like a lightbulb when all she'd needed had been a quiet reassurance that he believed her, he wasn't switching himself on again and expecting her to do a moth act. "You don't get to say things like that to me," she said coldly. "Not now. Not anymore." Though she *had* started it by telling him to bite her, and now she had to apologize to him yet again. This was becoming such a habit she was going to start running in the opposite di- rection as soon as she saw him—either that or write up a blanket apology, print out a bunch of copies, and simply give him one every time she put her foot in her mouth.

Before she could get the words out, though, his gaze dropped to her mouth. "Yeah," he said. "I do."

Her mind went blank, and her lips parted but nothing came out. Before she could recover he smirked again, and nodded in the direction of the minister. "Why aren't you wearing your special wedding planner do-rag?"

The urge to apologize was swamped by the urge to dump the remains of a big tray of banana pudding on his head. After humiliating herself with her own lack of control the night before, she clamped down on the vivid thought with every ounce of willpower she had. She refused, absolutely refused, to let him drive her insane. She'd be sane if it killed her. "I'm saving it for tomorrow," Jaclyn ground out. Excuses and explanations crowded her throat as if they had actual, physical presence. She wanted to tell him how much worse this wedding would have been if she hadn't been hired, she wanted to run through the whole horrible litany about the barn and the plastic flowers and Brad Paisley's tick song, but no way in hell was she going to explain anything to Eric Wilder.

She pulled her shoulders back and gave him a flat, unwavering stare. "Ask your questions, and make it snappy. I have another appointment, and I have to be there within the hour. What do you want to know?"

"I thought we could go over Wednesday afternoon again, see if you remember anything else about the man you saw or if you remembered anything Carrie might've said that—"

"Give it up, Detective," she said curtly. "I've told you everything I remember. How many times are we going to go through this?"

"As many as it takes." He looked at her hard, without any sign of the humor he'd displayed a moment earlier.

"Can't this wait until—"

"Officer," the minister called, and they both turned to the massive, mustachioed man who stood behind the bar. "How about a beer and some hot wings?"

Eric didn't correct the minister, didn't tell him that he was a detective and not an officer, to this crowd that wouldn't make any difference: a cop was a cop. "No beer, thanks, but I'd love some wings and maybe a tall glass of sweet tea." He moved past Jaclyn, heading toward the bar.

"You got it," the big man said. "We've got brownies, too. If you'd been a little earlier you coulda had some banana pudding, but it's about all gone."

There went her plan to brain him with the banana pudding. Jaclyn spun around and followed Eric to the bar. She was so indignant she felt as if she were caught in some Victorian melodrama. She wanted to point at him and demand *How dare you!* in her most outraged voice. What in hell was he doing? This was her world, her job, her life, and he was following her around as if he expected to catch her in the middle of some terrorist act. This wasn't good for business. Once could be explained away as an aberration, but twice? What if he showed up again tomorrow? Word would get around that something weird was going on at Premier, and people to whom that mattered would start looking at other event-planning businesses.

As soon as he was away from the door, a couple who weren't anywhere close to being finished with their large plates of food whispered a quick good-bye to the others at their table and slipped out the door as surreptitiously as possible, given that they were the first to leave. Another guy quietly got up and left. Mullet-head wasn't far behind them; he couldn't get out of Porky's fast enough. She'd known these people were different from her usual clientele, but what on earth had she gotten herself into?

"How many left?" Eric asked as soon as she appeared beside him.

"Four."

He grunted. "I was expecting it to be five."

She knew she shouldn't be drawn in. She knew she should answer his questions and leave as fast as she could. But curiosity got the better of her and she asked, "Who's the fifth one?"

Casually he looked over his shoulder, located the person he was talking about. "The woman with her tits hanging out of the red halter."

Oh, good God. It was the bride.

She hadn't recovered from that shock when he patted the stool next to him. "Come on, sit with me and we'll talk."

Abruptly she'd had enough. She had to

get out of here, and if he didn't like it, then tough. She pointed to a sign behind the bar that proudly read:

Kiss my butt.

Jaclyn turned her back on him and walked to a table where the only three women in the room who hadn't gone out of their way to show off their boobs sat, huddled together as if they were surrounded by aliens who might attack at any moment. The older woman looked so completely miserable Eric could only conclude her son was the groom. Looking around, he could even spot the guy, who was half-looped but still lacked that doper look he'd recognize in his sleep.

Lucky for them he wasn't working vice. He didn't care who was carrying pot or who had outstanding warrants. He'd have to act if one of them had a rolling meth lab sitting in the parking lot—in fact, he'd carefully sniffed the air before coming in—but other than that he'd give them a pass. They weren't his target tonight.

No, his target stood out like a diamond sitting in a bowl of rocks. Jaclyn had class, beauty, and balls. Other women might've cried or fallen apart, but she'd kept her cool. Sort of. Her walk killed him: sexy and slow and enticing. That sharp navy blue business suit clung in the right places, nipping in at the waist to show her trim figure, while the skirt ended just above the knee and gave him a good look at those legs. The glare she sent his way cut through him, but not in the way she intended.

After saying a few words to the three horrified ladies, she smiled at them and left the restaurant without looking back. Eric slid off his stool and followed her; no one was sorry to see him go, and no one noted aloud that he'd only taken two bites of a wing and one sip of tea. His feelings were almost hurt because no one said good-bye.

In the parking lot, he easily caught up with Jaclyn; her legs were long, but the snug skirt and high heels kept her from walking as fast as she'd like.

"I really do need to talk to you," he said as she reached her Jag.

"If you want to question me again, call my lawyer."

"Dammit, Jaclyn, listen to me," he said sharply, irritation flashing to life.

"That's Ms. Wilde to you," she snapped as she opened her car door and tossed her purse into the passenger seat. She got in the car, but before she had a chance to close the door he grabbed the top of it, held it.

"The man you saw, the gray-haired one," he began. "Do you—"

She gave him a disbelieving look that he could read even in the not-very-well-lit parking lot. "What do I have to say to get this through your head?" she asked incredulously. "I didn't pay attention to his face, and I can't identify his car beyond saying it was a silver sedan. I'm not a car person. I can tell you for sure it wasn't a truck or an SUV, and that's about it. The color might've been more of a champagne but I'm pretty sure it was just silver. Beyond that, *I don't know.* When I left Carrie— alive—I was flustered, I was *angry,* and I wasn't trying to memorize strangers in the parking lot. Are we through now? I have a job I'm trying to do, if you'll just get out of my way!" She jerked the car door closed, and he had to move his hand or get it crushed.

Without glancing at him again, she started the engine and almost, but not quite, spun her wheels on the gravel as she sped out of the parking lot. Probably she'd wanted to.

Well, that conversation had gone pretty much as he'd imagined it would. But even though he hadn't found out anything useful, he had taken the first step back to an intimate footing with her. Pissed her off, too. The connection was still there, though. Even when she was mad as hell, even though she fought not to show it, the connection was there.

He watched her taillights until they were out of sight, wondering if he should follow her to the wedding, but what was the point? A wedding wasn't like this circus of a rehearsal dinner; she'd be busy, and very unhappy to see him yet again. Better to give her a little bit of space tonight, let her cool down and do some thinking. He wasn't just using the man she'd seen as an excuse; sometimes people remembered more than they thought they did, they just needed to think about it, let the details surface. She *had* to have seen more than she'd just said.

Tomorrow was plenty of time to make contact again. Maybe by then she wouldn't look as if she wanted to take a swing at him.

Chapter Twenty

Maybe it was only because she was comparing it to the scene at Porky's BBQ, but the Bulldog wedding not only went off without a hitch, but it was remarkably charming. And thank God she'd had it to keep her mind occupied, otherwise she'd be at home, fuming over her last run-in with Eric, unable to sleep or eat or even concentrate on HGTV. Being busy was good. Being too busy to think was even better.

The guests had enjoyed the less-than-traditional theme, and everyone had gotten a laugh when the ring-bearer had walked solemnly down the aisle in his little tux and football helmet. It had to be good karma, to be in the presence of so many happy people. Jaclyn figured she was due some good karma, because lately bad karma had been jumping all over her.

The church was a large one, with several buildings other than the sanctuary, one of which housed a large reception facility. Instead of getting in their cars and driving to another location the guests had been able to simply walk, which had greatly simplified matters. The weather had cooperated, too; the humidity had backed off a little so the night air was actually comfortable, and a light breeze was blowing. A sliver of moon lit the sky, and a few small clouds were visible scudding along, backlit by the silver glow.

The entire event had been beautiful, everything had met the customer's specifications, and there had been no crises to be averted. All things considered, the night had been a success, at least professionally. On a personal level, Jaclyn had no idea where she was or what she was supposed to be feeling. Too much had happened in the past four days, beginning with the insanity of sleeping with Eric just hours after meeting him. She had been bombarded with emotions from every point of the scale, from ecstasy to rage, with fear, sadness, resentment, and even guilt thrown into the mix. She could no longer make sense of things; all she was doing was holding on, getting through each moment and hoping her mental equilibrium would return once this hellish week was past.

By midnight, the bride and groom were off, and most of the guests were gone. Because Diedra had arrived so early, she'd snagged a good parking space in the church lot; they walked out together, then said their tired good nights as Diedra stopped at her car. Jaclyn wasn't so lucky. She'd had to find a parking space on the street, across four lanes and half a block down. A couple of late-leaving guests were also walking across the street so she wasn't alone, though their car was parked about thirty yards before hers. She said good-bye to them, too, and they congratulated her on how well everything had gone. She thanked them and continued on her way, her heels clicking against the pavement.

The upper-middle-class neighborhood in a nice part of Atlanta was quiet this time of night; the big trees lining the street created deep shadows and a sense of lushness. Someone nearby had a flower garden, and the sweet, rich fragrance drifted Jaclyn's way, making her wish she could put in a small patio garden even though she knew she didn't have time to tend it. In the distance she heard car doors slam, and people laugh. It had been a good night. Amend that: the last part of the night had been good.

She unlocked the Jag and got in, then took a deep breath as she mentally checked off the tasks that had been completed during the long day. They were over the hump. Three weddings down, three to go. Her mother and Peach were probably wrapping up the Pink wedding about now, too. When she got home she'd call to see if everything had gone well with the Family Drama rehearsal as well as the Pink wedding, but there hadn't been any phone calls tonight so she knew there hadn't been any real disasters. Glitches, maybe; disasters, no. That was something.

The big wedding on Sunday would be

an all-day affair for Premier, but at least it was the only thing they had. After that was over, they'd have a breather, a few precious days to rest and regroup. She might even take Monday off. Since she and Madelyn had started Premier she'd never just not gone in to work. She'd taken one week-long vacation—three years ago—and she'd stayed home sick a couple of times when she wasn't needed, but other than that she'd always been there. After the week she'd had, she deserved a little break.

She started the engine and put the transmission in gear, but kept her foot on the brake as she looked over her shoulder to check for oncoming traffic.

Good thing she did, because a car pulled away from the curb behind her, back close to the intersection, and barreled down the street, wobbling a bit between the lanes. Jaclyn automatically tensed, keeping an eye on the speeding car as she waited for it to pass. The way the car was jerkily swerving, the driver was probably drunk. She hoped the drunk driver hadn't come from the reception; there had been some drinkers, of course, but none of them had made asses of themselves. No one else had been walking ahead of her and the couple who had crossed the street with her, but the driver could have come out earlier and been sitting in the car for a few minutes, maybe hoping to sober up a little, maybe fumbling for keys.

Thank God she hadn't pulled out into the street yet; if the idiot could just get past without sideswiping her, she'd be good to go. But as she watched the car in her rear-view mirror, sideswiping began to seem increasingly possible. The other car seemed to be aiming right for her. The distance was covered in just a couple of seconds but the time seemed to stretch painfully long. She gripped the steering wheel to brace herself, closed her eyes, and prayed.

The car pulled alongside; it didn't come to a complete stop, simply slowed with a jerk that barked the tires a little. Jaclyn opened her eyes and jerked her head around, but even with the streetlights shining the driver was kind of a dark blob. What she did see was the light reflecting off something metallic that was pointing toward her. There was a split second of incredulity before she recognized the metallic thing for what it was: a gun.

There was a loud crack and the window beside her head literally exploded, sending kernels of shattered safety glass raining over her. A concussion of hot air seemed to slap her in the face. Instinctively she ducked and threw herself to the side, across the center console. Another shot boomed, the sound much louder now with the window broken out. Again she felt hot air slapping at her, and she pressed her face hard into the smooth leather of the seat as if that would keep a bullet from hitting her. She could hear screams, and dimly realized that she was the one screaming.

Oh God, she was a sitting duck here! But if she tried to scramble out of the car she'd have to lift her head and give the shooter a target—and what if the shooter was even now getting out of the car and walking to the blasted-out window? She was caught; there was nothing she could do, nowhere she could go. She was going to die in some senseless drive-by shooting. A nauseating tide of regret swamped her, because she'd never get to tell Eric—

"Jaclyn!" That was Diedra's voice screaming her name, the sound rising high and sharp above her own screams. There

were other sounds, too, a man shouting, a door slamming—then, instead of the third shot that she expected, she heard the squealing of tires as the would-be killer peeled out and sped away.

Time slowed to the speed of cold molasses. Jaclyn heard the rasp of air in her throat, felt every beat of her heart thumping in her body. The smell of leather filled her nose, mixed with the sweetness of flowers and the sharp scent of gunpowder.

Slowly, as if she had aged seventy years in the space of a few seconds, she levered herself upright and looked around. To her surprise, the shooter's car was still fishtailing in the street in front of the church as the tires fought for traction. What felt like minutes had actually been no more than a few seconds. Feeling numb and oddly detached, she thought about getting the car's license number, or at least a partial, but it didn't have a tag. Then the driver finally got the car under control and it shot forward, tires squealing again as it reached the corner, took a right, and disappeared from view.

Diedra was sprinting across the street, still screaming her name while she punched a number into her cell phone. A couple who hadn't pulled out of the church parking lot yet was several feet behind her. The couple that had walked across the street in front of Jaclyn had already begun driving away, but when they heard shots they'd stopped and the man had pulled the car back to the curb. He and his wife were now both hurrying toward her. Lights were coming on up and down the block, doors were opening, people were spilling out into the night.

"Are you all right?" the man yelled, which struck her as odd, because if she hadn't been how could she have answered?

Her lips were numb, but laboriously she shoved the car door open and got out. Every move felt as if she were underwater, pushing against a strong current. Shock made chills roughen her skin. Oh, God, that had been so close.

Atlanta was a big city. The shooting could have been random, or she might have been mistaken for someone else, though the Jag made that kind of unlikely. She could have been the victim of a vicious prank, or a gang initiation.

But she didn't think so. Whoever had

been in that car had been gunning for her, specifically, and she had no idea why.

Eric's heart was still hammering when he arrived on the scene. When he'd gotten the call he'd jumped naked out of bed and already had his keys in one hand and his weapon in the other and was heading out the door before he realized he didn't have any clothes on. Cursing, he pivoted and returned to his bedroom to get dressed—in the first clothes that came to hand, which happened to be the pants he'd worn the day before and a dark gray T-shirt he wore when he was working out. Underwear hadn't figured into the scheme of things, so he was commando and sock-less, but at least he had a belt he could clip his badge to, and he'd grabbed his shoulder holster as well.

During the hair-raising drive into Atlanta, he'd called a buddy of his with the Atlanta P.D. and talked to him. They knew he was on the way, and he knew Jaclyn was all right, which were the two most important things. For one thing, he slowed down to a fairly reasonable speed. The second thing, the Atlanta cops weren't alarmed by the arrival of a half-dressed man who was apparently crazed and armed. A lot of the guys who'd been around awhile knew him from when he'd been on the Atlanta P.D., but they knew him with his hair combed and all his clothes on. The newer guys might well have shot him if they hadn't been looking for him.

He turned on his blue light, just to be on the safe side. By the time he arrived on the scene, it was the zoo he'd expected to find. When he got out of the car, he looked around until he spotted Jaclyn in the church parking lot, surrounded by her mother and friends, civilians he didn't know, and several cops, both uniformed and not. Even from a distance he could tell they were all talking at once. Madelyn had a supportive hand on her daughter's shoulder, and the other two stood close, offering moral and physical support. Spotting her car was easy; it was parked at the far curb in the center of a cluster of cops, the driver's side window shattered.

Of the four women, Jaclyn was the calmest as she talked to the Atlanta cops, but even from this distance he could tell how pale she was. He began threading his way through the tangle of hastily parked cars toward her. He had to remind himself not to run. She hadn't been shot. She was fine.

As he neared, her head snapped around in his direction, as if she had some built-in radar where he was concerned. "What are you doing here?" she said with open hostility.

"Hello to you, too. I hear you've had a little trouble."

"How did you hear?" she asked suspiciously. She narrowed her eyes at the detective she'd been talking to. "Did you call him? How would you even know to—"

Peach sighed. "I called him," she confessed. "I was worried out of my mind, so it seemed like the right thing to do."

"Why would you think that?" Madelyn demanded in a mixture of bewilderment and indignation.

"Well, why would anyone try to shoot Jaclyn? It had to be the same person who killed Carrie; it's just too much of a stretch to think the two incidents aren't related."

She was right. Eric already had his money on the gray-haired man, who probably thought Jaclyn could identify him.

"How did you even know his number?"

Madelyn's voice was getting louder as she tried to make sense of what she obviously considered nonsense.

Peach threw Eric a beseeching, step-in-here-any-time look. "His card was in my purse, and—"

"Where did you get his card?" Madelyn half-yelled, throwing up her arms.

"Your trash can," Peach admitted without shame. "The card was right there on top, and it seemed such a shame to waste it that way."

Yeah, like people didn't throw his cards away all the time. While the older women argued, lowering their voices, Eric caught and held Jaclyn's gaze. He could tell she was tired and scared, and he almost stepped forward to wrap his arms around her and hold her close, let her lean on him for a while. Yeah, like she'd go along with that. He did ask, "Are you okay?"

She answered with a nod, not that he believed her. She hadn't been shot, but she was far from okay.

Eric introduced himself to the Atlanta officers, stepped to the side with the senior investigator, and explained that Jaclyn was a witness in a Hopewell murder investigation. The Atlanta detective said, "She's all yours, buddy. I've been trying to find out what she saw, but the witnesses are a tad muddled, to put it lightly. The only two who haven't been drinking are Ms. Wilde and Ms. Kelley, but they're the two who were most scared. While you're talking to them, I'll interview the others."

"Muddled" was definitely putting it lightly. Jaclyn and Diedra, occasionally talking over each other, explained what had happened. The explanation didn't take long, and they agreed on the main points. As Jaclyn had been leaving, someone had pulled alongside her and fired two shots. Diedra and a handful of other witnesses who were also leaving the wedding could confirm what Jaclyn said.

When he thought about her sitting there, a clear target, his heart climbed into his throat.

"Tell me you saw the car," he said, aware there was a faint hint of pleading in his tone. One of the officers ruefully shook his head, so Eric had a good idea what was coming.

"It was a car," Diedra said, "not a truck or an SUV. It was black."

"I think it might've been more of a blue," Jaclyn said.

One of the officers spoke up. "According to the other witnesses, who were really too far away to be positive about anything other than there was a shooting, the vehicle in question might have been green."

"Make?" Eric asked hopefully. He knew Jaclyn couldn't provide the information, but maybe one of the other witnesses—

Again the officer shook his head.

Un-fucking-believable. "Surely you two can come up with some detail about the car," Eric said, looking from Jaclyn to Diedra and back. How could both of them be so car-blind?

Jaclyn just shrugged her shoulders as Diedra said, "Well, it wasn't a Mustang. I would've recognized a Mustang. I think."

"That's it? Not a Mustang?"

"All the midsized cars pretty much look alike," Jaclyn said. Her voice was a little thin; he could hear a faint tremble in it. "That's something, isn't it? It was midsized, not a huge car or a Mini Cooper."

"We can put out an all-points bulletin," he muttered. "Not a Mustang or Mini Cooper. We'll collect everything else, then sort them out. I don't suppose you got a tag number?"

"There wasn't one," Jaclyn said. "I *did* think to look."

The implication was chilling. Shooting at her hadn't been an impulse; the shooter had planned for this, had removed the car tag in case there were any witnesses. "What about the driver?"

Jaclyn shuddered, and her mother put her arm around her shoulder and hugged. After a minute Jaclyn took a deep breath, stood up straighter as if she'd braced herself. "I think he had something over his face, like a ski mask or a hood. I couldn't see any features at all, just the gun pointing at me. Right-handed. Dark sleeve. Um . . . gloves, too."

Diedra nodded. "I think so, too; when he went by me, I couldn't see a white blob where the face would be, so he had to be wearing a hood. But—" She narrowed her eyes in thought. "Come to think of it, the driver wasn't all that big. It could be a small man, but it might have been a woman. It's hard to tell when someone is sitting in a car, but I didn't get the sense it was a big person."

Jaclyn thought about that. "You're right," she said. "Looking through the window, I think I might be a hair taller than the driver."

Neither of them recognized any make of car, evidently, other than a Mustang and a Mini Cooper, but when it came to everything else, their sense of detail and proportion kicked in. At least that was something to go on.

"The shooter definitely fired right-handed?"

"Definitely. The car pulled away from the curb behind me, and I was watching it in my rearview mirror, letting it get past before I pulled out. It was weaving back and forth in the lanes, so I thought the driver might be drunk. Then he—or she—stopped beside me, right arm extended like this"—she demonstrated—"and fired twice."

He left her for a while to check out her car. The driver's side window was shot out, the interior covered with tiny cubes of safety glass. He also learned that no shell casings had been recovered, which didn't necessarily mean that the weapon had been a revolver. It could have been an automatic, but the casings had ejected inside the shooter's car. With luck, they'd find one or both slugs buried in the car's upholstery.

Her car was drivable, but he had it impounded so it could be searched for evidence. Rather, the Atlanta P.D. impounded it, on his suggestion. None of this happened fast. Crime investigations were, by necessity, extremely painstaking. Time wore on, past one-thirty, then past two. It was rocking on toward three in the morning when things began winding down. Eric kept an eye on Jaclyn, because her face was getting more and more pale.

She wasn't happy about losing her car, but she didn't argue, either. Someone had shot at her; it was in her best interest to find out who. "I'll arrange to rent a car until mine can be repaired," she said, then gave a rueful little smile. "At least this will stop Jacky from asking if he can borrow it."

"Who's Jacky?" Eric asked before he could stop himself, annoyed with himself at the slight burn of jealousy. Jaclyn just looked at him as if she couldn't figure out why he was asking such a dumb question.

Madelyn frowned at him. "Jaclyn's father," she said abruptly, the full stop in her tone telling him she wouldn't appreciate any further questions in that direction.

Huh. Okay. That explained Jaclyn's name, at least: it was a blend of Jack and Madelyn.

Madelyn turned back to her daughter, gently touched her arm. "I'll see if it's okay for you to leave now. You're exhausted."

"Thanks, Mom."

"I'll take her home," Eric said firmly.

"Thank you, but that's not necessary," Jaclyn said coolly. She was handling this well enough, but the night was far from over and the adrenaline overload hadn't quite hit her yet. When it did, the exhaustion would knock her on her ass.

"I want to ask you a few more questions," he promptly lied. Well, it wasn't a lie, because he did want to ask her some things, but it was more like the same questions he'd already asked, just phrased differently. Sometimes a little change in a sentence could trigger a memory. "I can do that on the way back to Hopewell, or I can follow you home and we can talk there."

"Fine," she said wearily. "I'd just as soon get this over with." She planted a kiss on Madelyn's cheek. "I'm glad you were here.

I'll see you in the morning. I'll be late, because I have to arrange for a car, but I'll be there."

"You should take the day off," Madelyn said, but Jaclyn immediately shook her head.

"No, I'm better off at work, where I'll have things to distract me. Besides, tomorrow's another hectic day. Remember my rehearsal tonight? You wouldn't believe. I have to tell you all about it."

Having been there, Eric completely, but silently, agreed with her.

Madelyn pressed her lips together. "You call me when you're safely home."

"I will." She thanked the others for being there, thanked the Atlanta officers and detectives, thanked the witnesses, apologized for the disturbance to the people who lived in the neighborhood. Recognizing the signs of impending collapse, Eric finally put his hand on her elbow and led her to his car.

She was stumbling slightly, and he provided more and more support as they walked. She said, "I'm not sure what questions you think you have, but I don't know anything I haven't already told you. Not about Carrie, not about tonight."

"Once you start talking, something of interest might occur to you."

"I don't think so."

"Then we'll talk about cars," Eric said as he opened the passenger door for her and she slipped in. She fumbled with the seat belt and he bent down, fastened it for her. He rounded the car, got in beside her, and clipped his own belt. "I swear, when this is over I'm taking you to a car show."

"When this is over, I'm never going to see you again," she responded.

"Every woman should know the difference between a Ford and a Toyota and a Cadillac."

"They have four tires and a steering wheel. Other than that, who cares?"

"If it makes you feel better, we can take Diedra, too. *Not a Mini Cooper,* my ass."

Chapter Twenty-one

A hard, warm arm slipped around her, tugged her sideways against a rock-solid shoulder. Half asleep, she sighed and nestled closer, because he was so warm and felt so secure, and she was almost boneless with fatigue. "You're home," he murmured, using his other hand to tilt her chin up. He slanted his mouth over hers in a leisurely kiss that slowly deepened until his tongue was in her mouth and sheer heat began to chase away her fatigue.

Yes, she was home, she thought vaguely. Jaclyn sighed again, slipping her hand around his neck and up into his hair. God, he smelled good, man smell mingled with heat and sweat and night air. Skin was skin; why did men smell so different from women? But they did, and his smell made something in her purr like a kitten.

His left hand slid over her breasts, rubbing and finding her nipples through her layers of clothing, catching them between his fingers and lightly pulling so that they tightened and stood out. Pleasure slowly grew, like a tide coming in, washing over her in incrementally higher waves and pushing the fatigue aside but still leaving her boneless. Her body knew his, knew the weight and heat of him, knew how he moved, knew the things that made him groan and the sounds he made when he climaxed. She shouldn't be kissing him, shouldn't let him touch her the way he was touching her, but she was tired and she'd almost been killed tonight and she wanted him even more than she had when they'd first met.

But this was exactly what she'd done wrong the first time, leaping before she looked, and that had turned out to be an emotional disaster. Throwing caution to the wind just wasn't how she operated—at least, how she operated most of the time. Eric jarred her out of her comfort zone, goaded her into saying and doing things that she would normally never say or do. The thing about comfort zones was that they were, well, *comfortable*, and getting out of them wasn't.

In the back of her mind, alarm bells began to ring. She had to stop, or the next thing she knew he'd have her skirt up and her underwear off, and there wouldn't be any stopping. She didn't want to go there again, didn't want to set herself up for even more hurt.

Bracing her hand against his shoulder, she tore her mouth free of his and pushed back, turning her face away. "No. I'm sorry. I was half asleep and . . . no."

He went very still, then slowly blew out a breath and eased away from her, straightening in the driver's seat and draping his left arm over the steering wheel. "Okay." If her refusal angered him, she couldn't hear it in his voice, but he was good at keeping his emotions hidden.

She should get out of the car and go inside; she was exhausted, and she needed to get some sleep, even if it was just a few hours, before another very busy day began. Sitting here in the dark with him was just asking for trouble, but she'd dozed off on the drive home and he hadn't asked those questions he'd been so determined to ask and she certainly didn't want to go inside with him. The car was the best of two bad choices.

"I'm sorry I fell asleep," she said, making her voice as brisk as she could, given that she felt like a limp rag. "What was it you were so determined to ask? I've told you everything I remember, so my answers aren't going to change unless you want me to make up stuff."

He was silent a moment, drumming his fingers on the steering wheel. She waited, wondering what was so complicated that he couldn't just spit it out so she could tell him she didn't know, then go inside and get some sleep. "We got the test results back on your clothes," he finally said. "No blood residue."

"Of course there wasn't," she replied irritably. "I knew there wouldn't be." Maybe it was because she was so tired, but it took a moment for the dime to drop; when it did, anger flared so hotly it blew away the fatigue, made her muscles shake with the effort it took to control herself. She refused to let herself lose it the way she had the night before, which had accomplished nothing except self-humiliation, so she hung on.

"Oh, I get it," she said, her voice tense. "You get the test results back, proving I didn't kill Carrie—at least not while wearing those clothes—so now I'm good enough again for you to kiss? You believe me now? No, that's right: you don't believe me; you believe your test results. You jerk." Her hand itched with the impulse to slap him as hard as she could; she curled her fingers tight to resist the impulse, locked her arms by her side. "You know what? You can kiss something, all right. You can kiss my ass."

"Any time," he said, his own voice low and angry. "I like your ass. And for the record, I believed you from the beginning. So did Sergeant Garvey."

"You had a funny way of showing it," she snapped back. "All you had to do was make one phone call, just tell me that you— Never mind. You didn't, which speaks for itself."

"No, what it *speaks* for is that, until you were cleared, which means cleared by evidential means, not cleared by anything *I* thought, I had to follow the book. I had to treat you as I would any other suspect. No, I had to be even more objective with you, or I'd have been jerked off the case. We're short-handed right now, which is the only reason I was allowed to work this case in the first place, but I wanted it because I was more motivated to dig deeper than maybe one of the other detectives would have been. I didn't know what we'd find, didn't know how strong any circumstantial evidence against you would be, but I knew I wanted to be in a position to look harder. I figured I was your best chance at getting cleared."

"Thank you so much," she said sarcastically.

"Get over your hurt feelings and *listen* to me." His tone was as hard as flint, and so was his expression. His mouth was set in a flat, grim line, the lights from the dash throwing harsh shadows on the rugged lines of his face. "I couldn't do anything to give the lieutenant or the captain—or the district attorney, come to that—any reason to think I might have compromised the case for you. I couldn't make any comforting phone calls on the side because that might have come out. For your sake, I had to be completely impartial, and I'll be damned if I'll apologize for doing my job."

"I might have to listen to you, because you're a cop and I have to cooperate or I could land in trouble, but *I'll* be damned if I have to *get over* anything. You know why? Because if you'd been deep down certain that I hadn't killed Carrie, you'd have known those test results would come back negative for blood. I understand about following the rules. I'm big on rules myself. But you know what? A single damn phone call wouldn't have changed the evidence any, and would have made a huge difference to me. You didn't make the call."

"So you're going to be pissy-minded and throw away what could be something good because I did what my job requires me to do?"

"*You* did," she pointed out, incensed that he was putting it all back on her. "If that makes me pissy-minded, then I guess you are, too. What it comes down to is you didn't trust me, and now I don't trust you. We're way past picking up where we left off, so keep your hands and your mouth to yourself. As far as I'm concerned, we needn't see each other ever again."

"Well now, that's where you're wrong," he said grimly. "In case you've forgotten, someone tried to kill you tonight. Peach was right in that it's too much of a coincidence not to be tied to the Edwards case. The man you saw likely killed Ms. Edwards, and he knows you saw him. But he's got a solid alibi, so as it stands now I don't have probable cause to get a search warrant, unless you could identify him, which changes everything."

"But I can't identify him," she said in despair. "I wasn't paying attention; I couldn't pick him out of a group of one. He doesn't know that, though."

"No. Obviously, he assumes that you *can* identify him. Probably it took him a while to find out who you are, but the information is a matter of public record. Now we need to figure out how he knew where you'd be tonight."

Then what he'd said clicked, and Jaclyn stared at him. "You said he has an alibi. You know who it is."

"I have a good idea. What I don't have is evidence."

"Who?"

"I can't divulge information," he said with eroding patience. "The case is still being developed."

"Someone who thinks I can identify him just tried to kill me. Don't you think I'd be safer if I know who it is? You know . . . just in case I see him again? Then I could even give you a call, and say, hey, here he is, come pick him up!"

He shook his head. "I can't tell you who I think it is because I can't prejudice you in any way. When I show you some photographs, if you can put your finger on him it'll be because you know you saw him at the reception hall, not because of anything I said."

Legally, that made sense. On a practical basis, though, it was enraging. "So you'll risk my life to keep your case pristine."

"No. *I* know who he is, which is why I'll be sticking to you like glue, to keep him from getting to you." He gave her a grim smile. "And because he knows who you are, he'll be able to find out where you live, if he hasn't already. Like it or not, sweetheart, you can't get rid of me just yet."

On a practical basis, that meant she couldn't sleep in her own home, that this hellish night wasn't over with yet. Eric went inside, thoroughly searched the house before he let her come in, and even then it was just to hastily pack a suitcase. She didn't argue, because she wasn't stupid enough to risk her life over where she slept. At the same time, she was completely prepared to put up a kicking and screaming fight if he tried to take her to his home, because no way was she doing that.

He must have known that, because he didn't even make the suggestion. Instead he drove her to an extended-stay hotel, where she got a two-room suite, a living room/kitchen combo with a separate bedroom. It wasn't home, but it wasn't bad. He even took the precaution of checking her in with his credit card, under his name.

"But what about work?" she asked, standing in the middle of the generic living room with anxiety eating at her. "He'll know where I work, too. Mom and Peach and Diedra are all in danger."

"This is Saturday," he said. "You told your mother you'd be better off at work, but did you mean you'd actually be in the office today?"

She was so tired she could barely think, but she focused on the question. "Maybe in and out. We don't have any appointments with potential clients, because our schedule this week has been so hectic. We do have two weddings today, and a rehearsal, so what I actually meant was that I'd be better off working."

"Then everyone should be safe enough this weekend. If the case hasn't broken by Monday, then yeah, maybe you should take some time off."

Wasn't it an ironic coincidence that she'd been thinking the same thing, though for a completely different reason? Somehow the idea of taking a vacation wasn't nearly as attractive when she was doing it to evade a killer. That took some of the shine off the idea of rest and relaxation, made it seem more like going into hiding, which of course it was.

"Is it on your website, which events you

personally will be working?" His mind was still working, worrying at the details like a pit bull. He had to be stretched as thin as she was; his eyes were shadowed, his hair was rumpled, and he needed to shave. Nevertheless, even with his sock-less feet shoved into running shoes, wearing wrinkled pants and a snug T-shirt that showed every line of his muscled torso, he was so masculine and sexy he made her toes curl. With a sense of sorrow, she realized she might never meet anyone else who made her react physically the way Eric did, and that hurt so much she had to force herself to concentrate on what he was saying.

"No, we don't post that information at all. Some—a lot, actually—of our clients put the information on their Facebook pages, but you'd have to know who they are to begin with, and then get on their friend list, so that doesn't seem feasible."

"No," he agreed. "But somehow he found you tonight, and when we can nail down how he did it, that's the link that'll connect him."

Dawn was approaching so fast that neither of them would be able to snatch more than a couple of hours of sleep, Eric even fewer, because he still had to drive home. As soon as he left, Jaclyn locked and chained the door, then stripped off her clothes and tumbled into bed after barely taking the time to hang up her suit. She did remember to set the alarm on her cell phone—and then she curled up between the cool sheets and cried, because when she'd thought she was going to die her last thought had been of Eric, that she wouldn't get a chance to tell him she loved him.

She didn't know where that thought had come from; she couldn't possibly love him. She didn't know him well enough to love him. The potential had been there, though, and she grieved its loss, with a sharpness that left her hollow and aching.

Chapter Twenty-two

The alarm went off at seven-thirty. Jaclyn stretched an arm from beneath the covers, fumbled for her cell, and silenced the noise. The feel of the phone in her hand reminded her that she hadn't called her mother the night before. Hastily she thumbed in Madelyn's number, blinking her eyes to focus them on the keypad.

"What's going on?" was Madelyn's greeting.

"I'm in a hotel," Jaclyn said, and yawned. "The detective thought I'd be safer if no one knew where I was, so I packed a suitcase and he brought me here. I didn't get checked in until around four-thirty. As soon as he left, I fell into bed."

"Safer?" Trust Madelyn's mom instinct to seize on the most trauma-inducing word.

"From whoever took those shots at me." Jaclyn sat up in bed and rubbed her eyes. "The good news is, I'm officially off the suspect list. The bad news is, the man I saw at the reception hall is probably who killed Carrie, and now he thinks I can identify him."

"Oh my God."

"There's more good news/bad news. Good: the detective said he's pretty sure he knows who did it. Bad: he doesn't have enough evidence to get a search warrant, so he hoped when he brings his photographs I'll be able to put my finger on a guy and say 'this is the one.' I can't, though. I honestly didn't pay enough attention," she said unhappily. She certainly wished there had been something outstanding enough about the guy that she'd memorized his face, so she could get this over with.

"But . . . I thought you and Diedra both said the person who tried to shoot you could be a woman."

"Or a small man," Jaclyn pointed out, then closed her eyes as she thought about the man she'd seen in the parking lot at the reception hall. Nothing about his face stood out, but she had good spatial memory, and she had a very clear sense of how tall he'd been in relation to his car. The man she'd seen hadn't been short; if anything, he'd been pushing six feet tall, if not taller. "I don't think it was the same man I saw that day."

"But that doesn't make sense."

"I suppose he could have hired someone," she said uncertainly. "Either that, or the shooting didn't have anything to do with Carrie."

"The odds against that would be astronomical. I agree with Peach; it has to be connected to Carrie."

"Or someone else whose wedding I did, and the bride hated everything."

There was a moment of silence, then Madelyn said, "Oh my God," again in a very unhappy tone. "There was a call yesterday . . . if it was a woman who shot at you, then I think maybe I told her where you'd be last night."

"What?"

"Someone called the office yesterday; Diedra answered the call, then transferred it to me. The woman, whoever it was, said she was an old friend of yours from college, that you'd talked recently and were supposed to meet for drinks after work but she'd forgotten the time. She rattled off a name, but we were so busy yesterday I didn't really take note. I told her you had a rehearsal yesterday, then you were going straight to a wedding and I told her where it was, and that it would be late when you got finished so probably there was a mix-up on dates. I gave her your cell number, to call and reschedule. Did she call?" Madelyn asked hopefully.

Jaclyn pinched between her eyes. "No, no one called. And I haven't talked to any old college friends."

"I almost got you killed," Madelyn breathed with horror, and her voice wobbled with tears as she continued, "Surely we can have the call traced, find out who it was—"

"Maybe. I don't know. I'll call Detective Wilder. Mom, don't cry. You didn't almost get me killed. Whoever shot at me is the one to blame, not you." Because this was her mother, tears welled in her eyes, too. "Please don't cry, or you'll have me boohoo-ing, and then we'll both have swollen eyes today."

"Oh, baby, I'm so sorry."

Soothing Madelyn took several minutes, during which they both cried. As soon as they disconnected the call, though, Jaclyn dug Eric's card out of her bag and dialed his cell.

"Jaclyn. Is something wrong?"

Startled, she took the phone from her ear and stared at it as if it were inhabited by aliens. It was one thing for her mother to answer the phone with a question, be-cause after all she would recognize the number and know who was calling, but she'd never called Eric before. Cautiously she put the phone back to her ear. "How did you know who it was?"

"I recognized the number."

"I've never called you before."

"No, but *I've* called *you.* Remember the occasion? I was inside you almost before your back hit the mattress."

A tidal wave of heat washed over her, because, yes, oh God yes, she remem-bered. She might want to forget, but in that moment physical memory was stronger and her flesh relived the feel of him pushing into her, thick and hot and deep. She vividly felt his arms around her again, his chest hair roughly rubbing her nipples, his hands gripping her bottom and lifting her into each thrust. Every muscle inside her tightened as if she was holding him again, clamping down around him as she came. Her nipples tightened on their own, standing out as flushed and firm as if he'd been sucking on them.

"I—" she said, then fell silent because there was nothing she could say, no rebuttal she could make. What had happened, happened. She squeezed her eyes shut and her legs tightly together, trying to make the ache go away.

"Yes," he said roughly, his tone making it plain he was reliving his own moments. "You."

She took a deep, shaky breath. She'd never understood the charm of phone sex until that moment, and this was a damn poor time for it, too. "Ah . . . someone, a woman, called Mom yesterday and said she was an old college friend and we were supposed to get together for drinks—" She was blabbering. She stopped, took another breath. "Anyway, Mom told her where I'd be last night. And, no, I haven't been in touch with any old college friends about having drinks."

"Caller ID?" he asked sharply, evidently making the transition from pleasure to business a lot more smoothly than she had.

"No, it was on the office phone. Mom said something about having the call traced. We don't have caller ID on the office line."

He muttered something that she doubted was complimentary, then said, "Okay, find out what time the call came in. We'll get the ball rolling with the phone company."

"It was a woman. That knocks a hole in your theory about the gray-haired man trying to kill me, doesn't it?"

"No, in fact, it doesn't. Look, I really need you to look at some photographs. If you can't come here, tell me where you'll be and I'll bring them to you."

A sense of alarm seized her at the words "come here." Surely he wasn't—

"Ah . . . where are you?"

"At work."

Her face heated as she thought of what he'd said. Had anyone heard him?

"Don't worry, no one's near enough to eavesdrop," he said in amusement. "Can you come now?"

She didn't know what devil seized her, but she did know that payback was sweet. "Almost," she murmured, and listened to the sudden fumbling and background cursing as he dropped his cell phone.

Garvey approached Eric's desk, some papers in hand. "The senator's alibied tighter than Dick's hatband," he said in disgust. "He was at a fund-raiser, with Mrs. Dennison, in Savannah last night. It lasted until midnight. He couldn't be in two places at once."

"He might not have done it, but he had it done," Eric growled. "The fucker screwed up. If he'd just left it alone, we didn't have enough on him to get a search warrant, but he was afraid Jaclyn could identify him. Now we're going to look real hard at his girlfriend. Jaclyn just called; a woman pretending to be an old friend called her business yesterday, and her mother told the woman where Jaclyn would be. That was a puzzle, figuring out how anyone knew where Jaclyn would be at any given time, but the answer was simple."

"The girlfriend."

"Yep." Eric pulled up some information on his computer. "Atlanta P.D. sent over their ballistic report. They found one bullet in the Jag's upholstery; the other one went through the passenger door. The weight of the bullet is consistent with a nine millimeter. Ms. Taite Boyne is registered as the owner of a Glock 26, which is a subcompact nine millimeter."

"If she's smart, that pistol is at the bottom of Lake Lanier."

"Problem is, she thinks she's smarter than everyone else. People like that make stupid mistakes. We'll trace the call to Premier's office, see what pops. Maybe she used her cell phone."

"She can toss that, too, say it was stolen."

"Pistol and cell phone both come up missing? I'd say that's suspicious behavior. Anyway, she might have been smart enough to use a calling card, so we can't bank on the call leading directly to her. But

the Atlanta P.D. didn't find any shell casings at the scene last night, which means
they ejected inside the car. There may be
scorch marks, gunpowder residue in the
car, on the steering wheel from contact
with her hands. At any rate, it'll be interesting to see if she has an alibi for last night."

Garvey rubbed his hands together. "I
love it when all the details fall in place," he
said happily.

"Jaclyn is on the way in, to look at photographs."

"Identifying Dennison won't count for
much, with him being all over television
these days. Seems like he's running an ad
every fifteen minutes."

"I've got another angle I'm going to try.
Jaclyn doesn't know cars. She seriously
doesn't know cars. About all she can tell
you is if a vehicle is a car, or a pickup, or
an SUV. But she's really, really good with
details, so she might have noticed something particular about the car, even without
knowing what make it is." He'd come in
early, started compiling stacks of photographs of cars, of both the kind the senator drove and the kind Taite Boyne drove.
He'd noticed a striking detail about the car

that the senator drove, and there was a possibility Jaclyn had picked up on it.

He also had a lot of head shots of gray-haired men, including two of the senator, one from each side. He didn't know which angle she'd seen him from, and one side of a person's face could be markedly different from the other side. If she picked him out, that was a bonus. Let a defense attorney argue that she'd seen him in political ads; that was the district attorney's worry. The important thing to Eric was collecting enough evidence that they could persuade a judge to issue a search warrant on that car.

Jaclyn walked in a little after nine. Eric watched heads turning her way. It wasn't that she was beautiful, because she wasn't. Objectively, he supposed most people would say she was attractive. She sure as hell attracted him. But what set her apart was her effortless, long-legged stroll, those dynamite legs, and a classy sense of style. Jaclyn couldn't look cheap if she tried. Everything about her was meticulously put together without being fussy. He hated fussiness, hated a lot of jangling things hanging off a woman. From the gold studs in her ears to the tiny gold chain around her right ankle, she was restrained and classy. It was funny how the very things that attracted him to her were what he most enjoyed messing up; maybe it was the challenge of getting her clothes off and her hair down, her nails digging into his back. *Oh, yeah.*

He stood up as she approached, directed her to the chair beside his desk. If he'd pushed it a little last night, he thought, they'd have ended up in bed, but what he wanted wasn't just sex. He wanted Jaclyn to decide that she wanted *him.* He wanted her to consciously, deliberately decide to give them a chance, because otherwise he'd always feel as if she had one foot out the door and was just waiting for him to do something wrong so she could leave.

Garvey came up as Eric turned to get the stack of photographs he'd put to the side. "I'm glad you're okay," he said to her. "That was a close thing last night."

"Thank you, Sergeant Garvey. Yes, it was. That was the most frightened I've ever been."

"We're making progress in the case. With luck, this will all be over pretty soon." He pulled up a chair and sat down—evidently he wanted to be involved in the process.

"I hope so." She glanced at the clock, then at Eric. "Ready?"

He gave her the head shots first. She flipped through them, taking maybe two seconds on each one, then shook her head and set them aside. "Nothing, but let me look through them again in a few minutes. Sometimes my impressions need to simmer."

"Take your time."

She gave a tiny smile. "Today? Time is the one thing I don't have."

Next she went through the photographs of cars in the same measured way. She went all the way to the end of the stack, but instead of setting the stack aside the way she had with the head shots, she went back to the beginning and started again, a tiny frown knitting her brow. She went more slowly this time, her head tilted to the side.

Eric and Garvey sat silently, watching and waiting. Eric almost stopped breathing. He was putting a lot of faith in her attention to detail. She might not know cars, but she knew style.

She pulled a photograph out of the stack and tossed it on the desk. "This one," she said. "The car was like this."

He glanced at the photograph. He wanted to smile with satisfaction, but he kept his expression noncommittal so he didn't inadvertently influence her. "Are you certain?"

"Yes. It had that same doohickey sticking up on the hood."

Eric picked up the photograph. The car she'd selected was a Mercedes S-Class, the S600, which ran about a hundred and fifty thou. Only the S-Class vehicles had the Mercedes emblem standing on the tip of the hood; on all of the other models, the emblem was made into the grill.

Senator Dennison drove a silver S600.

He gave her the other stack of photographs. These had been harder to come by, because they were photographs of the taillights of several different makes and models, taken at night. "Do any of these taillights look like the ones on the car you saw last night?"

"You're asking a lot," she murmured. "I was scared out of my head. I barely remembered to look for a tag number, and fat lot of good that did."

"Just see if anything rings a bell."

She did the whole methodical thing again, but when she reached the last one she shook her head. "Sorry. Nothing there."

That had been a long shot anyway. Still, she'd pulled out a piece of information that might sway a judge. She hadn't identified the senator, but she'd identified his car.

She picked up the head shots again, went back through them before finally shaking her head. "I don't recognize any-one."

Eric took the pictures back. "That's okay. Thanks for coming in."

She stood, gave him a quizzical look. "That's it? You aren't going to tell me if that hood doohickey means anything or not?"

He smiled. "It means a lot." It also meant a lot that she was being cordial, that she was keeping her hostility firmly under wraps in front of Garvey.

"Good. I'd hate to waste a trip here when I have a million other things I have to be doing. I have to run now. Have a nice day."

Everyone in the room watched her leave. Garvey heaved a sigh. "If it wasn't for my blushing bride, I'd give you a run for your money with that one."

Eric snorted. "Your blushing bride would cut your nuts off."

"I know. That's what I meant."

Chapter Twenty-three

"I have to take notes," Bishop Delaney said gleefully. "Forget notes; I have to take *pictures,* otherwise no one will ever believe it. I did the flowers for *Hee Haw* Hell."

"Hush," Jaclyn said in an undertone, casting a sharp look around. The last thing she needed was for anyone in the wedding party, or any of the guests, to hear him. But no one was close by; he'd had the good sense to wait until they were alone to share his observation. She wasn't worried about hurting anyone's feelings, but she was definitely worried that someone— like half the people there—would take umbrage and pull out their pocket knives. She didn't have anything against pocket knives; she carried a teeny one in her purse herself, and it was forever coming in handy. But if she had to vote on the wedding party she considered most likely to be in a knife fight, this one would win hands down.

She and Bishop were sitting in the back row on the groom's side, and since the venue, otherwise known as a barn, wasn't filled to capacity, there was no one seated in the two rows of folding chairs in front of them. At that precise moment the groom's mother, who remained silently horrified by her son's choice of bride and everything to do with the wedding, was being seated—to Garth Brooks's "Friends in Low Places"— by one of the ushers, though that term was a little glorified when applied to this particular usher, the bride's mullet-headed brother. At least he was wearing a tie. No jacket, and his pants were khaki, but he had on a tie.

Jaclyn kept trying to put herself into a party spirit and have some fun, because most of the people there, barring the groom's mother and two sisters, were having a blast. Fun didn't have to be color-coordinated. Fun didn't have to have a background of classical music. But what kept her from relaxing was the strong impression that this group's idea of fun didn't fit within the definition of "legal." She frequently handled guests, and wedding party participants, who drank too much or breathed through a joint, but she was afraid this group leaned more toward crack, meth, and a variety of crimes that made the words "warrant for arrest" of importance to them.

This wedding teetered on the edge of disaster; she could feel it. So far everyone seemed to be on his or her best behavior, but "best" was subjective. To call this *Hee Haw* Hell was insulting to *Hee Haw*.

The wedding was being held in a barn located in the middle of a field a good forty-minute drive from Premier's offices. The bride's grandfather owned this land, and though it was no longer worked as a farm, it remained the home place, the family stomping grounds. To get to the barn, one had to leave the paved road. The directions had read: *Turn in PawPaw's driveway, drive around the house, and follow the tractor road down the left side of the field until you get to the barn.* Maybe at one time the tractor road had looked like a real road, albeit a dirt one. Now it looked like a half-grown-up trail, with deep ruts that had threatened to rip the undercarriage of her rental car.

After driving down the dirt/grass road, everyone had to park on a grassy field, which made Jaclyn fervently thankful that the weather had cooperated. She was prepared to contact a vendor and order sturdy tents for the outdoor reception, if necessary, but she couldn't do a damn thing about a muddy field of cars and ruined shoes.

The interior of the barn was lit by open windows and a multitude of white Christmas lights, as well as a number of off-white candles. Arrangements of white and off-white flowers, along with the lighting, made for an almost quaint setting—"almost" being the operative word. There was old straw on the floor, which the bride insisted was "authentic," and while there were no animals present, the faint, lingering odor of past residents remained. The fans she'd arranged to be brought in were silent and effective, but maybe moving the air around so much wasn't a good thing.

On the other hand, without the fans everyone would be swimming in a sea of sweat. While this wasn't the hottest day of the year, the temperature was still close to ninety.

Many of the guests on the bride's side were in jeans and T-shirts; they hadn't even bothered to brush off the dressy jeans or, heaven forbid, drag a dress or a suit out of the back of the closet. On the other hand, the running shoes most of them were wearing might come in handy.

The groom's relatives had made an effort, and were dressed nicely. Jaclyn was wearing the lightest-weight business suit she owned. Bishop, of course, was immaculately dressed and, as always, fashionable and cool . . . seriously cool. Did the man have sweat glands?

"Why are you still here?" she whispered. The bouquets, corsages, and floral decorations, all paid for by the mother of the groom, had been delivered and set up to Bishop's specifications. He rarely stuck around for the ceremony.

"Honey, you couldn't pry me out of here with a crowbar and a quart of Vaseline," he observed, his voice low.

In spite of the events of the past few days, Jaclyn smiled. She was here, and as long as no blood was shed she couldn't deny the entertainment value before her. She might as well enjoy herself while she could. There was no telling what kind of challenges the reception might bring.

"It's like the Beverly Hillbillies meet Boss Hogg, with poor June Cleaver thrown into the mix," Bishop rhapsodized under his breath. "I've never seen anything like it. What the hell were you thinking when you took this job?"

She had thought that the groom's mother had a point when she said no one in the bride's family had any idea what they were doing; that she could help in some small way; that this bride and groom could use a little guidance. Unfortunately the bride and her mother had rejected most of Jaclyn's ideas, though some had stuck.

It wasn't necessary to have the bride's family and friends on one side and the groom's on the other to tell who belonged where. There was the inappropriate dress and abundance of mullets, shaved heads, and prison tattoos on the bride's side, and most of the groom's people looked shell-shocked. The groom's poor mother looked like she might pass out at any moment, and his sisters and their families were all but in shock, except for one brother-in-law, who wasn't trying very hard to hide his amusement.

"Imagine what this wedding would be like without us," she said to Bishop.

"Hootenanny," he whispered.

Someone entered the row from the far side and instead of sitting down at that end moved toward Jaclyn. Startled, she looked up as Eric took the folding chair next to hers, and instinctively she stiffened. She thought she had handled herself well when she'd gone to the police department that morning. She hadn't betrayed any of the tension and angry confusion, the hurt, that she felt every time she simply thought of him; actually being in his presence was worse. But this was her territory, and his intrusion in it was jarring.

Bishop leaned around her and gave Eric an appraising look. "Well, well," he drawled. "*Hee Haw* Heaven." She had to admit, in his jeans and boots and lightweight jacket thrown on over a collarless shirt, Eric kind of blended with the crowd, though on him the look was sexy.

Eric draped his left arm around the back of her chair and leaned around her. "I'm with the wedding planner," he said to Bishop.

"I got that," Bishop said, and winked before sitting back. With a small sense of shock, she realized that they knew each other. Well, not *knew*, but, of course, Eric had interviewed all the vendors who'd witnessed her scene with Carrie.

"What are you doing here?" she asked Eric in a sharp whisper.

"Watching over you," he whispered back.

Shock vibrated through her. Surely he didn't think there was any danger here? No way would Madelyn—or Peach or Diedra, either—tell anyone where Jaclyn could be found, not after last night's shooting. She was safe here. Well, as safe as one could be when at least half the people around her were armed with some manner of weapon.

She appreciated his concern, and his effort. Still, having him sit so close to her, his arm lying against her back, one long leg touching hers, was nerve-racking. She shifted her legs to the side, away from him and closer to Bishop. Why couldn't Eric wait outside? Did he have to put himself right here?

She supposed she could insist that he leave, but she already knew how much her insisting would gain her, so she saved her breath. He was stubborn and probably didn't give a rat's ass what she wanted. Not only that, she wasn't stupid. Like it or not she knew she was safe with him. She was afraid she might not be safe *from* him, but that was due to her own weakness, and that acknowledgment carried a sting.

The position of his arm meant she was almost in his embrace. For a brief moment their gazes met. He had on his cop expression, keeping all his thoughts to himself. Almost. He dropped his gaze, letting it slide down her body and linger too long here and there. She tensed again, because that look made her skin feel too hot and tight.

Then he turned his attention to the altar, and his shoulders heaved as he almost choked on laughter. The minister, the big bald guy who owned Porky's BBQ, wore a faded Lynyrd Skynyrd T-shirt and a black do-rag with a white cross positioned in the center of his forehead, so everyone would know his role in the proceedings.

The groom, at least, was dressed appropriately. A tuxedo would be out of place in the barn, but he did have on a nice black suit. He had a baby face and a new haircut, and he looked incredibly nervous. Not like he was about to run, but still . . . nervous. If he had any brains at all, she thought, he'd rabbit.

Evidently he was brainless.

Normally at this point in the ceremony Jaclyn was with the wedding party, making certain that everyone entered the aisle at the appropriate time, that they walked at the proper pace and were spaced correctly. However, the bride's aunt, who hadn't been at all happy that the groom's mother had hired Premier, had insisted that was her job, and she didn't need any help. Wouldn't accept any help was more like it. Still, it was Jaclyn's job to do what she could and resign herself to gracefully accept what she couldn't do. Some days that was easier than others.

Next, the bride's mother was seated, to a Garth Brooks tune of her own choosing.

Her dress was at least one size too small, and way too short. Spaghetti straps weren't what Jaclyn would have chosen for the occasion.

Her entrance was followed by the tulle-draped red wagon in which rode the bride's eleven-month-old daughter, who was dressed in flounces of white and had a baby blue bow taped to her almost-bald head. Who would have imagined that the something new and the something blue might come in the form of another man's baby?

That's not my concern, Jaclyn thought, and not for the first time. It wasn't her job to fix the couple's life, just their wedding ceremony.

The baby wasn't happy. One of her cousins, a sullen six-year-old boy, pulled the wagon, jerking it along. The baby entered the barn crying, her wails getting louder and louder until the wagon reached the end of the "aisle" and she saw her grandmother. "Mamamamama," she blubbered, holding out her chubby little arms. If the bride had thought the baby was going to placidly sit in the red wagon, looking cute, she was going to be disappointed. The baby wanted out of the wagon, and she wanted out now.

"Raquelle, hush," said the grandmother, then, when it became as obvious to her as it was to everyone else in the barn that the baby wasn't going to hush, she sighed and gave in, lifting the little girl out of the wagon, onto her lap.

The baby had a stripper name. At least, when she got older, she wouldn't have to go online to find out what it was, Jaclyn thought.

Next came the parade of bridesmaids and groomsmen. Garth was replaced by Shania Twain. Originally the bride had wanted to have the attendants line dance down the aisle; she'd gotten the idea from YouTube. In Jaclyn's experience, some things sounded good in theory, but rarely worked out as well as imagined. This was one of them, and thank goodness the bride had seen the wisdom of restraint in this case.

Except for a groomsman with a plug of tobacco in his cheek—Jaclyn wished she'd seen that earlier—and the occasional hip-wiggle aside, the procession went well.

The music stopped, then changed dramatically, swelling to fill the barn. Originally the bride had wanted her own country song, but Jaclyn had convinced her to walk down the aisle to Mendelssohn's "Wedding March." A touch of tradition in this very untraditional wedding was a very good thing.

Everyone stood and faced the aisle. The snow-white, ankle-length dress the bride wore was cut lower than Jaclyn would've suggested—the bride's philosophy was *If you have it, flaunt it*—and was a size too small through the hips. Jaclyn's sewing kit was in her purse. She prayed there wouldn't be a need for it today, but there was a definite danger of split seams. The hair, another job for the aunt who wanted no help but needed it desperately, was big. *Big* big. Bimbo big. But thanks to a makeover Jaclyn had recommended, the bride's makeup was tasteful, and the bouquet Bishop had fashioned was elegant and appropriate. The good helped to temper the bad, and Jaclyn supposed she had to be grateful for that.

After the bride was past them, Bishop leaned in and whispered, "They're not cousins, are they?" She didn't even dignify that with an answer. As they sat, Bishop added, "It must be true love."

Or temporary insanity.

Eric's shoulders were shaking from suppressed laughter.

The ceremony itself proceeded without incident. For her own peace of mind, Jaclyn spent the entire time leaning slightly away from Eric, trying not to touch him, but he was so blasted big he took up more than his allotted space.

Finally the unconventional minister said, "You can kiss her now," and then, as the newlywed couple turned to face their guests, he added, in a booming voice, "Now, let's eat! There's plenty of good vittles waiting for us outside."

"Vittles," Bishop repeated, his pronunciation precise and clipped. "Goody."

Chapter Twenty-four

The sun had gone down and the fierce heat of the day was abating, but the barbecue wedding reception party was still going strong. Beer was flowing—both in and out, judging by the number of trips people were making to the two portable toilets that had been discreetly located behind the barn. To Jaclyn's surprise, the party stayed within semi-acceptable limits, which meant that so far there hadn't been any fistfights and no one had pulled a knife on someone else.

Unfortunately, the bride and groom

showed no sign of going anywhere, and until they left, neither could Jaclyn. Neither the bride's mother nor her aunt had shown any interest in overseeing that part of the night. If the happy couple was in a hurry to start their honeymoon, it didn't show. The groom had shed his suit coat and tie, unbuttoned his top shirt button, and rolled up his sleeves so he could better enjoy the dancing. The bride and all of her bridesmaids had disappeared into the barn, reappearing about half an hour later to also join in the dancing, with all of them having changed into short, flirty dresses. A couple of them—okay, *several* of them—went past "flirty" straight into "slutty" territory, but at this point it wasn't Jaclyn's business if the bridesmaids drummed up some extra money on the side.

The live band was comprised of five middle-aged men, dressed in jeans and T-shirts, who weren't bad musicians. That wasn't to say they were good, exactly, but they did okay. They had a surprisingly extensive repertoire, ranging from classic rock to a lot of the more popular country tunes of today, all of which the crowd danced to with more enthusiasm than skill, but no one seemed to care if they could dance or not. Having fun was the point.

A huge tent had been erected, with a roughly built "stage" at one end, and at the other end were long folding tables laden with pretty much the same menu that had graced the reception the night before, and set off to the side were coolers filled with long-neck bottles of beer. Folding card tables and plastic lawn chairs had been arranged under the tent's canopy; Jaclyn had done her best here, covering the card tables with picnic-style tablecloths and arranging different-colored jugs filled with daisies in the center of each table. As the twilight deepened and the colored Christmas lights that outlined the tent were turned on, she had to admit the effect, though rustic, did have a certain free-spirited charm. Battery-operated votive candles flickered on the tables. Though real candles had grace, at least these lights wouldn't set the tent on fire if a table was knocked over, which, considering the amount of beer being consumed, became more and more likely as the party wore on.

Bishop was not only still there, he'd thrown himself into the party spirit. First he'd enticed the groom's mother—her name was Evelyn—into indulging in a beer, which had helped her relax enough that she'd actually smiled, for the first time that day. After half of another beer Bishop began teasing her about dancing with him, trying to entice her onto the dance floor, which was nothing more than rough wood planking laid in place on the ground and an equally rough frame nailed in place around the boards to keep them from drifting apart.

"Oh, I couldn't do that!" she exclaimed, a look of shock on her face.

"Sure you can," Bishop cajoled. "I'll teach you how to line dance."

"What's line dancing?"

"It isn't shaking your booty, it's more like the dancing people did on *Pride and Prejudice.* People stand side by side and do the steps—"

"But I don't know any of the steps." Her cheeks were flushed, and she darted a nervous but vaguely longing glance toward the dance floor.

By now Bishop had her by both hands, urging her to her feet. "It's easy to learn, I'll show you. C'mon, it'll be fun!"

Jaclyn watched, smiling. Bless Bishop,

not only for staying, but for paying attention to the poor woman and actually having her laughing now. She might never be happy with her son's choice of wife, the marriage might not last past next week, but she wouldn't look back and remember the wedding with total misery.

Bishop positioned them off to the side so they wouldn't interfere with the other dancers, who were whirling and gyrating, and began walking his partner through the steps. After the third pass-through, she began to get the hang of it, remembering when to clap, sometimes remembering when to kick. She was laughing, her cheeks flushed, her eyes bright.

The band wasn't slow. They saw what was going on, and swung into Brooks and Dunn. "Boot Scootin' Boogie" began blaring from the speakers. A couple of women squealed, and several of them hurried to align themselves with Bishop and Evelyn, stomping and scootin' and clapping. Bishop was laughing, his usual sardonic expression completely missing in action, and Evelyn was laughing in return whenever she missed a step.

"Thank you," the groom said, coming up

beside Jaclyn and handing her a cold, frosty bottle of beer.

Surprised, she automatically took the beer. "For what?"

He was a little sweaty from his own efforts on the dance floor, his hair falling forward onto his forehead, his eyes sparkling and his color high. He nodded toward his mother. "For making Mom laugh."

So he wasn't completely oblivious to the turmoil he was putting his family through, as she'd thought. If he was going into this marriage with his eyes open, he might actually have a chance to pull it off, though she was fairly certain that would mean separating his bride from her current crowd of friends. On the other hand, he might fit in with that crowd better than she thought, in which case Evelyn probably had some sleepless nights filled with worry in her future. You just never knew with people. And because you didn't know, because she couldn't fix things even if she did know, Jaclyn smiled and took a sip of the beer. "Don't thank me, at any rate. Thank Bishop. I had no idea he even knew what line dancing was."

"Who is he? Your boyfriend? I thought the cop was."

He didn't seem upset at the idea that people he didn't know were at his wedding, drinking and eating. "No, Bishop is the florist who did your flowers. He usually leaves as soon as he has everything in place, but today he decided to stick around. I'm sorry, I should have asked permission." The fact that she hadn't, that the idea hadn't even occurred to her, was a testament to how off-balance the whole day had been for her.

He waved her apology away. "That's fine. Doesn't matter to me. So the cop's your boyfriend?"

She opened her mouth to deny that, too, then realized that if she did, she had no ready explanation for Eric's presence. She could either explain the whole complicated series of events, which she didn't want to do, or she could let everyone think she habitually invited friends to the weddings she oversaw, which was in most ways worse than telling the truth. But if she said he was on duty—he *was*, wasn't he?—she ran the risk of half the guests bolting, and ruining the party. Evidently they had all decided he was there only because he was dating her, and for some reason that made him less threatening. "Kind of," she finally said, lamely.

"Thought so." The groom clinked his bottle with hers, winked, and wandered away in search of his new wife.

Jaclyn looked at the bottle of beer in her hand. She should set it down; she wasn't much of a drinker, and she never drank anything alcoholic when she was on a job. The problem with this job was that she was more bystander than organizer, she'd already done everything she could do short of getting the bride and groom in a car— please, God, *soon*—and, damn it, she was hot and thirsty and the beer was cold and wet. She wasn't crazy about beer, but what the hell. She tilted the bottle and drank some more.

She had almost finished the beer when an arm suddenly clamped around her waist and she looked up, startled, into Mullet Head's smiling face. "C'mon, sweet thing, let's dance!" And he began dragging her toward the dance floor.

Eric had been keeping his distance, more out of respect for the fact that Jaclyn was working than for any other reason, but he'd positioned himself, at the back of the tent close to the tables of food, where he could keep an eye on her. The location had turned out to be doubly advantageous. He'd had beer and barbecue pressed on him; he'd refused the beer and taken the barbecue, along with sides of potato salad and cole slaw. There were a few soft drinks and juices available, for the kids, so he drank a soft drink and ignored how good an icy beer would taste. The barbecue was damn good. The minister said it was because he set an open can of beer inside the barbecue grill and then kept the grill closed while the meat cooked; supposedly the hot beer added moisture to the meat and made it tender. Maybe there was truth to that, because the meat was outstanding.

If there was any public place where Jaclyn was safe, this was probably it. For one thing, very few people knew where she was. The other three women who worked at Premier did. Obviously Bishop Delaney had known where she'd be, which was a weak link he didn't like even though he didn't think Delaney had anything to do with either Carrie Edwards's murder or the attempt on Jaclyn's life. Eric had come to appreciate how linked the business of putting on a wedding was, with the same people running into each other again and again. Event planners had their favorite vendors that they recommended, in case the client didn't already have someone in mind. If Delaney mentioned to someone where he'd be, and who was directing, that someone could easily tell someone else and word could get to the wrong person.

But this place wasn't easy to find. The barn wasn't visible from the road. It was on private property, and there was only that one farm trail leading in. If he hadn't had Jaclyn's schedule and paperwork, and a GPS, he might not have found it himself.

Last but not least, he thought Jaclyn was fairly safe here because most of the people around her weren't the type to take kindly to someone being shot in their midst, and disrupting their fun. If all the vehicles here were searched, he was certain at least three quarters of them would have firearms in them. The pickup trucks had shotguns and rifles easily visible in rear window brackets; the cars would have pistols tucked in consoles and glove compartments, or under the seats. The shotguns and rifles were legal, and in any case all these cars were on private property. When he'd been in uniform, if he'd stopped any of these people for a traffic violation, a fair number of them would have been arrested on the spot.

He could make a phone call and have his people swarming over this field. A raid would probably result in that same fair number being hauled in on outstanding warrants, but hell, they hadn't broken any laws that he'd seen, and sometimes a cop had to make a judgment call. Most of the warrants would be on relatively minor stuff—"relative" being the operative word—and there was a lot worse going on out there that law enforcement could be spending its budget and man-hours on. He was cool with that.

Then he saw the skinny guy from the night before, the one with the worst mullet in the history of mullets, drag Jaclyn toward the dance floor, despite her protests and attempts to pull free, and he *wasn't* cool with that—not by a long shot.

He found himself stalking toward the asshole, and the expression on his face may have been a tad unfriendly, because even the people in this crowd took one look and moved out of his way. If he knew anything at all about Jaclyn, it was that she'd go out of her way to keep from causing a scene, unless she was tearing a strip off his own ass, which seemed to supersede everything else—so even though she was protesting she was trying to be quiet about it, trying not to be obvious that she was struggling with the guy, and that made him even angrier because it put her at a disadvantage.

Because she was pulling back, and because he himself was moving pretty fast, he caught up with them just as the jerk dragged her onto the dance floor. He stepped up on the planks and caught the guy by the shoulder; he didn't throw him to the side—he could have, but for Jaclyn's sake he tried not to create a scene. Instead he merely clamped down, digging his fingers into the shoulder joint and pulling him to a halt.

"I told you yesterday, she's with me," he growled.

The guy started to snarl something smart-ass in reply, then evidently thought better of it. Maybe he remembered he was dealing with a cop, or maybe the look on Eric's face was enough to dissuade him.

"I just want to dance with her," he mumbled sulkily.

"Well, she doesn't want to dance with you."

"You didn't have to—"

"Son, don't make me shoot your ass," Eric advised.

"You wouldn't—"

"Yeah," he said matter-of-factly. "I would. The paperwork would be a bitch, but it'd be worth it." He was lying. Maybe. He wasn't big on cops who threw their armed weight around, but he'd seen red when this asshole jerk put his hands on Jaclyn and started dragging her around. *Uh-oh.* Jaclyn. He hadn't looked at her since intercepting her and lover boy, and now he didn't dare glance at her to see how she was taking this. Probably she was embarrassed that he'd caused a scene.

Tough shit.

"Fuck it," the guy snarled. "She ain't worth it." He spun on his heel and pushed his way through the crowd, which had begun milling around watching them.

"I beg to differ," Eric said to his back, then braced himself for the ass-chewing he was probably about to receive.

Instead he found Jaclyn standing there visibly trembling, her face white, and without thinking he eased her into his arms. "It's okay," he said, lowering his face to her hair and inhaling the scent of it. With a sudden little jerky movement she burrowed closer, as if she wanted to completely hide herself. She stood probably five-ten in her heels, but she felt fragile in his arms, her slender body shaking against him. Maybe terrified was too strong a word to use, but she'd definitely been frightened, and that made him angry all over again.

"I'm sorry," she said against his shoulder. Her arms had slid inside his jacket and she was gripping the back of his shirt so hard he wondered whether the seams might give way under the pressure.

"Don't be. It isn't your fault that idiot decided to be a jerk as well as an idiot." Soothingly he ran his hands up and down her back.

"I don't mean that." Her voice was muffled, but even with the band playing valiantly on, he heard her.

He figured he knew what she meant. She was apologizing for clinging to him, even though she'd been scared. He'd noticed she was a tad uptight about some things, and to her, letting him hold her after she'd said they were a no-go would be like reneging on a promise, or something.

Who cared that she was uptight. That just made it more fun when she did lose control, because it was so unexpected, like now. He hadn't been prepared for her to curve into him the way she had, so he was caught flat-footed by the hot magic that had flared between them from the very first time he'd seen her. The feel of her against him, the smell of her, was enough to make his head spin and a heavy ache settle in his groin.

Then he felt her begin to gather herself; he knew she was going to pull away, and that wasn't what he wanted. The way to get to Jaclyn, he thought suddenly, was to keep her off balance.

Before she could say anything, he caught one hand in his, put his free hand on her waist, and spun her around. "Let's dance," he said, grinning at her, and before she could recover he had them right in the middle of Bishop Delaney's line-dancing group.

Normally Eric would rather have a root canal than dance, but in his younger, bar-hopping days, when "wilder" had been much more than just his name, he'd done some turns around a dance floor because that was a good way to pull the chicks. Now he clamped his arm around Jaclyn's waist, keeping her in place, as Delaney let out a whoop of welcome and the band swung once more into "Boot Scootin' Boogie," which was far and away their most popular number of the night, which was why they'd already played it three times.

He saw her blue eyes, wide and startled, but he ignored the expression and said, "Just follow what I do."

Her expression changed, her head tilted, and he saw challenge enter those eyes. "Please," she said with dripping disdain, then she pulled her suit skirt even higher above her knees and began sliding and kicking with the best of them. His heart almost quit beating at the sight of those killer legs moving in the steps. She threw herself into the dance, swinging her hips, clapping, stomping, with the fluid movements of a showgirl—or someone who had spent her own time on a dance floor. Like most of the people there, she sang along. At one point she and the groom's mother deliberately did a hip bump that wasn't part of the dance, both of them laughing as they got back in rhythm. Eric reeled her back in close to him, holding her so they moved in rhythm. Her eyes sparkled as she grinned up at him, and all he could think was: God bless beer, and God bless Brooks and Dunn.

The song ended and without pause the band swung into a much slower number, designed to give the dancers a chance to catch their breaths. Eric knew an opportunity when he saw it and he simply tugged her close to him, melding them together from knee to shoulder, and began swaying with her.

Being Jaclyn, of course, she tried to ignore the obvious, which was poking her in the belly. "You can dance, Detective," she said breathlessly.

He slid his leg between hers as they turned, his hand moving down to her hip to guide her action, which just so happened to all but grind them together. "So can you, Ms. Wilde. Drinking beer and line dancing ... does your mother know the things you got up to in college?"

"Some of them," she said, her smile and eyes still sparkling.

"Want to whisper them in my ear?"

"Not on your life."

He smiled and kept moving. She moved with him, fluidly, her legs sliding along his, her hips cradling his. Even through her suit jacket he thought he could feel the hard points of her nipples. He could definitely feel the heat rising from their bodies, smell the heightened sweetness the dancing had brought to her overwarm skin. He wondered how he could get her alone, because if he did, he was going to be inside her before she started thinking again. Just five minutes, he thought, pressing his forehead to hers. In five minutes he could have her biting his shirt to keep from screaming. He'd much rather be naked and have her biting *him,* but he'd take what he could get, so long as it involved making love to her again.

Abruptly the song was interrupted by some yelling and cheering, and they jerked apart in time to watch a full-package, customized pickup truck bumping along the farm trail, decorated with shaving cream, white shoe polish, dirty sayings, and trailing a jangling line of tin cans. Jaclyn's mouth fell open, and she blinked at the departing truck. "They left without me," she blurted.

Eric stared at her. "You were going with them?" he asked warily.

"No! I'm supposed to— It's part of my job . . ." Her voice trailed off and she waved her hand, then screwed her eyes shut. "I'm supposed to make sure they get off okay."

"I think they can handle that part themselves. Damn, this wedding planning stuff was beginning to sound kinky."

She laughed, the sound a little uneven, but it was still a laugh. "You know what I mean. I'm supposed to organize things, make sure the bride doesn't forget anything—though I guess, of all the weddings Premier has done, this one has gone the *least* according to schedule, so I shouldn't have been surprised."

Delaney swooped up beside them, planted a kiss on her cheek. "They sneaked off," he said in a comforting tone. "Evelyn didn't know they were leaving, either, and now she's pissed at her son all over again. I'm going to get her to dance some more, get her mind on other things. You've had a full day, girlfriend; why don't you go home and get some sleep? One more big deal tomorrow, then this insane marathon is finished."

That sounded like a good plan to Eric. Before she could come up with any reason why she should stay, he had her walking toward her rental car. "I'll follow you to the hotel, make sure you aren't followed." He thought of that sentence, grinned at her. "By anyone else, that is."

She gave him a rueful smile in return. Taking her car keys from an inside pocket of her jacket, she retrieved her purse from the trunk. Eric didn't wait for her to tell him it wasn't necessary for him to follow her; he was already striding away.

Jaclyn watched the headlights of Eric's car following her all the way back to Atlanta. She was so distracted that she almost took a wrong turn, heading toward her own town house, but she caught herself just in time and continued on into Atlanta.

She couldn't seem to collect her thoughts.

Nothing about the wedding or the entire day had gone the way she'd planned. The wedding, in all its unconventional, laugh-worthy glory, had turned out to be a lot of unexpected fun. Bishop had revealed a rowdy side of himself she hadn't known ex-isted, as well as a deep kindness. The wed-ding guests, many of whom she wouldn't be surprised to see on wanted posters in the post office, had been remarkably well-behaved. She'd been frightened by a rotten-toothed cretin who looked as if he'd had things on his mind other than danc-ing. And she'd been rescued by Eric, who could dance as if . . . as if . . . okay, as if he'd spent a lot of time in singles bars, picking up women. His dancing wasn't pro-fessional quality, but he was good, good enough that she'd been goaded into show-ing off for him because she knew she wasn't half bad herself. Then the band had gone into that slow number, and he'd al-most been making love to her right there on the dance floor, not that anyone had no-ticed. She hoped not, anyway.

But, God, it had been exciting, being in his arms that way, rubbing and swaying against him, feeling his erection prodding her and watching his gaze turn heavy and intent. Every move had heightened her own arousal, until she'd felt as if she'd come if he moved against her just one more time. If the happy couple hadn't surprised her by sneaking off . . . who knew what might have happened?

Now, deprived of his body against hers, she throbbed with a frustrated ache that made her press her legs together trying to contain the feeling. She should never have danced with him. She should never have had that beer.

She couldn't blame it on the beer, though, not just one beer. She should have had two. Then she'd have a viable excuse.

She turned in at the extended-stay hotel, parked in one of the two slots outside the unit he'd booked for her. As she stepped up on the sidewalk he pulled in beside her, got out of the car.

Jaclyn swallowed, tried to make herself say the words that would send him away. Silently he came to her, took the key card from her hand.

They made it inside. At least they did that. She flipped one of the light switches as they came through the door, and a lamp

came on. As soon as the door closed behind them, though, he had his arms around
her and his mouth on hers, and he used his
big body to crowd her backward toward
the separate bedroom—and she let him.
She not only let him, she had her arm
wound around his neck and one leg
hooked around his hips.

His hands were rough on her, pulling at
her clothes, tugging so sharply once that
she heard a seam rip. She didn't care. He
tipped her across the bed, came down on
top of her. A few frantic seconds later he
had her skirt up and her underwear off,
and one hard muscled thigh between
her legs, moving them apart. The thick,
hot slide of his penis into her made her
scream, then, because she was already
coming, the sound choked off as she buried her face against his shoulder. He said
her name, his voice guttural, then he
hooked her legs in the crooks of his arms
and began riding her hard and fast.

He didn't spend the night this time. She
woke a little after midnight, and he was
gone.

So, evidently, was her common sense.
She lay awake for a while, filled with an

aching sadness. Every time he touched her it was like being stroked by lightning, and everyone knew lightning destroyed. It was bright and beautiful, but it left behind nothing but scorched earth.

Chapter Twenty-five

"I don't think we should go to this wedding," Senator Dennison said uneasily as he and Fayre were getting dressed. "I mean, Sean is barely holding himself together, and with the funeral home visitation tonight—"

"Nonsense," Fayre said briskly. "If either of us had cared for Carrie it would be different, but there's no pretending, even to Sean, that we did. He knows we were prepared to welcome her for his sake, but that's all. Even though she's dead, I'm not going to let her turn me into a hypocrite."

Fayre's gaze was clear and unwavering. The senator sighed. Some people muddled through life, but not Fayre. She always knew who she was, what she was, and what she was doing—and apologized for none of it. She wasn't a cruel person, but neither was she a particularly comfortable one. He was human; he made mistakes; he blundered along, doing the best he could and always aware he fell short of her standards. What was really unnerving was the unspoken thought that she was always aware of that, too.

But what would he do without her? He loved Taite; he really did, because he could relax with her. She wasn't perfect, so he didn't have to be perfect with her. With her, he was the one in the driver's seat. With Fayre, he would always be the husband who rode on her coattails. It was her family money that gave them their social standing, her business sense that kept their income healthy, her connections that made things happen.

The worst part of it was, he loved her, too. Loved her, and feared her, and sometimes he couldn't tell which emotion was the strongest.

So, because Fayre said they had to go to this wedding, he finished knotting his tie.

Jaclyn was already at the church before she realized that, with all the recent chaos in her life, she could easily and legitimately have excused herself from the Sunday-afternoon wedding. No one at Premier would have batted an eye; they would have banded together and made sure that everything was taken care of. But of the six weddings they'd handled this week, this was the big one. Everyone who worked at Premier had had a hand in today's wedding and reception, and it was something they could truly be proud of. After all the stress of being investigated and shot at, after days of footballs, mullets, and family feuds, she needed to be involved in a wedding like this one. For her own sanity, she had to be here.

Besides, being at work was easier than being by herself, where she couldn't escape from her thoughts, and from the unavoidable realization that she was a coward.

No, being here was better. The last of the week's six weddings was the most traditional and definitely the most spectac-ular. Both families were big in business—one in music, the other in construction machinery, which was much duller than music but was evidently way more profit-able—so money hadn't been a concern. The bride's mother was from one of *the* prominent families in Georgia, which upped the social awareness of the event a hun-dred times over. By the time you put it all together this was the wedding to attend, and the place to be on this particular Sun-day afternoon.

The church was elegantly arrayed in white and pale peach roses, lilies, and so many flickering candles the overheads were almost an afterthought. A trio of vio-lins had provided the music—classical and without flaw—as the guests had ar-rived, and for the procession. Guests were appropriately dressed and so far had be-haved as they should, given the import of the day. Even the flower girl and ring-bearer were both adorable, and both had been well-behaved. There hadn't been a peep out of either of them: no tears, no temper tantrums, no throwing up in the aisle. She could count that as a definite success.

The bridesmaids were gorgeous in a shade of pale salmon that suited them all, and each and every one of them appeared to be happy to be a part of this wedding. If any one of them was suffering from always-a-bridesmaid-never-a-bride syndrome, she hid it well. Their gowns were simple and elegant, and Jaclyn had no doubt that, instead of being sold at a yard sale or even burned, these gowns would be worn again.

The bride had chosen a sweeping, traditional gown, and the groom's tux fit so well she knew it had been made for him—but then, this was the type of group where probably all of the groomsmen owned their own custom-fitted tuxes, as well. The church smelled of flowers and candles and a touch of perfume. Outside it was a hot day, but the air in the sanctuary was running at full blast so it was blessedly cool. For the moment, as the couple said their vows, all was right with the world.

Jaclyn glanced around the sanctuary and gave herself and her mother a mental pat on the back, and delivered a still and silent high-five to Diedra and Peach for a job well done. This was a day to remember for the couple at the center of it all, a perfect moment in time they would never forget. It was a relief to know that in a crazy world, such moments still existed.

She shouldn't have looked around, because her gaze fell on the tall, muscular man who was standing motionless at the back of the church, half-hidden in the shadows. He hadn't been invited, but the badge and weapon he wore were their own engraved invitations. When he arrived, the two fathers had gravely conferred with him, both of them had nodded, and Eric had gotten what he wanted, which was to be here. He'd stayed out of the way, but she'd never for one moment forgotten he was there, or been unable to pinpoint his location without even looking.

From the first second she'd seen him, her life had been turned on its head. In less than a week she'd completely overthrown her normally cautious nature to indulge in a one-night stand, then she'd been assaulted and fired by a client, *then* been suspected of and investigated for that client's murder—by the same man she'd had the one-night stand with. Oh, yes, she shouldn't forget that she'd also become the target of a would-be murderer, probably the same person who'd killed Carrie Edwards, and now her car had been impounded and she was living in a hotel because it wasn't safe for her to be in her own home. She'd always thought of herself as being strong, but she wasn't nearly strong enough to get through this ordeal alone. She was glad Eric was there. She might not be able to admit it to him, but she had to admit it to herself.

If Carrie hadn't been murdered, Jaclyn thought, she would *still* have him on her mind. She'd be waiting for him to call and ask her out, wondering if he really would. This week, she'd told him, after the craziness of six weddings in five days was behind her. If their first night together was any indication, they would have ended up back at her place, maybe starting something new and wonderful, maybe finding much more than what they had been looking for when they'd met. She'd heard that it happened that way sometimes, love coming out of the blue, surprising and unexpected, but she'd thought people exaggerated.

But, Carrie *had* gotten herself killed, and Jaclyn *had* been a suspect, and Eric *had* interrogated her and taken her clothes to check for bloodstains, and even if her blood and body did start to steam a little every time she looked at him, how could she ever get past that?

That was where the cowardice came in, because she wanted to get past it, yet was afraid to. She was tired of being alone, tired of watching other people find happiness while she stood on the sidelines, with only her mother and friends to keep her company. Not that she didn't appreciate how important they were to her life, but still, it wasn't always enough. She wanted to do what other women did, to reach out and grab for happiness. She had, once, only to watch it disintegrate right in front of her eyes. Had her marriage fallen apart because instead of completely committing herself to her husband she'd held part of herself back, waiting for him to let her down? Which, of course, he'd promptly done. Talk about a self-fulfilling prophecy.

But she was still holding herself back, still afraid to take that chance, to really love a man. The only man who had ever tempted her out of her comfort zone was Eric Wilder, and she'd let circumstance put him off limits—way, way off limits. And in spite of telling herself again and again that it didn't matter, she knew deep down that it did, more than she dared to admit.

Eric hadn't even tried to pass himself off as Jaclyn's date. Not only was it not necessary in this particular crowd, but she wasn't alone here; her mother and the other two women from Premier were here, and if he'd begun acting all lovey-dovey with Jaclyn he figured the three of them would try to take his head off. He'd have to do something about that, he thought as he did yet another narrow-eyed scan of the people in the church.

Did they think it was easy to do his job and keep an eye on her at the same time? He was doing double duty, literally, because Garvey could only occasionally put a uniformed officer on Jaclyn. Eric had to shower and shave, he had to eat and sleep, and, damn it, he had to work. Only Garvey's agreement that the person who'd tried to kill Jaclyn was almost surely the same one who'd killed Carrie had gotten the lieutenant to approve this duty, but if it hadn't been approved he damn well would've done it anyway, and they could kiss his ass. Probably Garvey knew that, and had asked Lieutenant Neille to do what he could.

After tomorrow, things should get easier. Franklin would be back to work in the morning. If necessary, Eric could hand over the Edwards case and take on guarding Jaclyn full time, though it would be better for continuity if he stayed on the case. But Franklin would be there, Garvey could go back to the sergeant's desk, and they'd get a little slack in the schedule.

Today though, today was hairy. Senator and Mrs. Dennison were here, guests at the wedding. Eric had no idea what would happen if the senator saw Jaclyn or she saw him, but so far neither had happened. The church was big, and Premier had all four women working, plus the Dennisons were seated at the front of the church. The enormous sanctuary had stadium seating so everyone had a good view of the altar, but people sitting at the front literally couldn't see what was happening at the very back of the church. He'd like to maneuver Jaclyn so she had a good look at the senator—without telling her what was going on—to see if actually seeing him again triggered enough memory for her to identify him. What he didn't want, under any circumstances, was for the senator to see her.

It helped that people on the Dennisons' level almost never paid attention to how things got done around them. They noticed only that the things were either done or not done.

At the moment Jaclyn was talking to the wedding party, arranging the line at the door of the reception hall, giving them last-minute instructions. Diedra and Peach were overseeing the layout of the food, and Madelyn was talking to the bandleader. She was safe enough for now, with the bulk of guests outside awaiting entrance.

The reception hall in Hopewell was very nice, yet this one in Buckhead almost put it to shame. The main hall was more than twice as large as the one where Carrie Edwards had been murdered. The parking lot was three times as big and surrounded by trees, providing precious shade on a hot summer day, and from the front entrance the hall looked like an antebellum mansion. If they'd been going for the look of Old South and Old Money, they had definitely achieved it, on both fronts. At the moment the room was decorated in the same colors that had been used at the wedding. It was all a little froufrou for his tastes. Personally he'd preferred yesterday's barbecue at the farm, a confession he wasn't about to share with Jaclyn. But this was nice. For froufrou.

The bride and groom were still being held hostage by the photographer, who insisted on snapping a jaw-dropping number of pictures, so there weren't many people in the reception hall yet. Soon the doors would be opened to the crowd for a well-mannered celebration. He could relax for a few minutes, at least until the doors opened. Nothing was going to happen right now, with no one other than the wedding party and a few workers present. He figured the Premier bunch would all be even busier once things moved into full swing, but now was the perfect time to do something about the hostile situation he found himself in.

Madelyn shook the bandleader's hand and turned away. She took a deep breath and surveyed the room with a critical but approving eye. Eric took his own deep breath—fortification was needed for this confrontation—and headed in her direction. As he got closer, she turned that critical eye on him, and there was nothing approving in it.

"Everything looks great," he said in an attempt at an icebreaker. "I like the orange."

Her chin came up, and ice filled her gaze. "It's peach and salmon, not *orange*," she said, as if he'd just presented her with a pile of dog shit on his outstretched palm.

Okay, so peach and salmon looked like shades of orange to him; so sue him. It was obvious beating around the bush wasn't going to get him anywhere, and just as obviously he was a failure at small talk, at least as far as Madelyn Wilde was concerned. Eric figured he might as well take the metaphorical bull by the conversational horns, or something like that. "I like your daughter," he said bluntly. "When this is all over, I'd like to take her out, see where it goes."

Her mouth fell open. "Are you out of your ever-lovin' mind?" she snapped.

"It's possible," he agreed, "but I don't think so."

Amusement was the last thing he wanted

to see on Madelyn's face, but there it was, chasing out the astonishment. "Do you really think Jaclyn will go out with you after the way you've treated her?"

Eric had to tamp down the rush of anger. It wouldn't help his case to go off on Jaclyn's mother. But at the same time . . . to hell with it. "The way I've treated her? I've busted my ass to make sure she was cleared and protected, and done the best I could in a bad situation. Because we dated once, I—"

Madelyn's head jerked back. "Dated? What're you talking about? Jaclyn would have told me if she'd dated you." The tone was very much the same she would have used if she was telling him her daughter would have told her if she had a fatal disease.

Probably Jaclyn had kept the news of their night together to herself because it hadn't really been a date, and because she wasn't the kiss-and-tell type—not that he could say that to Madelyn. "We'd just met," he explained. "But because I knew Jaclyn personally, I had to be even more objective with her than I would have with anyone else, or I'd have been jerked off the case faster than you can spit. We've been shorthanded, so I did what I had to do. That doesn't change how I feel. I'm interested in her—hell, I care about her—and when my partner gets back from vacation tomorrow, if I have to, I'll take myself off the Edwards case so I can keep an eye on Jaclyn full time until the killer is caught."

Was it his imagination or was there a subtle softening of Madelyn's eyes? She was easy to read, more open in her expressions than her daughter. "Will the Hopewell P.D. approve that particular duty?"

"If they don't I'll take my vacation and do it on my own time." And he would, too. He just hadn't realized it until the words left his mouth. Like it or not, Jaclyn had become important to him.

Maybe Madelyn saw that, because her mouth relaxed, though a touch of sadness filled her eyes. "All right," she said, then repeated it more firmly. "All right. I believe you. Go for it, young man, but I think you should know that Jaclyn has real trust issues."

A jolt of anger made Eric's spine stiffen, because too often, in his world, "trust issues" were directly related to physical abuse. "Her ex?" he growled.

Madelyn sighed and shook her head. "Nothing so dramatic, just a lifetime of dealing with her father. Maybe she'd have been better off if I'd divorced Jacky when Jaclyn was still a baby. I knew even then that, well, let's just say that Jacky Wilde is a walking emotional disaster. Not to himself—Jacky always looks after number one—but to everyone around him. All her life Jaclyn has been collecting broken promises from her father, and that's something that's hard for a child to get past even when she's all grown up. Then her own marriage fell apart so fast . . . She's afraid to trust herself, much less a man."

And in Jaclyn's eyes, he hadn't exactly proven that he trusted her, or that she could trust him. In fact, the opposite was true, not that he could have handled the situation any differently. Still, he felt as if he was on more solid ground now, because he not only understood exactly what he was up against, but maybe now he had someone on his side. He probably wouldn't have stood a chance if Madelyn disapproved of him, but with her understanding and support he at least wasn't going under for the third time.

As the photographer was finishing up, Jaclyn saw Eric talking to her mother and a stupid but powerful rush of panic made the blood roar in her ears. The only thing they could possibly have to talk about was her, which made her feel as exposed and vulnerable as if someone had walked in on her in the shower. Lovely. She'd feel a lot better about it if her mother continued to scowl at him, but even as she watched, Madelyn's expression changed, softened.

Great.

Then the doors were opened, and the guests began to file into the room. Instead of a sit-down dinner there was an impressive hot buffet, and round tables, each seating eight, were arranged around the glossy hardwood dance floor. The bride had suggested the more informal setup so her friends and family would be able to mingle, visit, have a good time. There was informal, and then there was so casual shoes weren't required. She couldn't help contrasting this reception with the one the day before, and an unwilling smile tugged at her lips. She had regaled the others with tales from *Hee Haw* Hell, as Bishop had named it, but she'd also had to admit that in the end she'd had a blast.

For a while Jaclyn was too busy with her duties to think about Eric Wilder . . . almost. Every time she turned around he was there, directly in her wake or just a few steps away, watching. His alertness worried her, made her wonder if he knew something he hadn't told her. He had a history of not telling her stuff.

She took a quick survey of the crowded room and had an unpleasant surprise. Movers and shakers stuck together, so she should have expected that she'd recognize two of Carrie's bridesmaids. If they were here—and that struck her as kind of cold, considering tonight was the funeral home visitation for Carrie—then how many other people in the room had been connected to Carrie? That gave her a chill, because likely Carrie's killer had been someone connected to her.

Suddenly she felt hideously exposed again, but this time in a very real, imminent-danger kind of way. Her head kept swiveling as she looked from face to face, until finally she thought she had to take a break or scream from the tension. The reception was proceeding well, people still filing in and offering congratulations to the bridal couple, and until it was time for the cake to be cut her duties were on hold. She grabbed a cup of punch, nonalcoholic, took a long sip, and retreated to a quiet nook where at least she didn't feel as if a gun was pointed at her back. All she wanted was a minute of solitude to get her nerves under control—

As if Eric would allow her that luxury.

He walked up, leaned against the wall beside her. "We need to talk," he said in a lowered voice.

How many times had he said some variation of that?

"Something's going on, isn't it?" she asked nervously.

"Yes."

She sucked in a quick, shallow breath. "Okay. What do you need me to do?"

"Just watch everyone as they come through the reception line. That's all. Tell me if anyone rings a bell."

She went pale. So she was right. The killer was here—at least, the person Eric thought was the killer was here, and what he thought was good enough for her to be scared.

"I can't stand here forever," she muttered some time later. "I really, really need to visit the ladies' room."

"Okay," he said, his expression unreadable, but Jaclyn thought he was disappointed. He'd hoped she would recognize someone—the gray-haired man, obviously— but the only people she'd definitely recognized were the two bridesmaids. She had carefully examined everyone, not just the gray-haired men, but no one had seemed familiar to her.

"I'm sorry," she said, wishing she'd been a better witness. More than anyone, she wished she'd been a better witness! "I know I'm no help."

"I wish you could make an identification," he said, "but I definitely don't want you to say you recognize someone when you don't. That would hurt the case, not help it. And sometimes, eliminating people is as important as including them, because that helps you know who's left."

That made sense. She didn't think he meant it, but it made sense.

She wound her way through the knots of wedding guests as she made her way out of the main ballroom. Long before she reached the doorway, he was following in her footsteps, watching.

And he saw her walk past Senator and Mrs. Dennison. Not close by them, but close enough that Mrs. Dennison saw her, recognized her as one of the event planners. It figured that she would notice things like that. The senator's back was turned; he didn't see Jaclyn and she didn't see him. Eric held his breath, hoping Jaclyn made it past without being spotted, because while he'd wanted her to see the senator he sure as hell didn't want the senator to see her, especially this close to him.

Mrs. Dennison gave a quick smile, reached out, and caught Jaclyn's arm, stopping her. Eric picked up his pace, all but shoving his way through the crowd. Senator Dennison continued talking to some other man and for a second Eric thought Jaclyn would make it through, but then Mrs. Dennison reached for her husband's arm, getting his attention so she could introduce the two.

Eric wasn't close enough to hear what was said, but he was close enough to see the senator lose every bit of color in his face. And Jaclyn was smiling, her calm, gracious manner never revealing that she was dying to pee. She even chatted for a few minutes, before excusing herself and continuing on toward the bathroom.

Senator Dennison stared after her with an expression gone as cold and blank as a statue's.

Since Friday night's failed attempt, it had been impossible to find another opportunity. Jaclyn hadn't been back to her town house; she was staying somewhere else, and locating her during the day so she could be followed hadn't worked out. No one seemed to know what event she was working; either that, or no one was saying. But now here she was, and following her from here would be easy.

In a way, it might make sense to wait a while longer before trying again. Locating her was the hard part. Just find out where she was staying, then let things rest. Eventually the cop would let his guard down; he'd have to leave Jaclyn on her own at some point. Eventually she'd go home. But what if Jaclyn remembered what she'd seen Wednesday afternoon before that happened? What if something—a visual, a scent, a dream—jogged her memory? The cops might try hypnosis or something, and then it was over. Done and done. Once the cat was out of the bag, it couldn't be put back in.

Today. Like it or not, complications or not, Jaclyn Wilde had to die today.

Chapter Twenty-six

Taite sat in the borrowed car, which was in the shade of a tree across the street from the huge church and reception hall. The businesses in the redbrick building behind her were all closed on a Sunday afternoon, so she had the parking lot to herself.

She kept her eyes on the building across the street, waiting and watching. Discovering that Jaclyn Wilde would be there hadn't been nearly as difficult as finding her Friday night. This was a big wedding, perhaps the wedding of the summer now that Carrie's had been called off. She supposed you could say the wedding had been called off, given that the bride had been killed. Anyway, a lot of the people who came into the boutique talked about their plans as they shopped, which was how she'd found out Premier was handling this wedding, and that meant Jaclyn would be there.

For the first time since this had all started, Taite was worried. Since yesterday morning, the Hopewell cops had been calling her again. Detective Wilder had left three messages, and the other one, Sergeant Garvey, had left one. Why were the cops calling her again? They couldn't know about Friday night. There was no way.

Was there? How could there be? She'd been so careful. But for the first time, a trickle of uncertainty made her doubt herself and her plans. *Damn* Douglas and his fucking fund-raiser, his airtight alibi. His Friday-night appearance had been so public, he couldn't offer her an alibi when she needed one. She'd provided him with one when he'd screwed up and was in a total panic, but when she needed him, was he able to reciprocate? Of course not. And this was all because of his stupidity, his lack of control. Douglas had his weaknesses—every man did. But she'd had no idea he could be so violent when pushed to the edge. If he'd only told her what was going on, she could have helped him. They could have come up with a plan, a good plan. Instead she was having to act spontaneously, and that was always dangerous.

Taite hadn't been home since yesterday afternoon, and she'd turned off her cell phone hours ago, tired of hearing it ring and seeing the same numbers come up on the display. If the cops kept calling they'd eventually just show up on her doorstep, and she couldn't be there when that happened. She needed time to construct an unshakable out-of-town timeline before she returned any of the official calls. She needed to psych herself up to present a completely provable case. A few phone calls, a few favors called in . . . she could make it work. Chicago, maybe. She made several trips a year to the city, and there were people there who owed her. The big thing was, she would have had to drive, because obviously her name couldn't appear on a passenger list anywhere, which meant she had to come up with a good reason for driving.

Or Jaclyn Wilde had to die. Without her, anything they had against Doug would just fall apart. Taite had had his car cleaned, because he'd been stupid enough to park at the reception hall, stupid enough to let himself be seen, stupid enough to act without thinking and risk everything she'd worked so hard to build. Being his mistress had worked out better than she'd ever thought it would. She had his balls in the palm of her hand, and they both knew it. The fool had actually fallen in love with her, gave her everything she wanted, and now she was in danger of losing everything. But Taite thought she'd covered his tracks fairly well. Unless Jaclyn could identify him, no judge would risk making an enemy of a future U.S. senator by issuing a search warrant without overwhelming cause.

For Taite, the solution was very simple. Eliminate Jaclyn, the only person who could put Doug at the reception hall when Carrie had been killed, and her very nice life could go on without disruption.

She wished she could simply have hired someone to do the job, put a layer of deniability between herself and the act, but it wasn't as if she had "hit man" on her speed dial. Besides, what assurance would she have that she could trust a hit man? Anyone who chose that line of work was automatically untrustworthy. Every so often a murder-for-hire would be reported in the news, and invariably it was some undercover cop a nitwit had tried to hire. She was determined not to be that nitwit. Besides, if she went that route she'd have to get rid of the hit man, too, once the job was done, and then she'd be back to square one. If you want something done right, you have to do it yourself.

She was coldly furious with Doug; this was all his fault. He'd let Carrie goad him, let her trigger a momentous loss of temper. Kabob skewers, for God's sake. If he'd wanted to get rid of Carrie it could've been done in a hundred different ways, all of them less ridiculous. Most of them wouldn't have led right back to him. She could have helped him plan a method of disposal that would leave people wondering where Carrie had gone. She could've been another runaway bride, and eventually people would have stopped looking. It wasn't as if anyone would actually miss Carrie, except maybe her parents, but if they had any brains at all it wouldn't take them long to realize how much nicer their lives were now that Carrie was gone. God, she'd been such a bitch. Taite had always been amazed that Carrie had been able to turn on the sugar and fool people whenever she wanted.

But instead of careful planning, Doug had lost his temper and now here they were: Taite was left cleaning up his mess so her own life wouldn't be ruined. Without Doug, her home would be taken away, her lifestyle would suffer. She wouldn't even have the dream that one day he'd leave his bitch of a wife and marry her.

He owed her. He owed her big-time. When this was done he was going to owe her a shitload of diamonds, and maybe a beach house. Make that *definitely* a beach house.

If she got good at this, maybe Mrs. Hoity-toity Dennison could be next. It was the time crunch that made the planning of Jaclyn's murder so difficult. Next time, she'd be able to plan properly.

Not that Fayre Dennison was the type to just up and disappear. Her murder would need very careful planning.

Douglas wasn't getting off scot-free. No, this was his mess and he had to help clean it up. Taite knew she couldn't very well drive all over town with no car tag, not after Friday night, and she didn't dare let anyone see her own car in the vicinity of Jaclyn's demise. So she was driving a borrowed car, one Doug had provided—one of Mrs. Dennison's vehicles, a BMW sedan. Taite thought that was a hoot. She almost wanted to be seen—well, the car, not her personally—so the high-and-mighty Mrs. Dennison could be grilled about her whereabouts this afternoon. Wouldn't it be cool if she didn't have an alibi? If the cops began to think that maybe Mrs. Dennison killed Carrie to keep her out of the family?

In fact, it might be a good thing if someone did take note of the car. Taite wore gloves, so she didn't have to worry about prints, and the hat and sunglasses made a decent disguise, at least from a distance. All she had to do was get off one good shot, then get the hell out of Dodge and ditch the car somewhere. It would eventually be found, but the important thing was there wouldn't be anything to link her to it.

It was early in the evening but still light

out—ah, summer—as the bride and groom made their getaway. Finally! Taite was getting a little cramped, sitting in the car for so long, and her hands and head were sweating beneath the gloves and hat. Soon after the bride and groom departed, wedding guests started climbing into their cars and making their getaways, car after car peeling out of the lot, heading in all directions. No one paid the car across the street any attention at all. Taite had made certain she was parked at the back of the lot, in the shade, so even if anyone glanced in her direction the car might look empty.

She even saw Doug and his bitch wife leave. Good. Now no one could place Mrs. Dennison at the church while Jaclyn Wilde was getting killed somewhere else. Now it would be Doug's word against his wife's, and the evidence would point to her. It struck Taite as a neat solution.

Finally, Jaclyn Wilde left by the side door. Twilight was deepening by then. She wasn't alone; she never was, damn it. There were two older women and a pretty black girl with her. They all hugged, and after a few words headed for separate parts of the parking lot. One of the women headed for a

Jag that looked just like Jaclyn's. Taite had wondered about that car when she'd seen it in the lot, had wondered if somehow Jaclyn's car had been repaired and returned so soon. It hadn't seemed likely, but the detail had jarred her. Nice to know there was a logical explanation.

Naturally, Detective Wilder was close by, following Jaclyn out to the parking lot. Taite was almost glad. The job she had to do would be easier if she could get Jaclyn alone, but he could go, too. She might as well get two birds with one stone, if she could. It would be best if she could concentrate on one at a time, Jaclyn first and then Wilder, but she didn't know what the night might bring. Besides, killing a cop wouldn't be so easy, and would rain all sorts of hell down on the scene, but she was prepared for anything. If she had the chance, she'd take it, just because he'd been such a pain in the ass.

"Where are you staying tonight, Jaclyn?" Taite whispered. She wondered if the wedding planner and the cop had come here in one car, wondered if that would make things easier or harder. It didn't really matter. From here on out she was going to have to play it by ear. When an opportunity presented itself, she'd make her move.

Jaclyn got into a Toyota, and Taite had to grin. Boy, wasn't that a comedown from the Jag? Detective Wilder continued walking, and now that the parking lot was mostly empty she could spot his car, at the far end of the lot. Separate cars, then. Probably just as well. Somehow, some way, she needed to get Jaclyn Wilde alone. A few seconds were all she needed.

Jaclyn said she just wanted to get back to her hotel room and fall into bed. Alone. Eric suspected she didn't *really* want to do that, but she thought it would be best that way. She was protecting herself from him, which annoyed the hell out of him but at least now he understood where her objections were coming from. He didn't intend to give up, though; they had something good. At the very least, they had something that had the potential to be very good, and eventually she'd admit it.

"I'll go straight to the hotel," she promised. "You don't have to follow me to the hotel and lock me in."

"Yeah, I kinda do."

She looked momentarily exasperated, but then she cast a glance over her shoulder at the church, and visibly shivered. "It's okay," he said gently. For now, anyway. Nothing could happen to her on his watch, because he couldn't live with himself if it did. Friday night's attempt had been too damn close, and the thought of how close she'd come to a bullet still sent his blood running cold.

She nodded tiredly, then unlocked her car and tossed her purse into the passenger seat. "I'll be right behind you," Eric said, and continued walking toward his car.

She had to wait on some traffic, so even though he had to walk farther, he was right behind her as she left the lot. She drove the speed limit, and stuck to the slow lane. He wondered if she did it to annoy him, and grinned at the thought. Everyone knew cops drove faster than the speed limit; it was kind of a job requirement.

Traffic was light, so as he followed her Eric had plenty of time to think, to consciously admit some things to himself. He wanted her. Not just for a night here and there, not for a date or two. She'd gotten under his skin in a big way, and he might as well not fight it. He wanted her, bad coffee, trust issues, and all. It had been a long time since he'd wanted anyone or anything this damn bad. He even liked the way she poked at him, like she was doing now with her overly cautious driving. If this was her normal mode of driving, she wouldn't have been paying a speeding ticket the first time they'd met.

His gaze was on her taillights, and his mind was definitely elsewhere, so the red light caught him off guard. He'd have been tucked right on her ass, otherwise. Jaclyn made it through on yellow. Was she trying to get away from him? Trying to annoy him? It wasn't like he didn't know where she was headed. Had she run through that light because she was driving as absent-mindedly as he was, and maybe for the same reason? Maybe she was thinking about last night, or last week, or the possibilities for tonight. Even better, maybe she was thinking about the possibilities for next week, or next year.

After checking oncoming traffic and finding none, Eric thought about going through the red instead of waiting for the light to change, but a woman in a tight exercise outfit made a quick turn and popped into the crosswalk directly in front of him, jogging, her ponytail dancing with each step. He made a disgusted sound in his throat. She had to be the slowest damn jogger he'd ever seen.

Headlights suddenly loomed behind him. A light-colored car, a BMW, flew past him on the left, blowing through the red light and almost taking out the jogger. The woman jumped back, directly in front of Eric's grill. She yelled at the car that had almost mowed her down, and then shot her middle finger toward the taillights.

Directly ahead the street shifted from four lanes to two, with turn lanes in between, and oncoming traffic began blaring horns at the Beamer. The Beamer swerved, then sharply pulled in right behind Jaclyn. Damn, that had been close.

And why take the chance of running the red light, and getting ahead of exactly one car? The payoff was way too small for the risk. Except—

"Shit!"

Eric popped the red light onto his dash, turned it on, and lowered his window to scream at the jogger, who was still standing in front of his car staring at the offending BMW. "Lady, get the fuck out of the way!"

The woman turned sharply, anger plain on her face. Maybe she'd been about to argue with him, maybe shoot him a bird, too, but she saw the flashing cop light and obeyed, lurching back onto the sidewalk. As he shot past her he saw her smug, vindicated expression as she sent a "gotcha" smile down the road.

Jaclyn and the other car were too far ahead of him. He could feel every foot that separated him from her, panic moving like shards of ice through his veins. If he were right, he couldn't get there in time. He knew it. He could see it happening in front of him, and there was nothing he could do about it. To make things even worse, as he shot through the intersection another car made a right turn in front of him, slowing him down even more. No one seemed to be registering the light yet; oncoming traffic wasn't moving to the side, and the asshole in front of him wasn't pulling off the road.

He grabbed his radio and began yelling into it, edging to the left as he tried to force a path past the car in front of him, who stubbornly refused to yield. No matter what, he thought, this asshole was going to get a ticket.

Jaclyn realized, too late, that she'd left Eric back at the red light. She slowed down a little so he could catch up with her after the light changed. He probably thought she'd left him behind on purpose, but she hadn't. Maybe he did turn her upside down and inside out, but she wasn't silly, and trying to evade him when he knew where she was going was worse than silly, it was downright stupid.

Because she was watching him in her rearview mirror, it was impossible to miss the speeding car that ran the red light. Instantly she saw the hazard, the car flying toward her, the road narrowing down to two lanes, the oncoming traffic. She flinched and speeded up, trying to give the car room to pull in behind her because there wasn't room on the shoulder for her to let it by, which she would have preferred doing. It was better to have stupid drivers ahead of her than behind her, anyway.

The car darted in behind her, then surged forward and hit her rear bumper.

The rental Toyota lurched, skidded sideways a little, regained its traction. Jaclyn
cried out, but knew to let the car's steering
correct itself. That's what the bells and
whistles were for. She wanted to fight the
steering wheel, but she knew better, and
sure enough the car straightened itself out.

What was wrong with the idiot behind
her? Her first thought was "drunk," and
then her heart skipped a beat. The last time
she'd thought a drunk driver was on the
road with her, that "drunk" had tried to kill
her. This wasn't the same car. Even though
every witness had remembered a different
color, they'd all remembered dark. This
car was light in color, kind of a tan. She
knew Eric would want her to try to make
out an emblem or a name, something by
which to identify the car, but as the car
rammed her again—harder this time, so
hard she was jostled and once more the
Toyota went skidding sideways—she gave
all her attention to the road. Thank God! In
the distance she saw the flash of light that
assured her Eric was coming.

The car behind her pulled into the now-
empty turn lane and speeded up to pull
alongside. Jaclyn turned her head, looked

at the other driver. Despite the wide-brimmed hat that shaded a large part of the driver's face, and despite the rapidly fading light, the headlights of the oncoming cars and the lights from the dash revealed a face she knew.

Taite Boyne, the maid of honor who had told Carrie to fuck off in such spectacular fashion. Her teeth were bared in a grotesque travesty of a smile. The passenger-side window was down, so Jaclyn also saw, very clearly, the pistol in Taite's hand. Instinctively Jaclyn hit the brakes.

The shot went wide, missing Jaclyn but shattering the driver's side window and the windshield. The car behind Jaclyn rear-ended her and sent the rental car up and onto the curb. The impact was incredible, rattling every bone in her body and throwing her forward against the seat belt, which jerked her back with a force that jarred her head as if she were being whipped back and forth on an unpredictable roller coaster. She held on tight, shaking and shaken by the gunshot and the jerking of the car. Her heart pounded, every muscle in her turning into a weak, trembling mush. The only thing that kept her from completely losing control was the fact that Eric was coming.

The car that had rear-ended her shuddered to a stop and the driver jumped out.

"You stupid bitch!" the driver screamed at Jaclyn, "what the fuck you doing?" He was scarlet in the face, shaking his fist at her as he advanced toward her car.

Ahead, Taite made a wide U-turn in the road. Panicked, Jaclyn turned her head and saw the light that signaled Eric would be here in seconds, but Taite was much closer, and seconds would be too late. She was a sitting duck; she had to get out of the damn car.

"Get down!" she shrieked at the angry man bearing down on her. "Gun!" As she screamed she fumbled for the release on the seat belt, trying to fight her way free, but the latch seemed to be jammed. The man glanced around, noticed the flashing light and the speeding car and the shattered windows, and with a curse he moved to the side of the road to duck around and behind his own car, flattening his body on the ground and covering his head with his hands.

Jaclyn threw an agonized glance at the

oncoming car. She couldn't get out; the seat belt held her pinned so tightly she could barely move. No, it wasn't the belt, it was her hands; they were shaking so violently she couldn't press the release. Three seconds.

She pushed the latch and the seat belt snapped away. Two.

She threw herself sideways, trying to reach the passenger door. She was too late, too late. One. Taite was almost there, almost even with the car.

And then Eric's car sliced by, light flashing, and instead of swerving around Taite, he rammed his car into hers, head-on.

Air bags had to be one of the best inventions ever, Eric thought foggily as he swam toward consciousness. Thanks to the impact his head swam, too. And, fuck, he hurt. He felt as if he'd been hit in the face with a baseball bat. He was going to feel like hell tomorrow. But he knew where he was, knew exactly what had happened.

He'd only been out a couple of seconds, because Jaclyn had just reached the car and was doing her best to open his door, frantically yanking on the door handle, screaming at him. Eric lifted his head. He could see just enough through the shattered windshield to tell that the front end of his car was smashed and twisted. The car might be totaled. Shit. The paperwork on this was going to take a week and a half.

"Eric!" Jaclyn was shrieking. Her voice sounded as if it came from the bottom of a well, distant and echoing, but it rapidly became much clearer.

"What?" he finally managed to say, and he sounded grumpy even to himself. Jesus. The interior of the car was full of the white air-bag propellant that looked like smoke, as if the car was on fire, but he knew it wasn't. Cars didn't burn as easily in real life as they did on television.

"Are you crazy?" Jaclyn yelled as she continued jerking on the door. She looked to her right. "Come over here and help, you asshole!" she bellowed.

"Maybe," he said, in answer to her question. "Just a little." Okay, things were snapping back into place. Damn, that had been some impact.

He'd radioed in as he chased the car that had run the red light, and patrol cars were beginning to arrive on the scene, boxing the driver in—not that her car was drivable. She had an air bag of her own—too bad—but from what he could see she hadn't moved yet. Other sirens, far away but getting closer, were added to the mix.

"Taite Boyne?" he asked.

Jaclyn nodded her head. "I saw her when she tried to shoot me—this time." Tears shone in her eyes as she struggled with the door, and Eric pushed away the deflated air bag and reached out a hand. He caught one of Jaclyn's hands, and she let him hold on. "Don't cry, sweetheart. She can't try to hurt you anymore. It's over."

Jaclyn swiped the back of a hand across her face and yanked the other hand away from his. "That's not why I'm crying, you . . . you stupid, moronic *idiot*!"

Oh. She was crying for him. That was okay, then. "I'm fine," he said, trying not to smile because he knew her well enough to know she wouldn't like it.

Her blue eyes flashed. Tears hadn't dampened her anger. "You rammed your car into hers. You could've been killed!"

She looked so pale, mascara was running down her cheeks, and even though he was no longer touching her he could see the way she was shaking.

"Police issue. They're built like tanks," he explained, but she didn't look mollified.

She kept jerking at the door, and some guy—must have been the one she called an asshole—came up and started jerking on it, too. Eric sighed and unlocked it—they could have reached through the broken window and unlocked it themselves, if they'd thought of it—and the guy managed to tug the door open far enough that Eric could unclip his seat belt and squeeze out. He was only a little bit unsteady. Okay, maybe more than a little, but even as he stood there he could feel the world steadying itself again. Blood dripped down his face, his shirt, from both his nose and a cut on his forehead. His nose felt numb; he hoped it wasn't broken, but if it was, it wouldn't be the first time. No, he was breathing through it semi-okay, even though it was bleeding.

Jaclyn wrapped both arms around him, lending him her support, and even though he no longer needed it he didn't think it was all that important to share that information with her right now. Holding on to her was nice.

She leaned into him, held on, and he watched as the Atlanta P.D. assisted Taite from her car. He'd radioed that she was armed, and they were treating her as armed and dangerous, which she was, which meant they weren't being very solicitous of her. Her nose was bleeding, too, and he felt a rush of satisfaction because, unless he missed his guess, her nose *was* broken. He hoped it healed crooked.

He'd have liked to coldcock the bitch, but he kept his distance. For one, he wasn't about to offer her the chance for a civil lawsuit, and it was more important to stay with Jaclyn. And two, if he decked her, the paperwork would damn near kill him. The car was going to be bad enough.

Taite wiped the blood from her nose, squared her shoulders even though her arms were being wrenched behind her back, and called to him, "I want to make a deal! I can give him to you. I can give you the man who killed Carrie!"

"Of course you can," Eric said softly, and smiled.

Eric couldn't help but smile, even though it made his face hurt. This time around, Senator Dennison was on *his* turf. Earlier in the day a warrant had been issued for the car Dennison had been driving the day he'd killed Carrie Edwards, and Taite Boyne was singing like a birdie. She still thought she could cut a deal and get off with probation, but she'd soon be disabused of that notion. With the blood evidence in the car, the district attorney didn't really need her testimony to make the case.

The senator fidgeted in the uncomfortable chair in the interview room. He hadn't asked for a lawyer yet, but he would soon. Eric was doing his best to make sure the senator was comfortable, for the time being. Maybe he'd say something that would make this process easier.

He gave a sigh and shook his head. "I guess I can kind of understand how it happened," he said in a sympathetic tone. "From everything I've heard, Carrie Edwards could be hard to get along with."

"Yes," Dennison said nervously. "She was." He glanced toward the closed door. "Is my wife out there? She really shouldn't be here, but when you called she insisted . . ."

"Sergeant Garvey is taking care of your wife, Senator. She's in good hands." Poor woman. She was about to get the shock of her life. She might've suspected that the dirtbag she was married to was unfaithful, but Eric doubted she'd had a clue that he was capable of murder. On the other hand, she was also a strong woman, and this wouldn't break her. "What did Carrie do? You aren't the type of man who commits cold-blooded murder."

"No, of course not!" the senator said, jerking back.

"She had to have done something, something that made you so mad you lost your head for a minute."

The senator paled. "I don't have any idea what you're talking about."

"Well, I'm just going by what Ms. Boyne has told us, so far, but of course she wasn't there. You were."

Eric hadn't thought it was possible for Dennison to get any whiter, but he did. "I don't know what Taite's told you, but she's just as unstable as her friend. You can't believe a word she says."

No, but they could definitely believe the smears of blood that had been found in the senator's car. Someone had cleaned that car well, but not well enough, because Taite hadn't told them to use bleach—and the tests could even work around bleach. It was harder, but it was possible. A detailer wouldn't have used bleach on expensive leather, anyway.

"Come on, Senator," he said softly. "What did she do? Was it blackmail? Did she keep pushing and pushing, wanting more and more?"

The senator must've seen the certainty on Eric's face, because the next words brought the interview to an end. "I want my lawyer."

Eric sighed and nodded. "I'll have someone bring you a phone." It would have been nice to get a confession, but it wasn't necessary. They had the evidence, and they had Taite's confession. Other people might have started singing, but Dennison was a politician. He knew all about lawyering up. This was something else that was rarely as easy as it was on television.

Eric left Dennison in the interview room to stew, while he waited for a phone to call his lawyer. He caught sight of Garvey talking to a very distraught Fayre Dennison. He hated that she'd be hurt by all of this. He doubted she was one of those stand-by-your-man types—she was too tough, too realistic—but it would hurt her.

Eric walked toward them, and as he approached Mrs. Dennison's head snapped around and she stared at his battered face. "Is this really true?"

He nodded once, and that was enough. Mrs. Dennison was going through so many emotions, and they all showed clearly on her face: disbelief, hurt, acceptance, and then rage. She'd loved her husband, once, maybe still did, but that strong streak of realism kicked in fast.

"Did you know?" he asked.

"That he'd killed Carrie? No. I'm still not sure I believe he could do such a thing." She somehow managed to remain regal, put together in spite of her pain. "About Taite . . . I knew there was someone. We haven't had a real marriage in years. But I had no idea he'd taken up with someone so young. Good heavens, Taite's younger than our son."

"He's asked for a lawyer," Eric said.

"That's too bad," Garvey said under his breath.

Fayre seemed to regain some balance. She lifted her chin. "I need to make some phone calls of my own. I'll be damned if Douglas will use my family lawyers, or my family money to pay his legal fees, or Ms. Boyne's. My husband doesn't have much money of his own; he's always been content to live off mine. I want him to feel every penny he has to pay out for lawyers. By the time he goes to prison, he won't have a dime left."

Nope, Eric thought. Not a stand-by-your-man kinda woman at all.

There had been interviews to give and paperwork to fill out, but finally, Jaclyn was home. She turned on the lights as she walked through, since it had been dark for a while. It was late, past her usual bed-time. Nothing made you appreciate home like having it taken away for a couple of days. Her couch, her chair, her kitchen. Her own bathroom. Her bed. *Home.* Knowing that the woman who'd tried to kill her was locked up added to Jaclyn's appreciative mood. For the first time in days, she could relax.

Garvey had picked her and Eric up at the scene of the accident and had transported them back to Hopewell, where Eric had very quickly managed to get another city car. He'd refused to go to a hospital to be checked out, of course, but Garvey had given him an order—the city's insurance demanded it—and he'd given in with bad grace. Garvey had also offered to arrange for a new rental car for her, but he also said he thought her Jag would be released tomorrow and he'd be happy to take her anywhere she needed to go until then. She declined the rental car. Who was she kidding? She'd been running from this for days, and the time for running was over.

Jaclyn walked into the kitchen and reached into a cabinet for a bag of decaf coffee. It was late, it had been a long day, but there wasn't any way she'd be going to bed anytime soon. She was absolutely too wired to sleep. She intended to just sit here, in her home, and *be*. It was over.

She was measuring the coffee into the filter when her doorbell rang. Mom, she thought, because of course she'd called Madelyn and given her the lowdown on everything. But when she looked through the peephole, it wasn't Madelyn on her doorstep. She opened the door and stepped aside so Eric could enter. He had on a clean shirt, and butterfly bandages closed the cuts on his forehead and across the bridge of his nose. He had two black eyes. He was the most beautiful thing she'd ever seen.

Silently she put her arms around him, and his closed tightly around her. Deep inside she felt herself surrender, let go of the fear that had all but paralyzed her life. She'd been fighting this since she'd run into him at city hall, and she wasn't fighting it a second longer. There was something real between them, and she wanted to find out what it was, where it might lead them. Maybe they'd had a rocky start, but he'd saved her life; without hesitating, he'd rammed his car into Taite's, put his life in jeopardy to save hers. How much more trustworthy could a man get? He was a good guy, her own Studly Do-Right. Hell, all he needed was a white hat.

She eased away from him, tried to think. It was so hard to know what to say to make this right. She'd been pushing him away for days: falling for him, holding on to him, then pushing as if her life depended on it. She didn't want to push anymore. This could be an important moment, a turning point in her life, and she didn't want to screw it up. She didn't have a plan for this, no chart, no neat list to check off.

"You snore a little," she finally said. "That might take some getting used to, but I'm willing to give it a shot."

His eyebrows rose, a bit. "You make the worst coffee I've ever tasted in my life, but you're worth the pain."

Her head jerked up. "I do not!"

He looped his arms around her waist. "Yes, you do. I spit it out. What the hell was that shit, anyway?"

"Hazelnut raspberry. It's one of my favorites." Well, not really. She could tolerate it, but mostly she'd just been using up what was in the bag. He could find that out later, though. But she really did like flavored coffee, just not that particular one.

She couldn't help but smile. "I work really strange hours, some days."

"So do I."

"Lots of weekends."

"Ditto."

She laid her head on his chest, listening to the sturdy thumping of his heartbeat. He held her tightly, but she could feel the difference in the way he held her, the very subtle shifting of his body. Already, she knew him surprisingly well.

"Sore?" she asked.

"Some," he admitted grudgingly. So like a man, not to want to confess that a car wreck might've left him less than one hundred percent.

It was a flaw, but one she could live with. "Poor baby. How about a nice, hot soak in the tub?"

Oh, she liked that sigh. The one that came from deep inside, that revealed without a word that he was affected. "Only if you'll soak with me."

Jaclyn smiled and rose up on her toes to kiss him. "Sounds good to me."

Eric just wanted a decent cup of coffee. Coffee that didn't taste like chocolate, or hazelnut, or—he still could hardly believe it—crème brûlée. A fine dessert when served with coffee, but damned if he wanted that taste *in* his coffee. Still, it wasn't as bad as it could have been. Turned out that god-awful swill from the first time had been a onetime thing.

It had been a couple of weeks since Taite Boyne had been arrested and had rolled on the senator. The case had fallen together perfectly, piece by piece. Of course, the resulting press had been epic. The paperwork had been epic. But things were settling down, and even his personal life seemed to be in order.

He was all but living with Jaclyn. At least, he had a toothbrush and a change of clothes at her place, and he was there more nights than not. She even had him watching HGTV, though to be fair they didn't spend a lot of time in front of the television. Soon enough they'd make the living arrangements full time—he could see it coming, wanted it surprisingly badly. By fall, Christmas at the latest, they might as well get married. He'd let Jaclyn do all the planning.

The arrangement was almost perfect. He hadn't yet worked up the nerve to confiscate her coffee and take command of her coffeepot; she kept thinking he would grow to love chocolate-flavored coffee in the morning, and he didn't want to hurt her feelings. He loved her, more than a little. Eventually, though, they were going to have a come-to-Jesus talk about her coffee. Maybe his and hers coffeepots were in order. Surely she'd let him keep a can of Maxwell House in the cabinet.

But for now, he wondered if it was safe to stop somewhere and buy a cup of coffee. He hadn't dared try it, but maybe that particular streak of bad luck was behind him. Still, he didn't want to go to the Mickey D's drive-through, and the gas station/convenience store was off-limits. Jaclyn had been bragging about Claire's, and he thought he could kill two birds with one stone. Muffins for Jaclyn, a cup of decent coffee for himself, and brownie points for bringing her the muffins.

Naturally, a place like Claire's didn't have a drive-through, so he had to go inside. He glanced around, liking what he saw. Plants— either real or very good fakes. Little round tables and uncomfortable-looking chairs. Gentle, unobtrusive music played through hidden speakers. Best of all, middle-aged, nicely dressed people—mostly women— were sipping coffee and nibbling at muffins.

Couples talked and ate. Women chatted. One woman sat alone and read a book, another was on her laptop. What could be safer? This was not the kind of place where he had to duck behind a stack of motor oil.

Eric ordered his coffee and a half dozen muffins. Different flavors, since he didn't know exactly what Jaclyn's favorite was. He fantasized about feeding them to her, one pinch at a time. The woman behind the counter was handing over his coffee—he didn't even have the muffins yet—when the door chime signaled a new arrival. The cashier who'd just released his coffee cup turned white, and she stepped back so abruptly she crashed into the coffeemaker.

An angry voice split the silence. "You bitch! I knew I'd find you here!"

Eric glanced over his shoulder. Then he closed his eyes and dropped his head forward. "Oh, shit, not again!"

About the Author

LINDA HOWARD is the award-winning author of many *New York Times* bestsellers, including *Ice, Burn, Death Angel, Up Close and Dangerous,* and *Drop Dead Gorgeous.* She also writes a paranormal romance series with Linda Winstead Jones. They have recently published *Blood Born.* She lives in Alabama with her husband and golden retriever.